GAY BLADES

Books by Ben Tyler

TRICKS OF THE TRADE

HUNK HOUSE

GAY BLADES

Published by Kensington Publishing Corporation

BEN TYLER

GAY BLADES

KENSINGTON BOOKS
http://www.kensingtonbooks.com

For Julia Oliver

ACKNOWLEDGMENTS

I am grateful to my editor, John Scognamiglio, for the opportunity to publish with Kensington. Also, to agent Robin Blakely.

I hope to never fail the following friends: Billy Barnes, Kevin Howell, Dr. Muriel Pollia, J. Randy Taraborrelli, Bill Relling, Mark Reinhart and Rick Lorentz, Les Perkins, Kym Langlie, Steve Sanders, Al Kramer, Mark Stroginis, Pat Kavanagh, John Fricke, Dana Gordon, Chris O'Brien, Peter Christensen, Michael Archer, Steve Trombetti, Michael Peirolo and Rene Martinez, and Julia Oliver.

Likewise, I hope the following will continue to live up to my expectations of them: Tonya Harding, Nancy Kerrigan, and Olga Olga (thank you, Judy!).

Evgeny Plushenko
And Viktor Petrenko
Were skating along on the ice
When on came a trio
With talent and brio
Ms. Fleming, Ms. Hamill, Ms. Heiss

Then enter Paul Wylie
All sunny and smiley
Scott Hamilton funny and fit
A wild hoochie koochie
From Ms. Yamaguchi
Then Kerrigan, Harding and Witt

It started for many
With Ms. Sonja Henie
Then Button, Boitano and Lynn
Those triples and quads
From the ice skating gods
Have for years kept the world in a spin.

There's nothing more thrilling
Divine and fulfilling
Artistic, athletic and nice
Than watching the greats
On their favorite skates
Give a preview of Heaven on ice.
—Billy Barnes

Chapter One

"Love his mane of floppy hair! And admire those wide shoulders with me, people! Yikes! Tonight, Tristan's skating to Something by Shirley Bassey. That's the song Something, not just something that I don't know the name of. Ha. Ha. Ha. Get it, Dick?

"Tristan's wearing black leather pants, and a black leather belt with a big buckle. Kids, you know what that means. Ha. Ha. Ha. His black shirt with the sleeves rolled up exhibits his famed forearms. Mmmm. Nice veins, Tristan. Let's all say that together. NICE VEINS, TRISTAN! Join the fun, Dick. Don't be such an old poop!

"Tristan's such a strong but sinewy athlete. He's one of the only males in skating with such a long extension—his leg position's not bad either. Ha. Ha. Ha.

"He carries himself so well on the ice. He could easily be a Calvin Klein underwear model, flashing himself over Times Square. Don't you think so too, Dick? You know you do! Ha. Ha. Ha.

"Just look at how precious this man is! He's wearing a choker on a leather string, with a medallion that falls right at the hollow of his throat. Yummy! Again with the floppy hair, deep cheekbones, luscious lips. He's the whole perfect package! Oh, my Lord, yes, indeedy.

"I, for one, do not care that he just missed his triple toe loop double Salchow combination. Do you care, Dick? I didn't think so. Ha! Ha! Ha!

"And there, you see Tristan's spread eagle? Yeah, spread 'em, Tristan! He's simply remarkable. After meeting him backstage during the pre-show, I know for sure that tonight I'll dream that I'm a big ol' slab of hard ice. He can slide his exquisite butt all over me. You know what I mean, Dick? Ha. Ha. Ha.

"Say something, Dick. Don't look so mortified.

"Okay, we have to take a station break so that those nice sponsor people can make a pitch for your heaps of disposable income. They want you to buy this new brand of what I'll euphemistically call sensual lubricant. *Don't knock 'em, kiddies. They're payin' for this altogether groovy program, so please stop your wankin' out there in TV land, and pay attention to what our hunky models have to sell you—oh, and the product, too, of course. Ha. Ha. Ha. Buy this stuff, babes. It works! I, Garry Windsor, big-time amateur competitive skating star, swear by it! You do too, don't you, Dick? Ha. Ha. Ha."*

Garry Windsor, the reigning champion of the Firebird Men's International Figure Skating Competition, sat in uneasy silence in the conference room/archive at the Icicle Skating Club of Dorset, New Hampshire. He was viewing his taped, on-air commentary from the recent *Celebrate Diversity Invitational Gay Men's Figure Skating Competition.* Also watching the spectacle was the female president of the American Skating Society, or A.S.S., as it was more popularly known. She was accompanied by two stodgy, old, male board members from the club. To Garry, in the looks department the president was a cross between Nikita Khrushchev and Margaret Dumont. The old men could have been rhesus monkeys on loan from a medical research lab.

The videotape went to snow, and Garry's sphincter tightened. The lights in the room were flipped back on, and Garry faced his inquisition panel. Krushchev and the monkey men were all former skaters from way back when Sonja Henie had been the Sarah Hughes of their day. Now, they were as physically decayed as George Burns. The moth-eaten, once-teal-colored, ladies skating costume plastered to a mannequin in one of the exhibition cases in the conference room/archive was younger than them by half a century.

For the moment, silence engulfed the room. *Oh, Christ,* Garry thought, *I'm in for more than my usual spanking.* "Poor Dick," he said. "I never let him get a word in edgewise when I'm gushing like that." Garry giggled, trying to lighten the hostile vibrations. "I suppose he's complained about my behavior again. Okay, so I'll send him another Timothy Goebel Strip-o-Gram, and he'll be handy-dandy. You know that Dick, he has a penchant for all things Tim!"

Garry felt as though he was back in school, in detention class. His practice session on the ice downstairs had been interrupted by a summons to meet with the president of A.S.S. All Garry wanted was to get through the slap on the wrist, which he resented but decided to tolerate in order to expedite getting back to his workout.

"You've got slush for brains, kid!" The older of the monkey men tried to shout, but his raspy voice was more of a spittled hiss.

Garry blanched. "Excuse me?" he said, seldom having been spoken to with such obvious disdain.

"We've had enough of your kind in competitive figure skating," said the other prune of a man who was, if not decomposing on the spot, certainly smelling like his overactive bladder pills weren't doing the trick.

"And you mean exactly what?" Garry said. Although he was completely out as a gay man, he was seldom aware of being such an obvious target of homophobia.

"Let's simply rip the Band-Aid off, shall we?" announced the president who, as Garry thought about it, looked more like Margot *after* leaving Shangri-La. "We've just returned from a meeting with the sponsorship committee. They're withdrawing all of their financial support for you." She pursed her thin lips in self-satisfaction. "No support. No skating club. No competitions. You're through with this and every other club in the Society."

Garry involuntarily gasped. He was speechless, nearly catatonic with shock.

"Your retarded comments to that *People* magazine reporter was a dumb move, too," the older old man wheezed. "Telling him—and the world—that you only got into skating in order to meet men. That took more than your average share of rust in the noggin, sonny."

"It was a joke, like all those actors who lie about getting into acting class to meet girls," Garry tried to explain. "Unlike them, I have nothing to hide."

The president tut-tutted and shook her head. "We should have put a stop to you long before that *Couples* profile. It's not like we didn't see this coming a mile away. Imagine," she huffed, "announcing in print that you had sex with your coach in exchange for lessons. Too poor to pay with anything but your . . ." she stammered, trying to verbalize something she had refused to visualize. "Your bedroom antics." She closed her eyes, put her fingertips to her forehead, and sighed heavily.

"It was just a stupid interview," Garry charged. "The same with that TV skating show," he stuttered. He was referring to his invitation to act as a commentator on the QueerVision Broadcasting Network's inaugural ice skating broadcast.

"You've freaked out the entire American Skating Society," the older man grumped. "We—figure skaters that is—used to be well respected and admired. Like Catholic priests. But because of you and your Nancy Boy ways, the Society has had to hire the Vatican's own PR firm to handle damage control. If mummies and daddies won't let their little angels sing in the choir, they sure as hell won't let 'em take figure skating lessons if they think it'll make 'em turn out like you."

"You mean, turn out to be champions?" Garry suggested.

"Mr. Windsor," the president said frostily, "you've placed us in a very precarious position."

"*I've* placed . . . ? You're in a . . . ?" Garry sputtered, stopping mid-sentence.

"Yes! You! Who else?" she continued. "We didn't force you into copulating with Coach Larson. And we're surely not responsible for that gushing television commentary either. Tristan Wright can do a spread eagle on your slab! Honestly! Oh, and just so you know, Coach Larson has been melted by A.S.S. too."

Garry's eyes widened as he fought to stay calm. "Coach Larson isn't to blame for any of this. You said it yourself. I'm responsible for my actions."

"It takes two to screw," the president sighed. "We're just being proactive. From now on, the only ice you and he will see is what's floating in the polar bear pool at the zoo."

"You show me a boy skater who hasn't been buggered by his coach, and I'll show you a skater who'll never make the Nationals or the Olympics—unless he's turning tricks with one of the judges," Garry spat.

"Mr. Windsor!" the woman declared, slapping the palms of her shriveled crone hands onto the table top. "Judges are incorruptible!"

"Is that like a secret that someone forgot to tell the French judges?"

The three codgers stopped to think about Garry's remarks for a moment. He took the opportunity to elaborate.

"As for my appearance on that television program, it was completely a put-on! Editorializing about a skater's wardrobe and such is as much a part of the job of commentator as dissing their quad and Salchow screw-ups," he persisted. "Dick Button is utterly euphoric whenever some tramp of a skater makes the smallest mistake during competition. He's so excited that he sounds as if he's just finished making up for an all-nighter at the White Party in Palm Springs!"

The older of the two octogenarians interrupted. "The fact is, we simply cannot have a homosexual skater at the club."

"Like you have even one *straight* skater," Garry parried.

"We're a private club. We cannot have a fairy representing us at Nationals. *Millions* of families tune in to watch those competitions. What kind of deviant message would we be sending?"

"No *gay* skaters," Garry deadpanned, still in a state of disbelief. "One ringy-dingy. Doesn't the name Rudy Galindo scream out to you?"

"That one again." The president rolled her eyes and groaned. "Mr. Galindo slipped under our gay—er—radar before he became famous," she said. "It's too late to do anything about him or his earrings or his Carmen Miranda halter tops."

"A lot of people, myself included, think Rudy's a hot pocket of tasty filling," Garry said. "You ask what kind of message you'd be sending to families? How about the idea that talent and determination to be the best is gender and sexuality neutral!"

"Mr. Windsor." The president smiled, as if trying to draw Garry into her confidence. "You're a very theatrical-minded young man. You must understand, at least from a political point of view, that we have to maintain an illusion—or shall we say an impression—that figure skaters are *real* men. Why do you think A.S.S. only selects masculine men to be our ice stars? I'm not suggesting that it's all predetermined. Of course it's not. But you must have thought it odd that none of the girly-girly boys at the clubs ever make it to the TV screens. Face it. Audiences want to imagine Brian Boitano with Dorothy Hamill."

"No one can imagine that," Garry said. "You won't get away with this. What you're doing to me must be illegal or something."

"We've checked the laws, my dear." The president smiled again.

"But I've worked my butt off for ten years to get this far. You're not wrenching my dream from me, just because I'm queer?"

One of the seriously old men shook a bent finger at the other man. "I warned you he'd get uppity when you mentioned Rudy!"

"Uppity?" Garry erupted, abruptly pushing his chair away from the table. He stood up and opened his arms as if to enfold the entirety of the dark-paneled, musty-smelling room. "Look around." He pointed to the walls, covered with cheap, gold-colored frames holding photos of smiling skaters wearing red, white and blue ribbons with medals, and holding silver loving cups. "There's Mitch. Sandy. Dana. Everett. Skipper. To name just a few. They're *all* gay!" he said, pointing to the various pictures of smiling young men.

"Son, if nothing else, your compulsory marks have been uneven this season," said one of the men, as bags of limp facial skin that used to be cheeks, jiggled with every word he spoke. "You didn't skate so well at the Regionals."

"What zip code do you live in, for Christ sake! I won my event," Garry pleaded. "It wouldn't be too far-fetched to think I might medal at the Olympics some day!"

"May we suggest you simply turn pro," said the woman. "You'll make gads of money doing guest appearances with the Ice Capades, or endorsing Atlantis cruise vacation packages. And professional shows are absolutely filled with your own kind."

"My own *kind*?" Garry parroted the woman. "By that you must mean other champions. You're flattering me." He feigned a smile.

"Mr. Windsor, please—"

Garry was, by nature, a soft-spoken, non-adversarial man. However, when cornered, he hurled back whatever was thrust at him. "Your attorney better be as good as mine, because if you follow through with this outrage, I'm suing the whole fucking A.S.S.!" he shouted.

The three waxworks became flustered. "There's no need to get hostile," the woman said, nervously patting loose strands of red dyed hair at the nape of her neck that had come loose from the pill-box bun she wore atop her head.

"I'm not hostile," Garry countered. "My lawyer is. As a matter of fact, Alan Dershowitz throws up before having to face him in court."

"Suit yourself," the older of the old men said, his own inadvertent double entendre apparently lost on him. "This is a private skating club. We carefully screen and select our members. No homosexuals or dogs allowed on the ice. Understand?"

"The question is, do *you* get it?" Garry said. "Don't you know what you're doing to me—and this dinky club? It's criminal! I'm not going anywhere without making a lot of noise! You'll all be sorry that you tangled with me!"

"You are excused, Mr. Windsor," said the woman, her clipped tone suggesting that Garry was the weakest link. She stood up in a huff, shuffled a sheaf of papers and swept them into a manila folder. With a quick snap of her head, she signaled for her colleagues to withdraw to a private office.

"What am I supposed to do now?" Garry begged as the trio retreated.

"Call Tonya Harding," the old woman sniggered over her shoulder. "That felon's bound to have a few post-career suggestions. Unless she's in solitary confinement."

As the trio exited the room, Garry slumped back down into his chair. For a long moment, he sat in confounded silence. Tears welled in his eyes as he thought of all the years of dedication and discipline and practice it had taken for him to earn a berth on the national team. Now, before he could say "Angela Nikodinov," everything that his father had predicted had come to pass. He had achieved an elevated level of success without any help, financial or otherwise, from his insensitive parents who never once acknowledged that their son was gay, let alone a figure skater.

"If you insist on joining us for Thanksgiving," he recalled his mother saying, "please don't mention anything about your personal life while my guests are here. As far as they're concerned, you're a flight attendant. I don't care which airline, just so they think you do international routes. Anything but figure skating." His beribboned medals and trophies weren't even on display at their home.

Thus, without parental support, Garry had done what was necessary in order to pursue his dream of skating: he gave his body and soul to both his art—and to his coach. As far as Garry was concerned, the barter had been worth it. He received superior training at a fraction of the standard cost, and he had sex as often as he wanted.

But even if they hadn't been master and student, Garry would have had sex with Coach Sven Larson in a heartbeat. Sven's twin dimples on his strong, handsome face, and the tattoo of the Olympic rings on his left biceps, made the blond stud from Sweden a wet dream fantasy. Sven's radiant smile and velvet-smooth skin stretched over his long, lean body—a huge distraction for Garry. The fact that Sven was a hot top with hard pink nipples and golden, cornsilk pubic hairs—and was also endowed with an 8-inch uncut piston—was incentive enough for Garry to work extra hard to please his coach—on and off the ice. Even now, while facing his inquisitors, Garry was getting hard just thinking of lying on his back and being hypnotized by the sight of Sven's tight abs and the beads of sweat that trickled down his sculpted torso as he worked his cock in and out of Garry's tight butt.

But now Sven was apparently ruined, too. Once the tabloids got hold of this story, Garry and Sven would be *People* magazine cover boys. By the weekend their sexploits would be fodder for a bad comedy sketch on *Saturday Night Live.* Garry cringed as he pictured Seth Meyers and Will Farrell wearing pink figure skates and ruffled taffeta tutus, and humping each other on an ice rink. The guest host—probably some seriously lyric-challenged hip-hop rapper—would try to impersonate Scott Hamilton, giving a running commentary. The repertory players, decked out in scarves and wool stocking caps, would hold up cards with pathetically poor technical and artistic scores.

Garry forced himself to rise again from the chair. He stood on the worn and slightly listing hardwood floor and looked at the wall-to-wall glass trophy cases that displayed some of his own medals along with those of such legendary skaters as Janet Lynn, Todd Eldridge and Brian Boitano. The muffled echo of canned music, mixed with the laughter of amateur skaters pock-marking the ice during the morning's public session, filtered up from the rink and wafted into the room. Garry corrected his posture, summoning the strength to open the door. "I'll be back," he said to the ghosts of skaters past, whom he firmly believed haunted the old building and rink.

He stepped out into the stairwell. The sounds of laughter, tinny music, and the scent of refrigeration from the rink, made him feel weak in the knees. "I love this place," he whispered to himself.

As Garry held on to the wooden railing of the stairs and descended, step by arduous step, he thought of the ass-kicking arguments he should have made to convince the triumvirate that they were making a huge mistake by eliminating him from the club. At the bottom step, before pushing the door that opened into the massive skating arena, he thought about calling his lover, international skating superstar Kurt Chrysler. "Can't do that," he quickly remembered. As of this very morning, Kurt was his *ex*-lover.

The reality of Garry's predicament triggered a collage of images that flashed through his mind: Tear-filled debates with Kurt over what appeared to be his lack of commitment to the relationship . . . Long stretches of silence between the two men as they stared at headline stories in *The National Enquirer* that suggested Kurt was romantically involved with a popular Russian singles skater . . . The final showdown, where Garry had decided that he couldn't trust a partner who was on the road performing in ice shows ten months out of the year.

Garry thought he was taking the high road when he offered the grand gesture, "It's not fair that I expect so much of you." He hoped for an argument to the contrary.

"You're right. You make me feel dishonest and irresponsible," Kurt replied. "It's not fair to either of us. I'll be out by the time you get home from practice."

Kurt's response was replayed on constant loop in Garry's head, and the weight of all that had transpired in Garry's life in one fell swoop of a single day, crushed him. "Just get me out of here," he sighed as he entered the cold, cavernous arena.

It was impossible to exit the massive, dome-shaped building without walking around the perimeter of the ice-skating rink. With lead feet, Garry moved along the black rubber-matted floor surrounding the chest-high, dirty-white, gouged wall that surrounded the ice. He was distracted for a moment by the sight of a teenage boy practicing his scratch spin at the center of the rink. The boy displayed all the determination and concentration that it took to be a winner. In a skin-tight white T-shirt that emphasized the Y-shape of his torso, he was wet with perspiration.

At any other time, Garry would have felt a pang of lust. He might also have dashed onto the ice to skate around the boy and show off his Lutz jump to get the boy's attention. Now, however, he was too drained with exhaustion and depression.

Garry watched as the boy's coach glided over to his charge and patted him approvingly on the back. The boy beamed. The coach beamed. Garry could see in their interaction that they were more than coach and student. "As I said, 'show me a boy skater who . . .' "

Garry stopped mid-sentence, shook his head in despair, and left the arena.

Outside, the day was bright and cold. Garry's eyes watered as he squinted into the painful, late-morning sunlight that reflected off the snow banks and puddles of meltwater in the parking lot potholes. He wasn't sure if the tears dripping down his face were from the sting of the light, or from his twice-in-one-day broken heart.

Now, more than ever, he wished that he and Kurt were at least friends. At this moment he wanted to be held in Kurt's arms. He wanted to bury his face in Kurt's strong, down-covered chest, and cry himself to sleep, safe and protected. Coach Larson was simply a fuck for fun and profit. Kurt was Garry's love. "No more Kurt. No more skating. What's left?" he sighed.

Garry opened the unlocked door of his ancient, rusting, Plymouth Fury III sedan and slid into the driver's seat. He mechanically placed the key into the ignition and turned the switch. Nothing. *Is Mercury in retrograde?* he thought to himself.

He listlessly pumped the accelerator and turned the key again. Still nothing. For a long moment, Garry sat looking out through the dirty, streaked windshield, too numb to think clearly. He watched some little girls in mittens and scarves. The white laces of their skate boots were tied together and slung over their narrow shoulders. With their pushy mothers leading the way for skating practice, the young girls reluctantly drifted from their SUVs to the rink.

Once again, Garry turned the key in the ignition. The engine coughed for a moment then came to life. He put the car into drive and slowly rolled away and out onto the street.

Presently, he was home in his now too large, too empty, and way too unhappy apartment. But he didn't remember how he got there.

"What to do now?" he whispered to himself as he stood in the middle of the kitchen, wondering if he should make a cup of tea, fix lunch, or wash the breakfast dishes. He could come to only one decision. He reached into the freezer for the Stolichnaya. He walked with the cold bottle to his bedroom. There he tossed the bottle onto the bed, stripped off his clothes and climbed under the top sheet. Settling himself with his back against the pillows and headboard, he pulled the sheet to his bare waist. Garry unscrewed the bottle top and put the lip of the neck to his lips. He took a long, slow pull, until he felt the vodka pervade his body.

The apartment was so quiet that he could hear the sound of a television two units away. "What will I do without Kurt?" he asked himself. "I can do without *Kurt* if I have my skating. I can do without *skating* if I have Kurt. But I can't live without both of my passions." He sighed. "Now, I have nothing."

Tears began again. *Fuck Kurt. Fuck A.S.S. Fuck anyone who ever stands in my way of happiness again*, he thought as he nursed himself into alcohol-induced unconsciousness.

Chapter Two

"Two shows a *day*? No per diem? I have to pay for my own wheels, meals, and digs?" Garry spoke in a petulant tone, as he read the *Gold on Ice* talent contract. He looked up into the large face of Charles Laughton's heavier brother—Ernie Shamanski—the production coordinator and artistic director of the ice show. "No HMO?" Garry asked. "Skaters are *always* pulling a groin muscle!"

"Which is why we can't offer coverage," Ernie said. "Too many casualties. Unaffordable premiums. You understand."

"What's a *three-month wage and job probation period*?" Garry balked. "A trial period? My reputation speaks fluently for itself. Why else would you have called me."

Ernie shrugged. "Standard contract, sweet cakes. Non-negotiable."

"Jeez, this salary is absolutely fry-cook rock-bottom, don't you think? Barely above minimum wage. No wonder you need skaters."

Ernie leaned back in his desk chair, which groaned in protest under his weight. He knitted his fingers together, then placed his hands on his globe of a stomach. He grinned with the smugness of one who holds all the strings as he covetously viewed the whole package of Garry's youth, thinking how tasty this young morsel would be.

After his expulsion from A.S.S., Garry had applied to all the top touring ice shows in the world. After months of waiting and ultimately receiving rejections from all of them, including *Stars on Ice*, *Holiday on Ice*, and even Nancy Kerrigan's *Stupid Things I've Said When I Didn't Know the Microphone Was On on Ice*, Garry had to seriously consider waiting tables to make ends meet. *Gold on Ice* was the sediment at the bottom of the barrel of shows—lower even, than Sterling Studios' *Mice on Ice*. *Gold* wasn't even on his list of shows to approach, which is what made it all the more curious when a representative from the production called inquiring about his availability. Garry had agreed to at least come in to discuss his possible participation.

Gold on Ice had a reputation as being the cheesiest of the touring ice skating productions. Skaters knew that it was far worse than *Medical Examiner on Ice*, or *The $1.98 Beauty Contest on Ice*. It was known among skaters as "the drain," because it circled the country like water in a hair-clogged pipe, slowly sucking talent into oblivion. Skaters pretty much knew it was the last stop before they were forced to hang up their blades and become what each feared most—a token taker in a tollbooth.

"I'm saving your ass, so to speak," Ernie smirked. He was teething on a Merit and blowing plumes of Philip Morris poison across his desk at Garry.

"Why me?" Garry asked, still confused about how the production had come to contact him in the first place.

Ernie waved a dismissive hand, then offered a pen for Garry to sign the contract. "Maybe it's a favor for someone."

Some favor, Garry thought, looking at Ernie whose girth could not be concealed under his blousy Hawaiian shirt. *Somebody up there hates me.*

"You've got the third lead, sweetums, if you want it. If not . . ." Ernie left the comment open as he continued to wantonly study Garry.

"Dozens of other guys are on the list if you don't want the gig." It sounded to Garry like a hint of a threat.

Garry's thoughts scattered like billiard balls rolling about a felt-top table. *To do or not to do? Christ, I wish Kurt were here to help me. Hell, if Kurt were here, I wouldn't have to take this crummy job in the first place!*

After a long moment of screaming silence and internal confusion, Garry leaned forward on the desk. *Scott Hamilton, you've failed me*, he thought, wondering why he wasn't interviewing with *Stars on Ice* instead. With pen in hand, and a sigh of resignation, he scribbled his name on the line with an X next to it.

"What choice do I have," he muttered testily. Then, checking himself, not wanting to show his true contempt, he smiled. "I thank you very much for the generous opportunity, Mr. Shamanski." Garry tried to muster what could pass as a tone of appreciation as he handed the contract back to Ernie. "I won't disappoint you."

Ernie grinned again. "So far, so good. Better pack up. After the evening performance tomorrow, we take a run down to Gloucester, Massachusetts." He handed Garry the show's itinerary for the next eight months. "All them horny fishermen are anxious to haul a catch like the perfect storm of my skaters' asses."

Garry gave a cursory glance to the itinerary as Ernie battled to hoist himself up and out of his chair to seal the agreement with a handshake. Most of the city names on the list were so obscure, Garry didn't recognize them.

Ernie came out from behind his desk and rested a moist mitt on Garry's shoulder. "Stay for the matinee. On the house. Starts in just a few minutes." Ernie picked up a ticket from his in-box tray and handed it to Garry. "Go and see what you've gotten yourself into."

Houdini's handcuffs is what I've gotten myself into, and I don't have a key, Garry said to himself.

Still, he was half delighted to finally have a skating job, although half devastated by the fact that he'd fallen so far down through a figurative crack in the ice that he had zero options but to accept the offer. "Tomorrow, then," Garry said, forcing a wan smile as he tried to liberate himself from Ernie's grip.

"Rehearsal's at ten," Ernie said, giving the muscles in Garry's shoulder a tight squeeze before lifting his hand off the younger man's shirt. "If you have any questions, I'll be around. I'm your best bet to succeed."

"Thank you, Mr. Shamanski."

"Everyone calls me Uncle Ernie."

"I don't think I'll be calling you . . ."

"It's not a term of endearment," Ernie said harshly. "That's how I'm addressed. *Capisca?*"

Garry stared at a black mole on Ernie's nose, then turned and exited the room. He wondered if Ernie buried bodies in the basement of his house. He looked like the type of perverted creep to do just that. John Wayne Gacy came to mind.

Outside at the box office, a short line of young attractive men were cued up to buy tickets. "Think he's as adorable in person?" one man said to another, presumably drooling over some skater.

"Oh, he's a doll, all right," the other man agreed. "He went to my gym the last time the show played here."

"Use the showers?"

"Mmmm."

Stepping up to the ticket window, the first man addressed the box office attendant. "Hi, hon. Listen, Jay Logan, the star of *Gold*, is a personal friend. He'd want me to be as close to the ice as possible? You're a sweetie. Thanks, tons."

"Smooth operator," the other man said.

Garry walked over to the entrance to the rink and handed his ticket to a teenage boy with red cheeks who ripped the ticket in two.

"Enjoy the show," the boy said without looking up at Garry. His monotone kept repeating, "Enjoy the show. Enjoy the show. Enjoy the show," as customers presented their tickets.

Garry merged with the crowd and entered the building. The seating was unreserved bleachers. Garry found a place and squeezed himself between a family of six with a picnic basket that reeked of egg salad, and two men in identical Army fatigue uniform pants. The guys, wearing tight-fitting red T-shirts, his and his matching mustaches, sideburns and earring studs, kept arguing about whether or not Brian Orser's ex-lover deserved the financial settlement he got when they broke up.

Garry flinched. Over the years, he had been to a couple of parties where Brian was a guest, and he thought that the Canadian star was not only sexy, but also one of the sweetest guys on the planet. Brian was among Garry's idols, and Garry loathed the fact that his personal problems were being so publicly debated.

"No way would I pay," one of the guys flatly stated.

"Yes, way, if you had his bucks and the courts made you," the other argued.

"No way, because I'd have a pre-nup."

"Yes way 'cause you'd never get me to sign a pre-nut for you."

"No way, 'cause it's not a pre-*nut*, you idiot."

"Whatever! Just shut up during the show!"

"You shut up!"

"Make me!"

"I'll make you later." The one grinned and nudged the other.

"You make me temporarily insane."

Mercifully for Garry, the lights above the rink dimmed, causing the two studs to stop their harangue. A hush began to filter throughout the crowd. Then the show started with a fanfare of canned music.

Immediately, Garry felt queasy. For the opening number, the entire cast assembled on the ice to perform a rousing tribute to *The Great Women of History*. Each performer came forth smiling under a bright spotlight as they skated to a musical rip-off of Andrew Lloyd Webber.

The show went into a steady artistic decline as one skater after another, boys and girls, strutted onto the ice dressed as Wilma Flintstone, Hillary Rodham Clinton, Venus de Milo (a tough balancing trick for the skater whose arms were bound inside her costume), Cher, Aunt Jemima, the Flying Nun, the Statue of Liberty, Lassie, and the lady in the cancer commercial who smokes through a hole in her throat.

The two and a half hour program was too long at half the length. When it was finally over, Garry was stunned by how humiliating the show was. He could only think of two reasons for *Gold on Ice* to exist at all. It boasted the best boy skater he'd ever seen, Jay Logan, who was also one of Garry's former competitors, and Amber Nyak, a name from yesteryear who still skated as though she loved every moment on the ice.

Jay, the brilliant boy skater, had performed a spectacular freestyle program to the music of John Barry, showcasing a superb triple Axel and a double toe loop combination. However, he was then forced to don a costume of indoor plumbing for the finale, which the souvenir program called *Great Modern Inventions*. For Jay's sake, Garry was happy that his old chum hadn't been given the role of the George Forman Grill.

Tired and depressed, Garry left the building without going backstage to say hello to Jay. With an eight-month-long contract to fulfill, there would be plenty of time for a reunion.

Chapter Three

Morning arrived too quickly and Garry was filled with trepidation. He was so nervous about joining the show and meeting new people that his morning ritual of jacking off before getting out of bed was perfunctory. Even with his favorite video, *Pochahiney*, playing in the combination television/tape player beside his bed, his first jerk-off of the day took longer than usual. Six months without Kurt Chrysler meant six months since he'd had sex with anyone other than himself. Even given such depravation, and fantasizing about being banged by Kurt, he had to force a climax.

Showered, shaved, and with a minimal wardrobe packed in two suitcases, Garry called a cab, said goodbye to his apartment, locked the door, and drove away from his building. His landlord, who furtively accessed Garry's apartment with a master key on a regular basis in order to bury his face in his tenant's underwear, had promised to water Garry's solitary plant and to forward his mail to the *Gold on Ice* office in White Plains, New York. "Don't bother to wash the sheets," the landlord had said.

Parking outside the building that housed the skating rink, Garry carried his skate bag into the building. He was greeted with his favorite scent: *eau de refrigerated air*. Garry pushed open the huge double doors leading from the long outer lobby area, which also housed a skate rental counter, and walked into the main rink.

An orchestral version of "Evergreen" from the soundtrack of Streisand's remake of *A Star Is Born*, squeezed through the tinny public address system. It seemed to be trying in vain to inflate the air of the cavernous room as well as the lethargic spirit of the twenty or so skaters on the ice whose morose physical vibrations were palpable. To Garry, they looked like they'd just skated over from Stepford.

As Garry walked closer to the barrier surrounding the rink, the ear-splitting shrill from a coach's whistle shredded the atmosphere and made him wince. "Listen up, you little cocksuckers," commanded the coach. He was standing at one end of the ice with a clipboard in his hand. The automatons stopped skating and slowly converged in front of the man. Garry, too, moved closer.

"Grant! Ric!" demanded the man, as if he were a Marine D.I. Two cute young guys tentatively glided away from the assemblage, looking nervously at each other. They stopped in front of the man with the whistle. "Turn in your ID's and get your asses off this ice!" the man shouted.

Garry looked at the two young men, both of whom had expressions of horror stamped on their faces. The one named Grant started to cry. Ric wrapped his arms around Grant then bellowed at the whistle blower, "Is this because I wouldn't come to Ernie's room on demand? Tell that hateful old cocksucking slug that we're in love!"

"Uncle Ernie has spoken!" the whistle man insisted. Then, to the others he yelled, "Get your asses ready for the matinee. Get!"

The young men and women sluggishly dispersed. Quickly reconsidering the next eight months of his life and deciding to disappear, Garry started to retrace his steps. But as he walked, with his head down, he was stopped by the sound of a loud, friendly laugh echoing through the vast rink. Garry turned toward the sound.

"Guess this is where they send all the naughty boys in figure skating." The guy smiled, walking toward Garry. He reached out his hand. "Jay Logan," he said. "Welcome to *the drain*." Jay laughed again.

Garry smiled, remembering the disastrous performance at Nationals a few years back that had ended Jay's competitive career. He then simply vanished from the limelight. But he was still as startlingly handsome as Garry remembered. With his thick, dark, JFK-Junior hair, and lips that, when parted, revealed perfect white teeth, Jay was worthy of a *People* magazine cover: *Sexiest Man Alive*.

"I can see how horrified you are." Jay snickered again. His honeyed voice and white smile warmed the chill around Garry.

Garry grinned back and held out his hand for Jay to shake.

"I heard you were coming aboard," Jay said. "Like it or not, welcome to your new life, man." In an aside, he added, "And we're all thrilled to have some fresh meat around here." Jay laughed again.

Garry was a bit embarrassed. Ever since his relationship with Kurt had ended, he didn't think of himself as anybody's *meat*. But he could tell that Jay was genuinely trying to be nice to him. "Remember beating me in Colorado Springs and Boston?" Garry said.

"And Seattle and Philadelphia," Jay added, giving Garry a small bow.

"How'd you ever end up . . ." Garry's voice trailed off as he remembered full well the reason Jay Logan was skating with this *Ice Charades*. He was immediately sorry that he had broached the subject.

Jay shrugged his shoulders. "There's nothing quite like fucking up your career while fifty million people are watching," he said. "I used to wake up during the night screaming from nightmares about that stupid quad jump."

"I never saw anybody freak out in the middle of a jump the way you did that night," Garry said, recalling the calamity.

"The worst part was flying over the barrier rail and landing on Peggy Fleming's microphone."

"Ouch, yes." Garry nodded. He'd watched the television monitors from back stage at the Olympic Center in Lake Placid and was as mortified as everyone else in the audience when Jay lost control while in midair. His marks were lower than those of Tonya Harding's in Lillehammer. But while that mascara-smudged crybaby and convicted felon got a made-for-television movie about her life in return for her despicable acts, Jay was simply excommunicated from his skating club and left with no sponsor for future competitions.

"Christ, what a cheesy show we're in," Garry lamented.

"It's only cheesy to you and me," Jay countered. "The people in the crowd think we're sensational. They have no idea what a first-rate ice show looks like. They think that just because we can do a waltz jump we're great skaters. Frankly, I'm grateful for the job. I wasn't as smart as Paul Wylie, getting his MBA from Harvard then joining the marketing division at the Disney movie studios. I just wanted to skate. So here I am. Do you think he's cute? Paul, I mean?" Jay answered his own question. "I do. Compact. Great dimpled smile. Moves like an angel, as if he's actually part of the music. Anyway, this is all I can do, and all I want to do."

Garry smiled. "At least he's shorter than me. Paul, I mean. I feel a hellava lot better now, just seeing you again and knowing that the show has at least one talent in the cast."

"Now there are two," Jay said. "Actually, three. Wait'll you see Amber Nyak. She's the real star."

"I saw the matinee yesterday. Yeah, she really sparkles." Garry spoke with genuine enthusiasm. "I wondered whatever happened to her. She got the Olympic bronze, then, phfft, she disappeared."

"We're best buds, Amber and I. Amber and me? Or Amber and I? I'm always confused about that. Must have been out skating the day they taught that in school. Anyway, you'll adore her. And the corps of skaters are mostly great kids. It's management you've got to watch out for. *Uncle Ernie,* if you can believe that guy."

"What the hell is *he* all about?" Garry cringed.

"He sees himself as the company's daddy. Or, rather, he wants to be the *boys'* daddy. As far as I'm concerned the measly three hundred and fifty bucks we get in our pay envelopes each week isn't nearly enough for me to call that slug *daddy* or *uncle.* Although a Rolex, or a Mercedes, might change my mind." Jay laughed.

Garry smiled again. "Rumor has it that there's no way to save enough to get out of this rat race," he said.

"Ernie will say you need a new costume and have one made for you. Then to pay for it he'll take a percentage of your check. Most of the skaters who get hurt or have to leave for other reasons, like poor Grant and Ric, end up actually *owing* money to the production."

"What did I ever do to deserve such an end?" Garry asked sadly, looking around the arena.

"You *did* Coach Larson, I heard. That's what you *did.*" Jay winked lasciviously. "Yummy. What a stud. Hell, my coach had a basketball for a stomach, and more hair on his back than on his head. But I did what I had to do for extra ice time or to pay for lessons whenever I used up my parents' skating money allowance on Pet Shop Boys CDs, or concert tickets to see Dame Edna. If Larson had been my coach, I wouldn't have gotten any skating done at all. I'd have been fluffin' him day and night!"

Jay gave Garry a high five. "What A.S.S. did to you stinks. You were *so* much a scapegoat. A pawn in their attempt to weed out all the queer boys—or at least make the public believe Boitano's theory that the sport has only a ten to fifteen percent gay ratio."

Garry shrugged.

"Never mind," Jay continued with a bright smile. "You're in for a treat. Every boy in the cast is so bored sleeping with every other boy, you'll be beating them off—pun intended—with a Jeff Stryker dildo. As I said, you're the fresh meat."

"I'm so *not* interested in sex," Garry said truthfully. "I just want to skate."

"Yeah, yeah. I've heard that line a gazillion times. We all get dumped at one time or another. You'll eventually find yourself another husband and settle down." Jay appraised him. "You're the type. I can tell. You're a real catch who doesn't know it."

"Ya think?" Garry wondered if maybe his celibacy trip was almost over.

"With your grace and good looks? You can have your pick of guys." Jay beamed. "In fact, the Prize Patrol is sneaking up on you even as we speak."

Garry turned to see what had caught Jay's eye. "Mmm. Tank top," he said, licking his lips as if he were devouring a messy plate of babyback barbecue ribs.

"That's Todd Bartlett," Jay said. "He only comes out from his web and onto the ice for the show, or when he's forced to practice. Or," Jay said, amused, "when he's sniffing for a ball sack to drain. Looks like he's picked up your scent of desperation."

"I'm hardly desperate," Garry countered. "I'm just in exile. At least until I'm reinstated in my skating club—or until this Todd guy asks for my hand."

"Whatever," Jay said, pretending to ignore the hunk whose made-up-on-the-spot choreography included a lot of poses where he had to flex his considerable brawn. "As I said, the welcome wagon stops here twenty-four-seven. That is until Mr. Ideal Husband waltz jumps into your arms. In the meantime, skating shows, especially this one, offer a boy/boy sex free-for-all. What *Gold* lacks in talent on the ice, it thoroughly makes up for with talent on the sheets."

Garry sighed. "I haven't been laid in eons. But I'm so not interested in anyone—except maybe every boy I've seen in the show thus far." He giggled.

"Three nights, tops, before you score. You play, or I pay. Guaranteed," Jay said. "And you need it, man. You're too young and cute to be stingy with your dick. Give the guys a break."

"What I need, is to get out of being in that totally lame opening production number," Garry pouted, changing the subject. "I suppose I'll probably have to take over one of the roles that Grant or Ric had. Didn't one of them have to be Ethel Rosenberg? Now there's a great lady," he said, facetiously.

"But the sparklers on that costume are outrageous! And you'd get to do a lot of spastic stuff. Like your nerve endings are being deep fried."

"I'd rather die!" Garry spat.

"Well, that's the point if you're doing Ethel Rosenberg!" Jay smirked.

"Corny, as Nancy Kerrigan would say," Garry whined.

"Trust me, it's a hell of a lot better than the *World Destinations* number we did last year. Ernie had me wearing a banner across my bare chest that read, youth in asia. The guy's not only a lecherous freak, he's a Darwin Award winner. God, did she goof up her image with that lame line or what? Nancy, I mean."

"And all the other dumb-ass lines she couldn't help blurting out," Garry agreed.

"She must have Tourette's syndrome or something. She could have made it big time, if her recurrent involuntary vocal ticks hadn't gotten in the way."

"When you've got ice chips for brains," Garry started to say.

"Not even the Disney publicity machine pumping out damage control press releases could save her. But I'm afraid nothing's as corny as the number *we'll* be doing together."

"We get to skate together?" Garry gleamed. "That's great. But how will the Clampets in those hick towns we're playin' in take to seeing two gay guys doing pairs skating?"

"First of all, you'd be surprised at how relatively sophisticated some of the 'burbs can be," Jay said. "Some places are a little more together than the big city meat markets. Plus, they'll be laughing off their coveralls 'cause we'll be dressed as Beavis and Butt-head."

Garry rolled his eyes. "I don't do costume characters!"

"They're dragging out the old outfits from a couple of seasons ago. There's no use making a fuss about it. We have no clout here. Just have to do as we're told and maybe, before too long, your gold medal–winning Prince Charming will return to sweep you off your blades."

Jay could see that Garry was suddenly close to tears. "Hey, I'm sorry about the gold medal Prince Charming crack, honest."

"It's not that." Garry waved away Jay's apology. "It's just that my career is almost over, and I still miss Kurt, and I didn't spend the past fifteen years of my life to skate around as a Butt-head, or as an electrical conduit for an innocent Red Scare commie, or a 1-800-Dentist spokesperson. I noticed she's in the *Great Ladies* segment too."

Jay put his arm around Garry. "Things could be worse," he said. "You could be a mechanical cat from the Moon in that cheesy *Mice on Ice* show from Sterling." Garry tried not to smile.

"They say that those costumes are never washed and they're used by so many sweaty skaters that they're crawling with what the cast calls *uninvited guests!*"

Garry nodded his head in agreement. Indeed, he could be worse off. He needed a job and one had appeared. He was grateful.

"At least Ernie gives us a weekly supply of Raid and Lysol disinfectant spray. Another perk," Jay grunted. "It's cheaper than dry cleaning the crabs."

"Oh, God," Garry said. "I'm a hypochondriac. I'm starting to itch!"

"Let Mr. Tank Top over there scratch it for you! Trust me, his magic wand'll satisfy your itch. Not that I know from personal experience." He grinned with a look of satisfaction.

"There's lots of time for him, and the others," Garry said. "Let's just take off and grab a bite. We can dish about Ernie and this crazy circus he's running."

"Please! We won't waste our time talking about Quasimodo's clone. I'll give you the complete rundown on who's spankin' whose monkey."

Chapter Four

Every *Gold on Ice* skater recognized the name Garry Windsor, mainly because they were aware of the scandal that got him canned from the world of amateur sports in the first place—and also he was the punch line of jokes on *Leno, Will & Grace* (delivered by Debbie Reynolds) and *Six Feet Under*. The skaters in the show were naturally curious about the infamous new addition to their family.

"Frankly," said one of the jaded chorines who only skated in the production numbers, "I don't give a rat's ass that this Garry guy is joining the show. I mean, he's gay, ain't he? So there's no dick in it for me." She snapped her wad of Big Red and groaned. "Face it girls, the really cute ones are always queer."

"Color me Barbra," said one of the chorus boys who at the moment was dividing his attention between dishing with his friends and applying a line of mascara under his eyes. "But I truly declare, we queer boys do have the good sense to know that men are more proficient in the art of fellatio than women. That is unless you're Julia Roberts. Those lips alone would make her worth three thousand dollars a night for poor, misguided Richard Gere."

"They turn queer when their skating classmates start developing those awesome butts," announced another girl who was also focusing her attention on her image in the lighted vanity mirror.

"One thing's for sure," added another boy skater, "this Garry Windsor has a package that's strong enough for a woman, but is made for a man."

"You're so queer!"

"La-de-dah!"

"You'll never get him!"

"Think he knows Michael Weiss?"

Another girl piped in. "Out of bounds, you silly little overactive glands." She laughed. "I suggest you keep your lips and your flies—whichever is more appropriate—zipped or buttoned, and your eyes open. Keep an eye on Garry. You might learn about something other than the length of his wee wee."

The entire company had stopped yammering to pay reverential attention to the girl defending Garry Windsor. She was Amber Nyak, the only member of the cast with a real Olympic medal. It was bronze—the medal that nobody ever brags about winning—but it was the closest thing to gold that the show could boast about.

They knew that Amber wouldn't stand to hear any of the boys or girls putting down another skater. Most of the kids in the show had very little ambition, other than to travel the world and find a husband. For the latter pursuit, the girls had joined the wrong aspect of the entertainment and sports world. There was only one Sergei Grinkov, and he was dead.

A dearth of straight male skaters seemed to rub off on them and they developed the cattiness of some gay men. But when Amber was around they'd never think to be antagonistic toward a gifted skater, even for the sake of a little fun. To all the skaters Amber was the queen of the ice. And if she heard the great Mike Ledgewood or Vladamire Klinkov referred to as "dinky dorks," the skater who voiced such a remark would be severely unbraided.

At age thirty, not only was Amber Nyak still beautiful and magical on blades, but she was the *Dr. Quinn Medicine Woman* of the company—quick to dispense assistance to anyone, boys or girls, who needed to improve a jump or spin. Amber was to the company of skaters what Mary Richards was to WJM-TV Channel 12—professional, levelheaded, calm-in-the-center-of-any-storm. Whatever she said was accepted as law.

Dressed in her first-act costume, Amber passed through the communal changing room shared by the chorines and chorus boys. Her outfit was a red, hand-beaded nylon affair made to look as though searing flames were licking her breasts. It was a knock-off of a Bob Mackie creation for Cher or Katarina Witt, and the dress never failed to earn great applause the moment the bright spotlights bathed Amber with pink and blue gels, as she came to the center of a rink.

Immediately after the skater who played the role of the woman smoking a cigarette through her trachea stepped off the ice, the entire arena went to pitch black. Amber, with an uncanny sixth sense, found her way to the center of the rink. She arranged her body like an Erté descending a staircase. She positioned her arms parallel with her shoulders, as if she was holding a bow and arrow preparing to spear the bull's eye of a target.

With her skate blades *en pointe*, her head up, and her smile fixed, Amber remained perfectly still until the key light found her. As though she were a music box dancer idle before her mechanism is wound, Amber remained in a pregnant pause, even as her music, a medley from *La Bohème*, began to fill the arena.

She then gave an almost imperceptible curtsy to the audience, did a half turn and slowly began performing back crossovers leading to her first jump. It was a double toe loop, followed by a series of relatively easy, but very dramatic jumps and spins as she expressed every note from Puccini's score.

Amber perfectly executed a flying Camel, followed by a series of spirals, interspersed with fancy footwork, and more back crossovers. Amber moved into a back sit spin and completed her opening routine with a back scratch.

Amber captivated the audience with her grace and signature triple Axel double toe loop combination that had earned her third place at the Winter Games.

As the music came to an end, so did Amber's breathtaking exhibition. She gracefully lay down on the cold floor of ice to mime the death of the character she was portraying. As always, there was a moment of complete silence as audiences came to grips with Amber's exquisite performance.

Then, thunderous applause followed. Amber, slowly, as if rising by strings from an invisible puppeteer, drew herself up and back onto her shiny skate blades. She had completed her program in the precise position in which she began.

As waves of enthusiastic applause bounced off the ice and arena walls, Amber curtsied again to the audience in front of her. Then she turned around and curtsied to the patrons behind her. She turned to the left and then to the right and gave each section of the old rink an acknowledgment of her appreciation for their kind response. After each performance she appeared to be genuinely touched by her audiences' ovations, truly moved by their approval of her work.

Gold on Ice boasted that there was something for the entire family in its show. Sure enough, immediately after Amber Nyak's solo, costume characters charged the ice, wiping out the essence of beauty and magic that had briefly permeated the building.

In Amber's place, a cavalcade of human Barbie Dolls (without permission from Mattel's character placement division) entered the rink as the tape-recorded announcer called out, "Malibu Barbie! Town and Country Barbie! Camilla Parker Barbie! Tow Truck Driver Barbie! Wal-Mart Greeter Barbie! Fear Factor Barbie!" They each carried props relating to their particular Barbie: a surfboard, a Neiman Marcus shopping bag, a bejeweled crown and scepter, a tire jack, a motorized wheelchair. The last Barbie was featured wearing a fishbowl over her head filled with gummyworms.

Then a skater dressed as a race jockey and wearing green-and-orange striped silks and tight white jodhpurs that emphasized his tushie, stepped onto the ice. He was followed in succession by Elvira, reclining on a chaise and holding a severed head. She was being pushed around the rink by Big Bird (no contract either from *Sesame Street*), trailed by a human-size Academy Award (no license fee from the AMPAS), and a naked-to-the-waist Catholic priest (no ID from NMBLA) decked out in a Cardinal's miter. His muscular body compensated for his minimal skills as a skater.

The crowd applauded wildly as this free-for-all spectacle worked its way around the rink. Then they nearly hospitalized themselves into a collective convulsion over pratfalls that were a chain reaction from the Kentucky Fried drumstick strategically colliding with the Doublemint twins, who tripped over the dwarfs who were Plain and Peanut M&Ms, who collapsed and slid into the Flags of The Axis of Evil troupe. The audience loved it. Uncle Ernie was having a meltdown and planning across the board terminations.

After intermission, the ice once again became the center for classic figure skating when the announcer's virile voice enthusiastically enunciated, "Ladies and Gentlemen! Please welcome! Former North American Men's Figure Skating champion! Mister! Garry! Wind-*sor!*"

Spirited applause greeted Garry who gracefully glided around the perimeter of the rink, his arms outstretched the same way a gymnast who has just dismounted the parallel bars brags with his body language. He found his way to the center of the ice, and, as the applause subsided, took his stance while he waited for his music—the love theme from *Nicholas and Alexandra.*

As the cascade of strings began to fill the air, Garry embraced the sound—a descending scale that gradually expanded to envelop the entire venue. Garry's body movements matched the fluidity of the orchestral arrangement. The artist and the material were one. He dazzled the crowd—as well as the other skaters—with his seemingly effortless leaps and spins. Garry never tired of being absorbed by the power he felt gliding over ice. He was on automatic pilot, absorbed in his own version of flying.

At the conclusion of his program, the applause was thunderous. It reverberated throughout the hollow building. Garry beamed from the sheer ecstasy of doing what he loved to do: soaring on thin steel blades. Nothing, including sensational sex, gave him a greater feeling of self-gratification.

Of course, Jay had been absolutely right about his prediction of the offers for sex that Garry would receive from both the other young skaters and also the men in the audience. Grandpas who looked as though they could be hawking Werther's candy on television, were as plentiful as (and perhaps more prurient than) the young country bucks who smuggled their brewskies into the arenas. After Garry's solo performance at each venue, bouquets of cellophane-wrapped roses were hurled to the ice from behind the bright lights by faceless men who hoped to express their affection on a mattress in some private motel room.

As Garry departed from the rink after every show, there was always a contingent of blatantly lustful men standing at what Garry,

Jay, and Amber affectionately called *Dysfunction Junction*. That was the alley, or as Amber put it, "the quarantine bay" outside of every venue in which they skated. The toadies who collected there were, more often than not, the variety of humanity one would find at sci-fi conventions or boasted about having season passes to Busch Gardens in Florida. Jay said that he suspected these men were probably responsible for the *Saved by the Bell* trivia website.

"Don't call 'em Neanderthals," Amber protested to Jay. "They're cute, in their cross-eye corrective glasses and wearing wrinkled T-shirts that say *Jesus Loves You, But Everyone Else Thinks You're an Asshole.*"

Jay usually cringed after signing autographs on souvenir programs that had been folded up in quarters or used as a plate for the nachos sold at arena concession stands. He politely declined invitations to midnight showings of such classics as *Christmas Evil,* and denied himself the fun and excitement of viewing someone's collection of Lucille Ball cover issues of *TV Guide.*

"It's not that I'm not grateful for their attention," Jay rationalized to Garry and Amber. "I'm just a little phobic about what grows under such long fingernails. I'm afraid that a rust-colored front tooth might fall out at any moment. I'm sure some men are very attracted to guys who look like Kathy Kinney with a ponytail. More power to 'em!"

But not every *Dysfunction Junction* was a toxic dump of other-world life forms. Occasionally, the quarantine bays were peppered with Brendan Fraser clones. For every ten Rob Schneider pathogens, one or two variations on David James Elliott or Patrick Dempsey appeared.

For the first two weeks, in consideration of Garry's self-imposed virginity, Jay tried to ignore the attractive prospects. His repeated excuse for passing on their generous offers for a beer and sex was that the show's producers were throwing a cast party and he couldn't get out of it. Garry always appeared grateful but a little guilty that he was keeping his friend from getting his butt pricked.

Then it happened.

One evening as Garry, Jay, and Amber were exiting another run-down rink along their grueling tour route, they were derailed at *Dysfunction Junction* by a six-foot-tall, green-eyed, auburn-haired definitive answer to the standard question, "Your father's James Van Der Beek and he fucked Joshua Jackson to get you, right? Right."

"Holy tits," Amber said without moving her lips. "I knew this day would come. Gay or straight, I'd take him on in a sec."

Almost too stunned to hear what Amber was saying, Jay made an effort to say goodnight to his friends.

"I should run along too," Garry said to Jay as they approached the dazzling creature stuffed into a faded T-shirt, a pair of frayed 501s and scuffed work boots.

Jay nudged Garry as they got closer. "Don't you dare move," he said.

"Well, it is a shame about his looks," Garry whispered.

When they were within striking distance, the poster boy for *Looks Are Everything* blocked their passage. "I'm in your way," the imperfection-challenged stud said.

Jay felt as though he was experiencing something close to astral projection—or a reasonable facsimile of the moment during a wet dream, just before ejaculation, when one is still unconscious but somehow aware of an awesome physical feeling. "Across the board six-point-ohs for artistic merit," Jay whispered out of the side of his mouth.

"I know what that means, but I'm really bigger." The guy smiled.

"Now I get what Cher was begging for when she sang, *Take Me Home*," Jay said to himself. Suddenly he couldn't get the song out of his head—or get his meat to stay still in his jeans.

There wasn't time for an awkward moment because the stud was as short on words. "I usually do it only for money. Or a meal." The kid paused. "But I've got a big one. Fantasy that is."

"Fantasy?" Jay encouraged.

"We're not psychic," Garry interjected. "What's your fantasy?"

"To be fucked by a skater."

Jay chuckled. "Yeah, we're at the top of everybody's wish list." He stared into the guy's eyes. "There's bubble butt–skaters, up here." He reached up at arm length and marked an invisible line in the air above his head. "And there's hairy-chested firemen putting out eight-alarm fires with their Municipal Pro-flow hoses, down here." He made another line in the air at knee level.

"Nothing like getting right to the point," Garry said, sardonically.

"Was that like a turn-off?" the guy said.

"Yeah. Crude and disgusting." Jay studied the boy for a long moment. "However, anyone with your shade of green eyes is for-given the impertinence. Real, or contacts?"

"Oh, my eyes? Don't need lenses to know that you guys would blow my head off. The one on my dick, I mean." The young man smiled, devouring Jay and Garry with his hungry look.

Just then, one of the bacterium with big corrective lenses and a prominently displayed Medic Alert bracelet shoved his way into the trio. "Mr. Windsor! Mr. Windsor!" he called like a Kotter Sweathog, "Can I get your autograph?"

Garry was obviously happy for the interruption. He signed the man's program.

"Far out! I betcha I can get five dollars for this on eBay!"

"Thank you," Garry said as the germ turned away with his prize, not paying any more attention to the skaters.

Garry shook his head. "Enjoy yourselves," he said, seeing that Jay was obviously digging the guy whose T-shirt should have read: *Yes, I Am A Male Model.* "I'm not in the least bit interested."

Jay meanwhile kept staring at the guy whose basket was filled with the entire hardware section of Sears. The guy's long, auburn hair fell to the collar of his jacket and the white T-shirt he wore under it. The shirt, filled with the outline of the kid's muscled body, made Jay salivate. He gave Garry a look that said, *C'mon, this is a win/win.* "How 'bout a three way?" Jay offered.

"Awesome, Jay," the guy said.

"You know my name?"

"And your friend is Garry," the guy said. "And I'm Gabe."

They moved down the alley and into the street. The neighbor-hood was more industrial than residential and very old. Abandoned brick buildings—box factories and coat hanger manufacturers—looked to be from the turn of the *nineteenth* century. The street was more ruts and potholes than tarred pavement. Screeching tires in the distance and the sound of Gabe's boots echoing off the walls of the old structures were the only sounds. They made Garry begin to wonder what they were doing just to have sex with an awesome-looking fantasy fuck.

As they turned another corner there were a few shacks that Garry decided were supposed to be houses. Uncut patches of grass surrounded by chainlink fences seemed as common to the area as those politically incorrect little statues of black stable boys in hunt-ing outfits and holding lanterns, that were ubiquitous beside drive-ways in the suburbs. Old Dodge Darts up on blocks seemed to be the ornamentation *de rigueur* in this part of town. The sidewalk was cracked and buckled from tree roots spreading under the pathway.

After two blocks they rounded still another corner where the buildings were even older and more run down. Garry and Jay con-tinued to follow Gabe until he finally stopped at the entrance of a fleabag flophouse of an apartment building. To Garry it was de-pressing to think anyone actually lived there—but enticing because it promised raunchy sex.

Gabe jiggled a few keys and unlocked the front door that was defaced with graffiti. "I'm on four," he said, leading Garry and Jay to an ancient staircase with a wobbly railing. The smell of onions and disinfectant permeated the stairwell. As they made their way up each flight, Gabe turned and put a finger to his lips signaling for them to be extra quiet. "Landlord," he whispered. "Rent."

Finally, the trio arrived at a door that had been painted and re-painted probably a hundred times during the life of the building. Quietly, Gabe inserted his key into the lock and slowly pushed it open. The hinges screeched. He reached around to the inside wall and found the light switch. He flipped it on. When they were all in-side, Gabe quickly closed the door and turned the security lock. "This is it," he announced, as though they had reached Bucking-ham Palace via the Paris sewers.

"Nice," Garry lied, looking around under the dim wattage from a bare overhead bulb. Chunks of plaster were missing from one of the walls. Dingy, once-gold-colored shag carpeting had entire sec-tions ripped out, exposing concrete. There were no shades or cur-tains on the two side-by-side double-hung windows, one of which was duct-taped to keep a wedge of glass from dropping out of its glazing.

Garry looked at Jay with Marty Feldman eyes. His unspoken words were understood: *What the fuck are we doing here?*

"I've got beers," Gabe announced, eagerly opening an old, personal-size refrigerator on the living room/kitchenette floor. He withdrew three cans of Bud, handed a can to each of his guests, and then snapped the pop-top on his own. He downed the suds practi-cally in one gulp while Garry and Jay took small sips. "You didn't want glasses did you?" he asked. "Don't have any anyway." Gabe tossed his empty can into an overflowing garbage bin. He retrieved another cold one.

"You might want to go easy," Jay said. "You know what they say: 'You don't buy it, you rent it.' "

Gabe looked quizzical, then laughed. "Oh, you mean I'll pee it all out."

Garry gave a slight smirk and a slighter nod.

"I'm just trying to loosen up," said Gabe. "I've got my sex dream fantasy about to come true." He emptied the second round of beer down his throat, crushed the can in his hand and tossed it into the trash without looking in the direction of his aim.

"Forget about your six point oh, here's what I've got," he said, as he peeled off his T-shirt, revealing the chiseled body.

His abs were as solid as a tortoise shell. The flesh on his stomach looked like it was a veneer over a steel form. There wasn't an ounce of extra body fat around his waist. His shoulders were wide and rounded. Garry's eyes followed from there down to Gabe's pumped biceps and thick forearms that were etched with more veins than he had ever seen on a man.

Gabe took Garry's right hand and placed it on his chest. "You like?" he beamed.

Garry took another swig of beer, put the can down and placed his other hand on Gabe's chest. He moved his fingers slowly over the satiny surface of the sculpted body. Garry held his breath for a moment then said, "Jeez, yes."

Gabe then unbuttoned the top of his faded 501s. "Here," he offered Jay, "you do the rest."

Jay put his can of beer down onto the floor and complied with Gabe's suggestion. He unhooked one button at a time. After releasing the last one he pulled Gabe's fly aside and gasped. The girth of the head of Gabe's meat was mesmerizing. If this was just the tip of the proverbial iceberg, one could only imagine the length of the shaft. To Garry's embarrassment, he actually drooled onto the floor.

"Hey! Help the trapped python out of its hole!" Gabe ordered.

Jay reached for the monster. Gabe inhaled loudly. He could feel himself leaking pre-cum.

"I'm just here to observe," Garry insisted, caressing Gabe's chest. Displaying his lust in front of Jay was an embarrassment he didn't want to risk. Garry was determined to exhibit all-but-impossible restraint.

Jay kneeled down, his face close enough to Gabe's crotch to feel the heat radiating from his penis. He shimmied Gabe's pants down to his knees. The guy wasn't wearing underwear, and his cock was pointing straight out, as if it was too heavy to stand up any higher.

Gabe's appendage was the girth of a turkey baster and as long as the shaft of a nighwatchman's flashlight. Awesome.

"Okay. I'm sold," said Garry, giving in to his carnal desires. He began to remove his own shirt.

Jay followed suit. Gabe saw Jay glancing at the window. "Let's hit the bedroom," he said, kicking off his sneakers and stepping out of the legs of his jeans.

Gabe moved the few steps into what was no more than a walk-in closet with a king-size mattress on the floor. Jay and Garry quickly shed the rest of their clothes. Gabe flopped backwards onto the unmade bed. Garry and Jay immediately joined him.

Gabe moaned in ecstasy as the men smothered him in deep kisses and dragged their tongues over his body, from his throat to his musky underarms, to his hard pink nipples and silky skin of his rock-solid chest. They attacked him with as much satisfaction as a deer enjoying a salt lick.

Then, unintentionally, Jay and Garry met face to face with Gabe's cock between them. Immediately, Garry pulled away. "You go first," he said, confused and astonished by his untamed, feral behavior.

"Mmmm," Jay moaned lustfully. He drew his tongue up and down Gabe's python. He then attempted to take as much of Gabe's dick as possible into his mouth.

Garry kneeled beside the mattress and observed as each man patronized the other. Back and forth they moaned, "Oh, God, you're killing me!"

Then, finally, Gabe announced, "Time's up for *your* fantasy. Let me have mine now."

Garry looked at Jay. "All yours."

"Dang right he's all mine," Gabe panted.

Garry reached for a tube of what was labeled *Axle Grease* next to the bed. He handed an *I Can't Believe It's Not Butter*–size plastic tub to Jay who lifted the lid and scooped out the Crisco-like substance. He slathered three fingers full of the grease over and into Gabe's puckered hole. Then he lubed himself.

"No condoms?" Garry asked, nearly breaking the erotic spell.

"Too expensive," Gabe gasped. "Just take it out before you cum," he said, looking at Jay who was pointing his member at Gabe's hot hole.

"You can afford beer, but you can't afford condoms?" Jay gave Garry a look that begged, "I know this is stupid, but don't spoil the moment."

Garry shook his head. "Hold on," he sighed with disgust and reached for his jeans among the pile of clothes. He found his wallet, opened the billfold, and withdrew a foil-wrapped condom. He pressed it into Jay's hand.

Jay acknowledged Garry's gallantry with a slight crook of his head as he tore open the package and quickly rolled the sheath over his shaft. He slapped his meat a few times against Gabe's ass. He positioned the head of his cock at the glistening bullseye. Slowly, he pushed the head of himself past Gabe's tight sphincter.

Garry, in the meantime, had decided to leave the other two men to do their business. He had given up any plans of losing his nearly year-old celibacy. And although he hated playing voyeur, he didn't know how to tactfully extricate himself from the scene.

Gabe's hands were all over Jay's upper body. Then he reached down for Jay's ass to bring him in closer and deeper into his hole. "Christ! Jesus fucking Christ! This is what I've been wanting. Christ to god almighty! Fuck me. God, yes! That's it! Fucking Christ!" he cried out.

Then: "Spit in my hand!" Gabe ordered Garry, who reluctantly complied. Gabe wiped Garry's spit onto the shaft of his cock. He began stroking himself, slowly. Clearly he could come at any moment, but he wanted the satisfaction to continue for as long as Jay could keep his dick buried in his ass.

They continued for nearly a half-hour. Then came the *fait accompli*. Gabe began to buck violently, thrashing his head from side to side. His cries came in staccato bursts.

Watching the scene, Garry thought it was pathetic irony that he was witnessing the sort of scene that he and Kurt once indulged in daily. Now, all he could do was watch from a distance. He thought that Gabe would lose his head from all the whipping back and forth.

Then, not so suddenly but still surprisingly, Gabe thrashed more violently. He cried out as if in excruciating pain. Then he pumped out as copious a load as would be expected from a man so young and well equipped. Jiz covered his stomach and chest. "Oh, god," he called to Jay, "take it out and shoot all over me!" Then, looking at Garry, he said, "You take his place!"

"Rain check," said Garry.

"Christ! Please!"

Garry stood up, then quickly left the room and retrieved his pants. "Oh, fuck!" he heard Gabe cry. "That's it man. All over me! Yes!"

Garry dressed, then stood in the doorway leaning against the molded frame.

Gabe lay on his back. His face, chest and stomach were covered with streams of semen that were sliding down the sides of his body. He reached up and slathered it around. He playfully wiped cum onto his face and put his fingers into his mouth. He sucked the collective jiz and instantly became hard again.

"So soon?" Jay said. He, too, was growing stiff.

"How 'bout if I watch you guys fuck each other," Gabe asked.

"No can do," Garry said.

"What're friends for?" Gabe asked naively.

"To help the other get laid in times of famine. Got a towel or something?" Jay said.

Gabe chuckled. "Your friend let you down," he said to Jay with a too-bad-you-dumb-fuck smirk.

"Not," Garry said. He wasn't the least bit distressed over not making out. But he had stopped to consider that after all these months without Kurt, he must look pretty silly being faithful to a non-existent lover. *I guess I'm just not made like other men*, he thought to himself. *I want sex, but I don't need it. Call me crazy.*

"It would put us in a different category of friends," Jay added, picking up the edge of the top sheet to wipe himself off. "Besides, strange as this may sound, I love Garry. But neither of us has ever had the least bit of interest in each other—sexually. Our love doesn't include fucking each other."

"That's cool, I guess," Gabe said. Then, to Garry he said, "Maybe you should try him out sometime. Might make you less miserable, you know?"

Chapter Five

Clarksville was smack in the middle of dairy and farmland. The local kids got a charge out of mucking out the cow stalls in their bare feet. However, despite the picayune size and population, and the absence of a pedicure parlor, the town boasted a fairly modern ice rink, The IceBox, as its sign announced.

The IceBox wasn't Madison Square Garden by any stretch, but it had a good skating surface and actual theatre seats. The *Gold on Ice* company was so used to playing to audiences who had to sit on wooden bleachers, that the place felt the way they thought Radio City must be like.

Garry was anxious to take advantage of practicing on well-maintained ice for a change, and he got up at five A.M. to beat the others to the rink, for what would probably be only a short amount of time by himself.

"We had Rosie O'Donnell do a concert here a few years back," the security guard proudly said when Garry tried to impress him with the fact that he was in the ice show. "She's one funny fat girl." The guard, a slender black youth, unlocked the control room booth to turn on the speakers and pop Garry's music cassette into the tape deck.

"Yeah, Rosie's a kick in the balls," Garry said in mock agreement.

Dressed in jeans and a white T-shirt that was quickly diaphanous with perspiration, Garry skated to his favorite classical music. No screeching *Star Search* divas for him. The rest of the world could have their Whitneys and Britneys and Krystals and Christinas. His tape played Ravel, Debussy and Satie, with solo violin arrangements.

The romantic music transported him. Vibrations filled the cavernous rink, as well as his soul. Garry's skating had more meaning when he was flying over the ice to "Pavane pour une Infante Defunte" or "Gymnopédies" or "Reverie." He skated from one end of the rink to the other, performing only for himself, and landing the quad jump with each attempt. "Damned A.S.S.," he said under his breath. "You'd think I was Robert Blake, the way I've been treated." With or without the support of his club or the Society, or even an Olympic medal, he knew that he was a world-class elite figure skater.

Garry listened carefully to the voice in his soul that said, *Back crossover. Back crossover. Slow down your speed just a little. Watch your left outside edge. Now, move your arms back. Bend your left leg. Now! Lift off! Swing that free leg around and bring your arms forward! Reach! Reach forward, Garry. Tuck your left leg under you and get ready for the landing. Great! Now rotate! Spin! Spin! Spin!*

Garry didn't notice that some of the other skaters from the show had begun to trickle into the building. However, rather than immediately join Garry, who was now skating to the theme from *Somewhere in Time*, they stood at the barrier around the rink and observed their star's virtuosity. He *tour jete'd* like a *primere danseur* for Alvin Ailey, springing into the air, landing on one blade, doing a pirouette then laughing as he whirled like a graceful hawk soaring on a current of air.

The chorus boys and girls ate it up. Some wished they'd spent more time as kids practicing on the ice and less time watching *Scooby-Doo* and *Mad-TV* or straying into restricted eighteen and older Internet sex chat rooms.

Driving his toe pick into the ice, Garry came to an abrupt stop. He noticed the crowd he'd attracted. "If you're waiting for this fairy to wave his wand and grant your ice wish, consider it done," he called, flicking an invisible magic wand and beckoning for them all to join him on the ice. "It's great! Sarah Hughes couldn't have it any better!"

Garry continued his practice at the center of the rink while the others warmed up and skated around him and in small patches.

Jay finally arrived, tired and looking like Gopher on *The Love Boat* with a Pacific Princess hangover. Immediately upon entering the building he was met with the frigid air of the rink—as familiar and comforting to him as any other feeling. He loved that he had the talent to skate. He never considered another career.

With his orange striped Adidas shoulder bag containing his skates and a dozen other things he might need at any given moment—gloves, boot laces, Band-Aids, Ben-Gay, Chap Stick, breath mints, sunglasses, Kleenex, and condoms—Jay moved along the long hallway entrance. He passed glass cases which held hockey trophies, figure skating medals and pictures of the local ice club's most accomplished competitors.

Posters announcing *Gold on Ice, Five Performances Only!* were stapled to cork boards that also advertised the Clarksville PTA's scheduled meeting to discuss their latest list of challenged books. Jay stopped for a moment to examine a black and white picture of a boy skater, apparently a local champion, holding a loving cup. "They're all so cute at that age," he said under his breath.

Jay took a quick look at the PTA poster. "Are your pre-teens reading Cardinal Law's *Boy, That Was Hard!*? Or does Britain's very own disciple of the devil, J.K. Rowling, possess them? Join us for a lively debate."

Jay frowned, shaking his head in distaste at the blatant attempt at censorship. *Change the punctuation of the Law book, and see what you get,* he smiled to himself. Entering the rink portion of the building, he walked toward a bench where he could sit and slide into his boots and blades. He couldn't help notice that standing at the rink's barrier was a dazzling, peach-skinned young man. His blond hair touched his broad shoulders. His tight, white T-shirt was tucked into equally tight blue jeans. He was wearing ancient, scuffed brown hockey skates.

"Priest bait," Jay said to himself, thinking of the PTA and their endorsement of the Cardinal Law book. The guy was staring intently at a particular figure on the ice. Jay followed the boy's gaze and saw that his eyes were glued to Garry, who was still practicing his sit spins and spread eagle.

Jay sidled up to the kid. He was so entranced with the spectacle on the ice that he didn't take any notice of Jay sitting down and lacing up his boots beside him. When Jay finished tying his knots, he stood up and moved close enough to the boy to pick up the scent of his warm body. The two watched in silence as Garry went through his long program for the show.

"Oh, jeez," the kid involuntarily sighed after one of Garry's jumps.

"He's pretty good, isn't he?" Jay said.

The guy looked at Jay with an expression of distraction and irritation. Turning back to watch Garry, the young man commented, "He's only my hero. I can't believe he's here in my hometown. At The Ice Box."

"You know who he is?" Jay asked.

"If you don't know who Garry Windsor is, you're not serious about figure skating," the kid said without taking his eyes off Garry's workout and in a tone that warned he was about to be pissed off.

"He's also only my best friend," Jay said with a trace of annoyance for the kid's unwarranted attitude.

That did the trick. The young man turned to Jay with wide green eyes. "You're Jay Logan! Oh, my God! I'm sorry! I didn't mean to be rude! I'm just so in awe of what Mister Windsor does on the ice! Oh, and you, too, Mister Logan!"

"Stop with the mister." Jay smiled, dismissing the hero-worship. "You want to meet him?"

"Garry Windsor?" the kid said with alarm. "No! I would never interrupt him while he's skating, or bother him even if he came through the line at the hardware store where I clerk. I mean, the guy's a god. You don't just introduce yourself to a god."

"I know what you mean," Jay said. "He's right up there with Captain Crunch and Spiderman. He's actually very human. He pees standing up and everything. C'mon."

"Thanks, but no. I'd have nothing and everything to say to him. I'd make a blithering fool of myself. It's enough just to see him in person. I can't afford to buy a ticket to *Gold on Ice,* so this is perfect. Better. Really."

"This way," Jay said, taking the young man by a muscled arm and forcing him to follow along to the opening in the rink barrier that led to the ice. "By the way, who should I tell him he's being introduced to?"

"Tag."

"Is there a last name? Or is that like Cher or Madonna?"

The boy blushed. "Sorry. Tempkin. Tag Tempkin. See, I'm too nervous!"

Nervous or not, Jay noticed that Tag was quite comfortable on the ice. He wasn't the least bit tentative or off balance. Together they glided to the center of the rink and stopped before a spinning Garry. When Garry came to an abrupt halt, driving the pick of his right blade into the ice, he noticed Tag and then Jay.

"Hey, pal," Garry said to Jay. "You're up earlier than I expected."

"Didn't want you hogging all the ice. You've got a fan here." Jay pushed Tag closer.

Garry offered a large smile and strong handshake. "A skater?"

"Skater?" Tag parroted. "No. I mean, I skate, but not really. Not anything like you. I'm a complete novice. Never had a lesson. Couldn't afford to hire a coach."

"Been there. Done that." Garry smiled knowingly at Jay.

"Maybe we could give you a few pointers," Jay suggested, winking at Garry.

Garry said, "Yeah. Let's see what you can do and we'll spend a couple of minutes imparting our legendary wisdom," he quipped.

"I can't!" Tag said. "I mean, I'd completely embarrass myself. Not to mention wasting your valuable time. Trust me, just meeting you has been a dream come true."

Garry seemed heady with flattery. "If you're such a fan, then let me repay the compliment by giving you a quick lesson. Yes?"

Tag blushed. "Well, when you put it that way. I mean, you're Garry Windsor!"

Garry stole a quick glance at Jay with a smile that said, *Isn't he precious?*

"Okay. Here goes. Promise not to laugh?"

"This is serious," Garry said. "My music's on. Just do whatever you can."

Tag glided backwards a few feet away from Garry and Jay. He

dug the toe pick of his right skate blade into the ice, then stood perfectly still for a long moment. Garry and Jay looked at each other, as if to say: *He's pretending to be Kristi Yamaguchi.*

Tag closed his eyes then raised his arms. As the music, "Pavane for a Dead Princess," began its fourth loop through the speaker system, Tag slowly began to move to the unhurried tempo. His fluidity on the ice was astonishing. As Tag performed ridiculously difficult maneuvers, the guys turned to each other with their mouths open. From flying camels to triple Axels to a beautiful spread eagle, Tag's body moved with grace and confidence. He used his arms and hands to nuance his performance. He had Jay and Garry—and the rest of the skaters—staring in amazement.

At the conclusion of his exhibition, Tag did an exquisite sit spin. As the music faded, he lay down and curled up on the ice in a fetal position. Spontaneously, all the skaters on the ice, including Garry and Jay, broke into applause. Whoops and hollers of "Bravo!" filled the arena.

Tag slowly got to his feet. He put his hands over his face as if in complete embarrassment. He wore an enormous smile but gestured for everyone to please pay no attention to him. "I'm just a beginner," he cried, placing his hands over his heart. "You're all pros. But thank you. I'm completely embarrassed, but thank you. Thank you so much."

Tag glided back to Garry and Jay who simply stared at him as if they'd just caught Ilia Kulik and Michael Weiss mating. "So, what can I do to improve?"

"You've got to be kidding," Garry said.

Tag turned pale. "I knew it. I knew I wasn't any good and I shouldn't have been so dumb as to skate in your presence. But you insisted."

"What I mean is, you're magic on the ice. If you think we can give you any pointers you're nuts. You're great! And you say you've never been coached?"

Tag protested, "Well, to be honest, in a way I have been coached. That is, I've watched tapes of all your competitions. I just sort of tried to follow along with what I saw you do. I hope you don't mind my kind of borrowing your moves. But I've added stuff of my own, so I really just studied you."

Jay cut in. "It doesn't matter where you got your program, Tag, the fact is, you've got a great gift. Hasn't anyone ever told you that before? Your mother? Your father? Someone at the rink?"

"Some guys, maybe. But I couldn't trust 'em. They all wanted something from me."

I wonder what that could be, Jay said to himself. Tag went on. "My folks don't know I still skate. When my dad found out I was spending all my allowance just to come to public sessions, he hit the roof. He said it wouldn't be so bad if I wanted to be a hockey player. But when I said I wanted to be Garry Windsor he threw up his hands and called me a fairy. Oh. Sorry. I don't think he meant . . ."

"Yeah. He meant it." Garry grimaced. "Heck, you want me to talk to him? I can vouch for your talent."

"No!" Tag pleaded. "He thinks only queers figure skate. Sorry."

"Stop apologizing," Jay said.

"He doesn't recognize the sheer athleticism of skating," Tag continued. "A four-minute free-style program is about as arduous as running a marathon. He sees it as sissy ballet or something."

"He's wrong of course," Garry said.

"*We* know that," Tag said, looking at Garry then to Jay, as if to say *I'm queer and I know you guys are too.* "But my folks already have their suspicions about me. The other morning, while Mom was making my lunch, she took a swipe at me. She said, 'I don't know what's wrong with my son. When I was your age, I'd had my heart broken at least five or six times. You're obviously not interested in girls.' "

Tag sighed. "I left my breakfast and walked to school instead of taking the bus. I bawled my head off all the way, 'cause my mom was my hero. I couldn't conceive that the one person I loved so much could be so cruel. I know I'm not what most parents want in a son, but I'm a truly nice guy. So I cried all during first-period math. I cried through English lit. And science. The whole time, I vowed to leave home just as soon as school was out and make a big success of myself. Somehow and somewhere far away. And nobody, and I mean *nobody* would ever hurt me again."

"That's every queer boy's best revenge," Garry agreed. "Get rich and famous and then play Lady Bountiful. It works wonders on the ego. But those unenlightened jerks will still see you as a second-class citizen."

"So why haven't you left yet?" Jay interrupted. "You're out of school, aren't you? I 'spect you're around eighteen."

Tag nodded. "A week from next Thursday. But I don't have enough money. I'm working at Lumber World and saving everything, except for what I need to get in here and skate. There's nothing in Clarksville for me. I have a plan worked out in my mind, but it'll be at least a year before I can split."

"Hang for a second, would you?" Garry said.

He pulled Jay to the side of the rink. "You have to agree, this kid's amazing!"

"You noticed his arms too? And that mind-blowing chest!" Jay snuck a peak at Tag in his still-wet shirt, clinging to what was obviously a sizzling hot young body.

"I'm serious! We've gotta do something!"

"He's still a minor!"

"Jay!" Garry said, clearly frustrated by his pal's pretending not to notice anything but Tag's ass. "Can't we get him a job in the show?"

"Whoa," said Jay. "I admit he's a terrific skater, but there are tons of talented guys there. He said it himself, he's just a novice. The kid's never been in a skating competition, let alone before an audience." Jay looked back at Tag. "Imagine having a piece of that," he mused.

"What better chance, than having him in the show?" Garry appealed. "Look, he skated well for us, and for all the kids. I know he's shy, but—"

Jay glanced over his shoulder yet again at Tag, who was now speaking to a couple of the chorus boys. "He's not shy. And I don't for a moment believe he's never had a skating lesson. But before someone else beats me to him . . ."

Jay shrugged. "Ernie's always looking for pick-up skaters in every town. Maybe we can at least get him an audition. It doesn't mean he'll get a job."

"But it'll show that we have confidence in him. That in itself might give him the balls to quit his job, tell his old man where to shove his prejudices, and move on."

Jay smiled. "Someone's got a sweet tooth," he teased.

"That's your department. I just want to help this kid, the way someone once helped me."

"Maybe he'd be so grateful that he'd put out for me."

"He's all yours. I don't want the baggage."

"Look at that butt," Jay lamented. "Am I turning into a lecherous old man who has to pay to get a cute kid? Although he's probably worth whatever the going price is."

Garry scoffed. "At eighteen, or almost eighteen, they're all beautiful."

"You were supposed to hassle me about not being an old man," Jay groused.

"Why would I contradict the truth?" Garry cracked a smile. "I mean, you *are* twenty-two!"

"Twenty-one until Monday, you dickhead!"

"What's the saying, 'When you're young, you sell it. When you're middle aged, you give it away. And when you're old, you buy it back!'"

Jay scowled. "I'm not *buying* anything!" He pretended to sulk for a moment. Then he announced, "Let me see what I can do about an audition for him. Just an audition, mind you. If he wants to pay me back in some small slutty way, so be it."

"No ulterior motives, eh?" Garry said. "You're such a saint."

The two skated back to Tag, who was accepting a small piece of paper from another skater and placing it in his jeans pocket. "Hey," Garry said, calling Tag to his side. Tag quickly came over.

"We've got a sensational idea," said Jay. "We think that you should audition to be in *Gold on Ice*."

Tag looked up at Garry and Jay with an expression of astonishment. "You can't be serious," Tag said, shaking his head. "That's impossible. Your show is for professionals, like you guys. I'm a hack. Audiences pay top dollar to be entertained. They'd never stand for an amateur."

"Look, it would only be for the chorus," Garry said.

"And only for the three weeks that we're doing shows in Wisconsin," Jay said.

Garry added, "Confidentially, anything these other kids can do, you can do twice as well. Of course I don't know if there's an opening, but we can try." He tried to sound hopeful but guarded.

"But my parents." Tag said, flustered. "My job."

"Your parents don't have to know that you're going on an audition. And I don't know what the chorus kids get paid. Minimum wage I suspect. But that's probably what you're making at your lumber job, isn't it? So what have you got to lose?"

Tag looked down at his pathetic old skates, then looked at the highly polished pairs that both Garry and Jay were wearing. He didn't say anything. But his body language spoke volumes about his apprehension.

"Look," Garry encouraged, "you said you wanted to get out of Clarksville. This might be the opportunity of a lifetime. You owe it to yourself to at least give it a shot."

"When? Where? The audition, I mean."

"In about three hours," Jay said. "We'll clear it with the production manager. Just show up here at ten o'clock. You'll skate for him just the way you did for us. Nothing to it."

"Put it this way," Garry finally said, "if you like me so much, and you get the job, you'll get to see me up close and personal, all the time."

With that, Tag beamed. "Great. Okay. Right here at ten o'clock. I don't know what to say. Thank you isn't nearly enough. I promise to find some way to express my gratitude. I promise. Honest!"

"Just do a great job," Garry said. "That's all the gratitude anyone needs."

"Now get out of here and change your wet shirt," Jay said. "But wear another one just like it for the audition. The production manager appreciates in-shape boys, if you get my drift."

Tag smiled. "Everyone likes my body," he affirmed. "I just hope your production manager likes my skating."

"We'll be here to cheer you on," Jay promised.

Tag skated backwards, and as he waved goodbye, his wide smile lit up the rink.

"He's right," Jay sniggered. "'Thank you' isn't nearly enough. We should both take him up on his offer to express his gratitude."

"He's still a minor," Garry reminded.

"Until next week. He made it sound like an eternity," Jay said. "Anyway, why do you think this kid has no self-confidence about his skating? You don't find guys with such polished talent very often."

Garry agreed. "He was as good as I ever was at his age."

"D'ya think anyone could really teach themselves how to skate the way he does?" Jay deadpanned. "Oh, I forgot, he watched all of your competitions and videotaped them. He just copied your moves. Yeah, sure. And Martha Stewart doesn't have a clever recipe for head cheese soufflé."

Garry frowned. "It does seem peculiar about him. Not having a coach, I mean. Maybe if he watched everything I did in slow-motion instant replay, with Dick Button criticizing my every move, and telling the world how a Lutz should really be done, then, maybe. Nah. Well, maybe. D'ya think?"

"Whatever. I really hope he gets in to the show. It would prove to his homophobic parents that they've got a super-talented son and they should be proud of him. Were your folks always supportive of your skating?" Jay asked.

"God, no. But I demanded to be on the ice when I was like eight years old. I think I saw Paul Wylie on television in the Olympics and I got my first hard-on. I remember I wanted to *be* Paul Wylie. Or Scott Hamilton. Or Brian Boitano—when he had his hair. Depending on who was skating at the time. I loved 'em all. Wanted to have sex with 'em all, too."

"It was Randy Gardner who gave *me* a boner. Still does! Did you jack off to that *Sports Illustrated* picture of Brian on the ice the moment he finished his Olympic program and knew he had the gold?"

"Yup."

"Me too!" Jay enthused. "I pretty much felt his lips on mine when I was wide awake in bed late at night. If they all knew!" he laughed. "I could never make up my mind which of those guys I was more in love with or which one I wanted to be. So I had to settle for just being me."

"They probably all watched you . . . Oops, I didn't mean just at the impaling of Peggy's microphone. Your idols probably envied you being younger and following in their footsteps," Garry said.

"That's a fun fantasy. The people I loved, loving me. Thanks for saying that," Jay said with sincere gratitude.

"C'mon," Garry said. "Let's go find Ernie."

Chapter Six

As Tag was leaving the rink, Ernie Shamanski was walking in. They passed each other, and Ernie made a one-eighty for another look at the boy with the wide smile and still-wet T-shirt plastered to his hard, muscled frame. The sight of Ernie's appreciation for Tag wasn't lost on Garry who, with Jay, was observing the departure of their new find.

They skated to the edge of the ice, then stepped off onto the black matted floor where they slipped on their plastic skate guards. "Hey, Unc!" Garry called, halfway giving in to Ernie's preferred salutation. He and Jay walked toward the production manager. "A little bolt of lightning to shatter the otherwise boring atmosphere, eh?" Garry knew full well that Ernie would probably go back to his Motel 6 room, and masturbate to some fantasy involving Tag.

"As I get older, you all get younger," Ernie said.

"We want you to give him an audition for the chorus," Garry said.

"That one?" Ernie asked, sounding optimistic.

"You won't believe how good he is," Jay said.

"We told him to be here at ten, and that we'd try to get you to see him," Garry added.

"For that one, yes!" Ernie said. "If he's halfway decent he's got a job! It just happens we've got a couple of openings."

"Too bad he's so *un*attractive, isn't it, Ernie?" Jay teased.

"Thanks, Ernie," Garry said as he and Jay headed toward a bench to unlace and remove their skates.

"Thank you!" Ernie called back.

"He's so transparent," Garry said, *sotto voce.*

Jay chuckled. "When you're as butt ugly as Ernie, you've gotta be pushy 'cause ain't nobody gonna be cruisin' *you.* Wish he'd shave off that soul patch on his chin. His breakfast is still there."

At ten o'clock sharp, a contingent of *Gold on Ice* creative executives arrived. In addition to Ernie Shamanski, the group included the show's choreographer, performance director, line captain and stage manager. Tag was already there with Garry and Jay.

Ernie was brusque in his introduction. "You're the kid we're supposed to audition?" he asked. Ernie's *modus operandi* was to intimidate the new skaters. Then when he invariably began to treat the special ones in a more civilized way, they'd often do almost anything to remain in his good graces.

"Yes, sir," Tag responded. "Mister Windsor and Mister Logan were kind enough to suggest that you might consider watching me skate."

"Where's your music?" Ernie snapped.

"Well, the guy in the booth has my tape. He'll play it as soon as you're ready."

"So let's stop wastin' my time," Ernie barked. "Get on the freakin' ice."

Garry and Jay both gave Tag wide, encouraging smiles. Garry was thinking what a shit Ernie was for treating their new friend so harshly. Tag smiled back at the guys and stepped onto the ice, gliding to the center of the rink.

The group from the production all took seats in what was a penalty box when the rink was used for hockey games. Garry waved and gave a thumbs-up sign to the guy behind the glass in the control room upstairs, who signaled back that he'd start the tape.

Tag posed on the ice with his right toe pick pointing forward and his left blade perpendicular behind him. He positioned his right arm and shoulder parallel with his right blade. He held his head high. His blue jeans and tight red T-shirt made him appear like some sexy mannequin from a Gap store window display.

The tape began to play, but Tag did not move.

Garry gave a nervous look to Jay.

The sound of a harp plucked out a brief introduction. Then, a solo violin began to fill the air—"The Meditation" by Jules Massenet. At the sound of the violin, Tag gracefully took control of the ice. Garry elbowed Jay in relief.

With his right knee bent, Tag pushed against the ice with the inside edge of his left foot. He moved forward on his right inside edge blade, shifting his weight from one blade to the other as he began to execute a series of turns. He transitioned to his right back inside edge as he approached his first spin.

Tag covered the entire length of the rink with powerful jumps and spins. He enacted the music's wide display of emotions, as though absorbing the music and filtering it out through his blades and body. Garry decided that Tag had selected the one piece of music that never failed to bring tears to Ernie's eyes, as if it reminded him of his old dog's funeral.

At the end of his program, Tag resumed the pose he had affected before his music began. Then, he bowed to his small audience. He stood at the center of the ice smiling as Garry and Jay led the applause.

However, Ernie and his group were merely giving an obligatory acknowledgment. "Thank you, Mister Tempkin," one of Ernie's lackeys called out. "We'll let you know."

Tag skated over to Garry and Jay. "They hated me," he said, his face red and his eyes brimming with tears.

"He's just the asshole who calls himself a choreographer," Garry tried to reassure Tag. "It's entirely up to Ernie. And I know for a fact he liked you."

"He said so," Jay added.

"Maybe the way I look. But I want them to like the way I skate."

"They have to think these things over," Jay said. "Anyway, you were brilliant, regardless of their decision."

"We'll let you know," Tag exaggerated a mimic under his breath. "That means I didn't get the job. Shit. What do I have to do, offer my freakin' cock to that freakin' pop 'n' fresh dough face of his?" Tag said petulantly. "Cocksucking, fuck breath dick-head."

"Tag?" Garry shook his head, perplexed by the unexpected response from this kid who previously seemed so happy just to be thought of as good enough for an audition.

"Gosh!" Tag quickly checked himself. "Whatever got into me? Mister Ernie obviously knows what's best for his show. And I'm certainly such an unfledged novice." He forced a smile. "I guess I just had some unrealistic hopes. Well, at least in fifty years or so I can remind myself that I once had a terrific opportunity, courtesy of two of the world's greatest figure skaters. You guys have been incredible. I can't thank you enough. What can I ever do for you?"

"You can let us take you to dinner after the performance tonight," Jay asserted. "And we won't take no for an answer."

Garry chimed in. "We're leaving a ticket for you at Will Call, then we'll all run off together someplace. Maybe Amber Nyak will join us."

"Gosh, I'm over the moon!" Tag said. "But it's Saturday. We're open late at Lumberland. Gotta work to earn my way out of this town. Still, I'll make this up to you somehow."

Tag sat down on a bench and began to untie his laces and remove his skates. He wiped the blades off with a towel. Then he looked up. Ernie was standing over the trio.

"We've been talking, my staff and I," Ernie said to Tag. "You were okay out there. Our choreographer thinks you're decent. So do I. If you want to be an alternate for the chorus we can offer you that right now. It doesn't mean you'll ever get to skate with the company, but at least you'll be around the other skaters. And it doesn't pay anything, except that you'll be able to practice with the corps and learn their routines, just in case. Take it or leave it."

Tag smiled. "You're too kind, Mr. Shamanski. But I still need to make money. I have a part-time job and I can't give that up."

Jay intervened. "It's just a crummy job at night, Tag. We rehearse during the day."

"There you have it," Ernie said and left the trio.

Tag looked at Garry and Jay. "What should I do?"

"You know the answer," Garry said.

"No," he whined. "I'm afraid of losing my job."

"Fuck hardware," Garry retorted. "You wanna get stuck doing the same ol' thing for the rest of your life, just 'cause you're waiting for something better to come along? Maybe you don't recognize when opportunity is hitting you in the face. If you don't take chances, you'll always wonder about what might have been."

"Anyone can put on a smock and sell nails and two-by-fours," Jay added. "But where would you rather spend your time? Demonstrating a table saw, or demonstrating a double Axel, toe loop combination? Sorry to be so harsh on you, Tag. But I don't have any patience for people who have a God-given gift, but refuse to take that gift and use it the way God intended. Whatever you decide to do, will be the right thing. But before you make your final decision, you'd better think about the consequences."

"You're right," Tag declared. "I can't pass up the opportunity. Tell Ernie I accept."

"Go tell him yourself. It's the professional thing to do," Jay said.

Garry and Jay watched as Tag approached the production group. Ernie nodded his head, obviously accepting Tag into the fold with a gesture of a handshake that lasted a little longer than necessary.

"Just keep us informed of where we can reach you and be prepared for a moment's notice to haul your ass over to the rink," Ernie declared, trying his best not to pat Tag on the butt in public.

Returning to his new friends, Tag smiled as though he'd just seen his picture on a box of Wheaties. "You did the right thing," Garry said.

"I feel it."

Quinn, the choreographer, a tall, lithe, long-haired man wearing a green turtleneck shirt that hugged his fit body, came over to the boys' bench. "I suppose if you're Ernie's boy you'd better learn the routines," he sniped.

"I'm not anyone's *boy*," Tag flared.

"Mmmm," the choreographer said, looking Tag up and down. "Be at rehearsal. Noon." He took one last look at the shape beneath Tag's wet shirt. Then he turned on his heels and walked away, a slight bounce in his step.

"I'm at Lumberland at noon," Tag said in a low voice.

"Rehearsal!" shouted the choreographer over his shoulder. "I won't tolerate a fuck-up in my squad!"

"You do have to know what the rest of the cast is doing," Garry encouraged. "Call in sick from work."

"But the money," Tag lamented.

"It'll be worth it in the long run," Jay insisted.

At noon, Tag found himself on the ice with twenty other kids going through a production number routine. To Tag, it was dumb stuff. He had to skate in a straight line, his arms were outstretched holding onto the shoulders of skaters on either side of him, and he was doing high kicks like a Rockette. The choreographer was a tight-assed tyrant, who kept screaming, "Keep it straight, you little ice queens!" Tag wondered how much of a dominant tough guy he'd be in bed. *Probably a submissive little puppy,* Tag smirked to himself.

Finally, after a grueling hour of the same repetitious stuff, the choreographer called out, "Take five."

The kids broke ranks and lazily filed toward the door in the wall of the rink barrier. As the group exited toward a bank of Coke machines, the show's middle ranking singles and pairs, as well as the featured skaters, and the *Gold on Ice* stars took to the ice for a short warmup.

Tag didn't join the other kids for refreshments. Instead, he took a seat in the penalty box where earlier in the day his judges had sat to determine his fate with the show.

Tag wanted to watch the more professional skaters go through their routines. Among those on the ice was the radiant and glamorous Amber Nyak, along with a couple of sexy boys who could have been tough competitors if they hadn't turned pro.

Tag watched intently as each of the skaters—especially the boys—warmed up before their routines. His concentration was interrupted when Garry's voice said to him, "You love it, don't you?"

Tag turned and beamed at Garry and Jay who had come to rehearse as well.

"Yes," Tag admitted. "It's the greatest thing in the world. This is the happiest day of my life. Gee, I got to meet my heroes and I'm skating in their show!" Tag gave out a sigh. "All these kids have the same dream that I have. For so long I thought I was completely alone in the world. With my fantasy, I mean. There was no support from anyone. But still I followed my heart. And look where it's brought me!"

"Everybody dreams about attaining some goal or another," Garry said. "But most people are too lazy to make 'em come true."

"You dreamed about getting your butt kicked by a jackbooted choreographer?" Jay laughed. "Welcome to my nightmare."

Garry pointed to a boy skater of less than average height and looks. The boy owned the ice. "That's Kerry Benjamin. He'll be the star of this show in no time. He's pretty great, don't you think?"

"Yeah," Tag said. "He introduced himself to me this morning, after you guys went off to discuss my future."

"Gave you his phone number too," Garry said. "We saw. Good for you."

"I just took it to be nice," Tag said. "He's not really my type. Rather arrogant, don't you think? When he found that I was with you guys he actually said it was only a matter of time before he kicked your butts off the ice."

"Jeez!" Garry said, incredulous. "He actually said that?" He looked at Jay. "God, you just never know about people's ulterior motives. He's never seemed the least bit conceited around us. In fact, I thought we were friends. Didn't you think he was a friend, Jay?"

"Of course. We hang out occasionally. Amber likes him, too."

"And you know how intuitive she is," Garry said.

Jay mused, "He's certainly not going to take over until we decide to leave. Nobody is. Too bad about him. I always liked him."

"Anyway, you skate better than he does," Garry said to Tag. "He's not nearly as focused as you are. He gets sloppy. Takes a spill too often."

The trio continued to focus their attention on Kerry as he practiced. He completed a beautiful triple Axel, double toe loop combination seemingly without effort. Then he launched into a dizzying scratch spin. He stopped, in complete command of his body and skates.

Kerry was sweating profusely. He began to circle the rink to cool down. He passed Garry and Jay. "Hey, guys," he panted. He winked at Tag, then he continued circling the ice with his hands on his hips, just gliding. He passed the guys once again.

Then, suddenly, Kerry came crashing down on the ice. Everyone in the rink let out a simultaneous cry of alarm as Kerry collapsed in pain. "My ankle! My fucking ankle! Jesus Christ! It hurts! Fuck! Christ!"

Immediately, the choreographer and the entire cast, including

Garry and Jay, raced onto the ice to surround Kerry. "What the hell happened?" the choreographer demanded.

"My right blade hit something on the God damned ice. Fuck, I think it's broken! Christ! Get a doctor!"

The company traveled with an LVN, not even a registered nurse. She was rarely around when needed, and this time she had to be summoned from her motel room. It took her twenty minutes to dress and gargle away her gin breath before getting to Kerry's side. "Hospital for you," she pronounced, hardly looking at him. She wasn't going to be responsible for attempting to take his tight skate boot off and risk further injury to his foot.

By the time the paramedics arrived, Kerry was sobbing from pain. "The show! I've gotta do the show tonight! Why did this have to happen! God, I don't even have any insurance!"

One of the chorus girls said, "I found this on the ice. A nail. Think this could be what your blade hit?"

"Oh, Christ. Who the fuck dropped that on the ice!" Kerry cried in agony and indignation.

"You're not to worry about the show, sweetheart," Amber said, leaning over Kerry. "We can manage without you for one night. The important thing is to just not worry. You'll be fine. You'll see."

Amber continued trying to soothe Kerry's concerns as he was being placed on a stretcher, and then strapped down and secured inside behind two red ambulance doors. The truck roared out of the parking lot, its sirens blaring.

"We won't manage!" screamed the choreographer. "My show is ruined! He's the number three man! What if he's really broken his ankle and can't skate for months? Huh? What if?" He bellowed at Ernie, "This is it! I give up! This fucking show doesn't even have understudies, for Christ sake!"

Garry looked at Jay, then spoke. "Tag can take Kerry's spot. Just for tonight. Or until he's back in the show."

"Pffft!" the choreographer snorted. "He's not even in the chorus. This isn't *42nd Street*. And he's not from Allentown. Are you?" He looked at Tag. "Are you from Allentown?"

"Clarksville," Tag said sheepishly.

The choreographer rolled his eyes.

"You saw him this morning," Garry piped in. "You can't say he wasn't brilliant."

"They're right," Ernie added. "Just show Kerry's routine to Tag once and see what he can make of it."

"Fuck!" cried the choreographer, as he stormed off to retrieve his skates. "This is madness! I should have stayed with *Mice on Ice!*"

Within five minutes both Tag and the choreographer were standing in the rink. "No, don't do anything, Miss Peggy Sawyer!" the choreographer said petulantly to Tag. "Just watch me! Pay attention! Try to memorize the moves! I can't do the jumps that Kerry does, but you'll get the general idea!"

Tag watched with intense concentration as he was shown Kerry's entire routine. When the presentation was over, the choreographer made a quick and immediate stop beside Tag, spraying him with ice shavings. "Think you can remember any of that? If you're not just somebody's boy toy?" He looked over at Jay and Garry.

Tag glided away from the boards and took to the center of the ice. Without music he began to move. Like an idiot savant whose I.Q. is barely 50, but who plays Bach and Brahams with virtuosity, Tag remembered nearly every move that Kerry had performed. He didn't try for a quad jump, but was able to land a triple without much effort. When it was over, Tag skated back to the choreographer. He repaid him with a bigger spray of ice chips.

The cast and production team in the rink went wild.

Amber and Garry and Jay were applauding enthusiastically as Tag stepped off the ice. The choreographer was dumbfounded.

"Can you do that again tonight?" Ernie asked.

"I can do whatever you want, sir." Tag gave him a stage wink.

"But he has to get Kerry's salary," Garry added.

Tag cut in. "And an announcement that says, Tag Tempkin is the show's newest feature, taking over for an ailing Kerry Benjamin. Play up the sympathy so the audience will still know they're getting their money's worth."

"Not a problem," Ernie said. "Be here an hour before the show, mister," he admonished Tag. Then he departed with his entourage.

"Oh. My. God!" Tag exclaimed. "How is all this possible? One day I'm simply skating because it's my passion, and the next thing I know I'm in a real, live, ice show!"

"Right place at the right time," Garry said. "Plus you've got what it takes. You know what they say, 'Success is one percent inspiration and ninety-nine percent preparation.' Or is it ninety-nine percent perspiration. Whatever. You've done all the work. Now it's time to reap the rewards."

Tag became sad. "I just feel so bad that someone had to be injured for me to get this chance."

Jay dismissed it. "Hell, accidents on the ice happen all the time. Some idiot dropped a stupid nail and Kerry's blades just happened to hit it. Weird though. He covered practically every square inch of the ice before the fall, but as soon as he passed us he went down. It probably wasn't the nail at all. He got a look at you and simply lost his concentration."

Tag smiled.

"The company is incredibly lucky that you were here," Garry said. "We'll get to share a dressing room. That is until you become the show's big star."

Tag simply smiled again.

Chapter Seven

"Smooch, smooch," said one boy skater to another, teasing, as they laced up their boots in the changing room.

"Get away, you orangutan," the other boy hissed then laughed.

"Nah, that's not how he'd respond to Uncle's kissy-kissy come-on. The dude's a first-class player. Manipulation's his middle name. He'd suck Fart Face's tongue in order to be a star. I've watched *Leave It to Beaver*. I know how these Eddie Haskell types operate. He's for sure fucked *Little Caesar's* pizza face. In the six weeks since he's been here he keeps getting more and more ice time. If you doubt me, just name one other boy who ever got a solo spot."

"There was Kerry. And of course Garry, and Jay . . ."

"Chorus boys, you dickhead," the first boy countered. "The point I'm making is that none of us ever get to skate a solo, let alone featured in the show. Even for one night. He's gotta be puttin' out."

Noticing that Tag was coming toward them, en route to the semi-private dressing room he shared with Jay and Garry, the first boy nudged the other.

Both boys giggled as Tag passed them. Then Tag stopped mid-stride, turned around and walked back to where the two chorus kids were lacing up their boots. He stood above them and looked down with a cold smile. "You're Chuck and you're Steve, right?"

The boys looked at Tag with trepidation. It wasn't necessary to respond to Tag's question. They knew that he was aware of who they were.

Tag beamed. "Gosh, you guys skate so well! I've noticed you both. Such a flair for interpreting the music. And you're both so dang cute, too. I'll call you Michael Weiss." He pointed to one. "And I'll call you Stefan Lindemann." He smiled at the other. "Would you like that?"

Chuck and Steve looked at each other and broke into smiles of relief. They bobbed their heads like the toys one sees in the back windows of cars. "Yeah, I guess so," they both said in unison.

"Gosh," Tag said again. "Kerry Benjamin was such a good skater too. Now his ankle hurts—a lot." There was no discernable melancholy in Tag's voice. "The break was bad. So bad, in fact, that he may not skate for a year. Or, maybe never again. Poor baby."

Tag paused for a moment. "Funny isn't it?" he finally said. "One day you're in the chorus, and the next day you're the fourth lead in an ice show spectacular. I'm kinda like a lottery winner, I guess. On the other hand, it's just as interesting to think that, gee, one day you're in the chorus and the next day you're clipping coupons and you can't meet the rent. Life works out in weird ways."

Just then, Tag noticed Ernie coming into the changing area, making his usual rounds to check on his skaters before the show. Tag said to the chorus boys, "I think Ernie's as sweet as apple pie. He's just like the rest of us, a little lonely. Like the Maytag repairman." He said this loud enough for others in the changing room to hear. "He's always treated me like a mamma kangaroo treats her little one."

"If you ask me, he's less than a urine specimen," someone else in the locker area said.

"He tries to get all the cute guys," said another boy.

"Not that he ever succeeds," another young skater added.

"Nobody is that desperate," still another boy said. "He's wanted to suck my dick ever since my first interview for the chorus. I've got true horror stories from a lot of skaters, past and present."

"You're all wrong. He's quite loveable," Tag said with a bright grin. "Oh my gosh! Speak of the devil," he said, looking to his right.

"Although you're more like an angel, of course," Tag smiled. "The guys were just talking about you."

Chuck and Steve's faces turned ashen.

"I've got ears," Ernie said, coldly. "Go change," he said to Tag. "I'll handle this."

With dead eyes, Tag looked at the first two boys and forced a smile. "Break a leg, Pat and Lynne." Then he turned to Ernie. "By the by, thanks for letting me add that new number to the program."

"Yeah," Ernie said with a distant tone as his slow-burn temper began to erupt. Tag walked away, but before he reached his dressing room he could certainly hear the two boys crying, "That's not fair! You can't do that! Where will we go?"

Chapter Eight

Tag was the first to arrive in the dressing room, which was actually a walk-in janitorial closet in another pathetic rink along their tour route. A few coat hooks had been nailed into the cinderblock walls for the guys' costumes. A bench and a full-length mirror had been placed in the dingy, windowless room, amid institutional-size boxes of Comet and toilet paper, mops, brooms, and electric floor buffers.

It had become routine that before any show, prior to Garry and Jay's arrival, Tag did stretching exercises in the nude. He slipped out of his T-shirt and paused to admire the planes of his chest in the mirror. He flexed his pecs and studied the ripple of muscles on his abdomen. He stood with perfect posture, his shoulders squared. He smiled. He loved his reflection. The hunk in the mirror turned him on.

Tag kicked off his Nikes and unbuttoned his jeans. He let his pants drop to the floor. He flexed his tight ass muscles and smiled at the dimple in his butt's two-dimensional reflection.

Then he sat, bare, on the concrete floor. It was chilling cold, but the sensation gave him a pleasure/pain rush when his warm skin touched the slab. Leaning back, he slowly stretched out completely until he became accustomed to the deep, penetrating chill. His body began to warm the surface of the floor. The physical effect on him was typical: a steel-hard erection. But he had long ago disciplined himself not to masturbate until he had completed his exercises.

After stretching, he rolled over onto his chest and stomach. The sting of cold wasn't enough to overpower the sensation of being fully aware of his body. He then proceeded to do three sets of forty push-ups. Each time that his fevered cock met the frigid floor Tag was more aroused. Until finally, lying on his back again with his eyes focused on his image in the mirror, he began to stroke himself.

He was an idol worshiper of his own perfection. He stopped long enough to retrieve a hammer he'd hidden behind some cartons of Borax detergent and a steel drum of institutional cleaning fluid. Taking a dollop of Vaseline from the dressing table, he slathered the wooden handle, and stroked it like a fantasy cock. With another three fingers of the petroleum jelly he buttered his ass, outside, then inside.

Tag knew he only had about thirty minutes before Jay and Garry arrived, and he intended to make his self-satisfaction last as long as possible. Stroking his penis with one hand and positioning the head of the hammer handle to the lips of his ass with the other, Tag maneuvered his feet in such a way that his soles clutched the claw and hammerhead. Now, hands free, he caressed his body. His fingertips sent a message to his brain, which sent more blood to his dick. His feet acted as a piston to force the shaft of the hammer into his hole.

All the while Tag observed himself in the mirror, making believe he was being fucked by porn star Vince Bandero. Caressing his nipples and abs with one hand and his cock with the other, he slid the hammer's handle in and out of his ass chamber. His eyes rolled up into his head, and his jaw dropped open as he lost himself in excruciating pleasure.

Absorbed in his actions and almost senseless with self-gratification, he nevertheless was careful to keep his moaning as quiet as possible. The fire stick of flesh that he wrapped his hand around, and the hard driving wooden shaft up his ass were making him delirious.

"Need some help?"

The words were as alarming as a telephone ringing in the night. Tag whipped toward the door, and the hammer handle popped out of his butt. It was Jay.

Without missing a beat, Jay walked over to Tag, bent down between his legs and picked up the hammer by its head. Without any words of direction, Tag raised his legs and put them over Jay's shoulders.

Jay placed the hammer's shaft against Tag's ass and slowly began to slide it back into Tag's pit. Then he began to rhymically move it in and out of the moist, slick crack.

Tag was now free to stare at his reflection, pump his python, and mentally sail off into a fantasy playground. Jay began driving and twisting the hammer inside his body. Tag gritted his teeth, exhaled several harsh bursts in a whimpering lament, and released more jiz than Tag had thought possible.

Tag finished milking his shaft, then lay back utterly exhausted. "Careful taking that thing out," he implored. With his climax came a loss of tolerance for pain.

"Relax," Jay said, as the hammer's handle slid out easily. Jay looked at it for a short moment wondering what to do.

"Wipe it off and put it behind the Charmin," Tag said, reading Jay's thoughts.

Jay looked around and found a cleaning rag. He ran the cloth up and down the shaft of wood. He then placed it out of the way. "You could get splinters in your ass using a thing like that," Jay said. "Don't you have a molded copy of Jeff Stryker's big one? Everybody else does."

As Tag began to recuperate from his ordeal, he slowly sat up and used the same cloth to blot and wipe himself dry of sperm. "Christ, there's no wash basin in this freakin' closet!" Then suddenly the full realization of being caught masturbating socked him in the gut. "Oh my gosh!" he said, returning to his characteristic innocence. "I'm so embarrassed. You caught me doing *that!*"

"Hell, Tag, everybody does *that.*"

"But it's a private thing and I'm so ashamed. You of all people shouldn't have to see another guy milking his meat. I mean, spilling my seed."

"Are you kidding? It was the highlight of my day to see you, and to take part in your fantasy," Jay crowed.

"No joking?" Tag asked. "You don't think I'm a perv? It would kill me if you thought less of me just because I was doing something that should only be done in a bed, alone, behind locked doors."

"You couldn't have known that I'd be early. Besides, I've done it in public toilets. A guy sometimes can't control the urge. And maybe you wanted to get caught. Fear is sometimes a turn-on."

"Not me," Tag declared. "I'd be mortified if I ever got caught. Don't tell Garry, please?"

"Our secret. I have a confession too," Jay said. "You're so fucking sexy, and I got so turned on by pretending that hammer was my own cock pumping into you that . . ." He stopped mid-sentence and looked down at his own pants. A dark wet spot spread over his crotch.

"What's that?" Tag asked. "Oh, my gosh! You came in your pants! Was it while you were doing me?"

"I couldn't help it," Jay said. "In my mind I was fucking you, and as soon as you came, so did I. Now, I've got to change. At least two of the twenty chorus kids won't catch the scent."

Tag gave a quizzical look.

"Chuck and Steve. They got fired. I heard that Ernie caught 'em sixty-nining in the dressing area. He let 'em go right there and then."

Tag looked shocked. "My gosh!"

"I always thought they'd be my biggest competition, when Uncle Ernie starts planning the new program next week," said Jay.

"New program?" Tag said.

"Next week. So I've heard," Jay said. "They'll find someone else."

"Ew, I'm a mess," Tag complained. "What's this about a new program?"

"Just some stuff I heard the other chorus kids talking about," Jay said.

While Tag and Jay were both still nude, taking turns cleaning the other up, and laughing as one wiped down the other with the same sticky rag, the door opened. It was Garry. "Hmmm. Now that's a perfect picture for *Unzipped* magazine," he announced. "Where's Ansel Adams to take a nature shot when you need him? Christ, Tag, where'd you get that salami, and why have you been hiding it from us all these weeks?"

"This little thing?" Tag said, as if surprised by the fuss. "I just came this way. I'm usually too embarrassed to undress in front of other guys."

Garry said. "Guess I shouldn't have stopped to buy postcards.

Watching you guys go at it would have been a more memorable souvenir."

"It's not what you think," Jay said, knowing full well that Garry wasn't in the least bit upset by seeing his pals naked, but just disappointed that he hadn't been around to enjoy the fun.

"You don't have a clue what I'm thinking," Garry sniggered. "Boys just gotta have *fu-un*," he sang.

"Trust me," Jay said, "we didn't have sex. Not together, anyway."

"Really. We didn't," Tag cried. "I swear."

"You don't have to convince me of anything," Garry said. "It's just so darn cozy in this room. If I'd only thought to bring along my video camera. Strictly for my own collection." He laughed. "Or maybe for auction on eBay."

Tag was red in the face. "You know I would never do anything that might jeopardize our friendship. I love you guys, and I want you to love me back. I'm really sorry if it looks like we had sex. Honest to goodness, Jay came in and just caught me yanking on my own chain."

Jay chimed in, "And I had an auto-ejaculation when I saw this beautiful guy cream all over himself."

"Too many details," Garry said, holding out one hand like Diana Ross when she was a Supreme. "Really. Even if you two got it on, I wouldn't mind. Hell, I admit it, I've had my share of fantasies about Tag."

"Me? No! Why? I'm not like some video porn star or anything." Tag blushed again.

Garry snickered. "As if you've ever even seen a skin flick," Garry said. "That's what's so adorable about you. You're so innocent. You don't even realize what an awesome-looking man you are. Every boy skater in this cheesy show, and most of the men in the audience, not to mention the company management, would probably give up a testicle to fuck you."

"Don't say that," Tag continued, putting on his skintight costume for his first number. "I hate to be teased. You guys are the hot ones."

Garry and Jay smiled at each other. "We are hot, aren't we!" they said in unison and bounced the palms of their right hands off the other's in a high-five.

"Shoot, look at the time," Garry said, glancing at his watch. He began stripping off his jeans and plaid lumberjack shirt, then picked up his costume from a hook behind the door. It wasn't that much different from his street clothes, except the jeans were freshly cleaned and pressed by the wardrobe lady, and the skintight black T-shirt had tiny filaments of silver threads woven into the fabric that made it sparkle under the spotlights.

"See what I mean," Tag said, admiring Garry's body. "You're stunning. You too, Jay."

"Okay. Enough mutual admiration society," Jay laughed. "We all agree, we're prize catches."

"So why can't I get caught again?" Garry said mournfully.

"As soon as you're ready, Mister Husband Material will come skating into your arms," Tag promised. "Gotta believe that."

"I do, actually," Garry said. "I can see him in my mind's eye. He's as cute as Paul Wylie is. As buff as Philippe Candeloro. As earnest as Michael Weiss, and as sexy as Dick Button."

The other two men cried in unison. "Dick Button! He's so old!"

"I'm serious. Dick Button is sexy! You know me, I'm a fool for that combination of talent and intelligence." Garry shrugged apologetically. "He's got both. A winner in every way. He single-handedly changed our sport. And, I'll bet he's got a nice rug of hair on his chest. Gray though it may be, I'd love to push my face into it and get a few strands caught in my teeth, like silver alfalfa sprouts."

"My funny friend," Jay said to Tag. "The really weird thing is, I know he's serious. Except for the gray hair chest part, he's just de-scribed his ex."

"Your old boyfriend is really your fantasy man?" Tag asked.

Garry nodded as he slipped into a sequined vest. "Not that any-one like him will come along again. But a guy can dream."

The three men were putting the finishing touches on their first-act costumes when a knock on the door was followed by a voice that called, "Showtime, guys." It was the stage manager, making sure the program ran according to schedule.

The three looked at each other, then embraced in a group hug, which had become their routine before every performance. "God, you both smell like Clorox," Garry said.

"Here," Jay said, removing a bottle of *Eternity* cologne from his Adidas bag. He spritzed Tag and then turned the spray on himself.

"That should mask the smell so those two little ice queens, Steve and Chuck, won't go blabbering to the other guys and starting rumors," Garry said.

"No need·to worry about those two," Tag offered. "Ernie canned 'em."

Garry was astonished. "They may have been dizzy little gossip mongers, but they were terrific skaters. Why'd Ernie get rid of 'em?"

"Jay said they were having sex in the shower. Ernie probably tried to join in and got rebuffed. So he fired 'em."

"That horny old prick," Garry said. "By the way," he said just before opening the door, "where's our Beavis and Butt-head costume? I thought there was something different about the room when I came in, other than catching my friends in a post-masturbation glow."

"I told you, mine was an auto-ejaculation. I didn't masturbate," Jay protested. "The wardrobe lady probably has your suit. We'll just tell the stage manager."

"I'll take care of it, guys," Tag volunteered. "Just get out there for your introduction."

"You're in the first production number, too," Garry reminded Tag. "Hurry or you'll miss your cue."

Chapter Nine

The audience was sparse in White Bluff, Nebraska, where the tour had stopped for two mid-week shows. The skating arena was another college campus rink with only hard wooden bleachers on which the audience could uncomfortably sit.

It was chilly inside the building, which made the patrons all the more restless. At exactly 8 P.M., the lights dimmed then went completely to black. A drum roll began from the pre-recorded soundtrack. Above the din of the orchestral fanfare, the announcer's voice greeted the crowd and welcomed everybody to *Gold on Ice.* "Now in our twenty-fifth record-breaking year!" he proclaimed the improbably long existence of the show.

Bright spotlights strobed the ice in pulsating colors. The chorus kids were costumed in French Maid outfits and knock-offs of Brian Boitano's military braided uniform that he wore when he won his Olympic gold. They darted over every square inch of the rink, skating as if they were chasing the red, green, blue, and purple blushes on the ice.

The music was "Putting on the Ritz," and the chorus kids performed simple waltz jumps and sit spins and single Axels. The lights dazed the crowd, as did the fact of finding more figure skaters all in one place than anyone from White Bluff ever expected to see. The music was muted and the chorus formed a fan line. The announcer called out, "Ladies. And. Gentleman. Please welcome. The lovely. The talented. Olympic Bronze Medalist. Amber. Nyyy-aaak!"

Thunderous applause greeted the radiantly smiling Amber, dressed in her flames-licking-her-tits costume. She glided onto the ice with a pink spot showcasing her layback sit to a back scratch. As she greeted her fans with waving hands and arms, the announcer's voice returned. With the same excited intonation he called out, "Ladies and gentlemen, Mister. Jay. Low-gan! And. Mister. Garry. Wind-*sor*!"

Both men appeared on the ice, smiling as broadly as Amber. They operated on opposite ends of the ice, performing double toe-loop jumps and spread eagles. They crossed paths and took to the other side of the ice as the chorus kids broke ranks and flitted around the stars of the show.

Finally, the announcer called out, "And. Our newest featured skater. Please welcome. Mister. Tag. Temp*kinnn*!"

Tag bolted onto the ice, executing split jumps from one end of the rink to the other. He followed these with a triple Lutz-triple toe jump, then a Russian split Lutz jump. Landing on his left toe pick and moving onto his right forward edge, his mastery was evident to amateurs and pros alike.

When the entire cast was finally assembled on the ice, the principals and chorus joined together, each taking a partner. Side by side they glided together in an intricate latticework, weaving in and out among each other. The music had changed to "The Skaters Waltz," then a chorus of voices sang "Moonlight Bay." The performance was a crowd pleaser. Even the skaters seemed to enjoy frolicking together.

Soon the music faded, and the lights dimmed. Only Amber remained on the ice, performing a scaled-down version of her Olympic program. No one in the audience could tell whether or not her jumps were any good, but as long as she landed even the smallest jump, she received a great ovation of cheers and applause. Amber had the knack of making figure skating look difficult but tremendously fun. She telegraphed every jump, and then smiled radiantly after her rotations. She gave the illusion that she was putting every fiber of her being into the program. In truth, she loved that she was skating. But she had long since given up doing the difficult compulsory moves that were required in competitions.

Amber segued into her *La Bohème* routine, then graciously surrendered the ice to Jay and Garry. After a few more appearances by the kids in the chorus, intermission was called.

"Time for Butt-head," Jay complained as he and Garry and Tag clomped back to their dressing room/closet. When they opened the door, there was the dreaded costume.

"I'd hoped it'd been stolen," lamented Garry.

"You were right, the costume lady had it," Tag said.

"What would we do without you," Garry said with a sarcastic edge. "Wonder what would happen if it was accidentally on purpose stolen?"

"They'd probably dig out those hideous Jack McFarland and Karen Walker outfits they tried last year," Jay said. "Trust me, boys, you wouldn't want to be stuck in those. Or the Bea Arthur and Elaine Stritch costumes they tried for the *Bitches on Broadway* segment. That was a huge flop, so they tried the cartoon equivalent. I hope Bea and Elaine are packed away for good! Hell, when Kerry Benjamin and I did that routine, the audience didn't know who we were supposed to be."

"I'll wager that you were Bea," Garry joked.

"It wasn't funny," Jay said. "At least as Beavis you can goof around with me in my Butt-head suit. It's more fun than those poor chorus kids who have to play *Animal Planet*. Ernie's contribution to nature awareness. One by one they each leave the ice because their species becomes extinct."

"A freak show," Tag said with an imperious tone. "I wouldn't ever let 'em put me in a costume like that for anything. They couldn't pay me enough to parade around on the ice as anything other than Tag Tempkin!"

He caught himself. "Oh, no offense, guys. Of course if Ernie said that I had to be a Butt-head I'd do it in a heartbeat. And you guys do it so well, and you're really hilarious. I just couldn't be as good as you. That's all I meant."

Garry and Jay looked at each other. Garry said, "Trust me, if we weren't contracted to perform in whatever fashion statement that management deems appropriate, we wouldn't be caught dead in these ridiculous get-ups either."

"But you're really great skating as a pair," Tag said disingenuously. "You look as though you're having a blast. And it's a star turn, so you do get a lot of attention."

The show resumed. Finally, after nearly two and a half hours, Amber, Garry, Jay, and Tag took their final bows. As they waved goodnight to the audience, the entire chorus, boys and girls, skated around dressed as Little Red Ridinghoods. From baskets hanging on their arms, they threw chocolate coins wrapped in gold foil into the audience. The gesture was met with thunderous applause and screams from kids trying to catch the candy coins. With Little Red, there had to be a big bad wolf lurking around somewhere and indeed, a salivating version of the wolf from *The Three Little Pigs* skated from one Riding Hood to the other, trying in vain to molest her or him. Then all the Riding Hoods turned on the wolf and pummeled him into the ice. He lay in a puddle of make-believe blood and guts until the lights were extinguished.

Then the announcer's voice was heard once again inviting the stars back to the ice and thanking the audience. He wished them a life filled with golden opportunities, just like the opportunity they had given the skaters to perform for them.

"Barf," Tag said as he stood with Amber, Jay, and Garry at the center of the rink waving goodnight.

"But we make people happy," Amber said. "I'm grateful that I have something to give to the world. Most of these people lead lives of quiet desperation. That's Thoreau." Amber smiled genuinely. "Bless their hearts. Mostly all they've got to look forward to in life is payday, sex, and reruns of *The Simpsons*. And probably, the sex is just because there's nothing else to do, or it's the boring baby-making kind. Which makes them even more desperate. Very few people have your talent, Tag. Remember that."

Unnoticed, Tag rolled his eyes. He knew that the star of the show was a sexless Pollyanna who always found something positive to say about everybody. She even defended Dave Sheridan after his Disney movie *Frank McKlusky, C.I.* was released with a thunderous career-crashing box-office thud. "He's got a real nice pack of abs," she said of Dave. "And after all, he at least had the good sense to be in a movie with Dolly Parton." Nobody would deny that universally beloved Dolly, even though her liver-spotted hands showed her real age, was an asset to any project.

When the lights were once again turned off, the cast followed flashlight beams to their exit. After the company had vanished into the back stage area, the rink's house lights were turned on and the audience began to move from their hard wooden bench seats and file out through the main lobby.

In their janitorial closet, the trio of skaters stripped out of their costumes. This time, after their little circle jerk before the show, each seemed to pay more attention to the other's bodies. As surreptitiously as possible, Jay and Garry stole more than a few glances at Tag.

As they dressed, they discussed what to do with the rest of the night. Garry kept a copy of *Cruising Across Middle America: Where Homos and Hicks Meat 'n' Greet*. It listed every gay restaurant and bar in every city from Minocqua, Iowa, to Little Division, Kansas, and Pudoff, Wisconsin. He prided himself at cutting a swath through the country and seeing how different the men were in each geographical area. The only thing he ever discovered that was vaguely unique was a regional accent. No matter where they went, the men in *Cruising's Meat 'n' Greet* bars all knew who Inga Stevens was, and Michael Feinstein, too. Some of them, mostly the older guys, even liked Michael's thin whiney voice.

Jay had also learned that gorgeous men weren't restricted to major meat market cities. Inevitably, Jay, Gary, Tag and Amber would find a bar in some small town and at least coax a few hot numbers to play pool. Ever since Tag had become the fourth Musketeer, there seemed to be more guys lining up to buy them all drinks. "Tag's like catnip," Amber observed. "He gets the fellas all hot 'n' horny."

Although Garry was more than satisfied with just accepting a beer and some conversation from a barroom admirer, Jay was easily coaxed into following a bear or a blond to an alley outside behind the bar. Pinned against a Dumpster, he welcomed the guys who would plant their beer-breath mouths onto his and force their thick tongues down his throat. As the guys squirmed out of their shirts and unbuttoned their jeans, Jay found that the young men in Smallsville came in all shapes and sizes. The common denominator being that they were horny and hungry to feel another man's hard body.

Jay reveled in the attention, and he always had a full load waiting to empty into a hungry mouth or butt. The guys were never disappointed. It was the straight-but-curious studs he had to be wary of. Usually, by the time they reached age twenty-five, their bodies had already begun to resemble John Goodman's.

By the time Jay and whoever was his anonymous partner for the evening returned to the bar, Garry was usually sitting alone watching television, telling the men whom he attracted as easily as credit-card debt, that he appreciated their attention but to please find someone else to flirt with. He explained to his friends that while he liked the smell of bars and the possibilities for sex, he was waiting for his Mr. Right. Tag, on the other hand, enjoyed a few beers but declared that most guys were beneath him, and that there was bound to be a better batch of men at the next stop on their tour.

On this night, as Jay returned sated from being fucked over a garbage barrel in the alley, it crossed his mind that Tag's standards were peculiar, considering how much he liked fucking himself with hammers. Jay reasoned that Tag's self-gratification was how he kept from going crazy with lust.

En route back to their Holiday Inn rooms, after escorting Amber to hers, an inebriated Tag said, "Who's a better skater than me?"

"Whoa," Garry said. "Where'd that come from?"

"You're one of the best," Jay said. "I admit that."

"Fuck, 'one of the best'," Tag shouted in the quiet, early morning air.

Garry and Jay looked at each other. "Someone's had too much to drink," Jay said.

"I know *I'm* the best," Tag said with smug satisfaction.

"Of course you do," Garry said. "You're cocksure, and we know why."

Jay chuckled at Garry's pun.

"Don't patronize me," Tag suddenly shouted at the men.

Garry started to say, "I wasn't—"

"Can you guys do triples and quads better than me?"

"Er . . ." Jay began.

"No," Tag answered. "You guys're getting older by the minute."

"Twenty is hardly old," Garry said. "Hell, you'll be twenty in two years."

"Now is all that matters," Tag said. "How long do they keep aging skaters in these shows, anyway?"

"Aging?" Jay was taken aback. "We're not exactly members of

AARP. My pension benefits don't kick in for another," he looked his watch, "oh, six hours or so."

"Ya know," Tag slurred, "Amber said if I played my cards right, I'd be the star of the show before too long."

"Amber has great intuition," Jay said. "Plus she's up on all that's happening in management. If she says you're going to be the star of the show, then she's probably right. She's a very positive thinker. Now here's your room. Let's go in. We'll put you to bed and maybe you'll wake up with a great big hangover to go along with your great big head."

Jay reached into Tag's pants pocket to retrieve his room key. He took the moment to squeeze Tag's dick as well.

"You like that, don't you?" Tag mumbled and smiled. "Nothin' gets past me."

When they had taken off Tag's clothes and placed him in bed, Garry and Jay left the room. They walked up an exterior flight of stairs toward the room they shared.

"What got into him?" Jay said. "A few beers and he just starts yammering about how great he is."

"He was doing shots while you were with that pierced nipple guy," said Garry.

Jay smiled, remembering the bear who had fucked him as a group of leathered bikers cheered on. "He's been getting less docile and less self-deprecating lately," Garry said.

"The guy's got an ego. Remember how he reacted after his audition that first day? I wondered how long it would be before his status in the show would bring that animal out of him again."

"I know what you mean," Garry nodded in agreement.

Garry and Jay immodestly undressed, brushed their teeth and slipped into their respective beds. The motel room was more comfortable than most of the motels they found themselves in. At least this one had heating and plumbing that worked. "Ready?" Garry asked before turning out the light between their beds.

"Yeah. Sleep well."

"You too."

After a moment in the darkness, Jay said, "What do you think Tag was talking about when he said that Amber told him if he played his cards right, he'd become the star of the show?"

"He was babbling. I'm sure she never said any such thing."

"Yeah, she'd have said something to me. We're best friends. Best boy/girl friends, I mean. If anything underhanded was brewing in management she'd be the first to warn us. You know, she told me to be cautious with Tag. I probably shouldn't have protested so much. She sees things that I'm a little blind about."

"She's pretty intuitive. And I certainly wasn't thrilled with the Mr. Hyde personality that took over Tag after just a few drinks," Garry said. "Makes you wonder."

Jay stared into the darkness. "Who is he really?" he whispered in a voice that sounded close to being asleep. "A fan. A great skater. A slut."

"Let's talk about it in the morning," Garry whispered. He rolled over clutching his pillow, and for at least a moment, wished it was Kurt that he was embracing.

Chapter Ten

In an abrupt change of itinerary, the *Gold on Ice* tour schedule was suddenly revised. The skaters found themselves hauled in rented cars across the plains states into the Deep South. It was a blistering August. The cool ice rinks in each Podunk town, dilapidated though most of them may have been, were a welcome relief from the sultry, screeching cicada-filled nights in Mississippi, Alabama, and Louisiana.

Being together nearly 24 hours a day, either on the road or practicing and performing, Tag absorbed every anecdote about his companions' lives, past and present. He learned that Jay was a rich kid whose parents lavished him with the best coaches, a choreographer, costume designer and special orchestrations for his music. All he had to do was skate. They even encouraged his homosexuality. "Let's just say that it wasn't any big deal when I came out," Jay had told Tag one evening at dinner after downing nearly an entire pitcher of beer. "My folks just wanted me to develop my art. Everything else was secondary. It was expected that I would be a champion. I couldn't let them down."

Amber, too, had had an exceptional family upbringing. "My momma and daddy were both skaters. They were in the *Ice Follies* and hoped that I'd want to skate too."

"Your daddy was a skater?" Jay asked. "I never knew that. A straight figure skater? I'll be darned."

"I didn't say he was straight. Just said he was my daddy. And I love him very much. And he loves me too. Of course they insisted that school had to come first. If I didn't maintain my 3.5 G.P.A., I would be off the ice before you could say Ekaterina Gordeeva. It only happened once. Damned French class. I was so miserable not being able to practice. I pulled those grades up right away. Now I can say, *Maintenant je peux dire, ne vous baisez pas avec moi peu de weasle cocksucking, en français!*" Amber laughed, knowing that her image was intact, and she was safe from any of the boys knowing exactly what she'd said.

"I got 'weasel' and 'cocksucking' out of that sentence," Garry said. "What the hell kind of progressive school did you go to?" he laughed.

Garry's youth was the opposite. "My mom and dad told me that they were what were called hippies in the 1960s." Garry laughed about his parents' past. "I saw their wedding pictures. They were so funny; flowers in their hair, love beads around their necks. My dad wasn't even wearing a shirt. Very cute! I think he's the reason I like guys with shaggy hair so much.

"But then they became what they called 'the establishment.' Dad taught anthropology and Mom was a psychotherapist. One year for Christmas they bought me a Tonka dump truck and a Susie Homemaker bake set. It was an experiment to see which one I was more interested in. They were disappointed when I didn't play with the truck, or the toy guns, and the G.I. Joe, and the basket-ball." He laughed.

"Then I gave them plenty to be nervous about when I hit pu-berty and started wanking to *Playgirl* magazine and inviting Kevin Bartlett to camp out in the back yard on summer nights. I think they were especially upset that Kevin was the proverbial son of a preacher man, and I was going to corrupt the horny little sinner. It was the other way around. Then I became a figure skater 'cause it's what they feared most!"

Tag was soon bored hearing stories about when his friends had begun to skate, and the long hours of practice, and going on to competitions and winning medals. When they complained about how difficult it had been to start their days at 4:30 A.M. to practice, then attended school classes, followed by more hours of practice, he wanted to scream out, "Of course it was tough! If figure skating was easy everybody would do it!" But Tag held his tongue.

He had the knack of making himself seem like an open book, without ever revealing anything substantive about himself. While the others boasted about past boyfriends, sexual experiences, future plans and current gossip about the skaters in the show, Tag sat quietly and just listened. He interjected enough personal information to make his pals feel that they knew him well. He would say, "Me, too," after someone said they thought Rudy Galindo had a big one. Or, "Been there, done that," when Garry or Jay made a reference to an episode of unrequited love.

But Tag seldom volunteered any real information. If someone had held a gun to Jay's and Garry's heads and demanded to know what Tag's astrological sign was, their brains would be splattered everywhere. The same was true about who Tag's favorite singer was, or which movie or book or movie star he'd take to a desert island. Although they knew what common building tool he'd take along as a playtoy.

As best buds, Garry knew what Jay's answers would be: *Pet Shop Boys, Mom and Dad Save the World, Valley of the Dolls, Hugh Jackman.*

Amber's answers would be: *The Carpenters, Ice Castles, The Long Program by Peggy Fleming, Hugh Jackman.*

For himself: *Judy, Auntie Mame, anything by David Sedaris, Hugh Jackman.*

Amber, in particular, was becoming exasperated by not knowing any more about Tag than what Jay had told her and a few personal observations regarding his meteoric rise to be one of the principals in the show. On the afternoon that they passed into Tennessee, en route to Nashville, she asked him outright, "Tag, what's your family think of you being in a traveling ice show?"

"Fine," Tag said.

Garry, at the wheel, exchanged a quick glance at Jay in the front passenger seat. "I thought your father didn't even know you skated," Garry said, looking in his rearview mirror at Tag in the back seat.

"Oh, he knows. He's fine with it now, 'cause I'm making money."

"That's such good news," Amber said. After a few quiet moments, she leaned her head against the door, and asked another question. "If it's not too personal, can you tell us about your boyfriend."

"Boyfriend?" Tag said, caught off guard. "Gosh, Amber, who has time for boyfriends? I've been too busy teaching myself how to skate."

"Don't sit there and try to convince me that a handsome boy like you has never had a boyfriend. I will refuse to believe such a monumental calamity."

"Well, nobody that you'd call a *real* boyfriend," Tag said, trying to squirm away from the subject.

"But you've had sex?" Amber asked point blank. "Oh, don't look so shocked. So help me, if you're saying you're a virgin, I'm gonna insist that Jay and Garry straighten you out. So to speak," she laughed.

"That's way personal," Tag said. "Of course I've had sex. I guess."

"You guess?" Garry laughed. "That's like being a little pregnant."

"I mostly abstain," Tag said. "End of subject."

"I am so amazed by you," Amber said and sat upright. "You're as handsome and sexy as those two movie-star buddies, what are their names, oh, Matt and Ben. Combined. And yet you're so focused on your skating that you don't let sex get in the way. I think it's a miracle. That's what it is! Also, that anyone can teach themselves to skate, with all the jumps and spins that you do. It's purely unbelievable. I guess you're just a big ol' alpha-male genius."

"Coaches are real expensive," Tag said.

"Didn't anyone at your club ever see you practice and suggest someone who might coach you for a lower fee 'cause you had such potential? Some coaches do that, you know."

"I never belonged to a club. Nobody ever helped me with nothin'," Tag grunted. "I had to get where I am by sheer hard work and strategy." Then, quickly, he backtracked. "That is except for Jay and Garry. They've helped me a lot. But no one else. Ever."

Amber nodded, accepting. "Well, my friend, you are certainly to be commended. If more people worked as hard as you to fulfill their dreams there'd be a lot fewer unhappy souls in this world. Seems most people don't even know what they want, let alone how to go about achieving a goal."

"I agree," Tag said. "I mean about most other people not knowing what they really want. I listen to some of the kids in the show, and they haven't a clue what to do when they leave skating. I know what I'm doing."

"What is that?" Amber asked, coaxing.

He became evasive again. "Just the usual. Coach, I guess."

"You are a very blessed man," Amber declared and put her head back against the door window. "Got your whole life mapped out. That is so refreshing."

Garry had been watching the exchange between the two in his rear-view mirror. Jay had pulled down the sun visor that had a mirror on the back to do the same thing. It was obvious to Gary that Tag was perturbed by Amber's attempt to draw personal information out of him. He tried to play the good sport, but Garry could see his discomfort discussing any aspect of his personal past.

The car became quiet, except for music from the radio turned down low, emitting twangy country songs. Amber slept, and soon Tag nodded off as well.

"Mind if I join the snoozers?" Jay asked, yawning. "I'll take over the driving whenever you feel like it."

"Nap for a spell. I'm fine. We'll be in Nashville in about two hours."

During this quiet time, Garry listened to Reba McIntyre, Trisha Yearwood, an oldie from Donna Fargo, and someone simply named Sylvia who he thought was sensational. He thought about how cool it was that those artists and so many more had recorded their songs right here in Tennessee.

His thoughts returned to Tag, and his evasiveness and contradictions about his past. Also, as flattered as Garry was about being Tag's inspiration and learning to skate simply by watching videotapes of his competitions, he never really believed that anyone could be as masterful on the ice without many years of training by a world-class coach. "It's rather strange, isn't it?" Garry inadvertently said aloud, which caused Jay to stir.

"Strange?" Jay asked, still half sleep.

"About Tag," he whispered. "Oh, nothing, really. Keep sleeping. Is the music bothering you?"

"No."

"'Kay. Go back to your snoring."

"I don't snore," Jay said.

"Right." Garry smiled.

Soon Garry could see the skyline of Nashville as he eased onto a busy highway. It was afternoon on Thursday. The passengers seemed to feel a change in the speed of the car and, thus, began to wake up.

"Are we there yet?" Tag asked. He sounded like a sleepy little boy.

"Pretty soon," Garry said.

"Mmmm. That was nice," Amber announced as she yawned and stretched herself back into consciousness. "You must be sick of driving," she said to Garry. "I'll take over anytime you like."

"Thanks. I'm fine. Maybe when we leave Nashville."

"Is that where we are this time?" Tag asked, not having paid the least bit of attention to what cities the tour schedule included. Every state and town seemed like every other place they traveled throughout the spring and summer. He simply followed along and let others tell him when to pack and head for whatever rental car Garry or Jay had picked up.

A billboard advertising a bank, announced the time as 3:30. The temperature was 97 degrees.

"God, I hope we find a decent motel," Jay said. "It better have air-conditioning. Otherwise, I'll sleep on the ice tonight."

"You get used to it," Tag announced.

"Been here before?" Amber asked.

Tag said quickly, "No. I've never been out of Clarksville. But I have relatives here. They tell me you get used to the weather quick enough."

"Relatives. Great. Bet they'll be thrilled to see you in a show," Amber said.

Garry observed the two in his rear-view mirror. "I don't know if they'll come or not," Tag backtracked. "We're not that close."

"Heck, I'm an Olympic star," Amber announced. "Bet they'd come if I called them for you."

"Oh, no, don't bother. I'll call 'em. But they live so far away, I doubt they can make it."

"I thought you said they lived in Nashville," Jay pressured.

"I said I had relatives here. But I meant here in Tennessee. In the Appalachian Mountains."

"Call me geographically challenged," Jay said, "but I thought the Appalachians ran from like Maine to Alabama."

"You must mean the Smoky Mountains," Amber added.

Tag was uncharacteristically flustered. "Yeah. The Smokies. That's where they are. They're somewhere down here. But like I said, we're not close. I probably don't even have their phone number."

"That's why they have Southern Bell and directory assistance," Jay offered.

"Don't tell me a great skater such as yourself would be intimidated by family coming to see you," Amber said. "Of course, I was always terrified when Momma would come to my competitions." She tried to make Tag feel that she understood why he was reluctant to contact relatives who might want to see him perform in *Gold on Ice*.

"There's a sign for a Ramada." Jay pointed to a billboard. "Wanna stop there and see if they have vacancies?"

"Perfect," Garry said, as he activated his right turn signal and pulled off the highway.

Not far from the ramp they saw the hotel sign and pulled into the parking lot. Garry stopped at a space that said, GUEST REGISTRATION ONLY.

"Back in a sec," Jay said as he exited the car.

The others watched as Jay opened a glass door to the dinky Ramada and walked into the hotel lobby. He stopped at the front desk.

The way he was nodding his head, the others knew he was flirting with the desk clerk, probably shining him on about being with the skating show that had come to town for a couple of nights. They saw him pull his wallet out of his back pocket and hand the man a credit card. "Great, there's room at the inn," Garry said.

After a short while—and an unrequired handshake with the clerk—Jay returned to the car. He handed out keys attached to plastic, miniature, old-fashioned vinyl record-shaped fobs. "The *Patsy Cline Room* for our star," he said to Amber. "The *Glen Campbell Goodtime Room* for the sexy little lad, wink, wink." He handed a key to Tag. "And, the *Harper Valley P.T.A. Room* for me and Garry."

"I'd rather you go back and get us the 'Achy Breaky Heart' Room," Garry joked.

"That one was booked," Jay said. "Some boy named Sue was registered there." Amber and Garry giggled. Tag didn't seem to have a clue to what the reference was.

Amber volunteered, "When we're settled, I'll call Phil to let him know we're in town. Then, after the run-through at the rink this evening, let's go across the street to that place we saw, The Pickle Barrel."

"Amber," Jay said in mock consternation. "Hanging out with a troupe of fairies all this time, and you don't yet have all of our list of rainbow-flagged no-no's? That chain of restaurants refuses to serve homos. And blacks too, I think. And probably Jews and anyone who doesn't display a rifle and the Stars and Bars in the rear window of their Ford pickup."

"Shame on me," Amber said in mock embarrassment, slapping the back of her hand. "You'll just have to educate me more. Cher, yes. Judy, yes. No on Kathie Lee and Dr. Laura. Yes to Pet Shop Boys, and no to burgers from Carl's Jr. What about Celine Dion? I always forget if she's in or out. How about going to that Hooters place we laughed at a few blocks back. Might be fun to see how the other half lives."

"Ah-ha!" Jay said triumphantly. "Now we're not just ten percent of the population, we're half!"

"I know you claim to be among a silent majority, dear heart, but I was referring to the everyday Joe and Josephine who patronize that tacky chain."

"Think they'd beat us up if we went to a place like that?" Tag asked. "Maybe there should be a place called *Big Ol' Johnsons*. Oh, there's Howard Johnson's. Think ol' Howie was queer?"

"Why not," Garry said. "Everyone's out of the closet these days—from Robin Hood to Abe Lincoln."

"Just flirt with the waitresses at Hooters," Jay said to Tag. "They'll eat you up, Mister Adorable."

"Meet you two back here in an hour? Enough time?" Garry asked Amber and Tag.

"I'll be in the tub for about fifty minutes, but back here on the dot," Amber said.

"Yeah. Cool. Here by the car," Tag agreed.

They retrieved their suitcases from the trunk and went off looking for their respective rooms.

Chapter Eleven

Settling into their accommodations, Garry and Jay lunged to turn on the air-conditioner unit. Just as hastily, they discarded their humidity-limp GAP T-shirts. "I stink!" Garry declared to Jay as he held his shirt to his face.

"Hey, it works for you," Jay teased. "Like that cute Italian boy we shared a cab with in Boston?"

"Ew," Garry scrunched up his nose. "I don't smell *that* bad!"

"Bad?" Jay said. "It's the aroma of a *man*! It intoxicates me! You have to admit he was incredibly sexy. I close my eyes and can still pretend I've got my nose in his pit," Jay said, knowing how much Garry valued CK's *Eternity* over the scent of perspiration.

"Aroma is freshly baked bread or rose petals," Garry insisted, removing his own shirt and holding it up to his nose. He made a face.

"I'd buzz around his pistol sipping nectar any ol' day. What a garden!" Jay tossed his shirt onto the floor. His jeans, briefs and socks followed.

Just removing the damp clothes from their bodies made them both sigh with relief. There wasn't anything quite like being naked and letting their skin breathe.

Garry and Jay took turns showering under an icy spray. Stepping back into the still-warm room, they dried themselves before flopping onto their beds for a short nap.

Meanwhile, over in the *Glen Campbell Goodtime Room*, Tag did what Tag enjoyed third most, after skating and fucking. He was admiring his own naked body. He positioned himself in front of the full-length mirror that was screwed into the bathroom door. He then stood before the air-conditioner and adjusted the vents so that the cool blower coursed over his sticky skin.

He raised an armpit to his nose and inhaled deeply. His cock jumped. He rolled out his tongue to taste the matted armpit hairs, pretending that they belonged to that new kid in the chorus, whatever his name was, the one who stopped by a few days ago for an autograph and left with a raw ass. "So glad I don't use Right Guard," he said, enjoying his all-natural scent.

He moved another vent flap on the air conditioner unit so that the breeze directly hit his fully erect penis. As the slimy moisture that had saturated his pubic hairs and balls dried, he stood with his eyes closed and his hands behind his head, gyrating to a dance mix from Thunderpuss that he heard in his head. Placing both hands on his shaft, he began to stroke himself, shaking his tool as though it was a fire hose. Feeling how hot his piece was he suddenly got the idea of jacking off with an ice cube. *Never tried that*, he said to himself, looking around the small room. Although there was no mini-fridge, there was a cardboard ice bucket, which meant there was an ice machine somewhere on the premises.

With less than an hour before having to meet up with his companions, he tugged on a pair of jeans for the short dash to the stairwell, where, if this place was like every other motel he'd ever stayed at, he guessed is where the icemaker would be. He didn't bother to button up his pants all the way, since he planned to just step out of his room, quickly find the ice dispenser, hoping it wasn't gravel-size crushed ice, and hurry back.

Tag opened his door to a blast furnace. He stepped out onto the landing and closed his door behind him. He hopped barefoot toward the stairs. Although it was late afternoon, the surface of the fiberglass deck was still hot. The soles of his feet burned, and he had to stop and stand for a moment on the mats outside each door along the outside corridor.

"Christ," he said, jumping to one mat. "Shit," he said, vaulting to another. At last a sign announced: ICE. He stood a moment on the mat outside room number 423. It was only a fraction of a moment longer than his other stops but it was long enough to change the destiny of the day.

Just as he was about to spring for the stairwell, the door suddenly opened, and the guy who occupied the room literally walked into Tag. It was a surprise for both of them, albeit a pleasant one. The man asked half-naked Tag, "Avon calling?" He wore a derisive grin. "Or are you here to offer your cookies for a merit badge?"

Also half dressed in swim trunks, the stud leaned against the doorframe, and Tag absorbed him with ravenous eyes. The man's powerful chest was planted with a bumper crop of dark hair across thick pecs. His tight, flat stomach was overlaid with a fuzz of dusky filaments, surrounding a deep inney navel. Although he looked around forty, there was no hint of lovehandles or excess body fat. If his dark brown eyes weren't enough to cause Tag's heart to beat a couple of paces faster, his large brown nipples, wide round shoulders, and swollen biceps were more than enough of a turn-on to give Tag a harder erection than the one he had moments ago while observing himself in his mirror.

The man's brown eyes moved from Tag's green ones, down to his smooth pumped chest and arms, then back to his eyes and again down to his stomach, his exposed hips—and the opened button of his 501s.

Tag could feel his own hard cock bursting against the denim of his pants. The movement in Tag's pants wasn't lost on the man.

"Got ice?" Tag asked seductively as he held his cardboard bucket to his crotch, as if to say, *fill this.*

The man looked to both sides of the landing then across the railing into the parking lot below. He jerked his head, indicating for Tag to enter the room.

Tag didn't hesitate.

He slipped past the guy, and before he could take in the characteristics of the room—which were identical to his own, down to the dusty Elvis on velvet hanging in the same place above the bed—the door was closed and the lock latched. Tag turned around and dropped his cardboard ice bucket to the side. Without a moment's delay, the men embraced.

Aiming for each other's lips, they forced their hot tongues down their partner's throat. Together, they both smothered each other's faces, tasting the wet pit viper that lived behind their teeth.

Wrenching themselves briefly away from their hungry tongues, they began exploring the rest of their lover's body. Seizing each other's shoulders, underarms, and chests, each man battled to dominate the other, only to relent for a moment and allow the other to command, then once again regaining control before submitting and allowing the other to direct the rumble.

Tag dragged his tongue over every inch of the man's face, chest and stomach. He dropped to his knees and put his mouth over the cloth covering the meat that was crammed into the guy's trunks. He forced his hot breath onto the other's crotch, while reaching his hands up and working on the elastic of the man's trunks. Tag gave a light pull, and the swarthy head of the guy's fully erect dick was revealed.

It was glistening with pre-cum. Tag slowly but determinedly put his nose to the head and inhaled the potent scent. His tongue darted out to lick the sticky fluid, then played with the helmet-shaped dick. Then, his entire mouth covered the shaft and swallowed the post until it hit his tonsils and he gagged.

"Swallow it whole, you little cocksucking asswipe!" the man demanded.

As Tag was sheathing the man's cock with his mouth, feeling the ridges of its large veins with his tongue, the man grasped tufts of Tag's blond hair in his clenched fists. It was exhilarating agony. The men whimpered as a million feral thoughts collided. Tag moaned with exquisite satisfaction, savoring the tang of pre-cum on his tongue, and inhaling the briny aroma from the steaming rainforest of the guy's pubic patch. The aroma made Tag ache.

The man groaned as if desperately trying, for as long as possible, to hold back a volcanic eruption. He was losing ground. Abruptly he bent down and dragged Tag to his feet. Once again, he thrust his tongue deep into Tag's mouth. He delighted in the thought that he was tasting his own pre-cum on Tag's tongue.

Working in unison, as if reading the other's mind, they both maneuvered to the bed. They fell back on the teal-colored bedspread that matched the drapes, that matched the rug, that matched the upholstery on the sitting chair. As the man stretched out on top of him, Tag wrapped his legs around the man's calves. The two continued kissing brutally.

Then Tag buried his face in the guy's chest, sanding his face against the brute's pecs as his hands played over his shoulders, his back, his ass, his face and returning to his hard chest. The man's tongue continued moving about as well. One minute it was aggressively exploring Tag's stomach and cock, then it was back to his mouth again.

Without words, Tag telegraphed his desperate need to be fucked. It didn't take long for Mr. Flesh Eater to pick up the signal. While still embracing Tag, he reached into the bed stand drawer and by touch found and withdrew a tube of *Glide Right* lube. He popped the flip top open with his teeth, then quickly propped Tag's legs up over his strong shoulders.

Squeezing a liberal amount of gel into Tag's succulent, pink, puckered hole, he worked two fingers into the warm, soft tissue; outside then inside, as Tag gladly agonized with the anticipation of having his ass impaled with the size equivalent of a prize-winning cucumber. The idea of how much it would hurt good going in, and the excruciatingly rapturous agony of having his sphincter muscles stretched to the max to make room for the full girth and length of this man's endowment, made Tag's cock all the more hard. He was satisfied that his routine with the hammer handle and other accouterment, living as well as inanimate, made it easier for the man to slide his thick, blue-veined tool inside him. He did so with alacrity after slipping on a condom.

Tag cried out with pleasure as the man forced himself inside. Tag's hands continued to explore the man's chest and stomach as his lover moved in and out of him like a steel drill punch; slowly then more quickly and slowly again, moving with purpose. The man was divinely brutal. There was no tenderness in what they were doing. And Tag wanted it that way.

"Just fuck the hell out of me," Tag moaned again and again. "Fuck my young ass."

He gritted his teeth as he continued to get the pounding of his life. With the man thrusting and retreating, thrusting and retreating,

Tag continued to navigate his hands over every centimeter of the guy's sensuous body. All along, he looked into the man's eyes and traced his fingers over his chest. Tag pinched the man's nipples.

"God yes," the man responded. "Do it harder. Squeeze them fucking titties, man."

Moments later while continuing to assail Tag's hot hole, the man clumsily reached into the bed stand drawer again and withdrew two clothespins. "Clamp these suckers on my big ol' tits, boy," the man commanded. Tag followed the instructions and as the man growled in sensual pain, Tag could feel the guy's meat grow larger inside of him.

Both men were sweating profusely, as if they were being poached in the steaming humid air outside. "Christ," Tag said, "I'm gonna come. It's so fuckin' hard."

"Don't touch that precious meat of yours," the man demanded. He grabbed Tag by the wrists, pinning his arms over his head against the mattress, as he continued to pound himself into Tag's butt. Tag winced but it was precisely what he wanted. He'd long fantasized about being with a lover who could make him shoot his load without so much as touching his cock.

"Okay. I'm coming," the man finally said. "I can't hold on."

"Do it, cowboy," Tag moaned. "Oh, Holy Christ, do me. Oh, fuck me, like right now! Holy shit!"

"Don't take the fucking Lord's name in vain, you freakin' cock-sucking asswipe." The man gave Tag a slap across the face that was meant only to sting. With that the man thrust harder and harder, and Tag suddenly lost any authority he had over his own body. He could feel his jiz rising from his ball sack, making its way through his cock. The man continued to punish Tag's ass, as Tag focused on the man's stomach. Tag nearly slipped out of consciousness as the eruption came. He discharged three swift jets of opaque sperm. The first load spit as far as the headboard. The second wave covered his face and chest. A smaller, but nearly as powerful, third copulation sputtered to his sternum and coated his abs.

And still the man rammed his rod into Tag's hole.

Then, with his eyes squeezed tight and his teeth bared, with a staccato of falsetto cries, the man unloaded a copious amount of jism. The guy pushed and retracted and screwed himself deeper into Tag as if he were fighting to make the sensation of his climax repeat and last as long as possible.

Finally, out of breath, he began to extricate himself from Tag's tight ass. Tag groaned in agony.

After removing his condom, the man milked the last of his jiz over Tag's still hard penis, shaking it down as if he were a horse thermometer. Then, he flopped atop Tag, whose body was slick with cream. He massaged his chest and stomach into Tag, the hairs on his chest practically cleaning Tag up.

After a few moments, still decompressing from the sex, he rolled over onto his back and lay beside Tag. Both continued hyperventilating. They didn't speak for what seemed a long while. Then, the naked man with the body of a leather fetish porn star put his hand on Tag's chest. He moved his hand up and down Tag's pumped pecs and stomach, reaching for his still solid cock. "Hot ass," he eventually said.

"Skater's glutes."

The man made a noise that sounded like a small forced laugh.

"I gotta go," Tag said, suddenly remembering he was supposed to meet his colleagues. "Get me a towel, will you?"

"What's the 911?" the man said, getting up to fetch a terrycloth wash rag from the bathroom. "I don't even know your name. I'm Derek."

"I'm just a boy who can't say no. Sorry. Got more important things to keep me occupied than hanging out with you," Tag said.

"Come back?"

"Sure," Tag said in his typical noncommittal fashion.

As he retrieved his jeans, and pulled the legs right side out, he looked at the man again. He was suddenly feeling as if he knew this guy from somewhere. He wouldn't necessarily have remembered if they'd ever fucked, since most of those guys in Tag's life blended together and become collectively invisible.

Then Tag noticed a stack of CDs on top of the television set. As he slipped into his pants and buttoned his 501s, he looked at the photo on the cover. It was this guy, with two other men. In bold, block, old West–style type font, the CD was titled: *the laramie brothers. spank me jesus, for i have sinned . . . and other classic country gospel overzealous right wing fascist favorites.*

Now Tag remembered. Derek and his family were big in country music. Tag recalled seeing them on talk shows and reading magazine profiles about them. They had started out doing local Jim Bakker and Tammy Faye-like church programs throughout the

South. Their concerts eventually became big-time events, and they'd parlayed their success to a recording contract.

In a flash, Tag remembered seeing them on *Ricki Lake* and hearing this very one, Derek, whatever his first name was, espouse how he was saved by Jesus while serving time in prison, and how he was called by God to devote his life to spreading the "good word," and to "expunging the earth of the Devil's disciples."

Cocksucking hypocrite, Tag thought to himself as he reached for the doorknob.

"So I'll leave my door unlocked?" Derek was saying. He was back lying on the bed, propped up against two pillows and fondling his still semi-hard cock. "Stop by anytime. I won't be able to sleep from thinking of impaling you with my fire stick and hearing you beg for mercy."

"Yeah. Great. I'll see ya 'round," Tag said. Turning the lock and then the doorknob, he walked out of the room—without his ice bucket.

Back in his own room, Tag quickly cleaned himself off with a washcloth that he'd lathered with the tiny bar of soap that had been wrapped in paper. He dried himself off and finger combed his hair. Then he slipped on a fresh red T-shirt, looked at his watch and cried, "Shit." He put his wallet in his back pocket as he simultaneously reached for his room key and bolted out the door, leaving the air-conditioner on full blast.

Although it was nearly dark, it didn't seem one degree cooler than when they had first arrived in Nashville. Tag looked to the right, then to the left, not wanting anyone—especially Derek Laramie, to spot him. Rather than have to pass by room 423, Tag walked in the opposite direction. It was the long way around to a stairway at the opposite end of the second level of the hotel, but he didn't want to encounter the Cheerleader for Christ, as he'd already named the fucker in his mind.

Descending the stairs, Tag raced to the parking lot. He was ten minutes late, but he knew Garry and Jay well enough to trust that they wouldn't leave for the rink without him. Standing in the center of the lot, in the dusk of evening, he surveyed the parked cars. A horn blasted behind him. Tag sighed with relief when he recognized the car and saw Garry was at the wheel.

"You and your playmate have fun?" Jay asked.

Tag was momentarily thrown off balance. Then he realized that it was impossible for Jay or anyone to have known what he'd been up to for the past hour. "Fell into a coma. Sorry."

"A likely story," Jay smirked, making a jerking-off gesture with his right hand.

Tag smiled. "I was just so exhausted from the drive I like zonked out completely. Sorry if I held you all up. Have a nice bath, Amber?" He tried to steer the conversation away from himself.

"Pure heaven," she said smiling. "By the way, I've already seen two country singing stars. "I was looking at tourist attraction brochures by the registration desk—Dollywood and the Grand Ole Opry and such—while I was waiting for the car to come around. You'll never guess who came in. It was that Larry and Jerry Laramie, from the Laramie Brothers family of singers."

Garry and Jay both seemed impressed by Amber's star sighting.

"They sing great, but I'm not too wild for their songs," Amber said. "'Make a Smiley Face for Jesus,' 'Burnin' Bush Blues,'—unless they mean ol' George W.—'My Hound's a Christian Too.' And they sure didn't seem as nice as they do on Oprah's show. They were kind of bossy to the man at the desk. They insisted that their other brother—you know, the best-looking one of the trio? He stands in the middle and plays a guitar that has *The Last Supper* burned into the wood—was at this very hotel shacking up with that other country star. The blonde? With the deep Kathleen Turner voice? What's her name?"

"Ginger Peachy?" Garry guessed.

"That's the Jezebel," Amber smiled. "The brothers got very mad, and then the man at the desk finally gave them a room key, even though he said he wasn't supposed to."

Tag sighed with relief, realizing how close he had come to being caught in what surely would have been a country music world scandal. Although he remembered that someone had told him that there were so many closeted country singers that whenever one of the stars gets suddenly hitched, it was common knowledge that it was because someone was about to out them. Tag smiled. He liked knowing more than anyone else about personal situations, especially potentially career-damaging ones. He thought of the Laramies' image, and how it would have freaked out the brothers if they'd caught one of their kin fucking another man.

Trying to change the subject, Tag complained, "I don't know

why Ernie insists on a freakin' run-through since we do a show somewhere practically every night."

"We've had a *full* three days off," Jay said sarcastically. "Ernie thinks we'll forget how to do a toe loop if we're off of our blades for more than the amount of time it takes for him to wank his little wee wee."

Chapter Twelve

"Curfew is supposed to be eleven o'clock, people," the choreographer snarled as he assailed his charges who were assembled for a pre-show meeting. "You all look like you were screwing half the night. I won't have this!"

"We dragged our butts halfway across the continent over the past couple of days," Garry interrupted. "Plus, we did another run-through last night. That could explain why we look so haggard."

The choreographer looked at Garry and sniffed. "We know *you* didn't get any last night." His snipe was greeted with a few timid chuckles. "But the rest of this sorry bunch were probably having an orgy. Christ almighty, every one of you freaks looks a mess! This is Nashville, boys and girls. This is the most important venue we've ever played in! Big time. You must look and perform at your peak!"

After practice, Garry, Jay and Amber changed their clothes and agreed to meet by the car. "I need a little more ice time," Tag said, dismissing Garry's urging to hustle and change. "I'll just spend another hour or so with the rink all to myself. Then I'll hitch back to the *Good Time Room*."

Jay said, "Meet us in the hotel lobby 'round sevenish. We'll all come back here together."

Tag watched Garry and the others depart. When the cavernous space of the arena was completely silent, Tag stepped back onto the ice. He was alone. No music filled the air. No squabbling chorus kids. No tyrannical choreographer. It was simply Tag, doing what he loved most, and doing it completely for himself.

He went silently through his routine, adding several new movements he had been rehearsing in his head. The ice was hard and smooth, *like that Derek Laramie's dick*, he said to himself.

He completed his routine three times before finally stepping off the ice. Then he sat in one of the spectator seats and pinched the steel of his blades between his thumb and index finger and slid the mushy ice off the hard, shiny blades. He slipped his skate guards on and walked with purpose to his dressing room.

This venue was at last a real sports arena. It was used for hockey games, basketball, and figure skating. The principals could each have their own dressing rooms, but Garry and Jay still bunked together. For the first time since joining the tour, Tag had a private space with a closet, a mirrored vanity and a shower. It was small, but it was completely adequate for his needs. The chorus kids even had a gymnasium locker room–like changing area with a large community shower.

After Tag had removed his skates and dried them with a hand towel, he checked to make sure his costumes for the night were in place. The costume lady had already completed her task of washing and ironing his clothes and placing them in the closet. He smiled. "My own closet," he said out loud. He placed his skates into his Nike bag, and pulled the strap over his shoulder. Then he left the room.

Closing the door behind him, Tag thought the hallway was eerily quiet. Not a sound could be heard, except for the squeaking of his rubber trainers on the linoleum floor. He walked past the next room, then did a double take as his eye caught something. A construction paper cutout of a star was pasted on the door. AMBER was written in pink ink. He knitted his eyebrows in consternation. The next door down also had a star. JAY/GARRY it read.

Tag backtracked to look at his own door. It didn't have a star. He blanched with indignation. "I skate rings around those three clits," he said.

He went back to Amber's door and ripped off her gold star. He then went down to Garry and Jay's and removed the star that had been taped to their door as well. Then he ripped the symbols of their superiority into halves, then into quarters and crushed them in his hands. He looked around. Seeing that he was still alone, he put his hand on the doorknob of Jay and Garry's room. The door was unlocked. He smiled, then cautiously entered the room.

Flipping on the light just inside the doorway, Tag was satisfied to see that the room was no larger than his own. He was further appeased to remember that two shared this room, which to Tag, counted for something since he had a dressing room completely to himself.

Then it occurred to him that this was the way Garry and Jay preferred things. They were best friends. They shared a room no matter what the accommodations were like. Even if they were working for *Stars on Ice*, they would still stay together. But nobody thought it was queer. If it ever occurred to anyone that the two might be lovers, the obvious fact that they were simply best buds quickly dispelled the notion.

Tag looked around, careful not to touch anything that might reveal an intruder had been present. His eyes went to the men's costumes. Clean jeans and shiny shirts were hung with care. The costumes were more theatrical than Tag's, and he made a mental note to find a silver or gold lamé shirt to wear for his second-act solo.

Then Tag saw the Beavis and Butt-head costume. He acted out a deed as though he had planned it for weeks which, in fact, he now realized he had done subconsciously. He gathered the garments, folded them over his left arm, and left the room. With his skate bag in one hand and the costumes in the other, he headed for the elevator. Without a free hand to push the down button, he used his elbow. When the elevator car arrived, he used his elbow again to push the button for the lobby.

Entering the lobby area, which encircled the arena, he nodded to a security guard seated on a plastic chair by one of the doors. "Have a good show tonight," the guard said as Tag walked out of the building. Tag didn't respond. He continued through a large concourse that boasted a shopping mall with restaurants and a multiplex movie theatre.

Where can I dump these fucking costumes? he asked himself as he looked around for an appropriate place to dispose of the clothes. "Hell, it's not like it's Robert Blake's stupid pistol," he said, knowing that the disappearance of the show's property would not cause an investigation by the Feds. "Aren't there any Dumpsters in Nashville?" He decided to simply go into the public men's room, enter a stall, hang the clothes on the door hook and accidentally on purpose forget the garments when he left. While in there, he also realized he was still clutching a few fragments of the gold stars he'd ripped from his colleagues' doors. He flushed them down the toilet.

Leaving the sports center mall, Tag realized he had no idea where their Ramada Inn was located. He stood on a street corner and realized that he was lost. He was totally stumped about what to do.

The sound of a horn blasting broke into his concentration. A faded and rusted orange and gray pickup truck idled up to the curb. "Hey," the driver called out over the voice of Tim McGraw singing on the truck's radio.

Tag leaned into the passenger side window. The guy was about thirty years old, and he wore his long dirty-blond hair in a pony-tail. He had dark, deep-set eyes, a mustache and at least two days' growth of hair on his face. Tag's dick swelled. Except for a tattoo of a headstone that said *Tammy Wynette* on his thick right bicep, the man's upper body was bare. He didn't have a great build, but nonetheless, Tag's blood drained into his cock and made it solid. If there was one attribute in another guy that turned Tag on second most, after the size of his tool, it was a tattoo. It didn't matter where the branding was done: the arms, neck, chest, ass. And the more tattoos the better. It gave a guy a certain danger appeal. To Tag, it said they were serious about sex, the way a necktie said a job appli-cant was serious about work.

"Hey, back at ya," Tag said, not smiling but magnetized to the sight of the guy kneading his crotch with his right hand, to convey that the thing in his pants was like a dog that needed to be taken for a walk. It had to be exercised regularly.

"Ya like to party, man?" the guy said.

"I'd rather fuck. *Man.*"

The driver smiled. "In," he insisted.

Tag tossed his skate bag into the back of the truck, opened the passenger side door—then heard another car horn. He shot a look in the direction of the sound, thinking it was probably an impatient motorist, and ready to flip him his middle finger.

It was Garry, Jay, and Amber. "Fuck," he said, closed the door, and quickly grabbed his skate bag. "Later man," he said to the stunned driver.

Tag walked to the car with a forced smile. "Just now leaving the rink?" Garry asked.

"I had a great session," Tag said. Then he coughed out a short laugh. "Tourists always pick me when they need to ask directions, especially when I don't even know my own way around."

"Glad that *tourist* didn't drive off with your skates," Jay said.

"You know we all hate you, Tag," Amber said with mock contempt. "Practicing when you don't have to. You make us all look like slackers."

"I hate you more," he said with a fake smile. "That's why I have to keep practicing, so I can try to be half as good as you guys."

"*Half* as good?" Jay said. "You're on par. Hamilton slash Boitano slash Missy Yamaguchi."

"Don't encourage him too much," Amber said, "or he'll be taking over my spot in the show. Wouldn't Uncle Ernie just love to have all boys as his leads? I may be from Iowa, but I'm no dummy. Ernie only pretends to be nice to me 'cause he needs a medalist in the show."

"Silly girl! You're irreplaceable!" Tag gushed to Amber.

She smiled sweetly. "I don't hate you anymore. At least not as much," Amber laughed.

"It's nearly two o'clock, so we have about four hours of rest time," Jay said. "Then we'll hustle to the arena. I've been warned about the downtown traffic so let's not take any chances. We'll start out just a little earlier than this morning. And so that *Mr. Glen Campbell Goodtime Room* can find his way, we'll all meet in the lobby at six sharp. Okay?"

Garry said, "Don't forget, after the show we're going to that place I mentioned yesterday."

"Dicks?" Tag said.

"Moby Dick's," Amber replied.

"That's just to confuse the locals," Jay sniggered.

Garry pulled his car into the Ramada Inn parking lot and dropped his friends next to the stairway that led to the second level where each of their rooms was located. He went on to park the vehicle. The remaining three dispersed to their respective rooms.

When Tag reached his, he pushed his hand into his pocket and withdrew the key. He rolled his eyes when he saw that the address and phone numbers as well as his room number were on the fob. He told himself that he needn't have been so panicked thinking he wouldn't find his way back.

It was another unforgiving humid day, and Tag decided to take his nap by the pool. Until now, he hadn't had the opportunity to use the bathing suit he brought with him from Clarksville. He'd thought it a waste of space in his suitcase, but was glad now he hadn't jettisoned it somewhere along their tour route. Tag didn't bother with any sunblock. He bronzed well without any extra help, and thought that he was too young to take into consideration the long-term consequences of unprotected exposure to the UVs.

He grabbed a bath towel and slipped on sneakers in which to walk outside. He locked the door to his room and headed down the second-floor landing toward the stairs and down to the pool.

The bathing area was a small patch of cement beside the hotel. The gate had a sign that said, "Don't pee in our pool. We don't swim in your toilet." Tag rolled his eyes at what tourists got a kick out of.

To Tag's dismay, the pool was crowded. Families with shrieking, hyperactive kids were acting as if they'd never been in a swimming pool before. But since they looked as though they probably hadn't, Tag checked his irritable disposition. There was only one vacant chaise lounge, and Tag tossed his towel from a distance of several feet, lest someone beat him to the seat.

He arranged his body on the chaise, positioning himself so that he could feel the sun directly on his face. Surprisingly, the hot sun and sticky air felt good on Tag's lean and muscled body. He closed his eyes and tried to blot out the sounds of the rowdy kids and their Diet Coke–slurping mothers who demanded that their young ones stop trying to drown Lurlynn or Billy-Ray or Dix or Embry.

Soon, all the noises melded together with the sound of traffic going by on the interstate. It all became white noise. Tag could feel himself drifting off to sleep. He set his mental time clock for twenty minutes, at which time he'd roll over and give an equal amount of sun opportunity to his backside.

The heat was soporific. In minutes Tag was unconscious. He had no idea how long he had been asleep, when a voice spoke. "Still at an age when you can get away with wearing Speedos, eh?"

Tag heard the words from just below the surface of consciousness. The voice returned. "Your dreams must have been outrageous. Your boner drove away all the mothers and their little no-neck monsters and knuckle draggin' daddies."

Finally Tag opened his eyes. When he focused he could see Derek Laramie.

"You don't even remember me, do you?" Derek said.

"I remember."

"What's my name?"

Tag cocked his head pretending to be drawing a blank. "Dude with a Heavy Pecker?"

"Forget it," Derek said, turning to leave.

"Hey. Derek," Tag said. "I'm just playing. Of course I remember you."

Derek smiled. "I didn't sleep last night. Kinda hoped you'd come knockin' at my little den of iniquity."

"I was busy with friends."

"Ya blowin' me off? I can take it. I just don't want to be strung along."

"No, no," Tag said truthfully. "I've pretty much been thinkin' of only you ever since . . ."

"You were so awesome, I thought we could exchange fluids again sometime. Like today. Or tonight."

"I've got a show at eight," said Tag. "It lets out around ten-thirty. Then I promised my friends to go to Dick's for dinner afterward. That takes us up till after midnight."

"What kind of show do you do? I haven't seen you on the country or gospel circuit," Derek said.

"Right. You're that famous singing dude. If you're rich why are you staying in this dump?"

"Publicity. Looks good to the peons who worship us if we stay in the same pit as our tech crew. Like we're just plain ol' folk."

"I'm not usually a star fucker either," Tag lied. "I'm a skater. With *Gold on Ice*."

"Then you weren't bein' a wiseacre when I admired your perfect butt and you said, 'Skater's glutes.' Hey, I'll keep my door unlocked again tonight."

"What time is it?" Tag asked.

Derek looked at his watch. Almost three-thirty."

Looking up at the country star, who was shirtless and wearing khaki shorts that didn't hide his basket, Tag considered. "I've got about an hour now. Why don't we go wreck the bed for the chamber-maids."

Derek grinned. "Get your skater's glutes ready to receive my face."

Acting out the role of perfect fuck host, Derek opened the door to his room and allowed Tag to pass through the portal first. Laramie whisked himself in right behind and closed the door with his ass. He walked two short paces to where Tag was standing in the middle of the room. Face to face, they stared into each other's eyes. Laramie quickly broke contact and buckled to his knees. He placed his mouth on the fabric that covered Tag's fully erect penis. Then he reached up and playfully toyed with Tag's bathing suit, easing it down from Tag's hips and butt just enough until the head of his dick was displayed. Pre-cum oozed from its hole.

Derek's tongue licked Tag's sticky moisture. He slid the suit down to the floor and Tag stepped out of the bikini-like garment. Holding onto Tag's hips, Laramie was literally drooling at the sight of Tag's steel-hard, blue-veined member, which throbbed with his rapid heartbeat.

Tag moved backwards until his legs hit the side of the king-size bed. He sat down and laid back, scooting himself up to the pillows. Laramie unzipped his shorts and let them fall to the carpet. He wasn't wearing underwear and his fevered cock was the center of the universe. Tag moaned when Derek revealed himself.

Derek climbed onto the bed and splayed himself over Tag's body. The two began to feverishly suck face, their mouths locked together as their tongues fought a stalemate war. Laramie raised Tag's left arm. He moved his face into the hairy pit. He deeply in-haled the scent of Tag's heavy perspiration. It intoxicated him. He made snorting noises as he greedily licked Tag's underarm, tasting the musky fibers of hair, which acted as a drug to take Derek out of his mind with satisfaction.

Tag began to copy Derek and reciprocated the actions of his partner, adding nipple play and biting the erect buttons on his hard, hairy chest. They wrestled with one another, and Tag fanta-sized about being raped by this tough-looking, even tougher lover.

Tag pretended to push Derek away as the bigger man laid on top of him, still kissing his mouth, his neck, his chest and stomach.

"You're gonna get it now, boy," Laramie said, intuitively knowing what head game Tag was acting out. He reached to the nightstand and picked up the bottle of *Glide Right*. He forced Tag's legs up over his shoulders and squeezed the tube until the cold gel was splattered all over the lips of Tag's butt.

"No," Tag pleaded, still play-acting.

"Oh, yeah, you little cocksucking skater. You're gonna get what you want."

"Yeah, I want it," Tag conceded, as Derek slathered the gel with his hands all over his young slave's hole. He used three fingers to coat the interior of his hot, steaming ass pit.

"God, no. Don't," Tag pleaded as Derek lubed himself then made his condom-clad cock connect with Tag's rectum.

"Shut your face, you little sissy skater," Derek demanded playfully.

"Fuck you!" Tag said, as Derek slowly pushed his boner into his moist chamber. "God!" Tag cried. "God, no, don't fuck me. Take it out!" he lied.

"Yeah, when I'm good 'n' ready. First, you're gonna sacrifice that hole to please me, you understand?"

Tag was in such ecstasy that his eyes involuntarily rolled back into his head as if he were about to have a grand mal seizure. His head moved violently from side to side as Derek drove his cock deeper into Tag's body and began a rhythmic grind and crush.

Tag's hands played with Laramie's tits and he grabbed at his chest hair, pulling strands out by the roots, which only gave Derek more pleasure. The two animals could not be sated. Tag slapped at Derek's face, which made the man grin, and he slapped Tag back in the same way. "Fuck me, you asshole!" Tag demanded, to which Derek slapped Tag's face again and said, "Who you callin' an asshole? Asshole!" Tag continued to pretend he was an unwilling partner in this sexual escapade, until he couldn't control himself any longer.

"Oh, Jesus," Tag said, "I'm gonna cum."

"Don't you fuckin' dare shoot that load until I say so, you little ass fucker," Derek demanded. "And I warned you about using the Lord's name, God damn it!"

"Can't. Help. It!" Tag cried out in sheer ecstasy as his cock blasted forth an explosion of jiz that was just as powerful as the day before. He sprayed his face, his chest, his stomach. Each thrust from Derek's dick seemed to uncork another load from Tag. Then, from the fierce look of pain on Derek's face, Tag knew that Laramie had just filled his condom with all of his baby-making juice.

Derek, still inside Tag, leaned his head forward and buried his face on Tag's semen-slick chest. He began licking Tag's body and spading up great amounts of the boy's load with his tongue, all the while whimpering like a lonely puppy. When he had finished his dessert, he finally withdrew his dick from Tag's ass and fell with fatigue on top of the young skater, who wrapped his arms around the torso of his muscled lover, enjoying the feeling of the smooth skin on his back.

After a few moments, Derek raised his head and planted his lips on Tag's. Tag could taste his own semen on Derek's tongue, which made his still-hard dick bounce with excitement. "Christ. Look at the time," Tag suddenly said, amazed that two and half hours had passed since they began their marathon fuck. "I'm late." He pushed Derek off of him and picked up his bathing suit. "Shit. My room key. Musta left it by the pool."

"Relax, Mr. Good Fuck. I'll get your key while you shower or douche or whatever you have to do."

Tag grinned and said, "Make it fast. I've got a show to get to."

Derek picked up his own room key and left. Tag took Derek up on his offer to shower. He scrubbed himself until even a coroner wouldn't have found an ounce of fluid to suggest he'd just had sex. When he stepped out of the stall, Derek was lying naked on the bed, trying to balance Tag's room key from his newly hard dick. "What do I get in return for finding your key?" he asked.

"You already got your prize," Tag said with a sullen tone. "My ass isn't enough?"

"Nope."

"Well it'll have to do, 'cause I'm outta here."

"Don't I at least get a kiss goodbye?"

"With your cum breath?" Tag grunted, grabbing the key from where it had fallen into Derek's pubic patch. Then he opened the door to leave the room.

"By the way, next time I see your brothers, I'll say 'hey' for you."

The color drained from Laramie's face.

*   *   *

Back at his own quarters, Tag pulled on his jeans and a T-shirt. He pushed his feet into a pair of moccasins, picked up his backstage pass, and quickly left the room again.

"Late, as usual," Jay called to Tag from the front passenger window as the car idled in the parking lot.

"No need to explain. We've grown accustomed to your tardiness," Garry said. "You never used to be this way. Is it the heat, or the southern hospitality of the men?"

"Tardiness is another word for being inconsiderate of other people's schedules," Jay said.

Tag apologized. But he said to himself, *Don't fuck with me tonight. I'm not in the mood.*

Amber sat quietly in the back seat next to Tag. She was never one to worry about being anywhere on time. Amber believed that she'd always get to where she was going and would never be late. She had a deep trust that all things worked out in her favor. And generally speaking, they did. For instance, she had not gone to the Olympics expecting gold. She did, however, know that she'd win a medal. It made no difference to her on which side of the podium she stood. She wouldn't have been any happier if she wore gold, silver or bronze.

She also knew that she'd become the star of a touring ice show. But again, it didn't matter one way or the other in which show she performed. Although the money would have been better had she joined *Stars on Ice*, again, she wouldn't have been any happier. She gave herself a direction in life, but left out specific details. She didn't care for trivialities. She simply knew that whatever happened was for the best for her. When the time came for her to move on, she would know it and follow whatever path opened up to her. She tried to make Jay see that this was a less stressful way to live. But Jay was the opposite when it came to making plans. He visualized every detail of how something would turn out. Usually he was in the ballpark, but often his big plans failed, like his Olympic dream. And he was left feeling like Brian Boitano after he did that lame, self-mastabatory effort of trying to wank another Olympic gold medal way after his prime as a competitive skater, and ended up not even making the final cut.

It was twenty minutes until showtime when the quartet arrived at the arena. Garry parked the car while the others jumped out and ran through the crowd of ticket buyers to the back of the building and the performers' entrance. They flashed their backstage credentials at the security guard and headed for their respective dressing rooms.

When Garry burst into the dressing room, he was out of breath as he quickly changed into his first-act costume. All four of them stepped outside their dressing rooms just as the taped audio of the announcer's voice began his welcoming remarks. Jay and Garry helped Amber down to the dark area behind the curtain in time for her to slip out onto the ice in pitch-blackness.

One by one, the stars' names were called to the ice. Tag was always peeved when the announcer said, " . . . and *featuring* . . . Tag. Tempkin." He didn't want to be simply featured. He wanted to be the main attraction, the star. Just the same, each night he bounded onto the ice with a wide smile.

After the opening production number, the stars returned to their respective rooms to change for the next number.

When Garry and Jay began looking for Beavis and Butt-head, they immediately thought of the costume lady. Garry went two doors down to Tag's room. "Hey, Tag? Could you find the costume lady and tell her she forgot Butt-head again."

Tag hated to play the role of lackey for Garry and Jay. However, it was the role he'd assigned himself when they first met. In the beginning, he couldn't toil enough for each of them. He'd take care of every major and minor problem, which immediately ingratiated him to the stars. Now, though, things were different. He felt that playing the sycophant was beneath him. He didn't want to waste his time pretending to search for the costume lady only to return and explain that she had placed B&B, as she referred to the costume characters, in their dressing room as always.

Tag pretended to complete his task. Sure enough the men were ticked off.

"Christ, I'd better let Ernie know so he can change the order of the show," Garry said.

"We're dead," Jay added.

"It's cool," Tag breathed a heavy sigh of impatience. "I'll take care of Ernie."

Garry and Jay looked at Tag doubtfully.

"You know he's hot for me," Tag explained. "I'll make him understand that this isn't your fault."

"He'll wonder why we didn't come to him ourselves," Jay said.

"'Cause you're in panic mode looking for the freakin' costumes. It's logical. Don't worry. Leave it to me. I'll make things work out okay."

"Ask him if he thinks we should cancel the number altogether or just skate without the costume," Jay called after Tag.

Twenty minutes later, Amber had joined Garry and Jay in their dressing room. The two men were strung out with worry. It was showtime and they didn't know what to do. Tag hadn't returned with instructions from Ernie.

Then they could hear over the house's public address system: "Ladies and gentlemen." It was Ernie's voice. "There will be a slight change in our program this evening." Jay and Garry and Amber cocked their ears. "In place of our ever-popular salute to the fun and lively world of those two moronic rascals Beavis and Butthead, *Gold on Ice* is proud to present, for the first time ever, the debut of an all-new program. Featuring our very own up-and-coming *star*: Mister. Tag. Tempkin!"

As Garry and Jay and Amber looked at each other in disbelief, they could hear the roar of the crowd. The applause filtered all the way back to the dressing room. The three bolted for the door. Together, they hurried as quickly as they could on their skate guards, down to the rink.

When they arrived, they saw that a bright spotlight with a pink gel followed Tag as he dominated the ice. Wearing black tuxedo pants, with a sparkling silver-and-gold lamé shirt, Tag performed a routine no one else in the show had ever seen. He skated to music from *Shaherezade*. Every jump and spin was carefully choreographed. His movements were completely in sync with the music. He received wild applause.

At the conclusion of his nearly five minutes of ice time, the audience was on its collective feet, screaming: "Tag! Tag! Tag!"

Garry, Jay and Amber stared with shock at Tag taking over the spot allocated to the two male stars.

"Feeling better?" The voice from behind Garry belonged to Ernie.

"About what?" Jay asked.

"Your food poisoning?"

Garry looked incredulous. "My what?"

"Tag said—"

"Well, Tag's gonna wish Jay and I really were ill when we pound his pretty face into the ice," Garry said.

"Hell," said Ernie, "he just saved the show. He said you both were too sick to skate, and he volunteered to try out his new routine. Went over well, don't you think? Besides, I think it's time to scrap B&B. It's old hat."

Garry could tell that Jay was burning with frustration and anger. Amber was apparently dumbfounded by the audacity of Tag; taking the principals' spot, and in such an underhanded way.

After what seemed like a five-minute ovation, Tag finally made his last bow and waved goodbye to the audience as he skated off the ice. When the curtain opened for him he walked right into Garry, Jay and Amber. Each had their arms folded across their chests.

"Hey, guys! Wasn't I great?" Tag enthused, still catching his breath.

"Yeah. A great *opportunist*," Amber said. "What's the idea of taking the boys' place in the show?"

"I had to do *something*," Tag tried to explain. "Ernie was so angry when I told him about the missing costumes. He was saying stuff like, 'This is the last fuck-up they'll make in my show.' I had to come up with a way to defuse the situation."

"As always, you took good care of us," Garry said in his most sarcastic tone.

"You're a wonder, Tag," Jay added. "What would we do without you?"

"Are you guys upset or something?" Tag asked, seeming perplexed. "I risked making a total fool of myself with an unfledged program all to protect you. Did I do something wrong?"

Garry didn't know what else to say. He looked at Jay and Amber, transmitting thoughts about the possibility that Tag really was just trying to be helpful.

Jay seemed to back down. "You didn't have to lie to Ernie that we were sick."

"He was so furious about the costumes. I just told him you were throwing up."

"That's not exactly the way Ernie explained it," Amber said. "Excuse me for butting in . . ."

Tag flashed a look of anger at her. "I didn't think I would get in trouble for trying to help."

"Just the same," Amber continued, "it's my opinion that you all should meet with Ernie and get to the bottom of this. Who's right and who's wrong is one thing. Taking away a principal's number is beyond reproach."

"I haven't taken anything away," Tag flared again. "I just saved the evening. It was only for one night. They'll find B&B by tomorrow, and you'll both be doing your pratfalls again."

"Our fine production manager has a different idea," Garry said.

Tag played dumb.

"Ernie is putting B&B back in mothballs," said Garry.

"Well, that is what you wanted, isn't it?" Tag dismissed the news. "You always hated that stupid number. What's he got in mind as replacement characters?"

"You," said Jay.

Tag stared blankly at the trio. "I don't follow."

"Don't play 'Daddy, what's beer?' with us," Amber challenged.

But as Garry, Jay, and Amber stared at Tag like a pack of ravenous coyotes surrounding a kitty cat dinner, the chorus skaters were on the ice doing their tribute to *Man's Modern Inventions for Convenience*. The skating electric toothbrush slipped and knocked down the George Foreman grill. The audience laughed, thinking it was all part of the act. Then the waltzing Ronko Slice 'n' Dice collided with the Natural Childbirth Dilator. Again, the audience was howling with laughter.

For a moment, the three principal skaters took their eyes away from Tag to watch what was happening on the ice. They looked up just in time to see Light Beer knock over Viagra, as the peppy costumed skater was doing high kicks. They laughed along with the audience.

For a short while, as calamity ruled the ice, Garry forgot about Tag. When the music finally subsided, Amber had left the group and returned to the ice for her final solo of the evening. As her last jump ended in a perfect landing, she received her usual applause and she curtsied again and again. She mimed *Thank You! Thank You! Thank You!*, and blew kisses to the audience. Then she skated backward to the red velvet curtain from which the chorus of skaters glided past her.

The familiar fanfare of music began, followed by the canned announcer's voice calling the principals one by one back to the ice. After Garry and Jay's names were called they skated out, beamed at the audience and waved wildly. The old tape replayed, "And our star. Miss. Amber. Nyak!" Amber returned for one final camel spin.

Then the unexpected happened.

Almost in unison the crowed erupted with a cacophony of, "Tag! Tag! Tag!"

Tag, who was skating with the ensemble, broke rank to appear at the center of the rink where he did a breathtaking scratch spin. He covered his heart with both hands, then shrugged his shoulders and opened his arms to the audience as if to say, "You like me? You really like me?" He received a standing ovation and was encouraged to perform an encore.

Tag skated over to the red curtain and yelled for Ernie. "What kinda fucking crowd-pleasing music ya got back there?" he demanded.

Ernie nervously raced through a shoebox of dozens of cassette tapes. "What'ya want? I got 'Birth of the Blues,' 'Greensleeves,' 'Rose's Turn,' 'Romeo and Juliet,' ABBA, a medley from 'Pump Boys and Dinettes,' the London cast album of 'Les Miserables.'"

"That's a good one. I saw Paul Wylie do that once. Put that on. Don't just stand there like a moron. The crowd wants me! Now!"

Ernie wasn't used to being ordered around, but then he wasn't used to an audience screaming for encores, either. He did as Tag instructed and ran to the control booth. Tag returned to the ice and found the center of the rink. He stood with one toe pick gouged into the ice and his left arm outstretched. His right hand touched his heart. The house lights dimmed. Finally, the music began, and the crowd settled down.

Tag didn't move for the first few bars of the song. Then, as if becoming one with the music, Tag turned on his left blade and did a grand *tour jeté*, flowing into a pirouette and arabesque. With his arms stretched out at shoulder level, he covered half the rink in back crossovers, finally jumping into a triple Axel, landing perfectly on the outside edge of his right blade.

As the music continued, Tag's entire body was vibrating with every note from the string section of the tape-recorded orchestra.

He made one final turn around the rink, then completed another triple Axel, triple toe loop combination, before gracefully coming to a slow and steady finale.

Again, the crowd was instantly on its feet. Tag bowed in supplication. He continued to bow and throw invisible kisses to his admirers until the house lights dimmed and he withdrew to the red curtain. Once he was away from the public, the house lights returned and the crowd began to disperse.

Chapter Thirteen

"HOT STUFF MELTS ICE," proclaimed the banner headline of the Sunday edition of *The Nashville Notice*'s entertainment section. On the first page, above the fold, was a six-column-wide picture of Tag Tempkin caught in the middle of a split jump. The sports reporter raved about Tag's performance in *Gold on Ice*. He noted that Tag had apparently been a last-minute replacement for one of the ailing stars (he didn't mention Garry's name) and that he had been completely embraced by the audience.

Amber scanned the article searching for her name. She was usually in the first paragraph with glowing compliments about her elegance and grace on the ice. In this article she found her name in the last paragraph. "Also appearing in *Gold on Ice* is former Olympic Bronze medalist Ember Kayak."

Amber was pouting as she presented the paper to Jay and Garry in their hotel room. "That reporter didn't even know who I was. Or didn't care! I'm an ice queen, for cryin' out loud. And nobody is ever a *former* Olympic medalist. You wouldn't say *former* Oscar winner."

"I didn't even get a mention," Garry sulked while sipping his morning coffee. "The Wonderbra in the modern inventions number got a mention, but not me."

"Guys," Amber begged, "it's time you caught on. Tag's doing something to you. He wants to be a star."

"Doah," Jay said. "Don't you think we figured that out?"

"He's going to get his way if it kills him—or one of you." Amber was pacing the floor of the guys' small room. "He's not into making distinctions between what's ethically right or wrong. There are no rules in his handbook for the upwardly mobile."

"I'm trying to comprehend what kind of person would hurt another just to get ahead," Garry said, slapping the newspaper. "He maybe got carried away last night, that's all. He's young, after all."

Amber shook her head. "You guys have got to watch your backs. God knows, I'm not the type to be paranoid, but it seems crystal clear that he's out for your jobs."

"And with reviews like this, he could probably have us out sooner than later," Jay agreed.

"What can we do?" Garry whined. "Nothing. Ernie adores him. He'd never listen to us if we complained."

"Ernie's not a complete dickhead," Jay reminded. "He may have the hots for Tag but he wouldn't let the show down by tossing us out."

"Don't be too sure," Amber said skeptically. "What if Tag could convince him that he'd be able to save the price of you two in payroll. Ernie would leap at that opportunity. This show expects our undivided loyalty. But there's no reciprocal exchange. They'd just as soon dump us all."

"It's all my fault for being seduced by the possibility of sex with an unbelievably cute guy," Jay said. "I should have known he was shining me on."

"No, it's my fault," Garry said. "I'm the one who first wanted to help Tag. I'm the one who was hoping to score enough dildo points so he'd be forever grateful."

"All that fawning and sycophantic shit," Jay said. "We should have known he was too good to be true. Nobody has ever responded that way to me, even when I was winning medals at competitions. His green eyes blinded me. He just seemed ripe for plucking."

Amber had picked up the newspaper and scanned the article again. "This reporter compares Tag to a young Kurt."

"Don't get me started on that one," Garry complained. "I was shaking the minute I read his name."

"He doesn't have enough glory without some jerk of a reporter stealing what little thunder we might have?" Jay added.

"I hardly think Tag's another Kurt Chrysler," Amber said, rolling her eyes. "He doesn't have Kurt's natural combination of athleticism and grace."

"Nobody is," Garry said distantly.

"Sorry," Amber said. "I usually try to stop myself from bringing up his name."

Garry waved away her apology. "Please. I'm completely over him. It only hurts when I laugh." He stopped for a beat. "That was supposed to be a joke."

"I think ol' Kurt just got too famous too fast," Jay said. "One day you're having a blast, then pfft, like that, Kurt doesn't want to associate with you."

Garry shook his head. "You really can't fault the guy. Someone explained it to me. They said that super successful guys can't be connected with people who aren't going anywhere. Meaning me." Garry sighed.

"He must have thought that way about me, too," Jay said. "I remember when he started being asked to chair all of those charities. I contributed a ton of cash to his stupid doggie walk-a-thon. All I got in return was a freakin' form letter thank you and color Xerox copy pictures of his Anthrax spore of a mutt, Missy Sonja. Ugh," Jay shivered.

"I'd always heard Kurt was the sweetest guy on ice," Amber said. "And cute! My god, he was—is, cute!"

Garry pursed his lips and nodded. "He was. Nice I mean. And cute, too. I was just too young and naive. I confused Kurt's making love to me as meaning we had a lifetime commitment. I was just one of many boyfriends—before *and* after."

"There weren't too many others, Garry," Amber said. "In fact, I know that Kurt loved—*loves*—you."

"So why did he drop me when I needed him the most?"

"That I can't explain. It was so not like Kurt to do such a thing. I've always felt there must have been other forces at work. Things in his life that you'll probably never know about."

"You're sticking up for him?" Garry asked, bewildered.

"No, no. I won't ever condone the terrible way it ended for you. But from my experiences with Kurt over the years, I would never have thought he was capable of being anything other than the proverbial boy next door. I just can't fathom what happened. But, if you say he was unconscionable, I totally believe you."

"Maybe enough time has gone by, and he wouldn't mind you contacting him," Jay said.

"There's nothing for us to talk about," Garry said.

"Maybe he's miserable without you," Jay said.

"Or maybe his success just went to his head," Amber said. "Same thing happened to me."

"Not our precious Amber!" Jay teased. "Not America's skating sweetheart who every mother in America hopes that their daughters will emulate."

"It's their sons who want to emulate me," Amber laughed. "Did you know that there's a drag queen in L.A. at a place called *The Queen Mary*, who portrays me? I hear she's spot on."

"Our little Amber would never allow anything as trivial as stardom to change her personality," Jay said.

The Olympic medalist smiled. "I was far from the sweet little thang *People* portrayed me to be. Part of my problem was being around all you cute skaters and never having a boyfriend. You were all fighting over each other."

"Can't help it if the boys are sexy *and* talented," Jay said.

"But you can't imagine what it does for a girl's ego, and her libido, to have such eye candy waltzing around all the time. I kept asking myself, 'Aren't there any straight skaters?'"

"I've heard they exist," Garry played along. "They're like ten percent of the population according to an *InsightOut* survey. I think some even get married and have a kid. But I've never met one. Of course, I've never met a free-thinking Republican either, but people swear they exist."

The three friends chuckled together. Then Amber reiterated that Garry should consider contacting Kurt Chrysler. "Send him a card. Or call him up," she pushed.

"I'm not ready to risk rejection again," Garry said. "But just as I'm starting to regain my confidence, this upstart, Tag, comes along and tries to steal what little of my star shine is left. I'd be devastated if Kurt rebuffed me again. I was too needy in that relationship. Unfortunately, things haven't changed in that respect."

Jay reached over and pulled Garry's forearm. "One thing's certain. Amber and I need you in our lives."

"Thank God for you guys." Standing up, he announced, "So, let's go meet the show's newest star, shall we? I wonder if his head will fit through the doorway this morning!"

Chapter Fourteen

Dressed only in blue jeans and an effulgent smile, Tag absently answered the door to his hotel room with one hand while holding the morning paper with his other.

Amber smiled and held her breath as she took in the sight of Tag's pumped torso and washboard stomach. His muscles seemed to be trying to escape the confines of his velvet smooth skin. She winked and said, "You just get healthier looking every time I see you." She playfully gave a finger-on-hot-iron tap to the pink button of Tag's right pectoral nipple as she eased past him in the doorway.

If he noticed, it didn't seem to register. "Guess you've seen the write-up," Garry said as he followed Amber into the room. "A star is born, my friend! The boys'll be lining up at the stage door tonight!"

"Like any other night," Tag said in a distracted voice as he divided his attention between the paper and his colleagues.

"I wouldn't be surprised if some big-time New York sports agent comes to the show tonight," Jay added, closing the door behind him.

Tag seemed to emerge from his reverie. "Really? This is just so awesome!" he acknowledged in complete agreement with everything his cast mates had said. He finally took his eyes away from the paper. "I am a star now, aren't I? This reporter got everything right. He really knows his stuff. Even his analysis of my jumps and spins was written as though he's competed and can tell genius on ice, as opposed to someone merely going through a slipshod routine."

"Um," grunted Garry.

"He especially liked my triple Axel." Tag either hadn't heard Garry's grunt, or else chose to ignore it.

"Yes, little star, we know," Garry said with more than a trace of sarcasm.

"And this guy's comparison of me to Kurt Chrysler? I mean, Kurt's the best in the world."

"Sorry Garry," Jay said to his best friend. "To think that just a few weeks ago our dear Tag thought that *you* were the best. How quickly the bloom fades when it's pruned from the bush."

"Oh, Garry, but you *are* the best!" Tag insisted. "I didn't mean that you weren't the best. I meant that this reporter just saw a flicker of something of Kurt in my work. That's all. You'll always be the best. Always!" Tag, in order to prove his point, picked up the paper to find where Kurt Chrysler was mentioned.

Garry looked at Jay, who was rolling his eyes and splaying his fingers over his head to demonstrate the increased size of Tag's cranium. Garry sniggered.

Tag noticed. "Hey, a good review for me does the whole show good," Tag bridled, but checked his annoyance. "And my ego is definitely not going Hollywood, I swear. This is just one critic. I'll bet the other reviews aren't nearly as good," he said with as much humility as he could muster under the circumstances of being heralded in the state's biggest newspaper. "As my acting coach in school said, 'If you believe your good reviews, you also have to believe the bad ones.' "

"You never mentioned being an actor," Amber said. *But it makes sense*, she thought to herself.

Tag became instantly guarded. "It was just school stuff," he backpedaled. "I needed some extra credits. Something easy."

"I bet you found it wasn't so easy after all," Garry said. "Acting's tough."

"As a matter of fact, it was real easy."

"Why am I not surprised?" Amber said.

"I even won a trophy at the end of the term for my role in *The Heiress*."

"A drag show, in high school?" Garry said, incredulous.

"I played the handsome suitor." Tag shot Garry a look of imperious disdain, then changed the subject. "Of course any good review I receive will still be completely due to all the help you three have given me."

Oh, Christ, stop with the modesty routine, Amber thought to herself. "You've worked so darn hard. You deserve everything you get," she said in mock support.

"I just wish the reporter had mentioned me, too," Jay added, smiling mirthlessly.

"They didn't mention you?" Tag looked shocked. "I didn't even notice that. I'm calling this stupid reporter right now and demand a correction in tomorrow's edition."

"Don't be silly," Jay said. "I've had my name in tons of papers and magazines over the years. I don't care, really. I was just teasing."

"I remember you were on the cover of *Sports Illustrated*," Tag said. "I suppose that should make up for a lifetime of getting your name in some stupid newspaper."

"If you do call that nice reporter, please tell him that my name is not Ember. Although I am very hot."

"Gosh, guys, it's just not fair that I'm the only one from the show that got a mention."

Jay said, "Garry's name was included at the end of the piece. Or didn't you get that far?"

"Oh, yeah, of course." Tag tried to sound as though he had simply made a slight mistake. "Anyway, I'm just the flavor of the day. You've all been there. Fame doesn't last very long."

"We're already has-beens," Garry joked. "Well I guess it's nice to watch a new star emerge. Obscurity one day. Fame and fortune the next. Only in America, eh?"

"Fortune?" Tag's eyes glazed over. "Nah. I don't care about the money. I just want to skate. I don't care about being well known or having cars and big homes. Where does someone like Scott Hamilton live anyway? Beverly Hills? Well, everything I've ever wanted is already mine. Just being with you guys, oh, and you too, Amber, is my dream come true. Honest!"

Jay looked at his watch. "This dream'll turn into a nightmare if we don't get over to the rink for rehearsal, mister," he said. "Put some socks on and let's get a move on."

"I notice you didn't tell him to put his shirt on," Garry said. Jay and Amber laughed. Tag, for the first time, seemed to notice that he was half-naked. He gave a quick surreptitious look at Garry and Jay's respective crotches. He smiled as he saw the outline of their stiff cocks giving an ovation to what he knew was his beautiful body. Then he hurried to get dressed.

There was a long line at the ticket window of the sports arena when the quartet arrived for rehearsal. The ice stars, with their skate bags slung over their shoulders, passed by the queue of young to middle-aged men and a few families with children. They caught a smattering of fragmented conversations.

"This Tag guy can melt on me any day," said one of the patrons to another man by his side, referring to the newspaper headline.

"Look at that split jump," offered another man, holding Tag's review. He offered an elbow to the ribs of a tattooed hunk who had discarded his perspiration-soaked tank top and tucked it into the back pocket of his black jeans. "Those legs have to be pretty pliable, wouldn't you say?" the first man said in agreement. "And look at that butt! Ohmagod! Where has this thing been all my life? Never saw him on ESPN."

"Guess he's been saving himself just for us Nashville boys," offered the second man.

Tag smiled as they passed the line. "They're talkin' about me," he whispered. "They're all here to see me!"

"Ya think those three kids hanging onto their daddy's pants have read that you're the Second Coming? I doubt that they're panting to see you undressed on the ice," Garry mocked.

"Bet their cute daddy is," Tag supposed. "I'll wager that he was desperate to get an up-close and personal look at me, but had to drag the little mistakes of nature along as an excuse to see an ice show. Looks pretty butch to me."

"You see how our Tag is taking it all in stride," Garry teased. "He's determined to show us that he can remain the same humble, down-to-earth guy we first fell in love with and took under our wings. No matter how much the audience adores him, he'll always be the same."

Tag smiled as Garry reached for the door handle of the performer's entrance. *But what's the use of living and learning, if we don't change?*, Tag thought to himself.

They signed their names on an attendance sheet that the stage door man pushed toward them on a clipboard. Tag huffed, "I'm a little disappointed that not one of those guys recognized me and chased me for an autograph."

"Nauseating, isn't he?" Garry said aloud, only half joking.

Heading for their respective dressing rooms, they all saw a white envelope taped to Tag's door. "A fan letter, already?" Jay said eagerly.

Tag pulled it off the door and stood for a moment, looking at his name, centered on the #10 business size envelope. He turned it over. It wasn't sealed, so he untucked the flap and pulled out a sheet of paper. Before reading it, he quickly looked at the name and signature at the bottom. "It's from Ernie. Christ, what does he want?"

Amber, standing by Tag's side, leaned in closer to read the note for herself, even as Tag was reading aloud. "Terrific program last night. Great reviews in all the papers. See me in my office, when it's convenient."

Jay looked at Garry, then looked at Amber. "That can't be from Ernie," he teased. "Ernie's never said to see him when it was convenient for a cast member. It's always when it's convenient for *Ernie*."

Tag smiled. "Guess I shouldn't keep the man waiting. See you guys on the ice."

Tag stepped into his dressing room, placed his bag on the cot that wasn't there when he left the room after last night's performance, and found two bouquets of mixed flowers on his dressing room table. He removed the first card from the plastic devil's pitchfork holder and opened it up. Tag grinned.

"HOPE YOU LIKED MY STORY. LET'S GET ANOTHER BREW AFTER TONIGHT'S PERFORMANCE." It was signed Parker Barnes, *The Nashville Notice*. "Screw you," Tag said as he pitched the card onto the table. He plucked the other from its holder in the second bouquet. It read, YOU'RE GOING A LONG WAY. It was signed, *Ernie*. Tag harrumphed. He pitched that card against the vanity mirror as well, then left the room.

"Congratulations," one of the male chorus skaters chirped as he passed Tag in the hall.

"Where's Ernie?" Tag asked as he strutted down the hall, not bothering to respond to the kid's praise.

"Doing a sound check, I think," the skater said to Tag's back as he turned around and headed down to the arena.

Minutes later Tag approached Ernie, who was deep in concentration at the motherboard of the computer-programmed sound system. Ernie was so absorbed in his chore that he didn't hear Tag.

"Let's play *Test the New Star's Patience*!" Tag trumpeted with obvious annoyance.

Ernie looked up, first with exasperation, then with a bright smile, as he took in the sight of Tag. "My new diva!"

Tag smiled. "I can be Kathleen Battle, if I have to be." Ernie probably didn't know who the hell he meant, and neither did Tag, really, except that he'd heard one of the chorus boys talk about some opera singer who was so difficult that nobody would work with her. They called her "a diva bitch."

"Look, I haven't got a hell of a lot of time," Tag huffed, changing his demeanor from the obsequious to the confident. He leaned against a steel pole and put his thumbs into the front two belt loops of his beltless blue jeans, which were unbuttoned at the top. "What'cha got on your mind?"

Chapter Fifteen

"Tag must have fucked Barbara Eden. That's it, isn't it?" Jay wailed as he flounced from his dressing room the following night.

Garry and Amber were already in the wings, dressed in their opening act costumes, waiting for the stage manager to call "places."

"I figured it out. He fucked a goddamned genie. He put his cock in a bottle and got three wishes. There's no other explanation. That freakin' stud drops his pants, and the whole world goes down on him. Now he's got another second-act solo, for Christ's sake." Jay fumed. "We've gotta get tougher, like Madonna. She wouldn't stand for some backup singer's double-crossing behavior. If my co-jones were as large as Ms. Ciccone's I'd have the son-of-a-bitch put out of our misery."

"Take a number," Amber murmured. "And the line forms to the right. My second-act number's been cut by five minutes. That's half of my program! Now I know how Michelle Kwan felt when she stood next to Sarah Hughes on the Olympic podium. God, how surreal that must have been for her, knowing that she should have been wearing the gold medal."

Returning to the subject of Tag, Amber mused aloud, "I'm thinkin' a dark country lane. Maybe a hockey-masked maniac. A chainsaw, for sure. Or a wild pack of somethin' nocturnal that stalks the local woods to feast on lost campers."

Then she poo-pooed her own idea. She waved away her Christmas wish list. "Nah. Nature walkers are always stumbling across the leftovers of sixteen-year-old nitwits with sticky bloody hatchets buried where their faces used to be."

"The moral of the story is don't leave your tent to pee outside in the night," Garry said. "Those bimbo slasher–bait types haven't got the brains of a graham cracker. That's why they keep gettin' swacked in movies."

"I know you're joking," Amber said, "but that's exactly what you two have done."

Jay and Garry looked at Amber with a look that said, *We wouldn't think to pee in the woods.*

"Metaphorically speaking, that is," Amber said. "You guys have left your zippers wide open and Tag has taken full advantage. What're we to do about him?"

"Foul play isn't as simple as it used to be," Jay said. "Not since science poked its microscope into other people's genes. You know DNA, and all that. And there's always that old standby: dental records."

Plotting *Law & Order*–worthy scenarios for Tag's elimination from *Gold on Ice* was becoming the trio's addiction. It was more fun than their previous avocation: Anna Nicole Smith. *Your sugar daddy dies tonight; spend his fortune by morning.* There were no other rules, per se. The first player to spot a big ticket item and yell out, *Anna Nicole Smith!,* scored a point. A Mercedes, or better: *Anna Nicole Smith!* A mansion boasting *Gone With the Wind* columns: *Anna Nicole Smith!* An ancient man with more liver spots on his head than hair, and a wellspring from his drooping lower lip: *Anna Nicole Smith!*

In strip mall jewelry stores, suspicious clerks kept an extra cautious eye on Garry and Jay. Although they'd enter with Amber, they'd instantly bolt for the diamond bracelet case and slip on the heaviest, most gaudy treasure they could select from the velvet cloth. They'd imitate Mae West. "Ooh. Anna Nicole Smith, indeed. Ooh," one or the other would coo covetously.

It was no different while watching television or eating in restaurants. *Anna Nicole Smith,* Garry would murmur when repeats of *Magnum P.I.* came on with Tom Selleck showing off a mat of dark chest hair under his Hawaiian shirt. Or, *Anna Nicole Smith* when the waiter undressed Garry or Jay with his eyes. No one ever won the game but the century's most successful golddigger, next to George W. Bush, had her name bandied about among the trio more often than by that gaggle of probate attorneys hired by billionaire J. Howard Marshall's spoiled brat rich son.

"Hate him or not, we've got a full house at the ice arena," Amber offered. She tried to come to terms with Tag's only purpose for being allowed to continue skating. "You'd think we had Kitty and Peter Carruthers in the show, for cryin' out loud."

"For. Get. It!" Garry cried out. "You can't cough up those three names in the same sentence! Peter's a darling specimen." He fanned his face with his hand. "Did I never mention that he was another boy skater who gave me a boner when I was a kid? My school library had videos of him and his adorable sister at the Olympics in Sarejevo. Each time I watched I thought I would literally gnaw the skin off my knuckles while I waited for the final scores, even though I knew how it turned out. Silver wasn't good enough! They were robbed. Another example of the incompetence of Olympic judges. I'm tickled that he's a commentator on TBS Superstation. Tag is no Peter Carruthers!"

As Jay was tucking in his gold filigreed black T-shirt into his blue jeans, the stage manager appeared. "Okay kids," he called. This was their cue to slip into their skate boots and head down to the rink.

"Let's try to be grateful for at least one thing," Amber said. "We should be happy that Tag is at least bringing in the crowds."

Murmurs of reluctant agreement issued from the guys as they left their dressing room and stepped into the hall. Clumping down the corridor, side by side on their cumbersome skate guards, the trio reminded at least one other cast member of Tom Hanks, Kevin Bacon and Gary Sinese, walking in their costume space suits toward the Apollo 13 gantry.

None of the skaters in *Gold on Ice* could remember a time when their show had so many people in the audience. The energy emanating from the bodies in the seats surrounding the rink was palpable, and the troupe could feel an electrical charge of having a capacity crowd pouring positive vibrations down to the ice.

The entire company assembled for the opening production number and the stars' names were announced, and the tide of approval became a tsunami when the spotlight hit Tag. The public's deafening response made it apparent that no further introduction was needed. Tag's newly recorded greeting was drowned out by the applause. Performing his signature triple Axel/double toe loop, he then stretched his arms high above his head and waved enthusiastically. Tag's heart swelled with emotion and pride. *They love me*, he said to himself. *They love me and I'm the greatest skater in any ice show.*

Intermission came too quickly for Tag's taste. However, he left his dressing room door open to allow other cast members to poke their heads in and offer their tokens of congratulations: "You're the best, man!" "It's a party when you're on the ice!" "Now I know what it must be like to be in a classy ice show." "The applause is better than sex, isn't it?"

That last remark was from a gangly teenage boy skater with a long body frame and, as Tag had already made a point to find out, an abnormally long dick. The comment made Tag laugh because although the kid was no virgin he probably had no idea just how great sex could be. To Tag, the adoration from the public was intoxicating, but nothing quite satisfied him like a good fuck. "Yeah," Tag said to the kid, "the audience is banging me with their applause."

Jay and Garry emerged from their dressing room, which was opposite Tag's. Garry witnessed the skaters in their second-act opening number costumes surreptitiously raising their eyes from the corridor hallway floor to take a quick peek into Tag's room as they passed by. Most were too nervous to say anything, so they settled for a glance at the new star stripping for his next number. Ernie had been convinced to allow Tag to skate without his shirt, à la Philippe Candeloro. "The audience will dig it," Tag had explained to an already persuaded Ernie.

After the fifteen-minute intermission, which was stretched to forty minutes to enable the audience to scarf down extra greasy helpings of artery-clogging nachos and cheese from the overpriced concession stand, the cast assembled in the waiting area behind the red curtain entrance to the ice. Many of the boys, and a few curious girls, changed in a fraction of their usual time because they wanted to catch Tag's new second-act opening number. Even the kids who didn't hate Tag, which were few, were curious about how the audience would react to his new program, which they had heard, was nearly pornographic.

When the pink spotlight found Tag at the center of the rink, he was dressed in a white tank shirt, tucked into the waist of his black jeans. Tag had gotten one of the chorus boys to paint the flag of Tennessee on his chest and stood with his thumbs pointing to the emblem. When the audience noticed the flag, they went wild with affection for Tag.

Tag was adept at reading the vibrations of his audiences. And although he had practiced to "Bolero," just before he glided onto the ice, he gave the soundman a different cassette tape. He chose "The Tennessee Waltz."

Knees slightly bent, back straight, head held up high and eyes looking onto the blackness beyond the bright spotlight, he moved for a few moments in silence. Only the sound of his blades scoring the hard surface of the ice could be heard. Then, the soft, haunting music began.

When the local crowd heard the first few strains of Patti Page, and witnessed Tag gliding spread eagle down the center of the rink, his hands outstretched as though taking the entire arena into his embrace, the applause was simultaneous and deafening.

By the time Tag concluded his program with Rudy Galindo's famous reverse Biellmann spin, holding one leg straight out then pulling it up in front of his face, he had endeared himself to Nashville. He knew he'd given the crowd everything it had hoped for, and more. If a two-minute standing ovation wasn't enough to make Ernie recognize the prize he had in Tag, nothing would be.

Jay, Garry, and Amber stood peering out from behind the velvet curtain that served as the artists' entrance to the rink. They were awed by Tag, and also at the same time, were more aware that their days as the stars of the show were numbered. The new kid on the block had taken over. Not just by sheer talent, but by manipulation.

"Again, he's got what he always said he wanted," Jay said. "The kid's a fucking star. I'm just glad that I never had to compete against him when I was an amateur."

"You're competing now," Amber said, not taking her eyes off the ice. "Tag's giving us all, but especially you two, the biggest competition of our careers. He thinks he's that little jumping machine, Tara Lipinski."

"He's clearly building a name for himself," Garry agreed. "I didn't pay much attention until this morning, but do you realize he's gotten an unusual amount of press coverage? You'd think Michael Weiss had done a quad in a g-string with all the fuss."

"Unfortunately, Tag's not the type to share his glory," Amber continued. "He won't stop until he's the last one standing on his blades. We've got to do something, and I mean right away."

"This production is hardly a democracy," Garry said. "He's in Ernie's camp. I wouldn't be surprised if the little cock tease weasel was actually letting ol' Ernie pork him."

Amber sighed. "I've tried to ignore the rumors I hear from the corps, but the talk is that Ernie is sure trying to build a cause to showcase Tag as the show's real star. I wouldn't be surprised if Ernie had something to do with all the press coverage Tag's gotten."

Garry took his eyes off the ice for a moment. "Makes sense. I was thinking that Tag had probably scrounged up the reporters himself. But it makes more sense that Ernie is the so-called brains behind the beauty."

Chapter Sixteen

TALENT MEETING AFTER SUNDAY MATINEE. ATTENDANCE MANDATORY. The notice, taped to the principal skaters' dressing room doors, was ominous. It was a lousy way to welcome the stars before a show.

Jay and Garry looked at the announcement as Amber was assessing the one on her door and Tag the one attached to his. "Ernie only calls a meeting when there's something important," Jay said. "Wonder what he wants?"

Tag looked at the notice without saying a word. He entered his dressing room and closed the door behind him.

Jay and Garry did the same thing, as did Amber. However, immediately after closing her door, Amber returned to the hall. Seeing that she was alone, she knocked once on Tag's door then opened it before he had an opportunity to ask who was there.

"Oh, this is cute," she said, in her sweetest voice, as she stared at Tag, who was kissing his full-length mirror and just beginning to jack off to his reflection. Startled, he turned toward her, his long, thick, hard dick at a 45-degree angle, glistening from being lubed with his own saliva.

"Oh, Christ," Tag exclaimed, "not you again. Don't you have to get ready for your performance?"

"And I thought those horny chorus boys were exaggerating," Amber cooed in mock surprise and approval of Tag's appendage. "Better not let Ernie see that. He's liable to have a coronary."

Tag nonchalantly bent down to pick up his jeans, intentionally facing his perfect white ass toward Amber. She whistled and said, "I should have brought my camera. The boys—and girls—would pay big bucks to see the photographic evidence."

"You're not interested in my butt, so why are you here?" Tag said, in a bored voice. "If it's about me opening the show, you'll have to talk to Ernie. I don't do the running order."

"You're opening the show?" said Amber. Then the obvious dawned on her. "How nice of someone to tell me." She was thrown off balance for a moment as she realized that her opening spot was being replaced.

"You'll hear more about the bigger changes at the meeting," Tag said.

"Bigger? What could be bigger than losing my star spot?" Amber said, looking dazed. "Anything coming that affects Jay and Garry?"

"As I said, you'll find out more at the meeting."

Amber regained her composure. She stared at Tag for a long moment then walked up to face him. "What's a good-looking, talented, young man like you, doing with the likes of Ernie anyway?" she said.

"This has nothing to do with Ernie," Tag said. "But if Ernie wants me to open the show and throw in a few more numbers, there's nothing I can do about it."

"A few more numbers, eh?"

"Just to fill out the extra space."

"The show's already too tight. There isn't any room for new numbers." Then Amber suddenly realized that Jay and Garry were about to be history. "But they both have contracts!" Amber cried.

"There's such a thing as a morals clause," he almost sang.

Amber looked at Tag incredulously.

"I'm not saying anything more," he went on. "The matinee today should be filled with anticipation, don't you think?"

Amber was stunned. She suspected that Tag was up to something, which is why she had barged into his room unannounced in the first place. But this news—or lack thereof—was more than she expected. "You *are* a lucky boy, aren't you?" she said, staring into Tag's green eyes. "I'll bet you never thought you'd be the star of an ice show and find yourself traveling all around the country and being in the newspaper. You've come a long way, baby."

"As a matter of fact, I did believe it," Tag said. "I counted on it."

"I'm sure you did." Amber offered a shallow grin. "How refreshing to hear someone come out and say that they believed in themselves completely. Too many people don't think they deserve success, so they don't reach very high. You reach for the stars, and darned if you don't pull 'em down. And I don't necessarily mean the ones in the heavens."

Tag smiled. "I don't believe in limitations. I should have reached for Olympic Gold."

"Why bother," Amber said, matter of factly. "It's just a lot of work, and you've reached the same payoff without having to pay your dues."

"The hell I haven't," bellowed Tag. "You've seen how well I skate. That doesn't come from sitting on my ass. I've paid more dues than you'll ever imagine. The things I've had to do just to skate would fill volumes."

"Good coaches can be expensive," Amber said.

"All they ever wanted from me was to have my dick in their mouths, or their cocks up my ass!" Tag exploded.

Amber seethed. "Never had a skating lesson, eh? What other obvious falsehoods have you told Jay and Garry? Who, by the way, have always given you the benefit of the doubt."

"They're no different from anyone else, skater or otherwise. Everyone wants me for something. I do whatever's required."

"You'd make a good whore," accused Amber.

"I *am* a whore." Tag smiled with satisfaction. "I'm a whore for making my mark in the skating world, and I'll become rich and famous doing it. Nothing wrong with that. We're all opportunists in our own way. You have to be. When a chance comes along you have to grab it."

Just then, Amber's cellphone rang out with "Für Elise." She looked away from Tag and retrieved the phone from her pocket. She pressed the keypad. "Hi. It's Amber." She smiled. "Kurt. Sweetie!"

she said. "So great to hear from you. Can you hang on for a second?" Amber looked at Tag. "We'll finish this conversation later," she said.

"Kurt?" Tag said, perking up. "Not Kurt Chrysler?"

Amber made a *keep your voice down* gesture with her hand. She turned and walked out the door.

As she entered her own dressing room, she put the cell phone to her ear. "Sorry about that. A little unpleasant business. Oh, you know how it is in these ice shows. There's nothing like showbiz to drag in the megalomaniacs. Listen, hon, I always hate to call someone for help, but I'm sort of stuck with a situation and need your guidance."

Amber explained to Kurt the predicament she and Jay and Garry were in. As soon as she mentioned Garry's name, she could hear a change in Kurt's voice. She said, "I know I shouldn't ask, but what was the problem with you guys? You're the sweetest couple on the planet. I can't imagine either of you being angry at anyone, especially each other."

Kurt sighed. "An old story. I made a few mistakes after I won the Nationals. I could never explain it. Except that maybe I suddenly had too much success."

"Garry thinks he's to blame," Amber said. "He still loves you, but thinks you stopped caring for him."

"That's ridiculous. He's gorgeous and talented and the nicest guy on blades." After a brief pause, Kurt asked, "Is he seeing anyone?"

"I think he's asexual. He's a catch but I guess no one has filled him in on that score. You're probably just an impossible act to follow. But listen, honey, he and Jay are in trouble. What do you know of a skater named Tag Tempkin?"

"Never heard of him."

"But you know all the skaters," Amber pressured. "Ahem. He's sabotaging Garry's career, and Jay's, and mine, too."

"Shades of Eve Harrington?"

"Only there are *three* Margot Channings, without our seatbelts fastened. Here's what I need from you."

Amber went on to explain how Tag had come seemingly from out of nowhere, and in a meteoric rise, became one of the stars of *Gold on Ice.* "He's a mysterious kid. A liar. A cheat."

"Cute?" Kurt asked.

"Not as cute as you." Amber smiled into the telephone. "Well, if you like 'em young and horny; blond, green eyes, peaches 'n' cream skin, gym bunny, and a helmet-head pee pee. Oh, don't be so shocked," she laughed. "I know something about the male anatomy. He's quite proud of his equipment. Doesn't mind waving it about for all the lads and lasses. And honey, he has every reason to be proud."

"You're sure that Garry hasn't had him?" Kurt asked. His tone expressed more curiosity than apprehension.

"Garry hasn't been laid since joining the show," Amber said. "He got close, once, but only because Jay coerced him into trying a three-way. Oh, you know Garry, always wants to please his friends. All the guys want him, but he just doesn't seem to want any of them. If I read him clearly, I'd say he's still pining away for you. Trust me. I know these things."

Silence from the other end of the line. Amber could hear Kurt clear his throat. "Well, first thing's first. I'll contact a chum at the A.S.S. archives in San Francisco. She's pretty helpful. I'm in their Hall of Fame, so I think they'll do whatever they can for me."

Amber said, "This Tag claims to have never been coached. Never belonged to a skating club. Supposedly taught himself to skate by watching videos of Garry. Total lies, I'm sure."

Kurt asked, "What do you think would happen if I arrived on the scene?"

"He'd probably pull down his tighty-whities, if he wore anything, which he doesn't, and offer himself body and *hole* to the great Kurt Chrysler."

Kurt snorted. "He'd have to be hung like Seattle Slew to be anything remotely unique to me."

"God *supersized* this one, my dear," Amber joked. "He uses that tool like a master key to unlock a lot of otherwise bolted doors."

"This is one reason I've always adored you, Amber," Kurt said, chuckling. "You look like Janet Lynn, but you can talk like Ozzie Osborne."

"Spend enough time back stage in ice shows and you get a serious education in skanky vocabulary." Amber giggled. "But seriously, Kurt, anything you can do to help us out would be above and beyond the call. I feel completely awkward about asking you in the first place. But you're like the only man on the planet who I think might be able to help."

"Leave it to me," Kurt declared. "We'll fuck this kid's ass."

"He'd enjoy that too much, I'm afraid."

"Metaphorically speaking, of course. Trust me, he'll be sorry he ever dug a toe pick into the ice or my friends' careers."

Amber and Kurt sent wireless kisses as they said goodbye and hung up their respective phones. Amber looked around her dressing room, and for the first time in ages thought about what she'd been doing with her life for the past five years. She'd given so much to the skating show, and now, it appeared that her days as the star attraction might nearly be over.

A fierce defender of the philosophy that all things work out for the best, Amber smiled and wondered what the next phase of her life would be like. She hadn't ever dated anyone seriously, not since just after the Olympics when she made the rounds of Hollywood parties on the arm of Barry Manilow. She thought the time might be coming soon when she would consider searching for Mr. Right and settling down to a farm in Iowa or Indiana. Although she didn't earn nearly as much money as Kurt did making TV specials of ice spectaculars, she had enough to buy a decent-sized house somewhere quiet and out of the limelight.

"But where will I find any man as cute or as intelligent and creative as my gay friends?" she asked aloud. "I suppose if it's true love I'll be able to overlook male pattern baldness and someone who doesn't get the message of *Hedwig and the Angry Inch*."

She looked at her Dorothy Hamill wristwatch. Dorothy's short arm was on the number four, and her long arm reached out for the six. "Time to get ready to greet Tag's new fans," Amber said aloud, knowing that the majority of ticket holders were coming to see what the newspapers were lately calling the Tag Tempkin Show. "You little twerp," Amber said in disapproval, as she went to the closet to select a different costume than she usually wore for her opening.

When the evening performance ended, a large group of men had assembled to greet the skaters at another *Dysfunction Junction*. Many of the men were holding the latest issue of *Stiff*, which included an interview with Tag. As the ice stars moved down the narrow alley beside the venue, men were thrusting copies of the magazine at Tag for him to autograph.

"What's this?" Garry asked Tag. "Why didn't you tell us you

were a *Stiffie*?" which was the name that all the models in the magazine came to be known as.

Tag shrugged.

"This is so amazing!" Garry exclaimed, genuinely pissed off. "What's next, *Time* magazine's *Queer of the Year*?"

Tag looked nervous, and Garry could tell it wasn't just the throngs of admirers crowding around him. Tag was used to the attention, and he reveled in it. Although he wasn't rude to the fans, he let it be known that he was in a hurry. He signed a few copies of the magazine, featuring a half-naked Ewan McGregor on the cover, before easing through the crowd and wending his way toward the car.

"Mind if I take a look?" Jay said to one of the guys in the crowd, who smiled and handed Jay his copy of the glossy magazine. He flipped through to the page on which the article began. The headline announced TAG, YOU'RE IT! Tag was pictured wearing nothing but ripped jeans, with his muscled arms outstretched doing a spread eagle. The caption read: *Grab hold of this stiff one.*

Garry sniggered at the picture as fans began to disperse. He saw his and Jay's names within the text. "We're mentioned," said Jay. Garry smiled for a beat, then furrowed his eyebrows and narrowed the scope of his vision. He noticed the words surrounding their names were a negative evaluation of his and Jay's skating.

Then: "You're the two dudes in Tag's show, aren't you?" the guy who had given Garry the copy of *Stiff* announced. "That's way cool. Can you give Tag my number?" The man handed Garry a business card. "Is it true, like Tag says in the article, that you dudes are getting too old to skate?" The man chuckled. "You both look pretty hot to me. Wanna go for a drink and unwind? Maybe convince Tag to join us?"

Garry looked at the man whose attire of black jeans and white stretch tank top over a powerful body seemed inappropriate for the freezing temperatures indoors. "I think we'll take a raincheck," Garry said. "But can I buy this copy of *Stiff* from you?"

"Keep it," the man said. He wrote a series of numbers on the cover. "You guys are studs. Call me if you want to party."

Garry and Jay looked at each other in disbelief just as Amber exited the building and came up between them. "Where's Tag?" she asked, looking around. "Did one of his fans abscond with that rascal?"

Her two friends had become mute with shock.

"What?"

"Hold on to your tiara," Jay said. He handed the magazine to Amber. After raising her eyebrow in approval of Tag's form on the ice as well as his physical form altogether, she read briefly then said, "Finally, I'm mentioned in the same publication as Tag." But her smile quickly turned to a frown. "What? What? This is . . . What on earth?"

"Let's go back inside and read the whole thing," Jay suggested.

Seated in Jay and Garry's dressing room, they picked out the most agitating pieces about themselves in the article, and each recited excerpts from the text. " *'The audiences don't really like Garry Windsor that much anymore, and for God damn good reason. He carries too much weight on the ice. His choreography is totally meaningless. It's very cheesy and just cheapens any artistry he has.'* "

Jay chimed in, reading about himself. " *'During his solo in the show, he wears the same blue velvet suit with the button down vest and peasant sleeve shirt that he's been wearing for ten years. There's got to be some yellow stains under there!'* "

Jay gasped.

" *'Sorry'*," Garry went on, reading Tag's quotes, " *'but they're both just too rigid. They both have dork haircuts. Jay skates around doing his dramatic "I'm on my knees, arms outstretched, here I am, gag me" stuff and Garry's idea of drama is to flail his arms and puff out his chest like a pigeon. Every night I count how many times he puffs out his chest during the freakin' program. I'm sorry, but that's not artistry. And, they're both inconsistent in their jumps.'* "

Jay stopped for a moment. He looked at Garry, who was biting his lip. Then he looked at Amber, whose arms were crossed in anger.

"What's the little twerp say about me?" Amber asked.

Jay found Amber's name. " *'In my humble opinion, we love Amber Nyak because she's kind of the Peggy Fleming of our day. She has a lot of grace. But,'* " Jay stopped and looked at Amber.

"What's the rest?" Amber asked, afraid to hear more but too curious not to continue.

" *'She's slacked off,'* " Jay read. " *'She's become a personality skater rather than a technician. She used to be known for her ice spirals. Now she just uses her arms a lot, and she overuses her fingers. It's very distracting.*

Amber really did have what it takes to be a champion. But she couldn't deal with the pressure when the time came to compete. Like Garry and Jay, she's more of a showman than an artist.' "

Amber was almost apoplectic. She stared straight ahead, looking into nothingness. In her mind's eye, she watched herself skate. From a flying camel to a back sit spin, to front crossovers to an inside edge spiral. She examined her performance. She observed her arms outstretched to her side, another inside spiral, then an outside spiral, a couple of turns, and into back circular crossovers, extending her arms again, preparing for a Lutz.

Suddenly, she was jolted out of her reverie. "At least he said I had a lot of grace," Amber deadpanned.

"He gets particularly nasty about me," Jay said, scanning the article for the most disturbing part of the piece. " *'His parents divorced when he was entering the senior level of competition, and his mom is like Brooke Shields's mom, except that Jay's mom is a lesbian. There was some real off-ice drama with her lover who was getting too involved in Jay's skating and trying to usurp his mother's control. It obviously screwed him up, because he was on his way to being a great skater.' "*

"I never said my mother was a lesbian," Jay continued to burn. "How'd he ever find out? I've never told anyone. Not even you guys."

"Where is that son-of-a-bitch?" Garry demanded. "Hiding his butt in Ernie's face?"

"He disappeared into the crowd," Jay said, remembering how anxious Tag seemed to be to leave the building. "With all those magazines being waved around, he must have known we would be reading the piece."

"He'd better stay out of *my* way, that's for sure," Amber threatened. "He'll be lucky if someone doesn't accidentally on purpose trip him during the matinee tomorrow."

"What's Tonya Harding doing these days? Think she's available for a hit?" Jay said. But no one laughed. They were each thinking of scenarios for revenge.

Chapter Seventeen

As Tag left the sports arena, he walked with purpose through the crowd. He fixed his sight on a group of three men who were walking a few paces ahead of him. When they split up to find their respective cars, and two of the men went together, Tag followed the third one. The man pulled out his keys and pushed the security button on his key ring. His BMW's headlights winked and a short beep was emitted from somewhere under the car's hood.

"Hey," Tag said, walking up behind the guy who turned around in surprise. "Wanna piece of a skater's hot ass?"

"That's succinct," the man said. He absorbed the sight of Tag. "Oh, you're that skater dude everyone's yapping about. What can I do for you?"

"Depends."

"On?" He returned Tag's lascivious smile.

"On you," Tag said.

The man looked puzzled, until realization crossed his face. "No thanks." He turned and opened the driver's side door. He bent into the car and sat down.

"Sorry. I'm not very good at pick-up lines," Tag said coyly.

"Better luck next time," the man said. He closed the door.

Tag rapped on the window. It slid down just far enough for them to communicate. "I saw you in the audience and thought you were really hot," Tag lied. "I couldn't wait for the show to end so I could find you. What's your name?"

"Carl. But that's all the information you need to know." He looked at Tag suspiciously. "With hundreds of men in the arena, you spotted me? That's a new one."

"Does it matter? The bottom line is you're a hottie and I'd like you to fuck me. Any more questions?" Tag looked over his shoulder, expecting Garry and Jay at any moment. "Look, could we talk about this on the way to your place?"

Carl looked at Tag for a long moment. He took in the sight of the younger man whose shirt was unbuttoned three notches, revealing cream-colored skin. Carl realized his dick was steel hard. After another moment he said, "Get in."

Without a word, Tag went around to the passenger door and slipped in beside Carl. He closed the door just as Carl turned the ignition and eased the car out of the parking space.

Tag leaned against the car door and stared out the front window, watching the street lights bathe the car's interior every several feet. He surreptitiously looked at the driver. *Not bad*, he thought. He could tell by Carl's posture and from his tight LaCoste shirt that he worked out. Carl wore a well-groomed mustache, and tufts of hair from his chest were sprouting from the V of his shirt.

"How far?" Tag asked.

"I'm about forty-five minutes out of the city."

"Jeez, that's a distance," Tag groaned. "Let's just pull over and do it in the back seat."

Carl frowned. "Look, you're the one who asked for this encounter. You're not even my usual type. So, if we're going to have sex, I'd like it to be nice and tidy. Got it?"

Tag said, "I'm just thinking about being back on time for the matinee tomorrow. You will bring me back to town in the morning, won't you?"

"We'll see. Depending on whether you're a good boy or not," Carl teased with a tone of lust in his voice.

Tag was sullen. The men remained silent for the rest of the journey. When Carl finally signaled a right turn into a driveway, Tag became aware that he was in a well-groomed subdivision development. Carl pushed the button on the garage door opener attached to the visor over his head and eased his car into an ultra-clean garage. Tag took note that the only other objects in this white space were a racing bicycle hanging on a rack on the wall, a clothes washing machine and dryer, and a spring-water dispenser holding a five-gallon bottle.

Carl closed the garage door before exiting the car. Then he walked around the vehicle and unlocked the door to the house. When he turned the knob and led Tag through the portal, Tag was impressed with the size and decoration. The place was immaculate.

"Drink?" Carl asked.

"Martini?" Tag was admiring an enormous floor-to-ceiling canvas painting of a well-pumped nude standing in the rain. Now that he had a view of Carl in the light, he felt himself getting hard. *Good choice*, Tag said to himself as he admired Carl's ruddy complexion, his blue eyes, and the black mustache above his luscious lips. His chest and arms filled out his shirt and his waist tapered perfectly into his Gap blue jeans.

"Wine. I don't drink hard stuff," Carl said. "Get comfortable," he added, removing a bottle from a wrought-iron rack on the kitchen counter.

At Carl's invitation, Tag moved to the living-room sofa. He looked up at the house's cathedral ceiling. An enormous wide-screen television on a black pedestal occupied an entire length of one wall, while a black grand piano bookended the opposite end of the room, beside French doors leading to a swimming pool. An outdoor light made rippling reflections on the stone wall dividing the property from the one next door.

"Hope you like red," Carl said, entering the room. He handed Tag a Bordeaux glass filled halfway with the dark liquid. "A San Sebastian Merlot."

"Like I know what that means," Tag said, taking a long pull from the glass. He looked up at Carl. "So, you like ice skating?" he said, not knowing how else to begin the mating dance.

Carl nodded. "I take a lot of ribbing from the guys at the station because I have a picture of Kurt Chrysler in my locker."

"The station?" Tag said. "What, like a gas station, or something?

Being a grease monkey must pay more than I thought," he said, looking around the room.

"A different kind of station. Police."

"Whoa," Tag said, coughing up his wine and practically spilling the glass. "You're a cop? A gay cop?"

"Whoa," Carl mocked. "And you're a skater? A *gay* skater?"

Tag considered. "Hmmm. I've always had a cop fantasy. How about another glass of wine. Then you can give me a sobriety test . . . with your tongue."

Tag handed Carl his empty glass. As Carl went into the kitchen for the refill, Tag took off his shirt and tossed it carelessly onto the couch. When Carl returned, he pulled up short when he saw Tag's bare chest. He walked over to the skater and rested the rim of the wineglass against the boy's lips.

"Drink," Carl commanded. He tilted the glass just enough for Tag to take a long swallow.

Carl pulled the glass away from Tag's lips and placed it on the coffee table. Then he moved in closer to Tag. With an edge of at least six inches in height, Carl looked down into his guest's eyes. He moved in and pressed his lips lightly onto Tag's. Then he reached behind Tag's head and placed his hand at the nape of his neck. He brought Tag's face closer to his own and pressed his lips much harder this time against Tag's.

The two sighed with pleasure as each began exploring the other's mouth with their respective grape-tasting tongues. With one hand holding Tag's neck and the other caressing his muscled back, Carl devoured Tag's face and then began licking the skater's bare torso. Carl slipped to his knees and pressed his face against Tag's hard stomach, licking out his navel. He began unbuttoning the younger man's 501s.

Tag moaned with intense pleasure. He tugged Carl's shirt out from the waist of his jeans, and pulled it up and over his head. Carl was indeed a bodybuilder. His chest was pumped, and he had a path of black hair running down his sternum and into his pants. His arms were thick with muscle, and his shoulders were wide enough to easily carry a five-gallon water bottle on each side.

When he'd succeeded in unbuttoning Tag's pants, Carl stood up and placed Tag in a playful half-nelson, one strong arm around his neck, the other holding one of Tag's own arms behind his back.

"You're under arrest," Carl whispered. Playfully he shoved Tag toward the bedroom.

Once there, Carl released Tag from his vice grip and gently nudged him toward the bed, where Tag lay on his back with his arms stretched over his head to the edge of the king size bed. Tag watched as Carl removed his own pants and socks. Like Tag, Carl wasn't wearing underwear. The cop's cock stood at attention above his scrotum, which was weighted by two walnut-size balls that seemed too heavy for the sack which contained them. Carl reached over to pull off Tag's shoes, socks, and jeans. Then Carl climbed onto the bed and laid his feverish body on top of Tag's and the two began again to smother each other with kisses.

"Oh, man, you taste so fucking good," Carl breathed as he explored Tag's armpits, chest and stomach with his tongue. He buried his face in Tag's crotch and began licking his balls and pubic hairs. He raised his head slightly and slid his face along Tag's throbbing shaft. He inhaled the warm scent of pre-cum and let his tongue linger at the head of Tag's cock. His tongue swabbed the delicate helmet. Finally, Carl opened his mouth and eased his lips over Tag's member, letting it slide far back into his throat.

"Mmmm," Carl moaned, as Tag flailed his head back and forth in traumatic ecstasy.

"God," Tag groaned. He forced his cock deeper into Carl's mouth. "God damn you, fucking asshole cop. God, you make me so fucking hot . . ."

Carl eased his face back up to Tag's and mauled him with fervent kisses. "I'm gonna fucking nail your ass, you little skating ice queen," Carl whispered in a voice hoarse with lust. "Be ready for the law to take over." He leaned over the side of the bed and retrieved his official police nightstick from the floor.

"I'm way guilty. Rape a confession outta me, you son of a bitch."

Carl was now kneeling over Tag, holding his riot nightstick and slapping the end into the palm of his hand.

"Which tool ya gonna use to fuck me?" Tag said in an alcohol-and-sex-induced daze.

Carl let his nightstick graze Tag's balls and cock shaft. Slowly, seductively, he let the wooden implement play with Tag's sex equipment. Tag raised his knees to his chest, exposing his pink, puckered butt. Carl let his nightstick linger on Tag's anus lips, then spat into the opening. With two fingers, he massaged the fissure for a few moments before sliding his digits into the warm hole. "You know, I could crack your nuts with this thing," he said with a satanic smile. "You'd never fuck or skate again," he said menacingly.

"Christ, just fuck me," Tag moaned impatiently. "Stick something up there bigger than your god damned fingers."

Carl tossed aside the nightstick. He opened the drawer to the nightstand beside the bed and pulled out a tube of lube. First, he squeezed a bit onto the head of his own cock. The cold jell on his hot flange made him close his eyes in ecstasy and the thrill of his forthcoming entry into heaven.

Then, he squeezed a copious amount of lube onto Tag's waiting hole. Carl rubbed the lube around the circumference of the pink playground before pushing the goo into the hole itself.

"Oh, Christ! Do it, man!" Tag begged.

"You're a fucking little whore," Carl said, putting on a condom as he acted out being a vice cop taking advantage of an arrestee. "You know what we do with whores down at the station?"

"Cock-tease 'em? Like you're doin' t'me?"

"I'll show you."

Carl held both of Tag's ankles with one hand and lifted up his knees. With the other hand, the cop guided his cock until it met the entrance to Tag's steaming hole.

He eased himself inside. Starting slowly, Carl began thrusting his hips forward, the better for Tag to receive his cock. Both men were vocal in their eager delight. They cried out as they tried to hold back their ejaculations.

Finally, after nearly twenty minutes of sweating and swearing and playful slapping, Carl commanded Tag to come. "I'm so ready, but I want to see you squirt your load first."

"Oh god, I'm so ready, too!" Tag moaned and quickly began convulsing with the release of his jiz.

Carl continued to grind his prick into Tag while scooping up his partner's thick sperm with his fingers and bringing the load up to his mouth and nose. He inhaled the scent then placed his hand in his mouth. Delirious with pleasure, he pumped faster until he cried out while holding Tag's legs up over his shoulders and slowly crushing his cock as deep as it would go past Tag's sphincter muscles.

The ensuing animal-like cries of pain/pleasure that roared from deep within Carl's diaphragm met with Tag's own groaning and whimpering.

When he'd spent his load, Carl eased his shaft out from Tag's ass and collapsed onto the other man's body. Tag's hot, sticky semen bonded the two men. They lay like this for a few minutes, decompressing from their marathon sex. Their breathing slowly returned to a natural rhythm, and Carl rolled off his partner. He massaged Tag's lukewarm, congealing pool of jiz all over the skater's stomach and chest.

For a while, neither man spoke. Intermittent sighs told Tag the man was satisfied and didn't want to break the spell of euphoria by entering into a conversation.

But finally, Carl got up and walked into the bathroom that adjoined the bedroom. Tag could hear him turn on the tap at the sink. A few moments later, Carl returned with a hot, damp wash cloth. He began bathing Tag's body to remove his gluey ejaculation.

Tag moaned, too tired to move.

"Climb in," Carl said. Tag lethargically moved into a position to pull the comforter and top sheet away from the mattress. Dead tired, he wiggled his body until he was under the covers. Before Carl could turn out the light, Tag was unconscious.

Carl simply looked at Tag for a few moments and started to get hard again. He wanted to touch Tag's face, chest and cock, but decided to let the kid have a long peaceful sleep. After performing on ice, the long drive to Carl's home in Meadowlark, and being fucked for nearly an hour, Tag deserved the sleep. Carl climbed in next to him and then turned out the light. He didn't think he'd be able to sleep, but within moments, he was dreaming of fucking a superstar figure skater.

"Get your cop-ass out of bed!" Tag demanded.

Carl squinted into the morning light. He saw Tag, dressed in his jeans and his T-shirt slung over his shoulder, standing beside the bed holding the car keys. Carl looked at the clock. 9:30.

"Get the fuck up," Tag insisted. "You've got to get me back to Nashville. Now."

"Good morning to you, too," Carl said, sitting up. The bed covers fell to his waist where his morning hard-on tented the sheet. He combed his fingers through his hair and yawned. "I need my Starbucks first."

"Get it at Seven-Eleven," Tag retorted. He threw Carl's jeans onto the bed. "I'm late for rehearsal."

Carl yawned again and rubbed his hands over his eyes. Then he got out of bed, displaying his erection.

"You fucked me with that?" Tag asked, impressed and momentarily distracted from his urgency to hit the road.

"You devoured it," Carl said, slipping into his jeans and pulling a size-too-small black T-shirt over his brawny frame. "Wanna go at it again?"

"Hardly," Tag said. "I'm late."

Carl pulled on a pair of Nike trainers, then walked into the bathroom. The sound of a horse peeing into the toilet was followed by a flush and water from the sink tap, where Carl splashed his face, then gargled with mouthwash.

"Let's move it," Tag called impatiently.

"I'm ready, for crying out loud," Carl said as he came out of the bathroom and walked down a short hall toward the kitchen. "Give me the keys," he said, annoyed at being told what to do by a trick.

Tag tossed the car keys to Carl and they both exited into the garage. Carl pushed the button for the automatic garage door opener and together, the men slid into opposite sides of the vehicle. They drove away, remaining silent until the Nashville skyline appeared in the distance.

"Which exit?" Carl asked.

"Whatever one takes us to the Ramada."

"It would help if you had an address," Carl said, exasperated.

"How many Ramadas can there be?" Tag responded.

"We'll be driving around all day. Was it close to the arena?"

"Kinda."

"Big help."

Then Tag remembered that the key fob would have the Ramada Inn address on it. He reached into his pocket and withdrew his room key. "First Street," he said.

Carl took the next exit off the highway. He made a couple of right and left turns before pulling into the hotel parking lot.

As annoyed as he was with Tag, Carl wanted to say something to reiterate that the night before had been one of the hottest sexual experiences he'd had in a long time. He wanted to invite Tag to dinner and to spend another sultry night fucking the kid. Instead, he directed the car to the space reserved for guests checking in.

"See ya," Tag said before Carl could utter a word. He quickly opened the door and stepped out into an already humid morning. The door closed, and Carl watched as Tag headed for the stairs leading to his room. The cop grimaced and shook his head, then backed up and drove away.

Chapter Eighteen

Silence filled the cavernous arena where the cast of *Gold on Ice* was seated for Uncle Ernie's meeting. Ernie had just made the announcement that he and Quinn, the choreographer, had re-designed the running order of the show, trimming more numbers and expanding Tag's role.

According to Ernie's edict, starting with the next stop on their tour, Tag Tempkin would open the show and close the first half. After intermission, Tag would return to the ice and skate to a medley of movie themes. The chorus would then perform their well-rehearsed modern inventions number, followed by Amber performing a pared-down version of her signature *La Bohème* routine. As a segue to Tag's return to the ice, the chorus of boys and girls would then bump and grind to "Like a Virgin." In the middle of the number, with a crash of symbols and multi-colored spotlights flooding the rink, Tag would charge onto the ice, and begin seductively removing his shirt and, eventually, ripping off his cutaway blue jeans, all in tempo with the beat of the music. "That'll slay the crowd," Ernie said, smiling at Tag and practically drooling.

"What about Garry and Jay?" a chorus boy asked while raising his hand.

"Our stars are our family," Ernie said with about as much sincerity as George W. Bush promising to place wilderness conservation over oil production in Alaska. He tried to placate the chorus boy who he didn't really know but thought he recognized as the cuspidor in the inventions segment of the show.

Intentionally not looking at Garry and Jay, he continued, "As long as they want to be with *Gold on Ice*, they'll have roles in making this show the best of its size on the circuit."

Garry was speechless while listening to Ernie describe the reorganization of the program. He looked at Jay, then looked at Tag. "As long as we can stand the humiliation of a public demotion, we'll be able to skate with the show. Lah-de-dah," he said loud enough for the entire company to hear.

Jay was pale. He looked at Garry. Then he moved his head to look at Amber, who was wiping a tear from her eye with a tissue. Finally, he looked at Tag, who stared straight ahead. He had to know full well, from the focus of the other skaters' eyes that Jay was looking at him. Most of the members of the company glanced back and forth from Jay to Tag, but no one could bring themselves to catch his eyes. Everyone adored Garry and Jay. Everyone knew that Tag had weaseled his way into controlling Ernie, and thus, controlling the fate of the show and everyone associated with it.

"I'm outta here," Jay said to no one in particular as he stood up.

Garry almost simultaneously stood up.

"We're still in the show, kids," Amber said in a soft voice to the younger boys and girls, who uttered a collective sigh. "This is really a good thing, 'cause you'll all have more opportunities to be on the ice without so many of us taking up time and space." Amber would be gracious to the end. And she knew that if she said another word, her tears would come flooding to the surface.

The trio sidled past other skaters, all of whom were silent. Like the situation or not, they all depended on keeping their jobs, and felt they had no alternative other than to do as they were instructed. If they hadn't completely hated Ernie and his treatment of them before this night, they were now completely disgusted with the big-bellied, sallow-skinned and rotting-toothed satyr.

All eyes watched as the stars of *Gold on Ice* moved down the arena's aisles and walked down to the next level that led to their dressing rooms. No one said a word, but Ernie could feel the hostility and hatred for him. "That's it," he finally said. "Get your asses outta here and ready for tonight's show."

Only when they had moved far enough away from Ernie not to be individually identified, did they start to mutter to the others.

As the other skaters moved out of the arena, Tag took a seat in front of Ernie. He smiled. "You sexy beast," he said with a smile. "You did a great job. That's why you're the guy in charge."

Ernie looked at Tag. "I wonder if I'm making a mistake."

Tag snorted. "No way, man. You're just getting a better program. When you finally make things so uncomfortable that they quit, Mr. Field will probably make you part owner of the show."

"I don't know. Amber always drew the families, and Jay and Garry were good for the horny guys."

Another snort. "I'm all three rolled into one. For mommy and daddy and their brats, I'm the boy next door. The reviews always say that. And, for the guys, like you said, I'll slay 'em by the time I take off my shirt. Already, I can get fucked by any of hundreds of guys who come to see me."

Recognizing Ernie's sudden look of jealousy and lust, Tag amended himself. "But you're the only one who really makes my dick hard. Come on, Ernie, you're doing the right thing. And I won't disappoint the crowds. Or you," he almost forgot to say as he reached out and cupped Ernie's crotch. "Hmmmm," Tag groaned. "Someone's got a woody. And somebody else needs to have his ass filled."

Both men smiled.

Tag stood up. "Don't make me wait too long or I'll have to jerk off without you," he said, turning away and walking in the direction of the exit.

"I'm right behind you," Ernie said. He caught up with Tag and placed a hand on his ass.

"That's the place," Tag groaned, leading Ernie back stage to the dressing rooms. "By the way," Tag announced, "since you won't be paying for three stars much longer, I want a better dressing room wherever we go."

"Here we go," Ernie said, "the diva starts making demands."

"It's for us," Tag said. "Get me a sofa couch so we'll have something to play on."

Ernie grinned. "Well, if it'll make you happy."

When the two arrived at Tag's dressing room, they found a white envelope taped to the door. "That's Amber's writing," Tag signed. "She's gonna make trouble, I know it. I can't believe you and the rest of the universe fall for her charade, acting as if she's Katie Couric, when she's more like Judge Judy."

He ripped the envelope off his door and untucked the back flap. Inside was another envelope. It was letter size and sealed. Tag looked in the upper left-hand corner. There was no name, only a return address. His own name and address seemed carelessly written.

"You can read that later," Ernie said, snatching the envelope out of Tag's hands and opening the dressing room door.

"But I love fan mail."

"God, your ego," Ernie said. Inside the door he was starting to unbutton his Hawaiian shirt which he always wore so he wouldn't have to tuck it into his pants and reveal how Pavoratti-like his gut was. He sat down at the chair in front of Tag's dressing room table. As he reached to untie his shoes, Tag grabbed the envelope back and turned away to open it.

"Take off your clothes you cocksucking wannabe star," Ernie said impatiently, to which Tag turned with anger.

"Don't you ever call me a *wannabe*!" he bellowed. "I'm a fucking star already. In fact, I'm almost the only star you've got!"

"And who's responsible for your meteoric rise?" Ernie asked, perturbed that he was having this argument instead of sucking on Tag's splendid dick.

"Me, you asswhipe! I'm responsible. You can take credit for recognizing my talent, but I'm the one who did all the work, so back off with your snide comments."

"Hey, baby, I'm sorry," Ernie cooed. "Now bring me your perfect cock and let me have a full load."

Tag turned his back on Ernie. "Cool your ass for a moment. I wanna read this letter."

Ernie sighed. He looked at himself in the vanity mirror. With his shirt off, he saw his own tits sagging like an old baboon's. His quarter-size pink nipples were barely visible under a carpet of black and gray hair, and his belly resembled that of a sumo wrestler's. He looked into his own eyes. Bloodshot. His facial complexion was dull from his two packs a day smoking habit. He then looked at Tag. *Who the fuck am I kidding,* Ernie asked himself. *Am I desperate enough not to care if I'm being used? Yup. But at least I'm not an idiot who can't see the impossibility of this stud being truly attracted to me.*

Nope. My mama didn't raise no idiot. Just a cocksucker who knows prime meat when he sees it.

"Hey, get this," Tag said with a wide smile. "It's from Kurt Chrysler."

Ernie set his shoulders back and adjusted his posture. Kurt's name was legendary in figure skating. Even Ernie was impressed that Tag had received a letter from the Olympic gold medalist.

"Shit," Tag grinned. "He's heard of me."

"You're in a lot of newspapers lately," Ernie offered.

"He says he wants to meet me when we're both in Chicago next week. Christ. Kurt Chrysler, of all people. He's cute too, don't you think?" Tag asked. "I'll invite him to the show and he can see how great I am."

"Show him how a real quad should be done," Ernie said.

"Yeah, I'll show him a lot of things," Tag said. He was paying less attention to what he was saying, and more to planning his first meeting with Kurt.

"If you don't get your clothes off and let me swallow that dick of yours, you won't have a routine to show off," Ernie demanded.

Tag rolled his eyes. "Will that get you off my back for a few hours?"

He turned toward Ernie and with sleight of hand that would make David Copperfield raise an eyebrow, he unbuttoned his 501s and pulled out his stiff dick.

Ernie smiled and dropped to his knees. Tag unbuttoned and re-moved his shirt while Ernie began kissing his cock. Tag faked a moan of ecstasy, then divided his attention between imagining it was Kurt who was sucking his dick, and planning on how to get him to do just that.

Chapter Nineteen

Tag now rode with Ernie between engagements. Although Amber, Jay, and Garry were still officially part of the troupe, it went without saying that Tag was not invited to travel with them. In fact, he had intentionally distanced himself from his former friends, as well as the entire skating company. When the kids all went out to bars after a performance, Tag was never invited, which suited him, since he didn't much like his fellow cast members; he felt that stars shouldn't associate with lesser forms of gas. His place was with the people who made all the decisions about the show that could ultimately affect him.

As the *Gold on Ice* tour motored toward Chicago, the cast had resigned themselves to the changes in the show. The pervasive feeling throughout the company was one of excitement. Instead of the crummy little rinks they'd been forced to play over the years, it seemed they were finally hitting the big time. Thanks to Tag's rising star status, they were booked into bigger sports arenas. For that, they begrudgingly gave Tag a small amount of credit. Even Amber, Jay and Garry seemed less annoyed with the show's newest star. At least they'd be skating on decent ice for a change. Although the short amount of time they were allowed to showcase their talents was hard to accept.

* * *

"Are you sure that seeing Kurt again won't make you a basket case?" Amber asked Garry as their car approached Chicago along the interstate.

"I still don't know how he can help us," Garry said.

"Kurt moves in mysterious ways, his wonders to perform," Amber chided, not knowing herself what information Kurt had been able to dig up about Tag, and what he might do to impact their nearly dire situation.

"I only wish we could have handled this ourselves. I hate to bring Kurt in to solve my problems," Garry said. "He'll think I'm a wimp who can't take care of myself."

"In this case, you can't. None of us can," Jay said. He flipped on the right turn signal and moved toward the Michigan Avenue off ramp. Jay moved the car toward the downtown skyline. "Keep an eye open for the Marquis," he said, slowing down for a red traffic light. "Can you believe we're actually staying somewhere decent?"

"It's six-thirty," Amber said. "Kurt'll have to cool his heels at his place for about an hour. I'll phone the Pump Room as soon as we check in."

"I'm actually excited about seeing him again," Jay said. "He always beat me in competitions, but let's face it, he was better. I never begrudged him those medals."

Garry remained silent. He was thinking of all the fun he'd had with Kurt the first year that they were a couple. He didn't much mind his near-anonymity when they'd go out. Kurt was the star. Although people were always nice to Garry, it was Kurt's attention they were interested in attracting. And Kurt was always magnanimous with his fans and the press, even when it interfered with dinner or some other social activity. The reflected glory of being in Kurt's presence was one of the aspects of their breakup that Garry missed most because it made him feel special that someone as handsome, athletic, talented and admired wanted his company.

Amber and Jay both recognized Garry's pensive attitude. "If you change your mind about joining us for cocktails, I'm sure Kurt would love to see you again," Amber said to Garry. "Think about it hon, okay? No pressure, but it might do you a world of good to talk to him."

Garry looked out the window. "Someone once said, 'If they don't want you, you don't want them.' That's how I feel about

Kurt. He can just skate on by and I won't pay him any nevermind. I can't be rejected by the same guy twice."

There was nothing more for Amber to say, and they all remained silent until Jay spotted the hotel's sign and pulled up to the valet. Stepping out of the filthy old Impala, he took on an imperious air. "Take care of her, my good man," Jay teased, using a phony aristocratic accent as he handed the uniformed valet the keys to his barely running car. "Careful of the rich Corinthian *leh-the*." For the first time in hours Garry laughed.

The Pump Room at Omni Ambassador East was as upscale as Jay had ever visited. Warned ahead of time by Amber (who had once dined there with Viktor Petrenko) that jackets were required, Jay had coaxed the concierge at the Marquis to let him borrow a sport coat for a few hours.

"So this is the place in Judy Garland's song," Jay said, as they approached the oak-paneled room. He felt some trepidation at seeing Kurt Chrysler again. He and Amber were both counting on Kurt doing the grand gesture and paying for dinner, because Jay was down to his last few dollars before his next payday.

Amber pointed to the famed Table One. "There he is." She giggled with expectation.

Jay felt seriously out of place in his borrowed jacket, in this room in which Gertrude Lawrence, Lauren Bacall, Natalie Wood, Beverly Sills and so many other luminaries had held court. The maitre 'd gave him a snooty once-over as he asked, "May I be of service?"

Falling into his fake old money accent, Jay gave a quick pull on the lapels of his one-size-too-large coat. "Lovely to see you again, Jeeves," Jay said. "Our usual table, my good man. We're dining with Mr. Chrysler this evening."

The maitre d' cleared his throat. "I believe that Mr. Chrysler is dining with colleagues, sir. And my name is James, if I may point that out to you sir," he stated in a condescending tone.

"Yes, of course, James. One meets so many people employed in service positions," Jay continued in his supercilious tone. "It's been far too long since our last evening here. We'll just find our way to Mr. Chrysler's table. Table One, isn't it?"

Although the maitre d' attempted to stop Jay and Amber, the two skipped over to where Kurt was sitting. "Honey, baby, cookie, sweetie," Jay changed from Boston hoity-toity to Hollywood syco-phant. Amber, too, squealed with delight at seeing her old friend.

Kurt's smile at seeing them was wide and heartfelt. He placed his flute of champagne on the table and stood up to welcome his old friends with kisses to their respective cheeks. "Please, please, sit down, you two," he insisted. He held up an index finger to beckon the waiter to the table. Kurt beamed. "May we have two more flutes?" he politely asked. The waiter seemed only too happy to accommodate any request from the great Kurt Chrysler.

After a few moments of telling each other how well and still very young and healthy they all looked, and how they'd missed being in touch but you know how it is on the road, never spending more than a few nights in any one location, Kurt picked up a large manila envelope off the table. "Shall we dish first or look at our menus? I'm starting with Truffle Ravioli. But I hear the Peeky Toe Crab cakes are great. And Scott Hamilton told me that the Amish Chicken is a really good main course."

"How about Pentecostal Pork, eh?" Jay chuckled. "Or the Christian Catch of the Day. Haven't had a good home-style sun-dried Jehovah's Witness, in ages."

"With a side order of Deuteronomy," Kurt quipped. "Ew, that sounds unappetizing, doesn't it?"

"Have whatever you like," Amber smiled, "because you're pay-ing. We haven't a pot, if you get my drift." She batted her eye-lashes.

"All taken care of," Kurt said, raising his hands in a don't-think-twice-about-it gesture.

"Dish! Dish!" Amber cried out. "Tell us what you've found out about dear ol' Tag."

Just then the waiter arrived with two more champagne flutes. He filled their glasses from the bottle of Veuve Clicquot that was chilling in the silver ice bucket beside the table.

The moment the waiter was out of listening range, Amber leaned forward across the table. "Kurt, my darling, please tell us that you've found out something incriminating about the little shit."

Kurt feigned shock. "Why little Amber Nyak! America's sweet-heart, you have a potty mouth!"

"Have not!" Amber protested. "But that little rat's ruined our careers. He's gotta be stopped."

"I do have a few interesting tidbits." Kurt smiled devilishly. He leaned forward to take the others into his confidence.

Although the miasma of conversation around them created a barrier of white noise, Kurt spoke in a whisper. As a celebrity he was constantly being watched, and his location at Table One was a focal point for stargazers. He couldn't take the chance that eavesdroppers might hear the smallest portion of what he had to reveal to his friends.

Observers of the table could only see Amber and Jay listening intently and occasionally moving their heads up and down in agreement to something. Then, their eyes grew wide, and their mouths dropped open. Both were shaking their heads, incredulous. Every few moments, Amber slapped the table to emphasize her excitement about the information being imparted. "What a dildo," she exclaimed, just as the waiter arrived to accept their dinner orders. He caught that part of the conversation and smiled. The waiter, a stunning Italian, recognized the trio and cast his dark, lascivious eyes on Kurt and Jay. "Sorry, honey," Amber said, smiling, "I just used that word to emphasize a point."

"You can do no wrong, ma'am," he said, dividing his attention between Kurt and Jay and their selection of starters and entrées.

After the waiter had withdrawn with their dinner orders, Jay and Amber once again leaned over the table toward Kurt. "Not from Clarksville!" Amber practically shouted.

"Bucks Hollar, Tennessee? I knew he'd been there before, that little perv," Jay said.

"Well, he didn't fool me with that nonsense about never having had a skating lesson," Amber said. "Honey, you don't perform a quad without years of practice and loads of moolah for coaches."

Kurt leaned back in his chair and folded his arms across his strong chest. He smiled and became silent.

"What?" Amber said, in a tone of eager suspicion.

Jay looked at Amber then at Kurt. He, too, grinned, alert to something looming ahead, as if a flash of lightning would soon follow distant thunder.

"I've saved the best for last," Kurt said. His right eyebrow arched. He picked up a manila envelope that had been resting next to his plate and withdrew a black videotape box. "Behold my pretties, the Holy Grail of our Crusade." He held the tape in the open palms of his hands, as if presenting a velvet pillow on which a jeweled tiara rested.

"What's on the tape?" Jay tentatively asked.

Amber's sparkling eyes looked into Kurt's baby blues. She knew, without him saying a word, that Tag was featured in some way on the tape.

Kurt nodded his head to Amber's unspoken understanding of the importance of the videotape. "We'll have a screening in my suite after dinner," Kurt joked. "I won't say anything more. No need to spoil your appetites for what will surely be a sumptuous desert."

Kurt sensed that his friends needed instant gratification. "Okay, here's a teaser," Kurt said. "Amber can't see this."

"I don't shock easily," Amber hissed, as Kurt opened the envelope again and withdrew a couple of sheets of paper.

"Got it off the Internet. Jeez you people need to get into the twenty-first century. You could have solved your dilemma by yourselves." He handed the pages to Jay whose eyes grew wider as he studied the printout. He smiled, chuckled and shook his head.

"Gimme those," Amber said, snatching the pages from Jay's hands. "I'm over twenty-one. Practically an adult, if the press would get over my sweet-sixteen image." She looked at the first page and brought her hand to her mouth to stifle a laugh. "The smoking gun, so to speak."

"Our evidence," Jay said.

"Yeah, but it's also the brainless caption under Tag's picture, or shall we say Ian's picture. That's the name here, but I'd recognize his penis anywhere."

"Let me see that again," Jay said, retrieving the papers. He studied the photo. "That's Tag's dick alright."

"You've had it," Kurt said, impressed.

"Are you joking? He saves his meat for men who can help advance his career. And for upwardly mobile cocksuckers in the chorus."

"You and Garry got him his job," Amber said. "Don't tell me you didn't get a reward."

Jay grimaced. "It's not that I'm too ethical," he said, adding quotation marks in the air. "Garry is the one with scruples. I would have dined on Tag that first day. But no, prim and proper Garry

Windsor said we'd be taking unfair advantage. Ha! Unfair, my ass! No doubt that he would have put out for me, and for Garry."

"Hell, you missed a big opportunity," Amber said. "And I do mean *big*," she joked, emphasizing the word using her hand to simulate masturbation. "Hell, he's screwed you anyway and you didn't even get to smoke a cigarette afterwards."

"Perhaps all this stuff I brought will be useful to you and Garry," Kurt said. Then, becoming silent for a moment, he asked, "So, how is Garry? Where is he? I was hoping he'd join us."

Amber looked at Kurt. "Truth be known, I think he was afraid to see you."

Kurt lowered his head. When he looked up again the waiter was beginning to place dinner plates in front of them. "Well, then, *bon appetit!*"

The dinner conversation consisted of the trio catching up on the past few years of their lives. With a little coaxing, Kurt disregarded his usual policy of never speaking about the personal lives of his friends, knowing he was among other friends who wouldn't betray a confidence. "I especially enjoy the shows I get to do with Rudy, Brian, Todd, and Timothy," he said. "And I never thought I'd have a weekly shopping date with Peggy!"

"Fleming?" Jay said with a mixture of embarrassment, reverence and awe.

"Such a goddess," Kurt said. "So regal. So smart. Just like you, Amber," he added, smiling. "I mean that. You're both class acts. She sends you her best."

"Ya think she's forgiven me?" Jay smiled sheepishly.

"Of course. But she'll never forget you. Count on it," Kurt laughed.

"Perfect Peggy," Amber sighed. "I'll bet she doesn't have an axe to grind with anyone. She'd never plot the downfall of another skater, the way we're doing."

"It's self-preservation, dear," Jay piped in. "We don't have a choice. It's Tag's career or ours. We're hardly in the show anymore. We're dispensable. You've got a few coins saved up, but Garry and I live from hand to mouth in this crummy freak show."

"Garry's not okay?" Kurt asked, genuinely concerned. "I only got him into the show 'cause I heard he was having a tough time."

"*You're* the one!" Jay said.

"I don't want him to ever find out," Kurt frowned.

"He's always wondered why *Gold on Ice* called him, seemingly from out of the blue," said Jay.

"You're a good man, Kurt." Amber smiled and patted their benefactor's arm.

"You know what these shows pay their talent," Jay said. "Diddly squat. And management treats us as if we're Rose and her Hollywood Blondes. 'Experience will be their pay,' to quote Mama."

"But . . . is he happy? Garry, I mean," Kurt said.

Amber and Jay were silent for a moment. Then they looked at each other. Jay shrugged his shoulders. "He's great, I guess. I mean he loves to skate almost more than anything else. Practice, rehearsals and performances take up the majority of his time . . . you know how that is. There's not much in-between, which I think is a blessing for him."

"Why a blessing?" Kurt asked between bites of his Coquille St. Jacques.

Amber seized the moment. "Okay, we're all friends, Garry too. You know that I don't ordinarily talk about other people behind their backs, but I don't think it's wrong to help friends help other friends. I'll be blunt. What happened between you and Garry?"

Kurt put down his fork and picked up his flute of champagne. He took a long pull from the glass until it was empty. "More champies?" he asked his friends as he reached for the bottle, only to be interrupted by the waiter who beat him to the bucket and lifted the white napkin–cloaked vessel and refilled each of the glasses.

"What has Garry said?" Kurt finally answered.

"We'd like to hear your version of the bust up," Amber coaxed.

"It was all my fault," Kurt began. "I confess. I loved Garry, but I had an affair with a guy on the Russian team. I don't even remember his name, Yuri or Petrov. That's how little he meant to me. If you guys hate me now, I'll understand. Hell, I hate myself for doing something so stupid.

"After nearly a whole year, I still don't know what happened." Kurt stared up at the chandelier. "One minute Garry and I were in love, holding hands and sending each other stuffed bears and Hallmark cards; the next thing I know, I'm starting arguments about really stupid stuff. Like he hired an incompetent cleaning lady, or his friends were boring to me. He knew that I was sleeping with someone else, but he thought that I was looking for reasons to dump him. Not true. I just wanted to feel a different body."

"That's kinda the way Garry tells it too," Jay said. "Only in his scenario, he blames himself. He says he should have been more mature and let you have whatever piece of ass you wanted, as long as you came home to him."

Kurt gave a sheepish nod. "No. He was right to be mad. I should never have done that to him. That freakin' gold medal made me attractive to a lot of guys. I turned down ninety-nine-point-nine percent of 'em. It should've been one hundred percent. I won't blame Garry if he never forgives me."

"But I think Garry *has* forgiven you," Amber said. "It's himself he hasn't forgiven."

Kurt laid his silverware on his china plate and sat back in his seat. "I did the best I could at the time. In retrospect, I wish I had made more time for the two of us to be together. But I had all these other commitments. Contracts to be honored. I had no idea what a toll winning the gold would put on my personal life. Don't get me wrong," Kurt added, "winning that medal opened tons of doors to me. I couldn't live the way I do without all the endorsements and television specials and the book. But the downside is that it also took away one of the most precious parts of my life. Garry."

"Why don't you tell him that?" Amber suggested. "He's an odd guy. I can't always read what he's thinking. But I do know that he still loves you."

"Yeah," Jay added, "when he first joined the show, I told him that all the chorus kids would be creaming in their costumes for a chance to have sex with him. Know what he said? He wasn't interested in sex. He just wants to skate to take his mind off the emptiness in his soul."

Kurt sighed. "That sounds like something silly he'd say. But I can't be rejected by the same man twice."

Amber and Jay both looked at each other. "Garry said those exact words," Amber said.

Kurt smiled sadly. "We could probably still finish each other's sentences," he said.

The waiter arrived. "May I show you our dessert cart?" he asked, as if begging to be appreciated by this triumvirate of his favorite skaters.

"Thanks, but we've got a fresh fruit tart waiting in my suite." Kurt laughed at his private allusion to the contents of the video that sat burning a hole in the leather banquet. "Just the check, please."

"By all means, sir," the waiter said, rolling away his trolley of crème brulée, crunchy Napoleon, Mousse du jour, Banànas Foster spring roll and Baked Alaska Volcano. He returned shortly and placed a leather check sleeve on the table beside Kurt. Opening the cover, Kurt immediately noticed that the waiter had boldly printed, "Buy you a drink?" He included his phone number on the customer copy of the check. Kurt smiled and pocketed the number without telling the others of the message. He signed his name, including a twenty-five-percent tip. "Shall we, my pretties?" he said, sliding out from the banquet.

"Our destiny awaits!" Jay announced and followed behind Amber gazing at the beautiful room, and watching guests watch Kurt. "Thank you again, my good man," Jay said in mock appreciation to James the maitre d' as they walked past his lighted lectern. "Ta-ta, for now. Cheerio and all that rot."

"Very good sir," James said looking over his bifocals and down his nose.

Chapter Twenty

Jay and Amber followed Kurt out of the Pump Room and into the hotel lobby. As they crossed over a thick Oriental rug toward the bank of elevators, other guests did a double take when they saw Kurt and then realized he was with Amber Nyak. A few seemed to recognize Jay, too. He cringed at overhearing loud whispers with phrases that included "busted Peggy's microphone" and "*The Globe* said he was a mental case."

The elevator car arrived. The trio entered and Kurt pushed the button for the penthouse, which required his room key card to access the floor. The ride to the top of the building was swift and the doors opened right into his suite. "Here we are," he announced. "My humble abode."

Wide-eyed and as impressed as one is when they first enter Buckingham Palace on a tour of the personal home of Queen Elizabeth, Amber said, "Wow! How can you afford to live up here?" Amber wasn't shy. She knew that she sometimes lacked tact.

"Trust me, I can't. The sponsors of my HBO special are footing the bill. Check out the bathrooms," he said. He played docent, leading his charges down the hallway.

"What more could a girl ask for?" Amber squeaked when she entered the master powder room. "You boys run along and play the video. I'll sit in this pool-size tub! His and hers commodes, for crying out loud! How decadent is that! Can't someone wait his or her turn? Or use one of the others in this huge place?"

The suite was large enough to hold a mass suicide of Enron and WorldCom executives. Floor-to-ceiling French doors opened onto a small terrace and a grand piano occupied a prominent spot in the sunken living room.

"Get her!" Jay said, looking at Kurt. "All this and a gold medal too. I'm very impressed!"

"Me too," said Kurt. He walked to a console and pushed a few buttons. Music issued from multiple speakers throughout the suite and the lighting changed to an almost candle-like softness. "The VIP tour train leaves the depot in five seconds. All aboard!" Kurt guided Jay and Amber through the old but exquisitely maintained series of rooms. He opened doors to three spectacular bedrooms, each of which was decorated with a different theme: contemporary, art deco and Tudor.

"The hotel manager told me that The Duke and Duchess stayed here," Kurt boasted.

"That trollop, Mrs. Simpson?" Jay sniggered.

The three other bathrooms matched their adjoining rooms. The library featured a writing space complete with computer and printer. Arriving in the kitchen, Kurt opened the refrigerator door. "May as well use this stuff up," he said, taking out a bottle of champagne and a bowl of caviar. "They just leave goodies all over the place, and I don't have a boyfriend to share it all with."

Jay leaned against a Corinthian column. "I didn't want to bring up the subject before, but now that you've mentioned it, how is it that a rich and famous stud such as yourself, doesn't have a partner? There has to be about a gazillion guys out there who would cream for the opportunity to be with you."

"It's not that I don't get laid a lot," Kurt said, removing the lead foil from the champagne bottle. "It's true that they're sorta lined up for me. I get this all the time." He reached into his pocket, withdrawing the restaurant check. "From our waiter. Maybe I'll get around to him eventually, but he's gotta take a number. I'm not being selfish with my dick, that's for sure."

"No, you don't sound at all like an arrogant egoist," Amber said with a smile. "Just telling the truth, I'm sure."

"But seriously," Kurt added, "I don't know if I'll ever settle down again. Garry was the only man I've ever been completely comfortable with. He had that elusive something special that made me nuts for him."

The cork on the champagne bottle made a small burp as Kurt eased it out of the neck. Amber had located the crystal and set three Waterford flutes on the granite countertop. Kurt filled each and set the bottle in an ice-filled silver bucket. Playing perfect host, he handed one flute to Amber, then one to Jay, before lifting his own glass. "But that's all in the past. I'll get over it. Now, here's to us! And to fate!" Kurt smiled. "May it wreak havoc on the life of your cute little ice queen!"

They each began sipping the effervescent potion, and rating it as the best champagne they'd ever tasted. "Shall we take a peek-a-boo at the featured attraction?"

"God, yes!" Amber cheered. "Let's see what our little Dennis the Menace has been up to."

"I'm a bit reluctant for you to see this, Amber," Kurt said as he picked up the videotape and walked down two steps into the sunken living room. He turned on the power button on the giant-screen television and pushed the remote control button for the VCR.

"I may be every virgin's role model," Amber said, "but I assure you, I've been kissed a couple of times. I may not be those shameless Bush twins, but I'm open minded."

"Okay, then. Everyone get comfy," Kurt said. He crossed to the wall console again and pushed a few buttons. The music subsided, and the lights went to starlight mode.

Wriggling into comfortable positions on the sofa, the three looked intently at a black television screen. Then, loud hip-hop music from Masta Storm T. Ruper blasted through the speakers in recurring pulsing tones. Then appeared a title card overlaid on the big screen: *LEAVES OF ASS*.

"Walt Whitman would love this tape," Kurt said.

The music was muted and the sound of boots echoing on a concrete floor filtered through the speakers. "I ain't your boy toy," came the stilted dialogue as a handsome muscled young man in a white tank top shirt was pushed into frame from someone off screen. "I ain't doin' this!" he declared to the unseen presence. Suddenly, both Jay and Amber's mouths dropped open and their eyes opened wide.

"Th-th-that's Tag," Amber stuttered.

"His name's *Snake*, at least in the credits of this video," Kurt said. "In *Jack the Stripper* he's the title character. In *Peter the Straight*, he goes by the name *Sputnik*. In that one, he's a laborer in a Russian palace. KGB operatives find him so sexy that it's pure torture for them. And in *The Hides of March*, he's a young Roman warrior billed as Big Pig. You can imagine what he does in that one."

A second, tougher-looking man, sporting a mustache, mirrored sunglasses, ripped blue jeans, and a black leather vest over his brawny, thick-muscled, dark hairy chest, entered the scene.

"Whoa, what do we have here!" Jay exclaimed as the bigger man grabbed Tag or Snake or Sphinx with an arm around his neck. Proving who was in charge, he ripped Tag's tank open to reveal his smooth, hearty body. "My friends'll come and beat you up if you dare touch me," Tag said without any demonstrable resistance as the man tied his wrists behind his back.

Amber was catatonic with amazement at what she was watching. "Wooo. This is a popcorn flick, if ever I've seen one!" She was clearly enjoying this revelation.

As the tape continued to roll through the VCR, the rest of Tag's clothes were ripped off his body by the strong hands of his captor. His wrists and ankles were tightly tied to the bars of an inclined jail cell door. He was gagged with a horse bit. Chrome weights dangled from his testicles. His nipples were squeezed in the vice of clothespins.

Tag moaned in painful ecstasy, as he was probed with a dildo vibrator. Squirming with pain throughout the tape, Tag was released from being tied to the jail cell door only to be roped to a chair, his hands tied behind his back. He was forced to suck off his nameless attacker. All the while the camera continued to focus on Tag's huge, throbbing cock.

"Clearly he's enjoying every moment of torture," Jay said.

As the non-story came to a close, Tag was dragged back to the jail cell door, where he was tied, spread eagle, with his dick between the bars, and fucked. The final scene showed Tag with his aggressor's dick up his ass, and the other man stroking Tag until he had an agonizing ejaculation.

"You rock, man!" Amber shrieked as the tough-guy had his way with Tag.

When the tape faded to black, Amber was practically doing a

cheerleading song, while Jay was dumbfounded by what he'd just watched.

"I need another drink," Jay said, getting up and moving into the kitchen. When he returned, the lights were once again on and Amber and Kurt were discussing what they'd just seen.

"What's to explain?" Amber said. "It's just hard-core sex. You're both acting as if it's the most disgusting thing you'd ever seen. Trust me on this one, we women have fantasies too."

"You liked that one?" Jay said as he sat down and leaned back into the sofa. "That's our innocent little Tag." He turned toward Kurt. "Where on earth did you scare up this thing?"

"It's an underground thing," Kurt said. "You have to know somebody who knows somebody. That sort of deal. After Amber's call I did some investigating. Seems your Tag talks too much. Someone knew a bottom who was a figure skater. It was almost a dead end because there were so many skaters who matched that description." He laughed. "Will it help your cause?"

Jay looked at Amber. They smiled simultaneously. "Oh yeah. Big time," Jay said. "The problem now is who to leak this to without our being implicated."

The trio sat together for the next three hours strategizing. They determined that they'd keep this evidence a complete secret until the right moment revealed itself. Then copies would be distributed to the A.S.S., *Good Morning, America, Access Hollywood, Larry King,* and *Montel Williams.*

"Way to go, Kurt," Amber said.

"Yeah, man, who would have thought that after all those times we faced off in competition, that you'd one day come around to save our butts. What can we ever do to repay you?"

Kurt smiled and was about to offer his standard line that he was just happy to be of service. Then he changed his mind. "There is something. Get Garry to meet with me. Here in Chicago. Before I leave for that Hillary Rodham Clinton re-election campaign thing on Friday."

Jay and Amber nodded their heads as if to say, we'll do our best.

Chapter Twenty-one

Tag lay in bed, on his back, visualizing the choreography he was creating for his next program. All the while Ernie held his legs suspended while grinding into him.

"How long is it going to take you, for Christ sake?" Tag finally said with irritation.

"All. Most. Ready." Ernie grunted. Perspiration was dripping from his forehead and flabby tits.

"Almost? Christ, you've been at it long enough. You get one more minute. I've got a rehearsal, ya know."

"Nothing. Like. Pressure." Ernie continued his systematic, boring push and pull routine. "I *love* your ass."

Tag was thinking. "I know. I know. You love my hole. It's hot and you're so horny. So what else is new? Get a myna bird to teach you a new phrase or two!" Tag upbraided Ernie.

Tag went back to visualizing his performance, and pretending to hear Scott Hamilton's commentary.

"*Skating to* Somewhere In Time, *Tag is cutting a lovely figure on the ice,*" he could almost hear Scott say. "*His outfit, his tone, his footwork, all matching the music perfectly in this artistic program. He is doing stuff that only the most mature skaters can do. He's feeling his music. He's in his edges. He's about to enter a Salchow. Beautiful triple Salchow! He landed it! That's the name of my book, by the way.* Landing It. *In case anyone in the audience wants to pick up a copy. He came into it as if it was accidental, like oops, it's a Salchow, and landed it with no big deal. It just fits this music perfectly. It was very well executed. Now, he's doing some back crossovers, preparing for a delayed single Axel, which you never see. They're dramatic looking. There's a double Axel on the same circle. Wow! What a performance!*

"It's *such a joy to watch Tag*," Hamilton continues in Tag's reverie. "*Those are Wallys that he just did, and there's a triple Axel. Very nice landing! And he ends with a rocker. Notice the compulsory edges? Lovely performance by one of the great stars in the figure-skating cosmos!*"

Suddenly, Ernie cried out. Orgasm at last.

"Okay, take it out now, please," Tag said, scooting himself away. "And please take a shower. You stink like garbage."

"The romantic in you always shines through," Ernie scoffed. "Such sweet phrases from your beautiful lips."

Tag sat up and put his feet over the side of the bed. "I'd like to put my new routine into the show by next week. I see it in the second act. Don't you think so?" Tag smiled sweetly. "You can cut the Inventions number down by five minutes. I promise, the new program will keep your dick as hard as the ice. It's another number without my shirt. Make you happy? And I'll also be applying a fake tattoo, because you said it would make me sexier than I am already. What sort of tattoo would you like me to wear?"

Tag noticed that Ernie's limp dick made an involuntary jump. "How about a real tattoo for that beautiful ass? Say a skull and crossbones, or *Fuck me, Ernie?* Printed in twenty-five point Helvetica?"

Tag rolled his eyes. "You're so creative, Ernie. You'll arrange it with the choreographer and cast?"

"Why don't we just dump the whole company and call it *An Evening With Tag Tempkin?*"

"You big ol' sexy tease," Tag said, squeezing Ernie's nipple buttons. "Give me a kiss."

"It wouldn't have hurt for you to have been a little attentive during sex this morning." Ernie smiled. His dick was growing hard again.

Tag noticed the physical response. "I was *very* lovey dovey this morning." He tried to sound convincing. "But honey, I gotta shower and run. We'll catch up later, you sexy beast, you."

* * *

Tag arrived at the sports arena early enough to practice without other skaters around. He hated it whenever he had to share the ice, whether in practice or performance. He felt an entitlement to the whole rink. With his boom box playing a CD of the soundtrack to *The Joy Luck Club*, Tag circled the rink to warm up. He began his practice with back crossovers into an Axel. As he felt the ice and the music, he moved with strong strokes. From his back crossovers, to an Axel, to a reverse sit spin and complex footwork, Tag was flying. Ecstasy. He landed his Lutz and segued into a camel spin, his arms changing positions and leading him into a back camel and a back sit spin. Finally, he went for the quad. He dug his toe pick into the ice and leaped straight into the air to a height he'd not achieved before. He came down with a bit of a two-footed landing but in otherwise beautiful position.

As the music ended, Tag concluded his newly self-choreographed program with a back scratch spin and stopped effortlessly. He bowed to an invisible audience. He skated around the rink a few times to cool down. Looking at his watch, Tag decided to call it quits. At any moment, the kids from the chorus would be filing in for their practice, and Tag never wanted anyone to see him creating a new program. He wanted his merits to be revealed only after all the kinks had been worked out.

As Tag stepped off the rink and placed his skate guards over his blades, he noticed an extremely handsome guy sitting a few rows up. The guy began to applaud. Annoyed that he'd been observed, Tag disregarded the guy and headed toward his dressing room. However, he had to pass by the man's seat to exit.

"You're quite the talent," the guy said, when Tag was close enough to hear.

Tag stopped and glared at the man. As he was about to read him the riot act—announcing that the arena was closed and how dare he sneak into a private training session—Tag realized the man looked familiar.

Then it hit him. "Oh my God!" Tag cooed. "You're Kurt Chrysler! You're only my hero. I got your letter, and you really came to see me. Oh, golly, I'm sounding so foolish. But you're my reason for skating!"

Kurt smiled warmly. "And you're the famous Tag Tempkin."

"Not so famous. Really. I'm surprised you've even heard about me."

"I keep up with everything in the world of skating. You've made the sports and entertainment pages of each city you've visited. With your show."

"My show? Oh, no. We're a family. The real stars are Garry Windsor and Jay Logan. And, we have a genuine Olympian like you. Amber Nyak. But you must know all that. You competed against Garry and Jay. I watched you. In fact, I learned to skate by watching videos of your competitions and television skating specials."

"It looks like you've learned well. But I'm sure your coaches had a lot more to do with your command of the ice than I ever could."

Tag shook his head. "I never had a coach. After all those years of watching you in competition, you could say that *you* were my coach."

Kurt smiled. "My quads have never been as pure and controlled as the one I just watched you perform. If you've never been coached, you're even more brilliant than I suspected."

Kurt looked at Tag for a long moment, staring into his sparkling green eyes and thinking how much he'd love to have his lips melt into Tag's, and to taste his pink tongue. He observed the way Tag's perspiration-soaked red T-shirt adhered to his pumped chest and tight stomach. He was steel hard thinking about Tag's sculpted body, the image of which he'd jerked off to after each viewing of *Leaves of Ass*.

Tag, too, was looking at Kurt, who was always considered one of the sexiest male skaters in the sport. Tag remembered a couple of years ago that Kurt had done a layout for *Sports Illustrated* in which various athletes traded sports attire to model. Kurt was photographed on a beach straddling a surfboard and wearing a regulation lifeguard-issued pair of swim trunks. His strong, oiled upper body glistened in the Malibu sun. It was said that he was singularly responsible that year for more young boys and girls begging their parents for skating lessons. The idea in the heterosexual boys' minds was that they could grow up to look like Kurt and have plenty of girls. For the young girls and queer boys, whose libidos were twitching off the Richter scale, their thoughts raced toward the prospect of becoming a skater so they could have sex with *guys* who looked like Kurt. He had something for everyone.

Tag realized that he now found himself face to face with the *SI* cover boy. "Er, I don't usually do this," he began with false trepidation. "But could I maybe buy you coffee, or breakfast, or . . ." His words trailed off.

"Sure. But I'm buying." Kurt smiled. "I know how much these cheesy ice shows pay you kids."

"At least it's a job," Tag said. "Gotta change my clothes. C'mon. My dressing room's the next level down."

He led the way through the hallways of the arena. As they made their way through the network of corridors, they came to Amber Nyak's name on a white card taped on a door. The next one had a card with Jay Logan/Garry Windsor stenciled in black lettering. After that there was a large gold star tacked to the next door. Written across the star was Tag's name.

Kurt asked, "So what's Garry Windsor like these days?"

"Argh. You want some really fun dirt? Look into that story about him and his coach. You probably heard all about that!"

"As a matter of fact—"

Tag cut Kurt off. "If you ask me, he and Jay Logan are holding this whole show back from being a first-class deal. Just between you and me, I think management's gonna cut them both loose before the end of the season. They've already tried once, but Garry and Jay and even Amber are too stupid to get the message, or too stuck in their ways to change."

Then Tag caught himself. "Oh, my gosh! What on earth am I saying about my co-stars and friends?" He had suddenly remembered that Kurt had worked with Jay and Garry in competition. "What I mean is, they're great skaters and should be with a much better company than this one." Tag opened the door to his dressing room. "I'll just be a minute. C'mon in."

"I'll wait in the hall," Kurt said.

"It's okay, there's a loveseat inside," Tag said, touching Kurt's arm.

Kurt shrugged and walked inside. He looked around. The room contained a vanity, a full-length mirror, a wardrobe rack on wheels, a couple of folding chairs, the loveseat and a bathroom. "Fancy digs," Kurt said. "You'd be surprised at some of the rat traps I've changed in over the years. Compared to them, this is the Taj Mahal."

"It'll do," Tag said, peeling off his T-shirt and holding it up to his nose. "Good for at least another day, don't you think?" he said, tossing the damp shirt at Kurt who flinched and missed the catch. "Sorry," Tag said, "I was aiming for the chair."

Shirtless, Tag sat down at the vanity to unlace his skate boots.

He effected a great effort to pull them off, the action of which show-cased his strong arms and chest. Then he stood before the full-length mirror looking into it a moment longer than necessary and patting himself dry with a hand towel.

Kurt was distracted by Tag's body, but not wanting to show his attraction, he pretended to be looking at newspaper clippings taped on the wall next to the vanity. But in the mirror, Tag could see that Kurt was surreptitiously enjoying the view of his lithe, mus-cled torso.

Tag finally turned around, making a show of looking for another shirt to wear. There were a half dozen colored T-shirts in the closet, but he wandered around the room as if he hadn't a clue where to begin looking.

"I didn't quite answer your question about Garry Windsor," he said, pulling back costumes on the wardrobe dolly. "He's a swell guy and completely professional on the ice. We can always count on him." Having exhausted his charade of searching for a shirt, Tag opened the closet and took three colored T-shirts off the shelf. "Which one?" he asked, holding them up.

"The black is good," Kurt said.

"You have a good eye," Tag said. He slipped the shirt over his head and slowly peeled it down over his chest and six pack of rock-solid abs.

"I know what you mean about Garry being so professional," Kurt said, dragging his eyes away from Tag. "We competed to-gether a few times. He was great to everybody, no matter what their final scores."

"But doesn't he remind you of someone who should be working in an office?" Tag joked.

Kurt gave him a quizzical look.

"I mean, bless his heart, he's sort of nerdy, don't you think? He could be selling Xerox products or something. He even dresses like an office worker. All those khakis and white Oxford cloth shirts."

Kurt smiled, remembering the distinct style of dress that Garry had. "Yeah, but a *cute* office guy."

"You think?" Tag said, wrinkling his nose. Then, remembering that Kurt and Garry had been on the American team at the World Championships, Tag veered from the path of his ridicule. "Oh, to-tally cute, yeah. Everybody calls him 'the gentleman skater.' He has a grace about him instead of an arrogance. So refreshing."

A gentleman skater. No arrogance. Kurt considered the commenda-tion. "I'm glad you like him so much," Kurt said.

"I'm ready," Tag announced. "Where to?" He opened the door and led the way out of the room.

"What do you like?" Kurt asked.

"I'm versatile," Tag said with a lascivious grin. He immediately checked himself, wanting Kurt to see an innocent young man who thought only of his sport. "IHOP's just fine with me."

Kurt smiled. "I'm no snob," he said. "IHOP it is. But we'll have to have dinner someplace a little more upscale. My hotel? The restaurant is five stars. It's in *Michelin*."

"Where's that?" Tag asked, wondering how far away Kurt Chrysler had come to see him.

"Not a 'where.' An 'it.' *The Michelin Guide* to restaurants. The most famous chefs."

"Right." Tag tried to sound as though *Michelin* had simply slipped his mind. "Sounds like you've got our day—and night—all planned," Tag said.

They retraced their steps down the corridor to the exit of the sports center. Along the way they made small talk about rust on skating blades, blisters on their feet, how cute the guys were who made the latest world team. Tag casually said, "By the way, what are you doing in town?"

"Preparing for my new HBO special," Kurt said. "We film in just a few weeks. I'm scouting for skaters to join me."

Tag stopped in his tracks. "Is that why you were in the rink? To scout me for your TV show?"

Kurt cocked his head to one side. "I'm looking at a lot of people. But hypothetically, is that anything you'd be remotely interested in? I mean, you're so busy with the *Gold on Ice* tour. Aren't you?"

"Are you kidding?" Tag said. "I'd do anything to be on your show! I saw your last one. You were awesome! The ratings were through the roof."

"They always are," Kurt said modestly. He continued walking. "Skating's extremely popular now. Televised competitions often beat football and basketball games with the number of viewers who tune in. I'm glad you're interested. Seeing you in person I can tell you'll probably look great on camera."

Tag had to boast, "I've done a couple of videos. I know I look good."

"Great. If you've got an extra copy, I'm sure the producers and sponsors would love to see them," Kurt said, baiting Tag. "They're the people who make all the decisions. I just give them suggestions."

Tag back-pedaled. "It was just local stuff on the news in my hometown. I don't think I even have them anymore."

"How about your mom?" Kurt asked. "Mothers always keep stuff like that of their kids. She'd get them back safe and sound."

Tag was silent for a long moment. "No mother. Gone to heaven. Dad, too. I'm completely alone. I have absolutely no one in the world. That's why skating's so important to me. It's an opportunity to give something back to my folks, who I know, are with me in spirit every time I'm on the ice. They're angels now. Sometimes I can feel them guiding me, especially when I'm skating to their favorite music. Mom was a concert pianist. Dad always wanted to be a skater."

They had rounded the corner of State and Michigan and found the IHOP. Opening the door to the restaurant, they saw that the place was jammed. "Yikes," Kurt said. "Wanna try someplace else?"

"I'll take care of it," Tag said.

He slipped through the line to the podium that had a sign that read: PLEASE WAIT TO BE SEATED. Kurt could see Tag speaking to an old woman who appeared to be the hostess. She was wearing a name badge and cradling menus in her arms. Kurt saw her shake her head. Then it looked to him as though Tag was engaged in an argument or a dramatic plea with the woman. At one point Tag turned around and pointed to Kurt. The woman looked up and shrugged her shoulders. She turned and walked away, for a moment. When she returned she had with her a corpulent young man dressed in a shirt and tie. Again it seemed that Tag was making a long explanation. This time the man nodded his head. At that point, Tag turned around and waved for Kurt to come forward.

Kurt wended his way past other patrons waiting to be seated, apologizing to them as they grumbled and reluctantly let him pass through. Then he and Tag were ushered to a table. "Enjoy your meal," the fat young man with a wispy blond mustache said, smiling at Kurt. "By the way," he said, "I never do this. I mean Oprah even comes in here sometimes, but I gotta tell you I saw you skate to something from *Les Misérables,* and you made me cry."

Kurt smiled warmly and shook the man's hand. "Thank you," he beamed. "You just made my day."

"No sir," the man said, "you've made *my* day. And my week, and my year."

Immediately, an elderly waitress arrived with a carafe of coffee. "Regular or decaf?" she asked in a whisky voice, without making eye contact and turning their coffee mugs over for filling.

"Regular," Tag said.

"Regular," Kurt confirmed. "Thank you very much."

"I'll be back to take your orders in a minute," the waitress said without an ounce of enthusiasm.

"We'll both have the Rootie Tootie Fresh and Fruity," Tag called after the waitress. "Hope you don't mind that I ordered for both of us.

Kurt smiled. "Tells me that you like to take charge of things."

They were silent for a moment.

Tag looked into Kurt's blue eyes.

"What?" Kurt said.

"Nothing. You. I can't believe I'm sitting opposite you. My hero. And you actually came to see me. Little ol' me, from Puberty, Massachusetts. A nobody who dreamed of someday meeting you, but never thinking about having a breakfast together, let alone plans for dinner. Wow!"

Tag was completely charming. He maintained eye contact with Kurt during the entire meal, as he answered Kurt's questions about his skating career. As if to prove his own sincere interest, Tag addressed questions to Kurt about his career. He slipped in a few queries about his personal life too. "Where did you and your boyfriend meet?" Tag asked.

"Boyfriend?" Kurt smiled. "I'm afraid I don't have one. Not any more. How about you?"

"Me? A boyfriend? I'm much too busy. Plus I don't think anyone would be able to put up with me." Tag sighed. "I don't think I'm boyfriend material."

"Then you must be dating up a storm," Kurt countered. "Anyone who looks as yummy as you do, has to be prime pickup meat, if you'll forgive the lewd expression."

"Thanks, but, nah, I'm about as lonely as they come," Tag said. "Don't get me wrong. I have a healthy appetite for sex. But I think guys are afraid to come on to me because I'm so good looking they think they haven't got a chance."

"Did you say you also have a healthy ego?" Kurt teased.

"I must sound like someone who thinks he's hot stuff," Tag said. "Maybe I'm just fooling myself."

"Not a chance. You're definitely a hottie. Even from my seat in the arena this morning I could tell you've got a great ass."

Tag forced a blush by putting his hands to his face and squeezing blood to his cheeks. "Mr. Chrysler, sir," he said, whisking his face with an invisible fan, "you are incorrigible. That's what a teacher used to say about me. So we're two of a kind."

"I'm only telling you the truth," Kurt said. Then he thanked the waitress as she delivered the bill. He left a fifty-percent tip.

As the two left the dining room and passed an even larger crowd of hungry people waiting for tables, Tag made a sudden offer. "I can get you house seats for the show tonight, if you like."

Kurt had anticipated the invitation, and he had also planned an excuse not to accept. He didn't want to take the chance that Garry would see him. Kurt was a star, and word was bound to get out that he was in the audience. He knew from past experience that this would make Garry nervous. "Thanks, but I have a meeting with the producers of the TV special. But I'll see you after the show for dinner, won't I? Unless I've already bored you too much?"

"Bored? Me? You're the most exciting thing that's happened to me since . . . well since I got into *Gold on Ice*," Tag beamed. "I just wish you could come tonight and see my numbers in the show. That might prove to you that I was right for your special. I'm outstanding. In fact they keep giving me more skating too. I'm a hit, I guess. Wait'll I tell Garry and Jay who I'm having dinner with. They'll freak!"

Kurt's heart skipped a beat. "No! That is, I'd appreciate it if you wouldn't tell anyone that we've got a date, okay?"

"Is that really what it is? A date?" Tag's eyes were wide.

"We are having dinner together, aren't we?"

"We are!" Tag gushed. "I know how it is. The other skaters, especially the guys you once competed with, might feel bad that I was the one you were scouting. Trust me, I won't tell a soul."

Chapter Twenty-two

Tag accepted his final ovation of the evening at 9:50. By 10:15, he was showered and dressed in black slacks, a deep blue dress shirt, a red silk necktie and a gray herringbone blazer, courtesy of the wardrobe lady. By now she knew not to deny Tag anything, lest he run to Ernie and have her canned. She had spent her lunch hour at Macy's buying this outfit and her dinner break altering the slacks.

"Perfect," Tag said aloud as he looked in the mirror one last time before heading out.

"And why so dressed up?" Ernie asked in a suspicious tone of voice. "You blowing me off again?"

"An interview," Tag lied. "Hey, don't be so judgmental. I'm pretty much everybody's meal ticket around here now, so I've gotta schmooze the press. You want publicity, don't you?"

Ernie's attitude changed slightly, as he looked Tag up and down. "Don't fly off the handle," he said. "A magazine?"

"*Rosie.*"

Ernie cocked his head and made a face of approval. "A fancy schmancy place?"

"The writer promised someplace nice," Tag said, making it

sound like he didn't know where he was dining. "I'll tell you all about it when I get back. Or in the morning. You'll probably be asleep when I get in."

Before Tag could get away, Amber opened her door and stepped into the corridor. She was dressed in comfortable street clothes. Within seconds, Jay and Garry had exited their room as well.

Amber whistled and cocked her head toward Tag. "Nice threads," she said, going up to Tag and giving the knot in his tie a quick little tug to straighten it.

"Smells good too," Jay said, sniffing the air. "Pheromone Number Twelve? Hot date I presume."

"An interview," Tag countered. *"Rosie."*

"I thought her muffin magazine got stale and crumbled after she left her show," Garry said, insinuating that Tag was not being truthful about the interview.

"You guys work it out," Tag said, as he turned on his Kenneth Cole heels and walked away, flipping his middle finger to a few people along the way who dared to whistle at him.

"Yes, sir. Mr. Chrysler is expecting you," the maitre d' said when Tag entered the Pump Room and announced himself. "Right this way, sir." He escorted Tag to Kurt's place at Table One.

"So sorry I'm late," Tag gushed, as Kurt stood up and shook his hand.

"Nonsense. I just arrived myself. Isn't that right, James?" Kurt smiled at the maitre d'.

"Just arrived, sir," James said, his eyes inadvertently darting from a nearly empty flute of champagne and back to Kurt's eyes. He smiled at Tag. "May I offer you an aperitif, sir?" James asked as Tag settled into his seat.

Kurt anticipated that Tag hadn't a clue what the maitre d' was referring to and chimed in with, "A glass of champagne?"

"Oh, yeah, great," Tag said with a smile that expressed his minimal comfort zone.

Kurt nodded at James, who immediately disappeared, back to his lighted lectern.

For the first few minutes of their evening together, Kurt asked about the show—if Tag had enjoyed himself, how many curtain calls he made before the audience would let him go. "You look very natty in that outfit," Kurt said. "The blue shirt goes well with your complexion."

"Thank you. Everyone who saw me thought so too," Tag said. "Jay and Garry and Amber were impressed. Don't worry, I didn't tell them what I was really doing," he said, anticipating Kurt's concern that their meeting be secret.

"You're a good liar," Kurt said in a tone that sounded approving rather than insulting.

Tag looked down, as if he were ashamed about making a falsehood. "It's not the Christian thing to do," he said softly. "I wouldn't want you to have the wrong impression of me. I try to do unto others . . ."

"Of course you do," Kurt interrupted, pooh-poohing Tag's self-deprecation. "So, let's get to know one another." He looked into Tag's sea-green eyes. "Tell me about your career. How did you start?"

Tag gave another variation on the story he'd given Kurt earlier, and to reporters dozens of times since joining *Gold on Ice*. From his poor childhood and self-taught skating, up to becoming a cast member of the show, he embellished every detail. Although he never mentioned Garry's name or Jay's either, as the catalyst for him becoming a pro.

"A scout discovered you on the ice at Crystal Lake in Puberty, Mass., eh?" Kurt said, pretending to be completely engrossed in the story and in awe of the youngster who had trained alone for twelve hours every day during the winter. "You certainly do get discovered a lot, don't you?" Kurt smiled, referring to their first meeting during the early part of the day.

"I guess if something's going to happen, there's no stopping it," Tag said. "But I've worked my butt off. I deserve everything I get."

"Indeed. You do deserve everything you get . . . and so much more. Like that great watch you're wearing."

For a fraction of an instant, Tag looked perturbed, and pulled the cuff of his sport coat over the wristwatch.

"Just a cheap knock-off," Tag explained. "But some day I'll have a real one." Changing the course of their conversation, Tag switched the subject to Kurt's career. He wanted to know all about his life as a competitive skater and what it was like after winning all of the sport's highest honors.

Kurt knew a genuine Rolex when he saw one. "They sure make

the fakes look real these days," he said, covering his skepticism, then launching in to the barest of facts of his skating career. Nothing that he said wasn't common knowledge, including his homosexuality. But when he returned the question to Tag and asked when he came out as a gay man, Tag became suddenly flustered.

"The truth is, and I'm embarrassed to admit this," Tag said, "but since I feel so comfortable with you . . ." He waited for a beat. "I'm a virgin."

Kurt laughed involuntarily, so loud that patrons at nearby tables looked up from their own conversations.

Tag wasn't laughing. In fact, he feigned hurt, as though his confidence had been betrayed.

Kurt quickly apologized. "I should never assume anything. I just figured since you were so damn sexy, that guys would be all over you, twenty-four-seven. You're one of the most seductive men I've ever met. I know for sure that any gay man would feel they'd found El Dorado if they had sex with you."

"Do you really think that I'm sexy?" Tag said, acting the innocent.

The look of bewilderment on Kurt's face was accepted by Tag as that of a state of astonishment at hearing that anyone as handsome as him could possibly be a virgin, rather than the absurdity of the lies, as Kurt was actually thinking. Kurt could only play along.

"We're often the worst judges of our own value," Kurt said.

"My only value is on the ice," Tag said. "But I'm sure that my self-confidence would improve if I had an opportunity to skate on your TV special." Tag looked into Kurt's eyes. "Guys who are confident get laid a lot. I think that's what they mean by cocksure."

He emphasized the first syllable, while staring intently at Kurt, who swallowed hard and picked up his champagne flute. He didn't realize it was empty until his lips met with little more than a drop of champagne. He reached for the bottle, then refilled his glass and Tag's as well.

"You know," Tag said, in a low voice, "it's time for me to know more about the world."

"*Disney on Ice* travels to Europe. Want me to put in a word?" Kurt asked.

"No, I mean, I'm still in my teens and I haven't been, you know . . ."

"Laid?"

"Exactly! It's time I found out what all the fuss is about. Facts of life? Don't you agree?" Tag looked plaintively into Kurt's eyes.

Kurt looked into Tag's eyes, thinking how easy it would be to have sex with Tag, who after all, was making the most obvious play for him. Kurt had lusted after this guy ever since seeing his videos.

Tag reached out to stroke the fingers that Kurt had wrapped around his champagne flute. "I'll bet you've got a nice one."

Kurt smiled.

"Room, I mean. Your room. In the hotel."

Kurt's pants were full and he was a little high on champagne. As he continued to stare into Tag's eyes, he could feel the sensation that radiated from his navel down to his balls. He pictured himself straddling Tag, the way the tough guy in *Leaves of Ass* had done. He could see Tag laying on his stomach, on an unmade bed. As if all in one flash of a scene, Kurt could see himself straddling Tag's waist and massaging his muscled back with hot oil. In Kurt's mind, Tag made guttural noises of satisfaction as Kurt's strong hands kneaded his shoulders and quadriceps, working down his spine, to his ass. There, Kurt's hands lovingly caressed each cheek, stroking them as if they were fragile.

Kurt became unaware of the miasma of conversation, silverware clinking against china and a harpist playing something probably by Ravel in the distance. Kurt could only comprehend his own fantasy. In his mind, he continued making love to Tag.

"So, Kurt . . . would you ever want to make love to a virgin?" Tag asked, taking Kurt out of his reverie.

"Naturally," Kurt answered. "Everyone has to start sometime."

Tag smiled. "You'll be gentle? I've heard that it hurts the first time."

Kurt smiled back. "You know what?" he said, reaching into the breast pocket of his coat to retrieve his wallet. "I've got a big meeting in the morning. May I take a raincheck?"

Tag blanched. "But don't you want me? I mean, wouldn't it be nice to hold me? That is . . . I guess what I meant to say was, I'm attracted to you, and just thought maybe you could find it in you to be attracted to me, too." In the space of two seconds he had gone from the fury that comes with unexpected rejection, to adjusting his temper to the acquiescence of a saint.

"I'm sorry," Kurt said. "But the meeting's for my special."

"A meeting? Oh, of course," Tag said with as much sincerity as he could muster. "I'm so awkward about these things. I hope you'll forgive me for being so bold. I mean, I have a great talent for misreading a situation. I just thought that we were having such a swell time together, and other men have . . ." his sentence trailed off. "I hope my stupidity doesn't hurt my chances to do the show."

"No, no, Tag, this is all my fault," Kurt said while thinking, *It always comes back to the show.* "You weren't being stupid about anything. You're extremely attractive, and a fun guy to talk to, and very talented." Kurt gushed. "I'd love to kiss you and touch you and feel your beautiful body against mine. And your famous dick!" Kurt suddenly stopped himself, realizing that he'd just revealed too much. However, Tag didn't flinch, and his smile never faded, as he heard Kurt's assessment of him. "It's just that it's been a long day, and I have to be up so early."

Tag nodded, showing disappointment. "Okay. As long as I'm not a complete turnoff to you." Tag watched Kurt sign the dinner bill. "I'm not nearly as sophisticated as the people you probably hang out with. But I was hoping we could become friends. Or more."

"Absolutely," Kurt said. "I'd consider it an honor if you were one of my friends. In fact, I think we're already very important to each other."

Tag took one last long drag of his champagne. "Any more of that left?" he asked.

"Afraid we knocked off the whole bottle," Kurt said, pushing back his chair. He rose to stand beside the table.

As they walked through the room toward the hotel lobby, Tag looked around. "What's he doing here?" he said to no one.

"Who?" Kurt asked, not paying much attention.

"Garry Windsor. From the show. Isn't that him?"

Kurt froze. He looked where Tag was pointing. It was Garry, or someone who looked a lot like him, heading out of the restaurant.

Chapter Twenty-three

"You've been amazingly quiet," Jay said to Garry during their Grand Slam breakfast at Denny's the next morning. "Everything all right?"

There was a moment of silence. Then, "I saw Kurt last night." Garry sipped a glass of grapefruit juice.

"That's great!" Jay said. "So what'd you guys talk about?"

"We didn't."

"Just jumped into sex?"

"He was making out with Tag," Garry said.

Disappointment and anger hung in the air. Jay looked perplexed. "What do you mean, making out? They don't even know each other."

Garry gave a weak laugh, the one that says, you may think I'm an idiot, but this time I'm right. "They had dinner after the show last night. At the Pump Room, *to say the least*. They were holding hands."

Jay made a face. "You don't know what they were doing. Maybe it just looked like they were holding hands. Besides, Kurt wouldn't do that in public, would he?"

"The only public opinion that Kurt ever cared about was the quality of his quads. He'd do whatever breeders would do, like holding hands and kissing at a shopping mall. He doesn't have any anxiety over his so-called image. They were definitely holding hands."

Jay pursed his lips in contemplation. "You went to his hotel unannounced?"

"I was taking your advice to go and see him," Garry said. "The hotel desk clerk said he was having dinner in the restaurant."

"What if he hadn't been there?" Jay said.

"I didn't know I was actually going until I got there. If I'd called him first, I would have chickened out. As it was I panicked a couple of times anyway. I had the cab driver pull over. He thought I was nuts. Finally, I figured that if he wasn't in, that would be cool. But now I agree with you and Amber. I have to close the door on my stupid past."

Jay said, "We just want you and Kurt to resolve unfinished business." He prodded for more details. "So you went into the Pump Room, and . . ."

"Some stodgy old maître d' pointed out Kurt's table, but he wouldn't let me go over without him announcing me first. When I saw him and Tag, I told him not to bother. They were smiling and laughing and carrying on as though they were Nicole Kidman and Mimi Rogers reminiscing about Tom's fuck technique. Remember how Tag was all gussied up last night? New shirt, new tie, new sport coat? He obviously had a date. With Kurt." Garry shook his head. "That kid's amazing. He gets everyone he wants to do almost anything for him that he asks."

Jay nodded in agreement. "That little cocksucker. Tag, I mean," he said. "Did you say anything to them?"

"Like what? 'Hey Tag, Kurt's a great fuck. I have personal experience. Hey Kurt, watch out for Tag's crabs.' Anyway, if Kurt wants to reach me, he knows I'm in town. He'd call if he had anything to say."

Jay said, "Garry, I'm sorry . . ."

"Let's face it, Kurt's free, and Tag's fresh meat. I shouldn't even be concerned. Neither of 'em mean anything to me." Garry's voice diminished to a whisper. "Gosh he looked good. Kurt I mean. One of the things I miss most is his sparkling eyes."

Garry put on a paper smile and changed the subject. "Well," he announced, "what's on the agenda for tonight, after the show?" He clapped his hands and rubbed them together. "Look at me," he said in a self-analyzing tone, "I'm the glad girl. Pollyanna. I think it's time to think of something fun. Like sex with Michael Weiss, or that dude from *Smallsville*. Frankly, it's time that I got back into the saddle!"

"Now you're talkin'," Jay said. He gave Garry a high-five.

"Wanna go to that place that *InsightOut* says is the Windy City's club of the moment? What's it called? *C-Men?* The article said that guy from *The Fluffer* hangs out there, so to speak. Yeah, I think it's time to go out and find me a boyfriend!"

"I heard that!" Amber came up to the table wearing a big smile. "It's about time you stopped being so darned selfish with your pee pee!" Amber cupped her hands over her mouth and looked around. "Did that come from me! Shame! Hope my public didn't overhear." There was a tone of naughtiness in her voice. She sat down at the table. "You guys know what I mean. Mr. Handsome Stud here should be enjoying the fruited plains. This is the plains isn't it? I'm afraid I'm geographically challenged. And God knows the guys who swarm to our shows aren't looking for a Madonna to liven up their sex lives. Can I have your bacon?"

"Garry had a little surprise last night," Jay said, pushing his plate to Amber and looking serious. He surreptitiously raised an eyebrow that only Amber could see.

"Yeah?" She took a bite from a strip of pig and looked at Jay then at Garry.

"He saw Kurt."

Amber's eyes widened. Before she could say anything, Jay shook his head in small bursts to indicate that it wasn't what she was thinking and hoping. Amber got the message as she crunched and swallowed her crispy bacon. She put on a somber face that she reserved for bad news.

Jay said, "He saw Kurt, alright. Someone was *tag*-ing along. If you get my drift."

It only took a fraction of a moment before Amber cried, "That little shit!" This time half the restaurant heard her, but Amber was too shocked by the news of Kurt and Tag to be aware of anyone else around her. "This is impossible. Kurt would never . . ."

"Let's not get into it, please," Garry said. "They were together and that's that. I just wish that someone would warn Kurt about Tag."

"You wouldn't be so concerned about his feelings, if you didn't still have feelings of your own," Jay noted.

Amber took a sip from Jay's coffee mug. Abruptly she said, "I gotta run, guys. See you at the matinee."

With that she stood up from the table, put on her famous Amber Nyak smile, and sashayed through the throngs of people waiting, some of whom gaped at her in recognition.

"Now she's got the right attitude," Garry said. "She didn't make a big deal out of the situation. She knows that whatever's meant to be, will be."

Jay smiled, sadly. "*Que Sera Sera*."

The waitress laid their check facedown on the table as she poured more coffee and asked if they wanted anything else. It was her less-than-subtle way of suggesting they should leave so that others could be seated. Jay recognized the hint and withdrew a clutch of neatly folded dollar bills from his pocket. He counted out enough to pay the tab and added another ten percent. Although he always wanted to leave more, he couldn't afford to do so.

"Got enough?" Garry asked. After being with Jay for the past few months, he knew better than to try to pay for his own meals. It seemed to give Jay enormous pleasure to do the grand gesture and play host to everyone. Mostly, he just hated to hassle over a check in public. If pressed, he would say that he was uncomfortable telling friends that they owed this percentage of a total, plus tip. The fact was that Jay was lousy at math. He couldn't add or subtract quickly enough or accurately enough to guarantee that someone among his group might be over- or under-charged. It was simply easier to pick up all checks.

"Kurt? It's Amber. When you get in would you *please* give me a call. It's urgent. Thanks, hon."

Amber hung up the telephone and looked at Dorothy Hamill's hands. Then she picked up the telephone again and pressed the keypad for another number. It rang twice. "Tag, honey? It's me, Amber. Wanna have lunch or something?" She listened for a moment. "Oh, you practice too much! I'll be at the IHOP at twelve-thirty. No excuses. I'll see you in thirty minutes. Don't keep me waiting, you precious thing." She hung up the telephone and pushed another series of numbers.

The walk from her hotel to the restaurant was a short one, but filled with trepidation. Amber didn't have a clue what she was doing going to lunch with the enemy. Often, she was able to parlay her cuteness to get around such obstacles as long lines at a rest-room facility or, once, to get a journalist from *The Globe* to go easier on a story about the back stage temperament of her skating pal, Allison Beckworth. Although most of her friends were gay, Tag was uncharted territory, because he was the only queer she'd ever known who didn't swoon when he met her.

"Sweetie! You looked so cute last night in your new outfit," Amber gushed when Tag walked in the IHOP fifteen minutes late.

Dressed in jeans, a tank top, and a baseball cap turned around backwards, Tag said, "I'm more comfortable in my everyday street clothes."

"Oh, I know how you feel," Amber agreed. "We wear so many costumes in the show—or at least I used to—that I just want to lounge around in my jammies when I'm not working."

Tag took a long look at Amber and thought, *This is why she's brought me here. She's upset because her role in the show is so limited. Or, she's found out about the upcoming changes and wants to beg me not to kick her bronze medal butt out of the show altogether.* "So what are you up to?" Tag asked.

Their waitress arrived with her order blank. She was a blonde twentysomething in a butterscotch-colored uniform with a white collar and trim, and a white paper tiara. Her plastic name badge said, T'FNY.

Amber said, "Let me try the tuna salad on toasted whole wheat. Oh, and a side of fries. What the heck, it's my cheat day. I can have a few extra calories. And would you ask the cook to burn them for me? I hate eating soggy French fries. By the way, that's such a cute name," she said to the waitress. "It's short for Tiffany, like the jew-elry place, right?"

"Naw," the waitress drawled. "That's just the way I spell my name." She was too busy flirting with Tag to take in Amber's chat-tering. Although she didn't recognize Tag from newspaper stories about his ice show performance, she did a double take when she first looked at him. She thought he'd make a hot lay. She didn't pick up on the nearly flashing sign in his eyes that blinked NO GIRLS ALLOWED.

"Now, why did you want us to meet?" Tag asked suspiciously as T'fny moved on to another table. "There's nothing I can do about the show, or how much ice time you get."

Amber gave him a *never you mind* wave of her hand. "I'm just so sorry that we stopped being as close friends as we used to be," Amber said. "Remember how much fun we all had, you and Jay and Garry and me, driving around the country together. Going from one dumpy rink to another? Those were the good ol' days. Don't you think? I'd really like for us to put aside whatever differences we may have. Do you think we can do that? It would mean the world to me. And I know Jay and Garry would be more comfortable, now that you're such a big old star on ice."

Tag smiled when Amber confirmed that he was, indeed, a star. It was the first recognition of his rightful place that he'd received from anyone in the original company of *Gold on Ice*. The words, coming from Amber, the undisputed queen of the show gave him a sense of having cleared a passageway toward his rightful position. For the first time, he felt that he was being accepted. "So, no hard feelings about all the changes in the show?" Tag asked.

"Heck, no," Amber pooh-poohed the notion that she was angry or unhappy. "Change is definitely good. That old show should have been revamped long ago. It surely needed the infusion of the fresh blood that you've given it. You should be so darn proud of yourself."

"Thanks, Amber," Tag beamed. "I guess I'm sorry if I made you, of all people, uncomfortable. Except for those few times when you practically punched me out, and I guess I had it coming to me. You usually made me feel as though I was part of the family."

"But you are. Always have been, precious. Siblings don't always get along, but they're always family. And I think the best part of being a family is that you can count on each other when the going gets rough. Now, I realize that you never had brothers or sisters, but the way a family works is that everybody accepts everybody else for who and what they are. Even if you don't necessarily agree with them, you still love them. You read their novels if they're a porn writer. You watch them skate if they're a big talent like you. No judgment."

Amber launched into a long story about growing up with five sisters and that they would be fighting one minute and telling all their deepest boyfriend secrets the next. "That's just how things are, at least in my family."

Tag was happy. Amber, as she had hoped to do, skillfully steered the conversation to a place where Tag might feel comfortable enough sharing bits and pieces of his life as never before. She weaved in anecdotes about her personal life, just enough so that he wouldn't be bored, and thus made him want to one-upman her stories.

"You think that was funny?" Tag laughed. "You should have been there the day that my father found me slipping my sausage to his new wife!" They both cackled the way old friends do when they get together and remember something that at a time in the past seemed like the worst thing that could have happened to them.

"So tell me," Amber said when her sandwich and fries arrived. "What's a gorgeous, talented boy like you, doing unattached?" She sounded incredulous. Then, in a conspiratorial voice, she added, "I know that most of the guys in the company, and lot of the girls, too, would love to get into your pants. Wink. Wink."

Tag laughed again. "Tell me about it. It makes them crazy when I pretend not to notice them." Tag leaned in closer and in a whisper said, "As a matter of fact, you know that boy Brad, the one who skates as Dolly, that cloned sheep, in the *Man's Great Inventions* number, I fuck him every night when you're doing *La Bohème*!"

Laughter exploded from Amber, along with the sip of Coke she had just taken. "I know!" she squealed. "I asked you about him way back in Tennessee, remember? So, while I'm out there working my butt off skating, you're working Brad's butt off?" she continued to laugh. "I always thought he made poor Dolly look a little wobbly and bow-legged, but awfully happy!" Tag and Amber laughed again. "Now you've gone and made me have to concentrate more in that number." She gave Tag a pretend slap on the wrist. "As poor Mimi is dying, I'll be thinking of you and that boy Brad!"

Again they laughed raucously. "This is so much fun!" Amber raved. "Go on, tell me another one. How about Garry or Jay? And don't tell me they don't screw each other's brains out every night. They're inseparable. They never tell me anything about their sexploits, with each other or anybody else for that matter. What are they really like in the bedroom?"

Tag snorted.

"Oh, c'mon, now," Amber coaxed. "Tell your Auntie Amber every intimate detail."

Tag looked around the room as if there might be eavesdroppers. Satisfied that their conversation was not open to public scrutiny, with the crook of his finger he beckoned her to lean forward and to meet him halfway. She did so with a wide smile and great expectations.

"Those two are the most boring old queens you can imagine," Tag said, rolling his eyes. "Not only do they *not* fuck each other—although, God knows I think they both want to desperately. If you ask me, I think Garry's turned back into a virgin. I've seen his dick, and it's a really nice slab o' meat. Even at his age, he could probably get a lot of men. But he won't do it. He says it takes more than a pretty body to make him get all tingly. Whatever that means. He has this stupid idea about waiting for what he calls a guy with *substance*. He once told me that the man of his dreams doesn't have to be especially good looking, or accomplished or hung as well as he is, or I am. Garry's big thing is finding someone that he calls *nice*. How boring is that!"

Amber continued to freeze-frame her smile, but looked at Tag as one would look at anybody who just didn't get the simple fact that George W. Bush is an utter moron.

"Now, Jay, on the other hand, he's a little more fun," Tag continued. "At least he gets laid. But you have to pry the details out of him. He and that guy Mark, the one who wears the Depends invention, had a couple of dates. *Real* dates. Not the pretend ones where you just go to dinner and a movie. They fooled around, or at least that's what I hear."

Amber knew the whole Mark/Depends story. Jay may have been a clam to everyone else, but he confided even the teeniest details of his sexual exploits to Amber, the way best friends share their most intimate secrets. What Tag didn't seem to know was that Mark/Depends had started seeing Brad/Dolly the sheep. She also knew that Brad was no longer Tag's *La Bohème* toy exclusively. Brad was fucking another boy skater while Tag was on the ice—which of course, had become more and more frequent.

"I'll tell you something else," Tag said with a grin. "I'm dating someone."

"Other than Brad?"

"That's not a date. He's just a ritual fuck. No. I've got my hands on a real catch," Tag said in a conspiratorial tone.

"Do tell," Amber said, trying not to scare him away with too much interest.

"He's rich and famous."

"Bill Gates? He always looked like he could be queer."

"No. A skater!"

"Skaters don't get rich and famous unless they're champions."

Amber waited a beat. Then in mock surprise she put her hands over her mouth. "Are you tellin' me that you caught one of the biggies?"

Tag smiled with smug satisfaction. He leaned back in his chair and put his hands behind his head. "You'll never guess who."

Amber giggled. "Oh, Tag, this is too much fun! I feel like we're girlfriends at a sleep-over, getting' all the dish on cute boys in the senior class."

Tag grinned triumphantly. "So, go on. Take a guess."

Amber feigned gullibility. "Let's see. Is he really really famous— like Olympic famous, or just one of the boys you see at Nationals?"

"Really famous."

Amber's eyes grew wider and she started biting her fingernails. "Oh my. Not someone like Brian or Yuri, or Michael?" She suggested a few of the household names.

Tag shook his head with each name.

"Give me a teensy hint."

Tag grinned. "Tall for a skater. Six feet. Blond shoulder-length mane of hair. Blue eyes. Brilliant smile. No more hints."

Amber's eyes widened with shock. "It can't be! No! How on earth did you two . . . ? He's so gorgeous! Are we both talking about the same . . . Kurt Chrysler?"

Tag nodded his head with a doublewide smile. "We're fucking night and day. He came on to me and I thought I'd go along just for the ride. But he's fallen in love with me, of course."

Amber didn't believe a word of Tag's scenario but she said, "Oh, you two make such a pretty couple!"

"And he's definitely not the type of guy I'd ordinarily go out with. He's way too old . . ."

"At twenty-four?"

"But he's rich. And he's got an awesome dick. In order of importance."

"So I've heard," Amber said, continuing to pretend that she had to recover from all the news that Tag had offered. "But for Pete's sake, when do you guys have a chance to see each other?"

"Just whenever we can. I admit that I can't get enough of him. He's the best lover a guy could ask for."

"My, my. You have the most interesting life. Yes, you do, indeed," Amber exclaimed. Then, in a nervous outburst, Amber looked at her wrist and gasped. "Oh, my, look at Dorothy!" She held her watch to her ear then showed it to Tag, effectively drawing an end to their gossipy conversation. "My dear young man, you're a much deeper wellspring than I ever imagined possible."

Tag accepted this as a compliment and shrugged his shoulders as if to say, *and you're just finding this out*?

Getting up, Amber said, "We *must* do this again! You're so much fun! I'll pick up the check. It was worth every dime just to hear you rattle on about all the exciting things in your life. I gotta run to the powder room, so why don't you just run along to the arena. We've got a matinee in an hour. Does matinee day count for two sessions with Dolly?" she quipped. "See you on the ice. I'll be thinking 'bout you and Brad during *La Bohème*!" Amber laughed as she blew a kiss to Tag.

On her way out, Amber hailed a waitress and asked where the pay phone was located. She hurried over to an alcove next to the restrooms. It seemed strange using an old-fashioned pay phone. She lifted the receiver to her ear and dropped in two quarters. She pushed the number for the Ambassador Hotel and asked for Kurt's room. Again there was only the automated voice mail system. "Damn. Of all the times to forget my cell," she muttered as she walked out of the restaurant.

"It's shit choreography," Tag was shouting at Ernie in front of the entire troupe, as Jay, Garry, and Amber walked onto the ice for the pre-show warmup. "The music sucks! And the costumes don't work at all!"

"Talk about mood swings," Amber whispered to Jay and Garry. "He was all dimples and pearly whites thirty minutes ago."

Tag was ranting. "I won't skate in that mess! Is it asking too much for a little creativity? Well, is it? I guess so!" With that final tirade, Tag stormed off the ice. He passed Amber with nary a look of recognition.

The chorus kids stood around snickering. Garry knew that none of them were the least bit intimidated by Tag. In fact, with his tantrums coming more frequently and with less reason, they found him to be more amusing and a nuisance rather than anything remotely upsetting.

"Paging George and Martha," one of the boy skaters dryly said to another. "And I don't mean the Washingtons, girlfriend." It was loud enough for Ernie to overhear and he looked at the kid with contempt. *"Di-va,"* another boy called out. He looked at Ernie, as if daring him to comment on his remark, then skated away with an imperious posture.

Ernie was steaming. He then barked at the choreographer and costume lady, demanding an immediate meeting to discuss Tag's complaints. Garry and Jay and Amber looked at each other. As principals in the show, they knew it would send a completely wrong message if they laughed with the chorus kids' appraisal of Tag's histrionics. Instead, Jay, *sotto voce,* sang, "Somebody's gonna get a spanking."

Amber winked at him. "We've got to talk," she said. "But not here. Someplace after the show, but don't let Tag see us. It's urgent."

She began to skate away, but she was summoned back by Ernie who asked where she thought she was going. "Have to freshen up before the show," she said with a light-hearted smile.

"Don't bother. Your number's been cut," Ernie snapped. "You'll skate as the McNugget in the Inventions segment," he said in a loud voice that was meant to convey to the entire cast that no one was indispensable.

Shocked, Amber stood motionless, as frozen to the spot as the ice beneath her blades. From the company, a low murmur of disbelief swirled around her.

Garry and Jay simultaneously shouted their outrage at Ernie's treatment of the show's star. Like big brothers coming to the rescue of a bullied little sister, they raced over to Ernie, spraying him with ice shavings as they came to a stop directly in front of him.

"Who the hell do you think you are, you fat-assed, cocksucking, dick head?" Jay roared.

"Amber's been the star of this freakin' excuse for an ice show for years," Garry shouted. "How dare you insult her! Apologize, you bastard. Do you hear me! This instant!"

"I've had enough of the three of you," Ernie yelled, standing his ground. "You skate around as if you're the lords and masters of the show. When was the last time any of you tried to infuse your programs with something new? You come out each night and skate the same mediocre shit that you've skated from day one. I can do your routines in my sleep. They're boring! No wonder this show was always playing in West Podunk, instead of Madison Square! Nobody cares about some *old* medalist and two also-rans!"

"Is that who we are to you? Also-rans?" Jay exclaimed.

"You're completely to blame, Ernie, 'cause you've got rotten directing and production design skills," Garry spat back.

"Listen here, you three," Ernie said. "We're making changes to the show. It's been rewritten and roles have been recast. If you don't like the way I run things, then by all means, I'll gladly release you from your contracts. Maybe it's time to pursue other options."

"It's all about Tag, isn't it?" Jay accused. "Be honest, Ernie. That little piece of ass that you get whenever he wants something has put you up to this, hasn't he? You think you can do without us because that little starfucker is the flavor of the month with the critics? If you're so stupid as to allow a great skater like Amber to get away from you, then I don't want to be in your show."

"Same here," Garry said.

"No. Please, guys, don't do this," Amber pleaded with Jay and Garry.

"*You're* the loser, Ernie. Not us," Jay said. "Wait'll Tag decides that *you're* dispensable. You'll remember this day, and maybe you'll feel sorry for the way you treated Amber. And us."

"Is that it then?" Ernie asked Jay. "You've decided to hang up your skates, at least as far as *Gold on Ice* is concerned?"

"Unless you tell Amber you've realized what a huge mistake you've made and kiss her skate blades to express your apology then, yeah, I've made a decision," Jay said.

"Does that go for you too?" Ernie said, looking at Garry.

"No!" Amber begged her friends.

Garry said firmly to Ernie, "I will not stand by and let you or anybody else treat Amber Nyak with such disrespect and lack of appreciation for her talents, and her enormous contributions to this show. If you don't want her, then you don't want me either."

Ernie looked at Amber. For a moment, he hesitated. He was reconsidering his decision to cut her one last solo number.

Amber stood silently. It appeared to her, and to everyone else, that Ernie was about to do as Garry insisted, to bend down and kiss Amber's skate.

Then, with a quick burst of anger, Ernie yelled, "Out! Clear your dressing rooms and get out! Now! Nobody gives me an ultimatum! Get out!"

Holding each other's hands, Amber and Jay and Garry lifted their heads high. Then, as if by telepathy, they each parted to skate once around the rink. As Amber was entering into an Axel on her left skate blade, Jay moved with strong strokes and landed a perfect Lutz. Garry performed a camel spin, into a back camel.

The cast of *Gold on Ice* erupted into spontaneous applause as the trio concluded their impromptu performance.

"We love skating, Ernie!" Garry yelled across the arena.

"We have a passion for what we do! We can do something that you can't, Ernie," Jay added.

Amber, always silent on her blades, simply did a deep bend curtsy for her former colleagues in the show.

As the trio stepped off the ice, the entire cast turned toward Ernie. They glared at him for a long moment. Then, one by one, each girl skater copied Amber and curtsied to the cast. The boys, too, curtsied, pulling on the fabric of the legs of their jeans. When they were all gathered on the black rubber mat surrounding the ice, they turned their backs on Ernie and walked away.

Chapter Twenty-four

"I for one, think it's fucked," Jay said of the *Gold on Ice* production, as he and Garry gathered with Amber in her hotel room.
"One slip, and Tag could wind up like Kerry. The show's too cheap
to hire understudies. Plus they're relying on Tag's name alone now.
What if he quits?"

"Quit?" Garry rejected the notion. "Only if he gets so famous
that those programming execs over at ABC give him his own sitcom. Could happen though."

"You're forgetting that little ol' thing called cause and effect,"
Amber added. "Like what OJ got, or those stupid Menendez brothers. Couldn't those two losers have waited a decent amount of time
before shakin' their dicks at every Rolex jeweler and Ferrari sales-
man in Beverly Hills? Talk about candidates for the Darwin Award."

"But back to Tag, he could be skating around the rink during
practice, and whoops-a-daisy. All fall down, go boom-boom! Like
poor ol' Kerry."

The two men and Amber sat on the carpeted floor of the room
with their backs resting against the bed. Sipping from a cheap bottle of Almaden white zinfandel that they found in the mini-bar, the
trio reminisced about particularly memorable performances from
Gold on Ice. Then they reminded each other how repulsive the over-

all experience had been. "It was like being held hostage on the set of a Barry Sonnenfeld flick," Garry said. He didn't really know what a Sonnenfeld movie set was like but he'd heard it was pretty intense with a lot of non-talented filmmakers blaming everyone else for the garbage they were creating. "Imagine anyone taking credit for making that flick *Big Trouble*?" he said to prove his point. "I only paid to see it in a theatre because it had that dreamy Rene Russo. Poor baby. How'd she get talked into doing that piece of refuse?"

"Let's look on the bright side," Amber said, always trying to find a silver lining. "No more Tag the Wonder Dick nipping at our behinds."

"If I hadn't been sidetracked by his cuteness, we'd still be the stars of *Gold*," Garry said. "This is what I get for letting Kurt get away. The irony is that Tag's got our show, *and* my ex!"

"Which reminds me," Amber said, getting up off the floor to sit on the edge of the bed. She reached for the telephone and picked up the receiver to once again call Kurt's number. She made a face. "Strange. No dial tone."

"Forget to charm the telephone man?" Jay teased.

"I'll have to use yours." Amber held out her hand for Jay and Garry's key card, then went to the door. The guys got up and followed her across the hall to their room.

There, Amber picked up the phone receiver off of its cradle and pushed the little square zero at the bottom of the keypad. "Hi, this is Amber Nyak in room 222? My little phone is having difficulty finding its voice. Can you have it fixed for me? No, this isn't my phone." She looked at the guys and rolled her eyes. "As I said, my li'l ol' ringy doesn't have a dingy. I'm in a friend's room. There you go. You catch on quick. Oh, before I hang up would you see if I have any messages?

"Bless her heart," Amber said as she waited for the hotel operator to return to the line. "Seven? Lord a'mighty!" She picked up a pen next to a scratch pad of paper next to the phone. "Okay, shoot."

Jay and Garry watched as Amber scribbled notes, shook her head to indicate disbelief about something, and scribbled more notes and numbers. "Right. Thanks much."

She pressed the disconnect button and held it for a second. "I can't believe this," she said lifting her finger. She began pushing a sequence of numbers. "Kurt tried to return my call seven times! He'll think I'm a flake for not getting back to him."

"Kurt?" Garry asked, surprised.

"I'll explain in a sec," Amber said. "Machine again! Kurt, it's Amber. I am sorry about not returning your calls, but I didn't get the messages until just now. The phone in my room was busted, and I didn't find out until only a wee bit ago. Honey, when you get this message, would you please reach me at Jay and Garry's room? Same main number but theirs is room 224. Please try to get back to me right away. There's lots to chat about, and we'll be leaving the hotel first thing in the morning. I don't have a clue where we'll be after that. By the way, we aren't in the show anymore. Bye for now sweetheart."

Amber hung up the phone. She looked at Garry. "You wanna tell him, or shall I?" Amber said, looking at Jay, who gestured: go ahead. "Okay. It's like this, Garry, sweetheart. Your Kurt's gonna try to help us nail that little weasel."

"Kurt's probably already nailed him," Garry said. "Can't blame him." He sighed. "Kurt's an all-American, red-blooded guy with a dick that responds well to cute young flesh."

"I have a good sense of what's going on between him and Tag," Amber tried to reassure Garry. "He's a clever guy, that Tag. But so's Kurt. And I don't believe for a moment that what you saw last night was anything other than Kurt playacting." She hoped that she sounded convincing.

Garry looked as though he was giving careful consideration to Amber's comments. "I'd hate to see him get pegged by that little prick," he said. "Unless that's what he wants."

Jay said, "Kurt's a big boy. He's done pretty well with his life. At least about most things." The unspoken thought, which they all picked up on, was that Kurt had certainly erred where his relationship with Garry was concerned.

Garry stood up and looked out of the hotel room window. It was dusk, and the sun reflecting off the silver windows of skyscrapers made him feel a little empty. "On any other night we'd be getting ready for the show about now. I think I miss it already," he said in a faint voice.

"There'll be other shows. Better ones, too," Jay said, trying to sooth Garry's melancholy. "I guarantee this was the best thing that could have happened to you. To all of us. I promise. Here, give me a squeeze."

Jay got up to embrace Garry. They held each other for a long moment.

"You, too, Amber," Jay said, beckoning her to join the group hug.

"You guys should be lovers," Amber said, sidling over to the men and wedging herself between them. "They say you're not supposed to marry the one you find most attractive, but rather the one you like to talk to the most. You care more about each other than most couples I know."

The men smiled.

Amber sighed. "I should've been a gay blade," she said. "But, my Lord, I wouldn't be able to choose between the two of you. Like that old song, 'Torn Between Two Lovers.' "

"We'd just have had to have a three-way relationship," Garry added.

"Well, you've both spoiled me for life," Amber sighed. She hugged her pals, resting her head on Jay's chest.

The phone suddenly rang, snapping them out of their reveries. Amber reached out behind her and picked up the receiver. "Kurt?" she asked.

She frowned, confused. "Kurt, is that you hon?" Amber asked again, letting go of Garry and Jay.

The line went dead. "Wrong number, I guess," Amber said as she sat on the edge of the bed. Dismissing the call, she said, "Hey, that mini-bar's beckoning again. Let's open a bottle of something else and celebrate our new freedom!"

"Absolutely," Garry agreed.

Jay unlocked the door to their small refrigerator and peered inside. "Champagne? Wine? Coke? Gin? What's your pleasure?" he asked.

"I vote for the champagne," Amber said. "And those little cans of Pringles, too."

As she was rinsing the wineglasses in the bathroom, the telephone rang again. This time Garry answered. "Hey," he said brightly. Then, in a solemn voice, "Oh, yeah, things are great. Couldn't be better." He paused.

Hearing the telephone ring, Amber had quickly returned to the room with the wineglasses wrapped in a hand towel. She put them down on the bed stand and stood beside Jay, watching Garry as he talked on the phone.

"That'd be nice," Garry continued. "Okay. Well, let me put Amber on. Yeah. Same here."

Amber accepted the receiver and immediately said, "Hey, Kurt. How you doin'? Oh, yeah, he looks fine." She glanced at Garry. "That is, considering what happened today. Oh, so Tag mentioned it too? That's a short grapevine. That's what I wanted to talk to you about. Can we meet? Wonderful. Twenty minutes? Great. On our way. Bye, hon."

Amber hung up the phone and said, "Pour me that drink. Amber needs reinforcement. We're goin' to see Kurt."

The small bottle of Andre champagne would ordinarily have been tough to get down, simply because Andre tasted like urine. But the three cheered, "Bottoms up," and quickly drained their glasses. "Let's hit it," Amber said. "Just gotta stop and pick up my purse."

"He sounded nice," Garry said. "He still thinks of me every day, or so he says."

"Told you," Amber taunted as they all entered the elevator and checked their teeth and hair in the mirrored walls of the car. "Wave and say hello to the nice security men watching from the cameras," she said, smiling.

"Jeez, Louise," Garry gasped when the elevator door at the Ambassador East opened into Kurt's penthouse suite. "I obviously didn't practice enough when I was a kid, if this is the payoff."

Kurt gamboled into the foyer. At six feet, he was tall for a skater. He wore black jeans and a sky blue dress shirt, opened at the neck and down three buttons. His sleeves were rolled up, revealing a gold wristwatch and muscled forearms. His warm wide smile complemented his dimples and light five-o'clock shadow. There was sweetness in his face. No one who was ever blessed to have his sapphire blue eyes gaze upon them could feel anything but a quick stab of lust.

"Garry!" Kurt called out, clearly delighted to see the man with whom he had once shared his life. "You look ... well ... just great."

Garry looked down at the marble floor for a moment, then was drawn back to Kurt's smile. "You look . . . pretty great, too," he said. "I mean you look the way you always look in my dreams." Garry held himself back. He didn't want to come across as someone who had spent the past year pining away for an ex-lover. "I mean, whenever you cross my mind, this is how I picture you. Except I never pictured a penthouse view." He indicated the extravagant accommodations.

"You cross my mind, too. Often." Kurt looked at Amber and Jay. "Sorry, you two. I didn't mean to ignore you. Let's have a drink."

Jay took charge, walking into the kitchen to select a bottle of Cristal from the wine refrigerator, and reaching for the Waterford. "You all go into the living room. I'll bring the tasties," he said, cocking his head toward Garry to indicate that he and Kurt should be together.

Garry smiled thanks at Jay and followed the others into the sunken living room. He walked over to the French doors that opened onto a small balcony.

"Here," Kurt said, opening the doors and leading Garry outside. Amber followed them. "There's the Sears Tower," he said, placing a hand on Garry's shoulder and pointing to the left. "And over there, beyond those buildings, is Lake Michigan. Have you been down to the shore? We should go tomorrow. It'd be fun."

Garry smiled as memories of their life together washed over him. He thought back to the first night they were together. Kurt was such a gentleman. He didn't try to be; it was just his natural state of being, as though he didn't have a choice. It was in Colorado Springs, where they both were training for the Nationals. They had dinner at the Broadmoor Hotel, then walked around the lake outside.

"Bubbly, my friends?" Jay said, coming up behind them on the terrace. For the moment, their mutual spell was broken.

"Absolutely!" Garry said, turning away from Kurt to re-enter the suite. He accepted a flute from Jay and went to sit down next to Amber.

When they all had glasses of champagne in their hands, Kurt announced, "A toast! To your newfound freedom! And to enduring friendship!"

He looked at Garry who suddenly wouldn't meet his gaze, but instead looked around the well-appointed room. "Okay, let's get down to business," Kurt said. "You won't *believe* that kid Tag."

* * *

Over the next hour, Kurt filled the trio in on the details of his breakfast and dinner with Tag, as well as Tag's attempt to come across as an innocent. "Shirley Temple, he's not," Kurt said. "You should have heard the things he had to say about all of you. Then he backpedaled when he realized that we probably knew each other from competitions. He was pathetic. But no dummy."

"And sexy," Garry interrupted, the champagne going to his head and making him slightly aggressive.

"I suppose," Kurt said. "I admit, I had hoped he wasn't such a good skater. But there's no denying the facts."

"The facts," Garry interrupted again. "Like how well hung he is, and that his chest and abs are about as delicious looking as anything you could imagine?"

Amber and Jay looked askance at Garry. Then they looked at Kurt, who didn't seem to know how to respond.

"Pretty obvious, I suppose," Kurt said. "What are you getting at, Garry?"

"Forget it. Nothing. I just know how he is, the prick. He wraps men around his little finger, then they're doomed. He's like some evil mermaid luring ships to run ashore and sink." He paused. "I saw you guys holding hands last night, and I completely understand if you even came back here and made love right in this room. He's gorgeous, and I remember how gorgeous guys always came on to you and they were impossible to refuse, and he's seductive and hot, and . . ." Garry ran out of words. He sat looking at Kurt. "The little shit. He's really bad."

"You're bringing up the past, and I don't think it's appropriate," Kurt said softly. "In all modesty, I admit Tag wanted me. That was clear. And, I'll admit, I wanted him, too. But we didn't do anything. We never will do anything. He's just a little whore who just wants to be in my next television special. He'll do whatever it takes to dump *Gold on Ice* and skate with me. So I have a plan."

Kurt explained to his friends how he'd set up Tag to think there would be a role for him in the next television special. "Tag said he couldn't wait to tell you guys, that it would be salt in your wounds after being fired from the show," Kurt concluded. "I explained to him that it was important not to tell a soul, especially you three, 'cause you would be jealous. I expected full well that he'd tell you."

Amber sat up. "Kurt," she said, "did you call Jay and Garry's room late this afternoon? Before you got my message to dial that number?"

Kurt looked perplexed. "I tried you at least half a dozen times, but always got the operator who said you weren't answering. I only called Jay and Garry when you left their number."

"I wonder . . ." Amber said. "There was a hang up a little before we spoke. I'm thinking maybe now it was Tag calling to rub Jay and Garry's face in his good news. At the time I thought it was you calling and said so into the receiver. If it was that little rat, he'd be wondering why I was there and expecting a call from you."

"If he gets the idea that we're in alliance, it could throw things off," Kurt said. He looked at his watch. "Oh, hell. It's nearly ten o'clock. He's probably taking his last bow right about now. We're supposed to meet for drinks at C-Men after the show. I'd better take off. You guys hang around and watch videos or something. In fact, why don't you show Garry this one?" He picked up a cassette and smiled evilly. "Just a short documentary you might find amusing," he said to Garry. "I'll be back as soon as possible."

With that, Kurt bounded to the front foyer and pushed the button for the private elevator. The doors opened and he stepped into the car. Before the doors closed together, his eyes made contact with Garry's, and both men smiled. They received a jolt of satisfaction, as though they had once again become connected.

Amber poured another round of champagne for her friends. "Take a long swallow, honey," she said, looking at Garry. "The feature presentation is about to begin."

Jay slipped the black VHS tape cassette into the video tape player and Amber pushed PLAY.

Within moments, Garry gasped. "What the hell is . . ."

Chapter Twenty-five

It was nearing eleven-thirty when Tag walked through the door at C-Men. The bass vibration of a disco remix of Elvis Presley songs was so strong that it almost stopped him in his tracks. He looked around the vast space through a forest of men, and finally spotted Kurt leaning against the top of a tall table. Kurt was holding a bottle of beer and talking to a guy who could have been Ryan Phillipe—if Ryan were about ten years younger. Tag walked up to the table and planted a kiss on Kurt's lips, to mark his territory. The Ryan Phillipe ten years younger lookalike took the hint. "See ya," he said, and wandered away.

Kurt smiled. "What was that for?"

"Just happy to see you. And I didn't want you getting any ideas about other boys."

Tag reached for the bottle of beer in Kurt's hand and seductively flicked his tongue around the green glass neck before bringing it to his lips and taking a long pull. He made the sound of someone whose thirst had been slaked, then tilted the bottle back and took another drink. This time he leaned over and planted his lips onto Kurt's again, and passed the beer into Kurt's mouth. This made Kurt's pants ready to burst from his erection. He smiled at Tag and locked eyes with him.

"So, what'd you do while I was out showcasing my spectacular ass on the ice tonight?" Tag asked.

"I took a few calls. Answered some fan mail. Watched a little of *Larry King Live*. Had to keep my eyes on something other than the clock and waiting to see you."

Tag smiled. "Me? Oh, come on. There must be plenty of hot kids you could be with. You don't need to wait for me."

As handsome men swirled about the room, some of whom seemed to recognize that there was a famous figure skating star in their midst, Kurt took a long hard look at Tag. He had to practically shout over the din. "I don't necessarily fuck everything that moves," Kurt said.

Tag smiled. "Sure you do. You have a reputation. When I told some of the guys in the cast that I'd met you, they all said you were a hell of a stud. Said that you'd have me begging for your legendary dick."

Kurt swallowed hard. "Legendary?" he laughed. "You weren't supposed to tell anyone about us, remember?"

"I didn't tell anyone about the special, just that I'd met you. Although, I was dying to tell Jay and Garry."

That's when Kurt knew that Tag had called their room. He was obviously aware that they knew Kurt was in town. Kurt could only imagine that he suspected something was going on. "You know, Garry and I were once lovers," Kurt said.

Tag was tugging on the back of a white tank top that held the muscled body of a bar boy, holding a tray of beers. He held up Kurt's bottle and two fingers. The boy nodded, then wended his way through the crowd, back to the bar. "I've done my homework," shouted Tag.

"That's one of the reasons I didn't want you to mention our meeting," Kurt replied, trying to find an alibi for not telling Tag earlier about his former relationship. "Amber, you know how she can be. She wanted me to at least call Garry. For old times sake."

"You let Amber know you were in town, but not your ex-lover?"

"She's an old friend. And I needed her to mediate a possible meeting with Garry," Kurt said. "I wanted to make sure she felt he'd be responsive."

Their beers arrived. Tag raised his bottle of Heineken. Kurt did the same and they clinked them together. "To our friendship. And more." Tag smiled.

"Absolutely," Kurt responded.

"So, you let me rattle on about Garry's shortcomings, when all the time you were planning on getting back together with him," Tag stated, matter-of-factly.

"Never," Kurt said. "We'll never be a couple again. I let you go on because everything you said reminded me of why we broke up in the first place. You're a very intuitive guy."

"I see," Tag said, taking another drink of beer. "Well, why see him at all then? You know what they say, 'You can't go home again.' Either you enjoy being a masochist, or you wanted to make sure he really hadn't changed very much, or you wanted to score with him one last time, or . . ." Tag's words trailed off.

"No. To all of the above. Well, maybe the last one." He chuckled. "I decided to take Amber's advice and see if Garry wanted to have a drink tonight."

"What if he'd said yes? Would you have blown me off? We had a date."

"Blow you off? Not on your life." Kurt looked deep into Tag's eyes. "I would have worked something out."

Tag smiled. "Let me work something out—of your pants." He placed his hand on Kurt's crotch. Kurt's boner was a swollen gland, ready for action.

Kurt smiled. He looked at Tag's peaches 'n' cream complexion, his green eyes, his full lips and his blond hair. Impulsively, he leaned over, secured his hands on either side of Tag's face, and maneuvered their lips into a tight lock. Tag automatically opened his mouth to receive Kurt's warm tongue. It tasted of beer. They held their position for a long moment.

Then Kurt withdrew his tongue and settled back into his chair.

"Sorry," Kurt said, picking up his beer bottle and downing the contents with one long swig.

"I'm not," Tag teased. "I want more than your tongue in my mouth. Let's get out of here. Your place alright?"

Kurt ached to take off Tag's shirt and to feel his smooth young flesh. Of all the men he'd fucked, he couldn't remember one that turned him on the way Tag did. He visualized the two of them naked in bed, mauling each other, their limbs flailing as their mouths feasted on the other's flesh.

"I can't," Kurt said. It was a voice he almost didn't recognize. Ever since he moved out of the apartment he shared with Garry, he

practically never said no to sex, especially when he was as overwhelmed with desire as he was at this moment.

Tag gave him a look of anger and confusion. "You're ready to
cum in your pants, so what's the problem? And don't say 'nothing.'
I know you want me."

Kurt looked into Tag's eyes again, debating with himself
whether or not, just for one night, he could have what would un-
doubtedly be the wildest sex ride of his life. He thought: *If Tag's
videos are any indication of his versatility, this is an opportunity I can't
pass up. Garry and I are no longer a couple. Yeah, but I'd sure like to be his
other half again. Anyone with a brain would understand that being with
Tag is simply about sex. But he's the type to kiss and tell. Would anybody
believe him? Even if they didn't, rumors have a way of being perceived as
reality.*

Kurt touched Tag's chest and could feel his hard muscles just on
the other side of the sheer silk fabric of his shirt.

Tag took Kurt's hand away from his pecs and placed it on his
crotch. Kurt involuntarily inhaled as though, for an instant, he was
suddenly short of breath. He smiled hungrily.

"We both need this," Tag said.

"Not tonight," Kurt said solemnly.

"Yeah, tonight," Tag said. "I'm not used to being so assertive,"
he slipped into his guileless character, "but when I want something, I get it. And I want you."

Kurt smiled. "I want you too. But really, not tonight. We've just
met. I'm not into one-nighters."

"Tell that to someone who believes in the Tooth Fairy."

Tag leaned over and harshly kissed Kurt, first on the lips, then
on the neck. He placed his fingers on Kurt's opened collar shirt and
unbuttoned the second and third buttons. He then kissed the hollow of his neck and dragged his tongue down the V of skin exposed from his shirt.

Kurt moaned. Again he imagined sucking the cock he'd seen
dozens of times on video. He visualized letting Tag do to him what
he had done to the model who played the tough KGB operative in
the porn flick, *Peter the Straight.*

"Move it," Tag ordered. "Your hotel. Now." He stood up from
the high chair and began to lead Kurt through the throng of men.

Kurt followed, drawn along as if by an invisible leash. The noise
in the room made it impossible for him to make any verbal objec-

tions. As he passed by the swell of beautiful men, without exception they all did a double take when they saw Tag. Then they gave Kurt a look of envy when they saw him being escorted toward the door. SEX seemed to be written all over his face.

Soon they were outside. The cool fresh air was a slap in the face after the hot, smoky atmosphere of the disco. The thick metal door and the sound of traffic muffled the din from the multiple audio amplifiers inside.

"Taxi!" Tag yelled to a cab wobbling down the street, trying to avoid potholes and pedestrians. Tag held up his hand, and the car pulled up beside the two men. Tag opened the door and got in, dragging Kurt with him into the back seat. "Ambassador East," Tag said, as he closed the door.

"No," Kurt said as the car began to move into traffic. "We can't go there."

"Who's gonna care?"

"The sponsors for my show for one, if anyone sees us."

Tag sighed with exasperation. "My place then. The Marquis, Michigan Avenue," he called to the driver. He then turned and grabbed the lapels of Kurt's sport coat. He pulled him close and their lips connected.

The pang in Kurt's stomach made him want to make love to Tag right there in the car. He didn't really give a damn what the driver or anyone else thought. Kurt wanted to unzip Tag's pants and pull out his perfect cock and go to work on it without another moment's delay.

He was no longer debating whether or not to fuck or be fucked by Tag. He was no longer in control of himself. Kurt decided that he had to have Tag regardless of the consequences.

Kurt was now resigned, or rather determined, to satisfy the vigorous sexual lust of the primal beast within him. "Christ, what am I doing," he whispered as he began to covetously tear open the buttons of Tag's shirt. For a split second he divided his attention between Tag's lips and the buttons on his shirt, and the cab driver whom he could tell was unruffled by the events occurring in his back seat, which he was watching in his rear-view mirror.

"God, you're beautiful," Kurt moaned as he unhooked the last button on Tag's shirt and pulled the fabric aside to reveal the young man's hard, smooth chest. "Shit, you're built!" He pushed Tag into a corner of the car and leaned into him, kissing the deep cleft between his well-packed pecs. His tongue then migrated to the pink buttons of Tag's nipples, on which he flicked his tongue like a viper.

Kurt's moans of sexual urgency collided with Tag's quick deep breaths of impatient sensual zeal. "God, I need you to fuck me," Tag insisted. "Fuck me hard." Tag was holding Kurt's head in the vice of his hands, and directing where on his chest and stomach Kurt's face would go.

Kurt could only whimper with the expectation of sex, as he worked his tongue deep into Tag's navel.

Then the car stopped. "We're home, guys," the driver said, sounding as if he was sorry to have to miss the finale of the back-seat performance. They were parked outside the Marquis. "That'll be twelve ninety-five. Want a receipt?"

Kurt clumsily reached into his pants and withdrew a money clip. He peeled off a twenty-dollar bill. "Keep the change," he said, handing the money to the cabby, who opened his glove box and reached inside. He withdrew two condoms. "You probably aren't prepared," he said. "It's important."

Kurt smiled in appreciation.

As the hotel's valet opened the car door, Kurt practically pushed Tag out. Drunk with ecstasy, Tag lost his balance and started to fall backward—smack into the arms of Derek Laramie.

Derek laughed. "You little fucker. You get around, don't you!"

"What the fuck are you doing here?" Tag bellowed.

"Oprah. Watch tomorrow. If you don't have anything better to do." He laughed, then playfully castigated Tag, steadying him on his feet and pretending to smooth out his unbuttoned and wrin-kled shirt. He looked at Kurt. "If you're goin' up to fuck this little weasel, be warned; he may be dang good in the sack, but he's a selfish little prick. Cold and callous after he gets his rocks off, if you know what I mean."

"Fuck off, you hypocrite!" Tag shouted.

An old couple, who had apparently just returned from a night on the town, tsk-tsked as they pushed into the hotel's revolving door.

"Just warnin' your new friend 'bout what to expect after he fucks your brains out," Derek continued good-naturedly. "But you're right, it's none of my business. You two go on up to the room and I hope both your heads cave in from mind-blowing sex." He gave Tag a slight shove, which sent him bumping up against Kurt.

The frenzy that Kurt had felt in the car had dissipated. He was now clear-headed again, and felt as though he'd just come out of a fantasy dream in which Tobey McGuire and Brendan Fraser were cast in an erotic production of Butch and Sundance, but the alarm had rung and he had been sucked back into conscious reality before a single close-up of the two, wielding their pistols, had been caught on film.

"This way," Tag said, his voice now cold from the altercation with Derek.

"What do you say we skip it," Kurt offered.

"I'm just up a couple of floors. C'mon."

Kurt looked at Tag. As he absorbed the long column of the young skater's muscled torso exposed where his unbuttoned shirt was parted, he felt a frenzy of lust. "Another time. Maybe," he said, sliding his fingertips down from Tag's throat to his rippled stomach.

"You're a freaking cock tease!" Tag erupted, pushing Kurt's hand away.

"Oh my gosh!" a woman's voice mocked from behind the two men.

Startled, they both turned to see Amber, Jay, and Garry seated on a wooden bench near the lobby entrance. Again, Amber said, "Oh my gosh!" She flipped her fingers as if they were a fan and began whisking the air around her face.

Jay and Garry joined in. "Oh my gosh! Oh my gosh!" they parroted Tag's obsequious line.

Tag looked at the trio, then at Kurt. "Are you coming?"

Kurt looked at Garry. Tag read the look on Kurt's face. Then, realizing that sex was not the way to audition for Kurt's next television special, he changed his approach. "Thanks, Mr. Chrysler, for rescuing me from those brutish men who ripped at my clothes." He winked. "Now you can have your reunion with Garry. Hope I get to see you on the ice again soon."

He turned on his heels and walked up the stairs and into the hotel lobby.

Kurt put his hand on his neck and began to massage himself. "Hey, guys," he said, looking sheepish. "You're probably wondering what was going on there."

"More like what *would* have gone on if we hadn't interrupted you," Garry said.

"Now, shush," Amber ordered. "I'm sure that Kurt was only doing whatever he had to do to help us out of our predicament."

Garry nodded his head in mock agreement.

"Can we all just go over to Tricks and let me explain everything?" Kurt asked.

"Sure," Amber said. "C'mon, guys. I'm sure that Kurt's buying."

"Better zip up first," Garry said, looking at Kurt's pants.

Chapter Twenty-six

Entering Tricks, the hottest gay club in Chicago, the quartet of skaters were met with loud bass thumping of music from the disco upstairs. The main bar/restaurant room was city-dude-faux-country, with hardwood floors, wood beam ceilings, and bales of hay stacked against the walls for customers to sit on while drinking their suds. A rusted tin sign warned: DON'T DANCE ON THE TABLES WITH SPURS!

A waiter dressed in boots, chaps, silver-and-turquoise belt—and nothing more—ushered them to a small picnic table for four with a red checkered cloth and a citronella candle in the center. He winked at Garry and took his drink order first. As he left to set their orders, he looked back over his shoulder and winked again at Garry, just before bumping into another waiter and accidentally up-turning his tray of beers.

"You still make 'em blind with lust, eh?" Kurt said, looking at a blushing Garry.

"So what was your meeting like with Tag?" Amber asked.

"First off, he's a lousy actor. One minute he's Mr. Been-There-Done-That, and then he's back to his self-deprecating, 'Oh my gosh, I didn't know that men could do that with each other'," Kurt mimicked Tag to perfection. "He can't keep his double identities straight."

"So what'd we interrupt as you were getting out of the cab?" Jay asked, knowing full well what was uppermost on Garry's mind, and probably Amber's too.

"It was too surreal," Kurt began. "When I left you guys, I went to meet Tag for a drink, just to get to know him a little better. Gotta know the enemy inside and out. So to speak. Before I knew it, he was coming on to me really strong."

"Big boy like you can't take care of himself?" Garry mocked.

"Jeez, Garry, I'm only human, okay!" Kurt frowned. "Look, I'll be completely honest. Tag's a total asshole. He's treated all of you abominably. He's a dinkwad. He's using me to get ahead. On the other hand, it's a no-brainer that he's one of the sexiest dudes I've ever met. Okay? Given the circumstances, if you guys had waited at my place, as I thought you were going to do, I probably would have fucked his brains out. So spank me."

Garry looked at Kurt with longing. For the past eight months he'd thought of little else than what it would be like to be naked with Kurt again. And, seeing him at his hotel earlier that evening, he thought that he could put all of his judgments and jealousies behind him. Now, being reminded of how everyone seemed to want Kurt, and how Kurt was led by his dick, he was on faltering ground.

"Sorry." Garry shook his head. "I'm being an idiot. We're not even a couple, and I'm acting like we're still lovers or something. My fault. Sorry."

Kurt reached over and put a hand on Garry's. "You and I have really got to talk. About a lot of things."

"I've got all the time in the world," Garry said. "Name the day."

"How about tonight? Later?"

Garry smiled. He nodded his head and looked deep into Kurt's eyes.

Kurt smiled back. "First, that little prick is going to pay for what he's done to you guys."

"Any suggestions?" Amber asked. "I see him being run over by the Zamboni."

"Too messy," Jay chuckled. "Plus, an ice rink is holy ground. What we have to do is ambush his career, the way he blitzed ours. What have we got on him so far?"

As the skaters reminded themselves of all the little pieces of the puzzle that became the sum of Tag, they toted up a list of his charades. "In one column we have the young innocent poor boy who teaches himself to skate. In another column, there's the porn star and sex toy," Kurt said. "In yet another column, we have the Judas who has somehow sold you guys out to take over as the lead in your own show. Christ, what a case!"

"I never bought the self-taught skating ruse," Amber said, sipping her beer.

"It should have been obvious from that first morning in Clarksville," Jay said.

"But we were so infatuated with the possibility of having sex with him, that we ignored all the signs," Garry said.

"Ah, ha!" Kurt teased. "So you're not immune to his charms either! So don't look at me as if I've got six dicks."

Garry smiled. "It was only wishful thinking. You actually had the opportunity."

"And what did I do with that clear field? As soon as I saw you, and your beautiful eyes, I sent him on his way. You guys are witnesses!" Kurt declared to Amber and Jay. "Okay, unless you can come up with another solution, here's what I think we ought to consider."

Kurt laid out a scenario for revenge. He peppered the conversation with references to friends of friends in the porn industry in California; what his pals at the Skating Society could do to find out about Tag's past; how his upcoming television show would play a part in mortally wounding Tag's burgeoning career. By the time Kurt called the waiter over for the check, Amber was practically salivating over how they were going to make Tag wish he'd never put on a pair of skate boots.

As Kurt reiterated their blueprint for revenge, he continued to study Garry. "Okay, you all . . . come over around four o'clock, and we'll see what I've come up with from my friends at A.S.S. and in L.A. Let's call it a night, shall we?"

The skaters stood up from their picnic table. "Why don't you guys head back to the Marquis," Kurt said, addressing Amber and Jay. "I'll make sure that Garry gets back in a little while."

Garry beamed. Amber and Kurt hugged Garry and Kurt good-bye.

"I'll leave the light on." Jay winked, as he and Amber walked out of the bar.

"Wanna walk for a bit?" Kurt said to Garry.

"Sure," Garry replied.

Outside, the night air was still humid. The city lights obscured most of the stars but a crescent moon was bright enough to catch their attention. Garry and Kurt walked for a while in silence. Then Kurt spoke. "You're looking great," he said, sincerely.

"You too," Garry said. "Fame and fortune obviously agree with you."

Kurt chuckled. "It is pretty much everything it's cracked up to be, I have to admit."

"I'll bet. I saw your last HBO special. Loved your guests. What's Paul Wylie really like? And Rudy?"

"Sexy. But the most fun was having the greats from the old days. Carol Heiss . . ."

"And John Misha Petkevich," Garry completed Kurt's sentence. "Yeah, they're legends. God, what great skaters."

"I know how much you admire Dick Button. I wish I could introduce you to him. He's really super. He just seems like an asshole when he's upbraiding some skater's jumps and spins. In real life he's a doll. And you're right, he's sexy, too."

Garry smiled, remembering how he used to get chided for saying how much he liked Dick Button. The same people who teased him about Dick, heckled him about his exalted reverence for Sandy Duncan. Garry remained silent for a long while, as they ambled down the street, walking in no particular direction. Then, with a sigh, he said, "I really envy your life."

"Please don't." Kurt waved away the comment. "It's pretty exhausting being Kurt Chrysler. Don't get me wrong, I'm extremely grateful for everything I have. I've worked damn hard, and I love the fact that I have a good reputation and that I get to skate for a living. But it can't last forever. Then what'll I do?"

"You used to talk about buying an old colonial house for us in some small town in Connecticut. You wanted to become a writer. And you wanted me to become a coach and support you. Remember?"

Kurt laughed lightly. "I bought the house."

"Ask and ye shall receive, eh?" Garry smiled, mocking Kurt's charmed life. "Do you get *everything* you say you want?"

"If I don't, I didn't really want it in the first place."

"What's it like?"

"You'd love it," Kurt began. "The wrap-around covered porch you always said you thought would be great for sitting on and watching a summer rainfall. The stone fireplace in the master bedroom for snuggling up next to during the cold winter months. There's even the pond you said you'd love to have so you could skate without anyone to share the ice with."

"No," Garry said. "I meant, what's it like to get everything—and everyone—that you want? You've always been the golden boy. You simply set your mind to something and, pfft, it's yours."

"Hardly," Kurt countered. "If that were true you wouldn't have left me."

Garry abruptly stopped, which forced Kurt to stop also. He bellowed, "You are such a cocksucking bullshit artist! You're blaming me for our breakup?"

Kurt was taken aback. "Whoa."

"Fuck you *and* your fame and fortune *and* your house. It's probably filled with every little starfucking wannabe Kurt Chrysler lookalike. Just like our old apartment."

Kurt blinked. "For crying out loud, you're not going to bring that up again, are you? I made one stupid mistake. How many times do I have to say *mea culpa* and plead temporary insanity by reason of my libido?"

"I was such an idiot to think anyone as gorgeous as you would want to be monogamous with me! You deceived me!"

"I deceived myself!" Kurt cried. "I loved you so much—I still do—I thought that you would be enough to keep me satisfied! But I couldn't help myself! After I won the gold, guys were throwing themselves at me! I did the best I could not to give in, but I failed a couple of times!"

"Now it's a couple of times?"

"It's not like you didn't have opportunities, too."

Garry said, "But I placed a hell of a lot more value on our relationship. I vowed that I'd never do anything to jeopardize what we had!"

"So you were stronger than me," Kurt sighed. "You score extra points. Just because I said yes to a few—and only a few—impossibly good-looking guys, doesn't mean I loved you any less."

Garry continued walking. Kurt drew up alongside. "That was a stupid outburst," Garry said. "I'm sorry. The weird thing is that being away from you all this time I've had a chance to think about our relationship. First of all, I confess that I confused sex with love. We never talked about monogamy, or what either one of us wanted from the relationship. I just presumed too much. I guess I figured that as long I was satisfied with our sex life, then you were, too. I wasn't fair to you."

"Yes, you were," Kurt said. "I was the one who made the mistake. I was afraid to bring up the fact that as far as sex was concerned, I might sometimes need some wiggle room, 'cause I was afraid I'd lose you if I told you that. I didn't really think anyone but you would give me a boner. I was wrong."

" 'Wiggle room'," Garry snickered. "Very funny."

Kurt tittered. "Wiggle this," he said, taking Garry's hand and placing it on his crotch.

Kurt took his hand away, and Garry smiled. "One of my favorite memories is of the first time we had sex. Remember? It was the North American Skating Spectacular at the Broadmoor Hotel in Colorado Springs. You'd just won the men's title, and I was the silver medalist. As we accepted our ribboned pins and shook each other's hands, I could feel an electrical energy surge between us. Coach Larson was furious when I said that I had a splitting headache and wanted to be alone." Garry laughed. "I'm sure he caught the way we were looking at each other. I think he must have been aware of why I begged off from our usual post-competition fuck."

"You were the hottest skater I'd ever seen." Kurt smiled. "I remember sneaking over to your room and when you opened the door, wearing only a towel around your waist . . . God what a perfect body you had . . . so smooth and hard. And your lips. Jeez. You won't believe me, but I get hard whenever I think about what it felt like when our tongues met. You always tasted of mint."

They stopped walking again. Kurt and Garry stood facing each other. Both remembered how great their bodies had felt pressed tightly against the other's. "I want to taste you again, so badly," Kurt finally spoke the words that both men were thinking.

"Me too," Garry said, almost bashfully.

"Will you come home with me?" Kurt asked.

"Why?"

Kurt was taken aback. "Why not?"

"Because I'm never playing second fiddle to another man again. And it would hurt too much to say goodbye to you. In fact, I'd better go."

Garry turned and began to walk away. He had no idea where he was, or which way to head to find his hotel.

"Wait!" Kurt yelled. He rushed up from behind to grab Garry, turned him around and held him in a tight squeeze. He began to kiss Garry passionately.

"Come to my place, please," Kurt finally said. "The hotel's just around this corner."

Garry felt powerless over his desire to touch and be touched by Kurt. He leaned against Kurt the rest of the way to the Ambassador East. When they arrived at the hotel, the doorman simply tipped his hat and opened the door.

If people were staring as they made their way to the elevator, neither man noticed. Inside the elevator car, Kurt pushed his key card into the slot that allowed them access to the penthouse. By the time the doors opened into the marble foyer, they were kissing ardently, tearing at each other's clothes. As they hurried toward the bedroom, they were carried along on a current of lust and finally, with their clothes strewn along the way, they fell upon the bed and began engorging each other.

"I've missed you so much!" Garry gasped between harsh kisses from Kurt.

"Oh, babe, I've thought of you so often and how beautiful you are and how badly I wanted to be with you!" Kurt panted as he ravenously explored Garry's lips, neck and chest with his tongue. "God, you're so fucking hot. I need to fuck you. Please, let me fuck you!"

"God, yes! I want you inside of me!" Garry moaned as Kurt kissed his chest and dragged his tongue from nipple to nipple! "I've missed feeling you. Christ, I love you."

"Oh, God, I love you too!" Kurt gasped, returning to Garry's lips.

To hell with past differences and future consequences, Garry thought as he quickly and heavily sank into an abyss in which he was aware of only one thing: that there was no place else in the universe he would rather be than making love to Kurt. As he reintroduced himself to the taste and intoxicating scent of Kurt's body, and his strong chest, sinewy arms, and flat stomach, Garry begged once again, "I want you inside of me. Forever."

Without another word, and in perfect sync with each other, Kurt quickly donned a condom, anointed Garry's ass with lube and began making up for all the time they had foolishly let slip away.

Chapter Twenty-seven

"Remind me not to think of sex every time I see you." Kurt smiled as he rolled over and cradled Garry in his arms. It was morning. The two had slept fitfully between long periods of deep kisses, and energetic wrestling and reexamining each other's bodies. They were tangled in a vine of bed sheets and legs and arms. "One look and I'll have to screw your brains out again. I'll never get any work done on our project."

Garry made a drowsy sound of contentment. Kurt rested his head on Garry's chest and allowed the pads of his fingertips to linger over his lover's skin. His tongue flicked Garry's nipples. "You taste so good," Kurt groaned. He began moving his lips toward Garry's. Within moments, they were once again exchanging deep sexual satisfaction.

After nearly an hour of intense frenzy and excitement, culminating in Garry happily and greedily receiving Kurt's eight-inch tool deep inside of him, the two collapsed and once again fell asleep in each other's arms. When they awoke next, it was nearly ten o'clock.

"You stay here and rest," Kurt cooed into Garry's ear as he prepared for the pain of extricating himself from the bed. "Gotta make those phone calls I promised."

Garry held onto Kurt for a moment longer before giving in and allowing his lover to leave his side. "What can I do to help?" he asked.

"Just stay in bed. I'll order room service. Still like egg whites and hashbrowns?"

"You remembered," Garry said, now holding on tightly to his pillow. "Don't forget the salsa."

"And grapefruit juice?"

"And a rose on my tray," Garry joked.

"Don't push it. " Kurt was chuckling as he got up from the bed. He hit some buttons on a wall panel and soft classical music issued through speakers hidden in the walls. He went into the adjoining bathroom and turned on the shower.

Garry could hear Kurt making the call to room service from inside the bathroom. Then, above the din of the music and the shower raining down on the tile, Garry could hear Kurt gargle, followed by the sound of his electric toothbrush. They were sounds that Garry had forgotten that he missed. He lay in bed, staring up at the ceiling and smiling. *Nothing can be this good*, he said to himself. *It's as if we were just starting to date, but having known each other intimately in another lifetime.*

Then the telephone rang.

Garry rolled over and picked up the receiver. "Hello?" he asked. No response. "Hello?" he asked again, this time a bit annoyed because someone was clearly on the other end of the line. Garry gave up, reached back over the bed and put the phone on its cradle. One of Kurt's boyfriends? he wondered, starting to lose his perfect contentment.

The door to the bathroom opened and Kurt, naked and hard, was followed by an enveloping fog of steam. He smiled as he moved to the bed. "Just one more teensey-weensey fuck?" he asked, laying his body down on top of Garry's.

"I haven't brushed," Garry said.

"You taste fine," Kurt assured him. The two began stroking each other's bodies and grinding their solid cocks together. Garry happily let Kurt dominate him.

Then, just as both were about to climax, the doorbell rang. "Tell 'em to go away," Garry panted, clenching Kurt's ass cheeks and not allowing him to extricate himself from his body. "This is all the room service I need!"

They heard the announcement chime from the elevator door

opening, and a voice tentatively called out, "I'll just leave it in the dining room."

"Oh, Christ," Garry called as he felt his cock swelling.

"Me too," Kurt cried.

Whimpering, they discharged their loads simultaneously. Once again, they lay down together, heaving breathlessly.

After a few minutes, Garry finally said, "Okay, now I'm hungry."

"Beat you to the table," Kurt exclaimed as he jumped from the bed and ran down the hall laughing, followed by an equally jovial Garry.

"Careful not to spill coffee on your dick!" Garry admonished playfully. "I don't want that precious piece of meat to be scalded by anything other than my ass."

When they arrived at the table, their place settings had been neatly arranged. Silver domes covered their plates. Juice glasses with clear plastic wrap secured by elastic bands covered the tops. Two silver coffeepots were marked as *Regular* and *Decaf*.

"I'm starving," Garry said. "I haven't eaten since lunch yesterday. Let me have some of that jam."

With that, Kurt plunged three fingers into the jar of raspberry preserve and withdrew a glob of red jelly.

"Don't," Garry cried, catching the mischievous gleam in Kurt's eyes as Kurt slowly brought his hand toward Garry's face. "Don't you dare!" Garry giggled as Kurt moved quickly to plaster Garry's chest with the red slime. "You're sick!" Garry protested. "Stop! Don't! You're making a mess! What'll the maids say?"

Kurt got down on his knees and pressed his face against Garry's sticky skin. He smothered himself in Garry's jam-covered flesh, snorting like a pig while licking him clean.

Garry howled with laughter as he played along and his dick once again became as hard as a rubber dildo.

"My eggs are getting cold!" Garry fussed with impish protest as Kurt sat in his lap, straddling the chair. Kurt's cock quickly stuck to Garry's stomach as they kissed, the taste of jam on their tongues.

Then Kurt pulled back. He looked at Garry, turning his head to one side. "I've missed you," he said. "You're not getting away from me again."

Garry broke out in a wide smile. He didn't have to wonder if the proposal was legitimate. Kurt's look spoke volumes about his sincerity. "Fuck me again, you gold medalist, you!" Garry said, falling onto the carpet. "Lube up with raspberry jam."

Kurt smiled.

The day was half over by the time Garry got out of the shower and dressed in yesterday's underwear and jeans. When he emerged from the master bedroom, pulling on his wrinkled T-shirt and finger-combing his hair, Kurt was on the telephone and only wearing his blue jeans.

"Can you fax that to me here at the hotel?" Kurt asked into the telephone. "No, there's a private machine here in the room. You're the absolute best. I owe you big." He hung up just as Garry sidled up to him and nibbled on his nipples. "Mmmm. You smell sexy," Kurt said, inhaling the clean aroma of Garry's body.

"Good news?" Garry asked as he raised his head and kissed Kurt.

"Interesting."

"Tell me. What?"

Kurt kissed Garry back. "I'm waiting for a call from a friend in Los Angeles."

"About what?" Garry moaned with a kittenish playfulness.

"Seems your little protégé . . ." Kurt stopped when the telephone rang. He picked up the receiver. When he heard the voice on the other end, he smiled. His conversation was cryptic, and Garry sat listening to: "I see. Yikes! Where? How many? Police? *Gold on Ice*? Garry and Jay? Impossible! I've seen a few. Okay. Thanks. You're a pal."

Garry's attention was diverted by the sound of the fax machine ringing. He rose from the living room sofa and went to a desk where the machine was situated. As the sheets of paper issued forth, he picked them up one by one.

The top sheet had the seal of the American Skating Society in black and white. The text was single-spaced. It presented the personal stats of a member whose name was Mark Bennett. Age, weight, height, hair color, eye color.

Garry looked up at Kurt. "Who's this?"

"Doesn't it describe anyone we know and love?"

Garry continued reading. He stopped every few lines and looked up at Kurt with a look of incredulity. As he turned to page two, he shook his head in amazement. "Holy moly," he heard himself say. He continued reading.

Halfway down page three, Garry let out an involuntary laugh. "Sorry. It's not funny. Just stupid." He looked up at Kurt. "Let's not wait. Call Jay and Amber. Tell 'em to get over here right away. This news is just too weird."

Chapter Twenty-eight

"How could you *not* know it wasn't Garry?" Amber demanded, looking around the motel room. She made a face at the disorder.

"I was practically asleep. I told Garry that I'd leave the door unlocked for him. I wasn't expecting anyone else."

"But you said you turned the light on, for cryin' out loud," Amber cross-examined Jay.

"Only for a moment."

"Long enough to know who it was!"

"I lost all control. He was too sexy," Jay pleaded for mercy.

"Alright. So, what was he like? May as well tell all the news that's unfit to print."

"In a word: sigh! I have never, repeat *never* been ravaged by anyone like him. It was every fantasy I ever had."

"Is it possible you just haven't been screwed enough lately?" Amber asked. "Maybe you're confusing love with getting your colon cleaned out by someone with a stick of dynamite in his 501s?"

"Yeah, it was just one night. But I know there'll be more. I've been burning for this guy for what seems like eternity. Sure, it's like an impossible union. I never thought I'd get fucked by him, not in a million years. But just the same, he says he's wanted me for a long time too."

Amber sighed. "You realize that I think you're a total lunatic don't you? Him too." She sat down on the bed and took Jay's hands into hers. "Hon, he's got a ton of baggage. He's a liar and a fraud; not just to everyone who worships him, but more importantly, to himself. But you know I'll support anything that you decide to do. That's what friends do." She heaved a heavy sigh. "I don't mean to be judgmental. I'm scared, that's all. For you, and for me. And for Garry, too. This could break us all up."

"No way," Jay insisted. "In fact, Garry'll be thrilled for me. Notice he didn't come home last night."

"Lucky for both of you."

"I'm sure he and Kurt have made up. Look, we'll all get through this. But let me be the one to tell Garry."

Amber grinned. "Trust me, I wouldn't be the one to break this news to him, or to anybody else. First off, nobody would believe me. Or they'd have you locked up in an insane asylum. Where is Mr. Wonderful anyway? He should be holding your hand instead of me."

"He's afraid of being seen coming out of my room."

"Well, that's a nice start for a relationship," Amber deadpanned. "Frightened of the publicity, eh?"

As Amber was standing up and preparing to leave, the phone rang. "I'll leave you to chat in peace," she said as Jay picked up on the second ring.

"It's Garry," he said to Amber, as she was reaching for the door-knob. "Yeah?" he said into the phone. "Give me a few minutes to shower . . . I know it's late. Rough night. I'll tell you about it later."

Jay hung up, then told Amber that Kurt and Garry had some important news. They wanted them to get over to the Ambassador right away. "I'll meet you downstairs in twenty," Jay said. "Okay?"

"You don't sound too concerned," Amber said. "Aren't you worried about what they've found out? What if it hurts your new romance?"

"I hardly think that's possible," Jay said with confidence as he took off his T-shirt and moved toward the bathroom.

"Guess you *are* in love," Amber said, and she walked out the door.

Chapter Twenty-nine

"**K**nock-knock!" Jay called into the penthouse apartment as he and Amber stepped out of the elevator. The concierge had been instructed to use his master key card to allow Jay and Amber access to the penthouse suite. The foyer was empty, but Jay and Amber could hear classical music wafting from recessed speakers. "It's us," Jay announced as he walked past a lighted painting by Picasso, hanging over a hall table on which two baseball caps had been casually tossed. Cubs. Betty Bowers.

"Kurt, honey?" Amber tentatively called. "Garry, sweetie?"

Jay gave Amber a questioning look as he stepped down into the sunken living room. "Hey, sports! You around? Guys!"

"Right there!" a voice called from somewhere down the hall.

"Still making up for lost time." Jay winked at Amber, who rolled her eyes.

"There you are!" Amber called as Kurt and Garry entered, with their arms around each other's waists.

"We were just about to drink up everything in your champagne stash," Jay giggled. Looking at the two men, he enviously observed the look of contentment on their faces. "Hey, you invited us over, but if we're interrupting your reunion . . ."

Kurt kissed Garry on the cheek. "Right. No, we're cool. We've been catching up plenty," he said, looking into Garry's eyes and once again kissing his smile. "Okay, everybody have a seat. We've got a lot to discuss. Drinks? I'd highly recommend it."

"It's way early, but I've already had one shocker for the day," Amber said. "Make mine a double."

"Same here," Jay added.

"What's wrong?" Garry said, looking at Amber.

She rolled her eyes again and made a face that said, *We'll talk later.*

"Hon, would you turn down the tunes just a tish," Kurt cooed to Garry.

Presently, they were all gathered together again, peppered throughout the vast room on various chairs and sofas.

"First of all, as you can see, Garry and I have been getting reacquainted," Kurt smiled.

"You were right about a lot of things, Amber," Garry said, acknowledging that what she had suggested about what might have been the root of his breakup with Kurt was, indeed, the case. "Kurt and I talked about a lot of things that we never talked about before. So, it looks like I'll have three best friends instead of just two."

"Oh, hon, my eyes are gonna perspire," Amber said, with a sniffle. "You know I'm so happy for you. But I'm losing both of my best friends in one day! I don't know that I can handle the emptiness!"

"You'll never lose me," Garry gently protested. "Who else have you lost today?"

"Nothing. I mean no one," Jay answered the question. "But this is great news for you and Kurt. Congratulations."

"Yeah. Really. Congrats," Amber enthused. "But let's change the subject." She looked at Kurt. "You must have found some potent dish about Tag. Am I right?"

Kurt laughed. "Your analytical reasoning puts Columbo to shame." He looked to Garry. "You wanna tell 'em?"

"It's your news."

"Ours, you mean."

Amber became impatient. "Just tell us, before I drain that bottle of Cristal and I'm too anesthetized to understand what's going on."

Garry stood up and went over to the writing desk. "These came over the fax," he said, handing a dozen pages to Kurt.

"Thanks, babe," Kurt said, taking the papers, then passing them to Jay and Amber. "You can see for yourselves. This one is from my pal, the archivist at the Skating Society museum. She has reams of stuff about all the clubs and skaters who belong to the Society. When I gave her a list of names that my other pal at the Greenwood Skating Club in Tennessee faxed over, she checked her database. Sure enough, here's our Tag. That's not his name, and the picture isn't all that clear, but the info stacks up."

"So, what's it all mean?" Amber asked.

Garry said, "Remember that scandal from a few years ago, the one with the Marines who got caught doing porn flicks but they were too stupid to think the videotape would be used for anything other than for this one guy's personal pleasure? Tag—or Mark Bennett, that's his real name—is the kid who lured them to some funky apartment and got them to suck and fuck him on camera."

"*Semper Fi*, eh?" Jay smiled.

"I remember reading about that," Amber said, "but I never heard anything about any kid being involved."

"A minor," Kurt said. "The press never mentioned his name. Still, his skating club and everybody else in his town found out and sent him and his family off to another city."

"Clarksville?" Jay asked.

"The last train to," Kurt said. He took a long pull from his champagne flute. "But that's not all."

"Goody, more dish! Sorry Jay," Amber said, trying to stifle a smile.

"No, I'm curious too," Jay said. "Do tell."

Kurt said, "According to my pal in Greenwood, this Mark, or Tag was a fantastic skater. But as soon as Marine videos started selling like tickets to the International Drag Ball, his parents forced him to keep a low profile. No more regional competitions. He was destroyed."

Garry took over. "His parents moved the family into a house in Glen Ridge. They were very conspicuous by their seclusion. The neighbors hardly ever saw anyone come and go from the house. Their automatic garage door opener would let the car in and out and close before they were seen outside the vehicle. They didn't subscribe to newspapers or have mail delivered to the house. Then, one day, some birthday flowers for a neighbor were accidentally delivered to the Bennetts. They reluctantly called the florist to say there was a mistake. The florist called the rightful recipient—a neighbor—and told him the address where the delivery was made. When the neighbor knocked on their door, Mark answered and handed him the bouquet."

Kurt said, "Turns out, the neighbor was this old geezer who frequented the bushes in the local park. Apparently, he had quite an impressive gay porn collection, too. He immediately recognized Mark from his Marine tapes. He told another snoopy neighbor, and before they knew it, the Bennetts were on the road again. This time, *without* Mark, who was tired of hiding and didn't care what anyone said, as long as he could make more gay porn and skate. That's when he fortuitously ran into you guys."

"I'm so sorry for you, Jay," Amber said, giving him a motherly pat on the arm.

Jay looked surprised.

"Why? I'm thrilled we've got something on him that's potentially detrimental to his career. That is, if we use the material wisely."

Garry grinned sardonically.

"How can you say that about the man you love?"

"Love!" Jay bellowed. "I loathe and despise that asshole! What are you talking about?"

"You had sex with him last night," Amber argued.

Garry blinked. "You had sex with Tag? Are you nuts!"

"I never! What the hell are you talking about?" Jay demanded.

"You have to tell Garry the truth," Amber implored. "Oh, Garry, honey, now that you've got Kurt back, it's okay for Jay to be in love."

"I swear, I have never had sex with Tag!" Jay insisted.

"He told me all about it this morning," Amber said to Garry.

Jay exclaimed, "That wasn't Tag! I told you about Derek Laramie!"

"Derek Laramie?" Amber said, stunned. "But you said you've known him for a while and always found him to be really sexy."

"I've known *about* him, just like everybody else who watches the CMA Awards! He's hot shit! He thought I was, too. He followed me to my room last night. I left the door unlocked for Garry and instead Derek came in."

"You fucked the same guy that Tag fucked?" Garry said.

"Actually, he was pretty hot. Don't you think so Kurt?"

Kurt smiled. "I only have eyes for you."

"No seriously," Garry said. "But I didn't know he was gay."

"Those country music people are queer, in their own way," Kurt said. "They're like skaters. But they're less obvious."

"Oh, I'm so embarrassed," Amber said. She turned to Jay. "Everything you said this morning sounded like you were talking about Tag. And I just presumed . . ." She started to laugh. "Here I was thinking you'd totally lost your mind. But my support should tell you how much of a true friend I am!" she said.

Kurt looked perplexed. "This might complicate things a bit, you sleeping with Derek Laramie, I mean. He's had sex with Tag, and Tag could make things unpleasant for Derek's career if we try to out Tag and he finds that you two are involved. I don't want us to accidentally hurt someone else's career."

Jay looked at Kurt. "But why does Tag have to know about me and Derek?"

"He doesn't. But he's a smart kid. He'll use any ammo he can against you when he finds out what we're doing to get rid of him."

"What exactly do you have in mind?" Amber asked.

Kurt leaned forward conspiratorially. "Garry and I were discussing this. It's a win-win situation for all of us. Here's what I'm thinking."

The afternoon slipped by quickly. Soon it was early evening. The skaters had spent so much time discussing the elements of their plan for revenge against Tag that they didn't even bother to eat lunch. Finally, Kurt suggested they call for room service.

During dessert, Kurt said, "Can you imagine when Tag finds out that you three are the guests on my HBO special, instead of him?"

"The best part is that he'll be so amped up about doing the show that it'll come as a complete shock when he's fired and we come out skating instead," Garry said.

"Oh, I think the best part will be the way he'll leave *Gold on Ice* when he thinks he's got a shot at stardom," Amber said. "Of course, knowing Tag, he'll completely burn his bridges with Ernie and the ice show. He'll probably just tell 'em to go to hell, that he's skating on television with the famous Kurt Chrysler. What a thrill it'll be to see his face when he discovers, like the kids he had fired . . ."

"And us, too," Garry reiterated. "But of course, he's not going to take this without retribution against us."

Kurt said, "And that's where *Leaves of Ass* comes in. And *Jack the Stripper*. And, my pal, the pornographer, is overnighting the complete collection of candid Marine videos. If Tag tries for any type of retribution, those tapes are going straight to Peggy Fleming and Dick Button, and the heads of all the ice shows. Even *Mice on Ice* won't touch him after Liz Smith runs her column about the skeletons in his closet."

"Don't you all feel just a little bit of sadness for him?" Amber asked.

"Hell, no!" the men said in unison.

"But he was our friend."

"He *used* us!" Garry insisted.

"We all use people to get ahead," Amber protested. "Don't we?"

"You never did," Jay said.

"That's what I had a mama for. I could play good cop to her bad cop," Amber revealed.

"He got you fired," Garry said. "Don't you have any animosity toward him about that?"

"Of course I do. But if he could have been any better he would have been."

"Bullshit," Jay retorted. "He's a bad seed. He stepped on each of us, like we were the rungs to the ladder of his success, which we were. He may be one of the most beautiful men on the planet, but he's pure evil on the inside."

"I'm sure you're right," Amber agreed. "Still, I'm kinda sorry to see all that talent wasted."

"He'll land on his blades," Garry said. "That type usually does."

"I'm utterly exhausted," Kurt broke in. "We've got a huge day tomorrow, what with me calling Tag to say he's got the job. I'm going to have to start rehearsing him."

"If he's not really going to be in the show, why make him rehearse?" Garry asked.

"It's gotta look legit," Kurt said. "I'll practice with you guys at night. You have to know the choreography, too."

"You know, Kurt, for the first time ever, since I've known you, I'm not in the least bit jealous or suspicious," Garry said, smiling at his lover.

Chapter Thirty

"Let's face it, Ernie, I'm way too hot for you and your cheesy show," Tag said as he officially resigned from *Gold on Ice.*

Ernie sputtered a few words about Tag being an ungrateful little ice queen who owed him big time for making him into a star.

"You're the one who owes me!" Tag bellowed. "Not only did I let you put your pathetic, slimy tongue on my dick, I gave this equally pathetic, migratory, shit-house production some badly needed luster! And no, I don't have time to give you two weeks' notice! You can cruise for a while on the show's newfound reputation! Thanks to me, you've got a little credit to dine out on! At least until you get your old stars back."

Ernie was livid. He stamped out a Merit into an overflowing ashtray and cried about how he literally scraped Tag up off an ice rink and personally made him into a headliner. As far as he was concerned, Tag would never work in another touring skating show.

"Like that's a problem or something?" Tag rolled his eyes and flipped Ernie his middle finger. "I'll be stealing so much of the thunder of that aging Kurt Chrysler that I'll have my own television special before you can say Evgeny Plushenko. Hell, I'll be making so much money, I might even buy this tragic excuse for a show. So you'd better be nice to me, Ernie. I could be *your* boss in the near future."

Tag returned to his hotel room to change his clothes and ring for a cab. Determined to look his sexiest for his first time on the ice with Kurt, he selected faded blue jeans and a white tank top shirt. He accessorized with a silver medallion that was an Oriental symbol for love, which he wore on a rawhide choker around his neck. He slipped his right hand through a silver and turquoise wrist cuff.

Tag stood before the mirror and viewed his appearance. He smiled. "A perfect score of six-point-oh, if I do say so myself! And I definitely do say so! Yummy!"

He ran a hand lightly over the silky skin of his bare, round, muscled shoulders, and caressed his shirt, feeling the mass of his chest and stomach muscles under the nearly diaphanous fabric. "Hell, if I make *myself* horny, I can only imagine how Kurt is going to feel." He laughed to himself. "Who'da thunk, you devil, you!"

Tag fussed with his hair for a moment, checked his teeth, then he glanced at his watch. He picked up his skate bag and left the apartment. Outside the heat and humidity hit him hard. The doorman blew a whistle, which ushered a cab to the curb. "The ice arena," he snapped at the driver. "And, for Christ sake, don't you use deodorant! Jeez you stink. You should carry Lysol in this car!"

The driver didn't respond with words. Instead, he took the most circuitous route he knew to the arena, ostensibly to avoid major construction-caused traffic jams. He smiled sweetly when they arrived and said, "Twenty-four fifty, please."

The cool air inside the arena was heaven to Tag. He signed in with the security guard and was directed to follow the corridor through two sets of large swinging double doors to the main rink. Stepping into the vast domed stadium, he found himself at the second tier of seating. He smiled with genuine enthusiasm as he looked down and then spotted a lone figure on the ice below.

Indolently skating from a right forward inside edge to a left forward inside edge, then quickly maneuvering to his left and right back outside edges, Kurt Chrysler was covering the ice. His scratch spin and back sit spin were executed with ease, as was his transition to a Death Drop. Tag was impressed. He stood for a long moment, a private witness to the master running through what was once his competitive free-skate long program, in the utter silence of the building.

When Kurt completed his program with a Reverse Double Lutz into a Russian Split Lutz, he circled the rink a few more times to cool down. He glided down the right side of the barrier with his knees slightly bent, shifting his weight from his left foot to his right, rotating his arms and shoulders in a right inside edge, then a left outside edge. Right. Left. Right. Left. Repeating the movements, until he was suddenly interrupted by the sound of one person applauding.

It was Tag, giving a standing ovation. "Come on down," Kurt called.

Tag walked down to the arena floor. He leaned over the barrier wall. "Oh my gosh," he said. "You are so sexy on the ice! Off the ice, too! I didn't mean only when you're skating. Oh my gosh, I'm so nervous that I'm babbling!"

"There's no need to be nervous," Kurt said. "And, if I'm sexy, there must be a new word to describe how fabulous *you* look!" he said, his eyes absorbing the way Tag's chest filled out his shirt, and his butt put shape into his jeans.

"Do you think it's too much for the audience?" Tag asked.

"I'm your only audience today. Trust me, it's not too much." Kurt showed a lascivious smile. "For my audiences, you can even be a little more seductive. Remember, this is for cable television. We can get away with tons more than ABC, so go for it. You've got a lot to show. We'll score huge ratings if you let it all hang out. So to speak."

Tag gave a toothy Dennis Quaid smile as he locked eyes with Kurt and telegraphed his complete understanding of what he knew were his major physical attributes. "So I'll just lace up and join you in a sec," he said, sitting down on one of the cushioned theatre seats.

Presently, Tag and Kurt were moving across the surface of the ice. "Woo-hoo!" Tag roared at the top of his lungs. "This is the greatest rink I've ever skated on! It's huge! The ice couldn't be any better!" As if to demonstrate his utter ebullience, he suddenly vaulted into the air. His left leg crossed over his right, his arms hugged his body, and his head looked over his left shoulder as he opened his arms and legs and landed on the back inside edge of his left blade, with his right leg extended out.

"Just from watching videos of my competitions, eh?" Kurt smiled, indulging Tag's vitality and excitement.

"And lots of practice," Tag added.

"Well, that's what we're here for, so let's get to it," Kurt reminded. "Now here's the choreography I've planned for your first solo. For your music, I've selected a medley of the theme songs to *Sex and the City*, *Six Feet Under*, *Queer As Folk*, and *Powerpuff Girls*. How's that?"

He began to demonstrate the various spins and combinations in the program, until he was suddenly interrupted by Tag.

"Gee, Kurt, I'm sorta disappointed. I have a whole program choreographed in my head that I know'll be sensational. I was sort of planning on doing that in the show. And since I'm technically a star, even though I'm only billed as a guest star, I think I should be able to do whatever number I want to. That is of course, if you don't have any objections."

Kurt was completely taken aback by Tag's chutzpah, but he tried not to show how overwhelmed he was with stupefaction. "Yeah. Well. Ah. Sure. I guess you can at least show me what you've planned. But we have a really famous choreographer who's worked a long time with the music director to make this special a big hit. You have to let them and the producers be the final word."

"They'll love my routine. So will you. I promise. So here goes." Tag glided to the center of the ice. "This'll be performed to the music from *Thoroughly Modern Millie*. Think of that when you watch me."

By the time Tag had completed his last scratch spin, Kurt grudgingly admitted to himself that the program was quite good. His opinion was reinforced when Tag came to a stop, and the sound of people applauding echoed over the ice. Kurt and Tag simultaneously turned toward the sound. "Bravo!" two male voices called in unison. "Far out!" said one voice. "That was sensational!" said the other.

Tag beamed. Kurt was ashen. "My producers. Harlan and Markus."

Kurt skated over to the barrier with Tag pulling up the rear.

"Who's the champ?" one of the men asked, giving his partner an elbow in the ribs and dividing his attention between Tag and Kurt.

"This one'll be good for ratings," the other man said, returning the jab to the ribs as if their actions weren't an obvious gesture that they liked Tag for his perspiration-soaked tank as much as his authority on the ice.

Kurt made the introductions. "Harlan Walhberg. Markus Schnell. I'd like you to meet Tag Tempkin. He's from *Gold on Ice*."

"What's a sport like you doing in a pile of dog crap like that?" said Harlan, who, Kurt knew, had about as much tact as hair on his balding head.

"Oh, I'm outta that show," Tag said. "Now I'm in *your* show."

"That a fact?" said Markus, who had a pronounced overbite and large round eyes that immediately reminded Tag of Homer Simpson's nefarious boss. "Well, aren't we the lucky ones," he added, focusing more on the triceps of Tag's sculpted arms than his green eyes.

"I guess you guys should know, since Kurt . . ."

"What brings you guys down here before rehearsals officially begin?" Kurt quickly asked, desperately trying to avoid any more interaction than necessary between Tag and the producers.

Harlan said, "Just wanted to tell you some good news. We got Marina Anissina and Gwendal Peizerat to come in from Moscow to do the special. Is he adorable, or what! We're still trying for Michael Weiss, too. Should know by the A.M."

Markus said, "To hell with Michael. This Tag kid's just as good."

Tag blanched. Rather than being pleased to be mentioned in the same sentence as Michael Weiss, his ego was bruised and his curiosity peaked about why the producers didn't know he was in the show. "Michael's old," Tag said, flippantly. "Plus, he's too serious. No fun. Audiences want more than a great performance, they want star quality, which I've got in spades."

"Indeed, you do," Harlan smiled, reaching out to finally shake Tag's hand. What he really wanted was to lick the beads of sweat off of Tag's underarms.

"You're a clever one, Kurt," Markus said as he, too, took Tag's hand and pumped it a few times. Markus flashed on what Tag must look like under his damp shirt. "You saved a good surprise for us. Well done."

"So, we'll leave you two alone." Harlan winked at Kurt. "We'll let you know about the Ruskies." Looking lecherously at Tag, he added, "I'm tempted to call Michael's people and say forget the whole thing. We may already have a star."

"You may at that," Tag said with more than a small degree of bravado. "Kurt said I'm the guest star."

"I have every confidence that he did, indeed." Harlan smiled, looking at Kurt knowingly.

Harlan and Markus took one last long look at Tag and then turned around. They whispered and giggled all the way down the aisle and out the door.

"Well, well, well," Tag said, this time in a tone that meant *what the fuck's going on*? "They must not be very good producers if they didn't know that I'm your guest star."

Kurt's mind raced. "Don't worry. They're nobodies," he finally said. "They're just the co-producers. The HBO execs are the real guys in charge. Those two duffuses are just upwardly mobile pricks. Used to be at Disney, I think. The guys probably didn't get the memo."

"Well, I'll be damned if I let my show be spoiled by having that Michael Weiss character around," Tag said.

"*Your* show?" Kurt smiled. "Aren't we kind of getting a little ahead of ourselves?"

"Oh my gosh!" Tag exclaimed. "Listen to me! Don't pay any attention to what I say. I'm just so thrilled to be on the ice with you— even if I wasn't here to be in a TV special—although, of course, I am—I'd still be completely out of my mind. I hope I never come down from this high. This is the best thing that ever happened to me." Then, in a soft voice that reeked of conspiracy, he added, "And of course having you kiss me the other night. Even though it was wrong of me to push myself at you the way I did, I can't regret it. I only do those things when I really, really, really, like somebody."

Kurt smiled. "Oh, I'm sure," he said.

"Hey, since we're all alone in this big ol' arena, can you show me something," Tag cooed as he sidled up beside Kurt.

Kurt was on his guard, but some things were unavoidable. Looking at his self-professed protégé, Kurt realized that his dick had completely filled his pants. He swallowed hard. His body language was not lost on Tag.

"I could use your help on my rotation before the landing of that last triple Lutz-triple toe combination," Tag said with about as much sexual suggestiveness as if he'd just implied that Kurt should teach him about blowjobs. "My problem begins when I spring back into the air for the second jump. Here, let me show you."

Two hours of rehearsal passed quickly. During the majority of the session, Kurt divided his attention between reflecting on the great sex he'd had with Garry, and the great sex he could have with Tag. He realized there was no use trying to pretend that even being completely satisfied with his lover didn't mean that other guys didn't turn him on. Although he was determined not to act on his desire to taste Tag's dick and to fill his ass with his meat, he was still conscious of his struggle to be a one-man man.

Tag didn't help matters. As Kurt glided over the ice, Tag was always close by. Even when they were working on their individual routines, Tag would slide by Kurt and make a comment about his great smile, or how much he admired Kurt's strength, or the sexy shape of his butt. Kurt was so horny, that if Tag's teasing had occurred forty-eight hours earlier, he would have nailed his ass right on the ice. But now there was Garry, again. Kurt prayed that Tag wouldn't do something that he would be too weak to resist.

When they got off the ice and finally called it a day, Kurt yelled to the fire sprinklers on the ceiling of the men's room, "I'm *not* a whore!" He sounded a lot like the Elephant Man imploring, "I am *not* an an-i-mal!"

Chapter Thirty-one

When Tag arrived at the arena the next morning, his dressing room contained an enormous array of cut flowers arranged in a cheap green vase. "Oh my gosh!" he exclaimed to Kurt. "From you?"

Kurt shrugged his shoulders. "Mine are supposed to arrive the day we shoot the special."

Tag plucked the envelope from a plastic fork in the center of the colorful garden. He pulled out the card and skipped the message. "They're from Harlan!" He read the message to himself first, and then decided to share the last line. "Expect a forty share!"

Tag scrunched up his face. "What the hell does that mean?"

"Expect huge ratings," Kurt said.

"He sure wants me to feel welcome," Tag said. He thought about the private part of the message that he hadn't read aloud. "Those co-producers are friendly. Not anything like you said."

"I never said—"

"I'd better phone Harlan. Will you excuse me for a few minutes?" Tag said as he opened the dressing room door and practically pushed Kurt out.

* * *

The next few days were filled with grueling work. Although their call time was for seven A.M., Tag wandered on to the ice closer to eight. The following week, when the principal cast was set, the choreographer waited impatiently each morning, for all of his charges to be assembled before going through the day's skating routines. Kurt's reputation for being cooperative and professional was true to form. However, on more than one occasion, the choreographer had to take him aside and plead that he discuss Tag's lack of teamwork and his snubbing of Michael Weiss.

Tag also managed to leave early each afternoon. He complained of an ache in his groin or a blister on his ankle. Or he had to get the screws tightened on his boots. Regardless of whether or not he'd achieved the level of accomplishment demanded of the Russians—or Michael Weiss, whom he loathed because he was nearly overshadowed by Michael's brilliance—Tag found an excuse to leave by teatime.

At least Tag kept busy. He had so many maladies and personal errands it kept him and Kurt apart after hours. His ducking out before they wrapped each day meant that Kurt could hang around and wait for Garry, Jay, and Amber to sneak in for their nighttime rehearsal sessions.

It was a grueling schedule for Kurt, rehearsing all day with Tag and the other cast members, then working late with his friends. He rationalized that at least he had time to spend with Garry.

"Where does that little queen go every day?" Jay asked late one afternoon.

Kurt shrugged his shoulders. "Everybody's actually glad when he leaves. They all hate him. Michael thinks Tag's getting special treatment because he's rumored to be my pet. I'd like to know who spread that insane idea. Probably Harlan, that hairball who masquerades as a co-producer."

Each night, after the quartet had spent four hours learning what the choreographer had given Kurt to teach his friends, they changed their clothes and went to dinner. It was either room service at the hotel, or at Mary's Place, a popular bistro that was their favorite, not because of the food, but because it was decorated with Mary Tyler Moore memorabilia. The small establishment was created to resemble the set of her 1970s sitcom. Even the waitresses wore MTM smiles and their hair had to be worn either as Laura

Petry, Mary Richards, or under a nun's habit, à la Mary's Elvis Presley movie role.

Each night, while Kurt and Garry stared at each other and *played here's the plane, open the hangar* with French fries or breadsticks, Jay and Amber talked about what they'd heard from the chorus kids at *Gold on Ice.*

Ernie had lured Kerry Benjamin back to the show. He had recuperated from his broken ankle and was thrilled to be back on the road after doing temp secretarial work in the New York office of Miramax Films.

Then, one evening while they were all sipping Chianti and savoring an asparagus risotto, Amber looked up when two men entered the restaurant. "Holy cow," she said in a controlled panic. "Don't make it look obvious, but get an eyeful of what just came in the door."

Like characters in slasher films who are vehemently warned not to go down into the basement of a house where unspeakable murders have taken place, the three men all turned around together.

Tag and Harlan were being ushered through the room. The table at which they were seated was already occupied, by another man. Markus.

"Christ, has he been here for a while?" Kurt asked. "Think he's seen us?"

"Can hardly miss the great Kurt Chrysler," Amber offered. "How many autographs have you signed already tonight?"

"God, we're trapped," Jay said.

"What the fuck could they be doing together?" Kurt asked without expecting a reply. "I've noticed that they were kind of smitten with him."

"Guys, I hate to be paranoid . . ." Amber started to say.

"It's time for a little perception check, right?" Garry interrupted. "We've been really stupid and naive and trusting, so I think paranoia is totally appropriate."

"So what if dear ol' Tag, or Ian or whatever his name is, has spread his cheeks for those two pervs in exchange for a bigger role on your show?" Amber looked at Kurt who looked incredulous. "Hey, hon, not that anything's going on, but wouldn't you rather consider the possibility and take precautions?"

Kurt sat silent for a long moment. He stared into space, his mind clicking away a montage of images that might support Amber's theory. Finally, he said, "I just remembered something. The other day, after Tag left the ice, Michael skated over to me. He said, 'My gaydar's on super high alert. Make sure yours is too.' "

Amber made a face. "Fantasize all you want my super-stud darling, but here's a news bulletin; Michael's the only skater whose sexuality I'm on the fence about."

"Please," Kurt said. "I'm not a complete moron. I know he wasn't coming on to me. I think he was looking out for me, offering a red flag or something."

"To be guarded around Tag?"

Suddenly, Amber looked up and flashed her grab 'n' grin publicity shot smile. "Oh my gosh, if it isn't Tag Tempkin!" She squealed, as if happy to see an old friend.

Tag was at the table smiling back. "It's the old gang. What are you guys still doing in town? I mean, I'm really happy to see you, but I thought you would have been glad to go home and get off the road."

"We're not in any hurry," Jay said. "Plus, we couldn't leave without having a farewell dinner with Kurt."

Kurt said, "We've been so busy that this is the first opportunity I've had to get together with them."

Tag stood behind Kurt and placed his hands on the skating star's shoulders. He gave them a quick squeeze. "Yeah, this blessed man has been up to his ass, so to speak." His tone of voice implied that they were fuck buddies, but the others knew better. "Guess you've heard the news."

"What news is that?" Garry forced an Amber-like smile. He was not about to give Tag the satisfaction of thinking that he was the topic of every conversation.

"Nothing much. I just sort of got rich and famous."

"You're only getting union scale." Kurt looked up at Tag. He tried not to show that he was perturbed by the younger man's ego.

"For now," Tag checked himself. "But when Kurt's special airs I'll be in millions of homes around the world." He was careful to refer to the program as *Kurt's special*. "He told you about our working together, didn't he?"

"Yes," Amber said. "We think it's amazing. Kurt certainly knows star shine when it flashes before his eyes."

Tag gave an extra-wide smile when Amber used the word star.

He took it personally. "I'll never be able to repay him for all that he's done," he added, giving Kurt another squeeze on his shoulders.

"Heard that one before," Jay said, the statement not lost on Tag.

"Hope you don't repay him the way you repaid us," Garry sniped.

Tag smiled. "You guys should be happy that you're out of that pissy show. It wasn't doing anything for your careers. Now you're kind of forced to find something worthy of your talents. Still, I defended you to Ernie, but you know how he is. When I have my own special, I might call you up to be guest stars. How'd you like that?"

"What a lovely bone!" Amber mocked. Tag didn't get the less-than-subtle message. "Imagine being on the television, in a skating special starring Tag Tempkin? Marvey-do!" Amber's tone reeked of condescension.

Tag looked at Amber as if she were less than the crumb from a breadstick on Garry's lips. "Tag has to be careful of what he wishes for, because he usually gets what he wants," he said, speaking of himself in the third person. "But I'm sure you've all noticed that."

"We've noticed that you're hanging out with Harlan and Markus. Glad you've made friends with the executives, 'cause you're not doing such a hot job with the cast," Kurt said. "You've got to start being on time for rehearsals, Tag. I mean it. If you're not there for the taping, it could cost HBO about a gazillion dollars."

"I'm sorry. It's just that those people in the show don't like me." Tag frowned. "The Russians intimidate me. 'You a soft American! We tough Russian'," he imitated the speech pattern of Marina Anissina and her partner Gwendal Peizerat. "And that Michael Weiss is a fart, who shouldn't be in the special at all! He said mean things about you, so I avoid him."

Kurt narrowed his eyes and gave Tag a look of skepticism. "Michael and I are old friends. He'd never say an unkind word about anyone."

"Well, he seems to think that he should have his own TV special. I told him that you were my friend and that he was totally wrong to say that you're a has-been. I think he's just jealous. And, he's probably hot for you. Maybe you should show a little interest in him. Oh, but then your ex-boyfriend would be upset," Tag said snidely, looking over at Garry. "Oh my gosh! I'm ignoring my hosts." Tag smiled. "They're not as butt ugly as I thought when we first met. *Ciao*. Watch me on the special!" he called over his shoulder, drawing attention to himself from the other diners.

"Suck my nads," Amber said, when Tag was no longer within listening range.

Chapter Thirty-two

After a weekend break, the cast of Kurt Chrysler's special returned to the arena for one more week of rehearsals. The atmosphere was less than convivial.

Kurt's shows were famous for having a family-like spirit. The members of various previous casts adored each other and usually remained friends long after their programs aired. But this early Monday morning, Kurt felt a definite negative vibration among his skaters.

Instead of returning Kurt's warm greetings, the Russians simply gave a non-verbal grunt. "Okay, they had too much vodka last night," Kurt said to himself.

"Hey, Michael, how's the new baby?"

This was greeted with a simple but cold, "Why?"

From Timothy Goebel, Kurt only received a yawn and deep sigh in response to his attempt at a morning high-five.

The day progressed with each skating star simply phoning in their performances. Except for Tag, who Kurt thought must have taken his suggestion to be more serious. Tag appeared to be more accepted by his castmates too. At least they were talking to him. But they weren't talking to Kurt.

At precisely four o'clock, as was his routine, Tag announced that he had to leave. "I'm out of contact lenses," he said, making another excuse.

"Please remember that the crew is coming by first thing in the morning to do up-close and personal interviews with each of us," Kurt called after Tag. To Kurt's unhappy surprise, the Russians both called out testily, "Give him break. Nobody stupid enough to forget interview."

Kurt was taken aback and the entire cast knew it. They simply turned away and presented him with cold shoulders. "What?" Kurt said to the choreographer. "God, the vibes have been like daggers all day."

"What do you expect? They're really hurt by your interview with *The National Enquirer*."

"The what?" Kurt asked, bewildered. "It's the same old publicity stuff I always do before a show airs."

With her lips pursed in contempt, she reached deep into her canvas shoulder bag and withdrew a copy of the tabloid that had been folded in half. "Not a nice thing to do," she said, slapping it across Kurt's chest and then turning on her heels.

The paper fell into his hands. Kurt held it in front of him and his eyes grew wild with anger. The Russians walked by and said something in Russian that he didn't understand—except for his name.

"Where'd they get this stuff?" Kurt ranted to his audience of Amber, Garry, and Jay. "Yeah, I spoke to a reporter the other day, but it was supposed to be for publicity about the special."

"You've certainly got publicity," Amber said.

"But this makes me sound as if I'm some kind of monster! I never said Michael was a 'hot massage oil love machine'! I distinctly recall saying 'Michael's the eye candy in the show, and that boys liked him as well as girls. I said I'd open my closet for him, if I had one. But I was being facetious. And the words riding crop were never used in the same sentence with Timothy!"

"You should know better than to kid around with those tabloid morons," Jay said. "They take a kernel of what you say and twist it around until it suits their agenda."

"No wonder Michael's upset with me! And Timothy. Yikes! I swear to God, I never said 'Dinkwad Munchkin!' My reputation for being the Betty White of the ice is gone! People believe what they read in these rags. I know this is why Harlan has called me to his office tomorrow."

"You can certainly point out all the nice things that you said," Amber said sarcastically: " 'Tag Tempkin is everything I ever wanted to be,' she quoted his alleged comments. " 'He's a once-in-a lifetime talent whose charm and elegance on the ice is matched only by his generosity to other skaters. If there was a Mister Congeniality Award from the A.S.S., he would be the hands-down winner'."

"Jesus Christ!" Kurt put his hands over his face. "Can you imagine me saying those words?"

Reading allowed from the paper, Jay picked up where Amber left off. " 'Chrysler, an openly gay skater said, 'Tag's a true star, alright. Plus he's about the sexiest Dirt Devil on two blades.' A pal confirmed, 'Kurt says Tag is pretty darn distracting to him, and to all the boys.' Chrysler's shows are known to be 99.9% gay. A source close to one of the behind-the-scenes technical people said, 'Kurt has made it clear that it's tough to concentrate on his quad/triple/double combination when he's drooling all over the ice!' Another pal of the star said, 'Kurt's got it bad for Tag. All he talks about is how he'd hang up his skates and give up his TV specials if Tag agreed to marry him.' "

"It's the end of the world," Kurt lamented. "After my meeting tomorrow there won't be any more specials. Sorry guys. There goes your part in the show too. He's really done it this time, hasn't he?" Kurt gave a heavy sigh. "Betcha Tag is the new star of *Chrysler's Ice*. Or, should I say, *Tag Along: An Evening of Duplicitous Cocksuckers on Ice*."

That night, Garry and Kurt lay together in their bed enfolded in each other's arms. Although they were both hard, and they kissed tenderly, neither initiated sex. Their minds were spinning with thoughts about Kurt's upcoming meeting with the executives of his show and they simply wanted to feel the security of being held in loving and protective arms.

Morning arrived and found the two men nuzzled together in their spooning position. Kurt's right biceps was a pillow under his lover's neck. His other arm held Garry at the waist. Even before returning to consciousness, Kurt was somehow aware of Garry's smooth skin against his bare body. Involuntarily, his free hand had begun to caress Garry's stomach and then he reached down to find his lover's cock, prominent and solid.

In the moments before comprehending precisely where he was, as he felt his body being stroked, Garry began to make sounds of contentment. He rolled over and, with his eyes still closed, found Kurt's lips and slipped his tongue into his mouth. The two wrapped each other in their arms and kissed passionately, their sleepy vocal chords issuing deep guttural sounds of satisfaction. "Good morning, you," Garry finally said.

Kurt smiled. He was nose to nose with Garry. "The only thing good about it, is you," he whispered, touching Garry's chest with one hand and his cock with the other hand.

Despite the anxiety that Kurt was feeling about his impending meeting with the HBO executives, he couldn't resist sex first thing in the morning. He was always at his horniest between the time when he woke up, and when he had to tear himself out of bed. There was something about being in a bed that turned him on with a fierce emergency for sex.

Without another word, Kurt drew his face down to Garry's stomach. He kissed his abs and felt Garry's throbbing penis hitting his throat. Kurt moved down further and began licking Garry's ball sack.

Garry moaned with pleasure. His hands reached down to touch Kurt's shoulders.

Kurt drew his tongue over Garry's pubic hairs and up the side of his pulsating flange. When he reached the head of Garry's cock, he opened his mouth and sucked in the whole package. His tongue could feel the contours of the meat, and his own cock felt ready to explode.

In a short period of time, Garry started to whimper with the sound that always preceded a mind-crushing climax. He jerked his head from side to side as he tried to stave off the ultimate pleasure. He was helpless. He felt his hot load rising to the surface. The pressure was accelerating until, with a loud cry from the depths of his soul, his body ejaculated an enormous load.

Hyperventilating, and still whimpering, he pulled his cock out of Kurt's mouth and slightly tugged on Kurt's elbows to bring him back up to the head of the bed. "Now you," he said.

Kurt sat up and straddled Garry's waist. With one hand he

worked his own meat and with the other, he grasped at Garry's pecs and nipples. He began to grind his hips and slide his cock through the tunnel of his hand, as if he were fucking Garry's ass. Gritting his teeth and whimpering as Garry had moments before, Kurt could hear his own heart beating through his chest. Then, suddenly, he threw his head back just as he gave up his load.

"Oh, yeah," Garry moaned along with Kurt. "That's a boy! Give it all up! So much! My man. My very own hot man."

Kurt heaved a huge sigh. He looked down at his semen puddled on Garry's stomach and oozing down his pecs. His eyes moved to Garry's, and he smiled. "Whoa, man," he sighed. "Whew!"

Garry reached down and put his fingers in the sticky fluid. He made little circles, massaging Kurt's cum into his skin. "I love it when you shoot all over me," he said, bringing his fingers up to his lips and sucking on them. "They say you can't live on love. It certainly tastes good."

Kurt sniggered as he lay down on his back next to Garry. Both men were still breathing rapidly. "This would be a perfect day, if . . ."

"It'll work out." Garry tried to sound positive.

Kurt looked up at the ceiling with its crown moldings and Victorian chandelier. He wondered how his star could be shining so brightly one day, and the next, have it crash and burn out. He looked at the digital clock on the bedstand. He sighed. "Better get this thing over with," he said, sitting up and resting on his elbows, then leaning over to give Garry a kiss.

"Hey. I'll always be here for you," Garry said.

Although Kurt smiled, he still felt a deep sadness about his future as an ice-skating icon. However, he also felt a surge of gratitude toward Garry. "I'm hitting the shower. You rest a while."

The HBO executives were in temporary offices in the Pliable Plastics building on Concord Street. Kurt arrived by cab. He paid the driver and walked up three steps to the smoked glass doors of the building. He stood for a moment looking at his reflection in the double doors, adjusting the knot on his necktie. He opened the door and stepped into the cool lobby. A security guard in a blue uniform stood at a lectern in front of the elevator with his thumbs hooked over his leather gun belt.

Kurt first looked at the office directory on the wall. He didn't see a name that matched any of the men he expected to meet. "Excuse me," he said, walking toward the guard. "Do you know where I can find the offices for HBO? Specifically Harlan Wahlberg?"

The security guard was a well-built black man with bright eyes and perfect white teeth. He smiled. "I know you," he said. "My boyfriend and I are huge fans. That's your special they're doing here, isn't it?"

Kurt smiled back. "Well, that remains to be seen. But I'm trying. God knows, I'm trying."

"We've seen every one of them. Wouldn't miss a Kurt Chrysler special even if it was on opposite *Six Feet Under*. Just go up to the tenth floor." He looked at his clipboard and flipped through a few pages. "They're in room 1027."

Kurt noticed a record book with a lot of names and times of arrival and departure next to them. "Want me to sign in, Franklin?," Kurt asked, having read the guard's name on his I.D. badge.

The guard pushed the up button on the elevator. "Not necessary, Mr. Chrysler. I'll vouch for you. Anyway, my boyfriend would only come down here and tear it out for your autograph," he cackled.

The elevator car arrived with a ping and a green light. Kurt smiled and thanked the guard for his help. "I'll see you on the way out," he said, pushing the button that was imprinted with 10. The doors closed and Kurt could feel his sphincters tighten.

"Wait a minute," he said aloud. "I'm Kurt Chrysler. I'm famous. Why should I be nervous?"

Too quickly the ping sounded again and the floor number appeared in a small rectangular box above the pad of buttons. The doors parted and Kurt stepped into the hallway. He walked to the right and found a door that had #1027 painted in black. He took a deep breath as he placed his hand on the knob. He pushed the door open.

Seated at the reception desk was a bleached blond young man wearing a hands-free telephone head set. He smiled and less than furtively looked Kurt up and down. He admired what had just walked through the door. Kurt smiled back and before he could identify himself, the young man beat him to it. "May I get you some coffee, Mr. Chrysler?"

"Great. Sure," Kurt said as the boy eagerly slipped off his headset and walked a few paces to a Mr. Coffee machine that sat on a small glass table. He picked up a black mug with gold lettering.

Kurt could see that it said *Sex and the City*. Kurt wondered if the boy's choice of mugs was a veiled come-on. He decided it didn't matter. The young man handed the cup to Kurt.

"I'm Scott, if you need anything . . . Oh, let me just tell Mr. Wahlberg that you're here," the boy said, and returned to his desk. He pushed an extension number on the keypad and announced Kurt's presence. "It was only a moment ago," the boy explained into the mouthpiece, obviously being reprimanded for not letting his boss know the very instant that Kurt arrived. "No sir. Yes sir. Right away, sir."

The kid's face was bright red. "Harlan wants you to come right in. I'm so sorry I kept you waiting."

"You didn't keep me at all," Kurt said, feeling a genuine distress for the put-upon young man. "I'll tell Harlan how great you were to me," Kurt said. "I promise."

The young man smiled broadly. "You're just as nice as everybody says," he beamed. "And I don't believe a word they write in those rags!"

Kurt's smile faded slightly. "Thanks Scott," he said, reaching out to shake the young man's hand. They stopped for a moment outside Harlan's office. "Wish me luck," Kurt said, looking into Scott's brown eyes.

"He's in one of his usual rages this morning," Scott warned as he knocked on the door and then opened it for Kurt.

As Kurt entered the room and closed the door behind him, Harlan looked up and gestured for him to take a seat in one of the two chairs opposite the desk. Harlan's office was relatively small and only had a white leather love seat below two side-by-side windows. White vertical blinds accented the white wall on which a couple of poorly framed posters of *The Sopranos* and *Oz* were hanging askew.

Harlan leaned back in his executive desk chair. His elbows rested on the chair's arms. His fingers were in a *here is the church here is the steeple* position, and he was talking rapidly into the mouthpiece of his own hands-free telephone head set. "It's your ass if the ratings aren't better on Thursday," he barked at whoever was on the other end of the line. "Of course you're responsible for the world staying home to watch that piece of shit special. Do what you have to do to make 'em stop fucking for an hour and watch

Mariah!" He abruptly leaned forward and pushed a button on his telephone while simultaneously taking the headset off and standing up.

"Kurt!" he exclaimed, reaching out for his star's hand. He noticed the coffee mug. "That little shit gives you coffee and not me! Figures!" Harlan complained and picked up the telephone. "Coffee," he barked.

"You've got a great assistant out there," Kurt said, keeping his promise to Scott.

"Think so?" Harlan said, looking bewildered, as if he'd never even considered the possibility. "At least he's a bit of eye candy, eh?"

Kurt smiled. "Whatever turns you on."

"That, my friend, is why I've asked you to come over today," Harlan said.

Kurt was prepared for the worst.

"Who's gonna turn you on? Audiences I mean, after the kind of story that ran in the *Enquirer*?"

"I swear, I never said any of the things they printed in that trashy rag!" Kurt challenged. "It's a huge fabrication. I'm sure you're upset. I know I'm history. If I could get my hands on that son-of-a-bitch . . ."

"Whoa. Stifle for a second," Harlan said. "I think you need a doggie downer. Who said anything about me being upset over the piece?"

"But the special? My shows are always family events. My reputation."

Harlan laughed. "At long last, Kurt Chrysler has an edge! And I don't mean on your skate blades! Quite frankly, Kurt, the test audiences for your last show all pretty much rated you the same way. For skating, ten. For balls, three. Sorta like that song in *A Chorus Line*." He laughed at his own joke. "People see you as Mister Goody Two Shoes. You're the freakin' Pat Boone of the skating world. A Sandy Duncan-eating-Wheat-Thins-in-a-fake-crop-field, for Christ sake. Boring!"

Kurt was taken aback. He cherished his image. Although he was out as a gay man, families adored him. He thought it was because of his clean-cut character. "So why am I here? I expected you to fire me."

Harlan looked completely stunned. "Fire you?" he repeated.

"Why would I do that? After that *Enquirer* piece, half the country'll be tuning in to see the show. Enquiring minds'll wanna know if you're as much of a shit as the paper said."

Kurt looked perplexed. "Why summon me to your office?"

"I need your help." Harlan sounded as though he were about to cry. He checked himself when the door to his office opened and Scott brought in a mug of coffee on a tray. "Where are your manners!" he shouted at Scott. "What about a cup for Mister Chrysler!"

"I'm fine," Kurt immediately responded. "Scott made me the best cup of coffee I think I've ever had."

"Oh," Harlan said. Then, not knowing what else to say, he bellowed at Scott, "Aren't you forgetting something?"

Scott looked at him blankly.

"Here's a hint," Harlan said as if speaking to a four-year-old. "It's brown and it's cold."

Your asshole, Kurt wanted to say.

Harlan waited a beat. He rolled his eyes and waited for a response from Scott. "It's as plain as the *two* cups of coffee on my desk!"

"You want me to take your old cup?" Scott asked.

"Sharp as a tack, this one!" Harlan jeered, as if his assistant wasn't in the room.

Scott picked up the mug that read *Hallmark Sucks* and walked out of the room.

"Great kid," Kurt said.

"Yeah. The best. Now, we were talking about this favor I need."

Kurt leaned forward in his seat, now feeling as though he was the one in charge.

"How do I say this," Harlan gulped. "I need you . . . to get that fucking . . . Tag Tempkin off my freakin' ass!"

Kurt was stunned. "Tag? What's going on. I thought you two . . ."

"Yeah, he thinks so too. Don't get me wrong, he was probably—make that *definitely*—the best fuck I ever had. But he's so fucking manipulative. Hey, you don't fuck a fucker, so to speak. He's a first-class asshole, and it takes one to know one. Know what I mean? So there's not room for two of us involved with the same show. He even had his journalist friend from *The Nashville Notice* call in some favors to get that *Enquirer* story filed. He had the nerve to say, and I quote, 'Your freebies with my ass are over. Get rid of Chrysler and make me the star of the show or your dick'll fall off before I ever let you fuck me again.' As if I don't have a hundred other holes to drill if I want.

"Hot? Yeah, he is," Harlan continued. "Bright? Sure. Fuck my friends? Never! I've got *some* scruples. Not many. I admit it. All those years of working for Shari Draper in Hollywood left most of 'em in the gutter, along with my nuts. But once I got that whore off my back I managed to escape with some semblance of humanity."

Kurt smiled wickedly. "Harlan, you've always been a sweet man," he lied. "Whatever you'd like me to do about Tag, I'm more than happy to help out. My pals from *Gold on Ice* will help too. I think they'd just love to nail Tag's ass, and not in the way you did. Got any plans?"

For the next hour, Kurt and Harlan brainstormed ways of eliminating Tag from the show. "How would Scary Shari handle this?" Harlan asked himself aloud, referring to one of his nefarious old bosses in Hollywood. Then to Kurt, "My cojones are made of regular-grade steel. I don't have the really thick stuff that holds nuclear waste like Shari's."

"Turn everything around," Kurt suggested. "Tell him you discovered that the *Enquirer* piece was his fault, and HBO won't stand for being an accessory to libel."

"Deceit is part of the publicity game. He knows there's no such thing as bad PR. He'll make the charge that the ratings will go through the roof if we get rid of him and make this more of a scandal. And he'd be right."

"Hell, use me as the bad cop," Kurt offered. "I'll do the firing. I'd like nothing more than to kick his butt right off the ice." Kurt thought for a long moment. "I've got an even better idea. Call Tag in for a meeting. Tell him that because of the tabloid piece I'm history and you have to cancel the special."

"He'll have a fit. This is his big break," Harlan scoffed. "He'll back me into a corner. He'll insist that he can carry the show on his own, then he'll blackmail me into giving him the chance."

"Pride goeth before a fall," Kurt smiled, waiting for Harlan to catch on.

It took longer than expected but eventually Harlan's eyes grew wide and his smile beamed. "A comeuppance?" he asked. "Do tell!"

"Just take a meeting with the little gold digger. Then be at the rink right around ten A.M. for the taping," Kurt advised. "And wear a hard hat."

Harlan issued a sigh of relief. "If I'd known a beautiful body would get me into so much trouble I'd stop fucking," he said. He looked at Kurt. Their eyes met. In unison they said:

"No, I wouldn't."

"No, you wouldn't."

They were still laughing as Harlan opened the door and ushered Kurt into the hallway. "Speaking of beautiful bodies," Harlan cocked his head toward Scott.

"You be nice to that kid," Kurt admonished. "You don't want him to turn out like you. The way you almost turned out like that Shari creature you're always talking about."

Harlan nodded his head in agreement and smiled. "See you Friday morning."

"So long Scott, and thanks for the great coffee," Kurt said. He gave the receptionist a salute as he left the office.

Scott beamed. It was then that he knew what to look for in a life partner. The ideal man was anything remotely resembling Kurt Chrysler.

Chapter Thirty-three

A taxicab was waiting at the curb of the Pliable Plastics building, courtesy of Scott and his conscientious anticipation of the needs of those he served. Kurt made a mental note to hire the sharp young man away from his unappreciative boss, Harlan, and bring him aboard his own team.

Outside the Ambassador East, Kurt tipped the driver fifty percent of the fare and smiled warmly at the doorman who greeted him by name. As he rode the elevator to the penthouse, he imagined how he'd tell Garry the good news. Kurt felt like celebrating with sex.

The ping of the elevator bell announced his arrival seconds before the doors opened. As the mirrored panels separated, three smiling faces greeted him: his friends. They had gathered to be supportive. Kurt smiled as he stepped into the foyer. He gave Garry a hug and a kiss. "A drink is in order," he said evasively.

"Already chilled, honey," Garry said. "Go have a seat in the living room. They've sent up your favorite Chinese foods."

"Fuck HBO, anyway," Jay said. "No other skater has the easygoing friendly demeanor for television audiences that you have. They'll never get a replacement."

"I'm so proud of the way you're handling all this nonsense," Amber said, patting Kurt on the back.

When Kurt had plopped himself onto the brown leather sofa and accepted a flute of champagne from Garry, he looked at each of his friends. He raised his glass and they followed suit. "A toast," Kurt began in a somber disposition. "To my beautiful lover Garry. And to my two supportive friends, Jay and Amber. I love you guys."

He was about to take a sip of his bubbly, when he stopped just before his lips touched the rim of the glass. "And"—he waited a beat—"to *Chrysler's Ice!* The show must go on!" Kurt smiled. "It's not over! I didn't get fired! We tape Friday, just as planned!"

Champagne spilled to the carpet as Garry practically leaped to his lover and planted a passionate kiss on his lips. "I knew they couldn't let you go!" he cried.

"What's the deal?" Jay called enthusiastically.

"What did Tag say?" Amber interrupted.

"Filler up again, and I'll explain everything in detail," Kurt said as he pushed his glass toward Garry.

For the next hour Kurt painted a detailed picture of all that had transpired that morning. He discussed the scenario that he had suggested to Harlan for eliminating Tag. "This is where you guys come in." He began to include his friends in his scheme. "Jay, you're responsible for getting Derek Laramie. Amber, would you please call his coach in White Crystal and send him a plane ticket. The same for Tag's mother and father. Garry, sorry, hon, but would you mind meeting my pal with his videotapes at the airport?"

"The porn king," Garry asked with a smile. "Happy to be of service."

"The taping will begin promptly at ten. I'll work out the rest of the details with our director. As for your own performances, you guys have skated enough. You know what to do once the cameras start rolling. So let's take tonight off and celebrate!"

"Places, everybody! Places, please!" the assistant director called over the microphone as a chorus of glitter-clad skaters filled the ice rink.

It was the day of taping the HBO *Chrysler's Ice* skating spectacular. Tag, dressed in blue jeans and a bugle-beaded vest over his bare chest, impatiently paced the floor beside the arena in his sequined skates. "No, no, you idiot," he yelled at the director. "That kid over there, the second one from the far left, yeah, him. What's he still doing here?"

"Sorry, Tag. Give me a hint. I'm too busy to play twenty questions."

"I told you I didn't want him in the show. He's trying to upstage everyone!"

The director, who had worked in feature films with the likes of Rob Schneider, Bill Murray, and Ashley Judd, was usually adept at the diplomacy required for dealing with temperamental egos. But even he was losing patience with Tag. "The cameramen have been advised that he's never to be in close up. I didn't think you could possibly mind . . ."

"Don't play me for an idiot," Tag said in a voice that conveyed that there was a lava flow of rage ready to erupt at any moment. "I've been around. He's probably sucking your pencil dick, and you'll edit him into the final cut. Not on my show, you don't! I'm not skating if he's on the ice!" Tag stormed away and threw his half-full bottle of Evian against the cinderblock wall of the back stage area.

The director called after Tag. "He's staying! And you'll be on the ice in five minutes! I'm calling Harlan!"

Tag turned around, folded his arms across his chest and stared at the director. "Is that supposed to intimidate me? Harlan's a little cocksucking weasel. He's damned happy that I was available to step in for America's favorite skating homosexual. In fact, give me the phone. I'll call Harlan myself. I'm sure he'd love to hear how you're making my life a living hell."

Tag was secure in his trust that Harlan was neatly tucked into his back pocket. Although he had to beg for the opportunity to headline the skating special, and go back on his vow to never let Harlan touch his ass again, he was still proud of the way he had maneuvered himself into the star position. *Big cock trumps dispensable directors every time*, he thought as he stared down his nemesis.

The director pinched the bridge of his nose with his thumb and index finger. "You're holding us up, Tag. We're on a tight schedule. Do you want to do this show, or what?"

Tag snorted. "Your schedule just got as tight as your butt, 'cause

I'm not going on until you take care of that kid, or Harlan takes care of you. Directors, at least second string directors, like you, are a dime a dozen."

"Alright, already," the director said. "He's gone. History. Now, would you be kind enough to step on to the ice and introduce the show?"

Tag smiled. "Temper. Temper. First the kid."

The director went out to the ice. Tag could see him in conversation with the male skater who had been too good during rehearsals. Tag didn't want anyone from the chorus to shine. As far as he was concerned, there was always another someone like himself, just waiting in the wings to ride on a star's coattails. The skater nodded his head. He looked up and found Tag, staring at him for a moment. Then he left the ice.

When the director returned he said to Tag, "If you're satisfied, would you please take your place. This is the intro."

"I know what it is," Tag snapped. "So what are you waiting for? Roll the fucking tape!"

Tag glided to the center of the rink and dug his toe pick into the ice. He combed his fingers through his hair, pulled on the bottom of his vest, straightened the Chinese good luck medallion around his neck and took a stance.

A kettledrum roll began, followed by a lush fanfare from a live orchestra. Tag maintained his pose, waiting for his cue, which was a chorus of voices singing a medley of "Sunshine and Lollipops," "Don't Sleep in the Subway," the theme from *The Love Boat*, and "From This Moment On." Muscle memory kicked in. Suddenly Tag was flying across the ice, performing his most practiced and beautiful program.

When he came to a quick stop in front of the camera, an announcer's voice immediately called out: "Tag Tempkin!"

With the music muffled in the background, Tag smiled warmly and introduced himself. He was out of breath but offered his winning personality and perfect white teeth. "You folks may not know me yet, but you will."

He launched into his monologue—a self-deprecating poor-boy-makes-good speech in which he gave an abridged version of how he came to be in his own television special.

As the director and the cast and the crew all watched him on monitors back stage, they had to admit, albeit reluctantly, that Tag had that something extra of which stars were made. He was devastatingly handsome, he came across as a sweet young man who didn't take himself or his newfound fame very seriously, and he appeared to be utterly grateful for the opportunity to skate for his audience.

"Oh my gosh!" he enthused. "I am so very excited, and so very pleased and so honored to be able to share the ice this evening with legends! And you'll get to meet them. They're the most wonderful skaters you'll ever see. I'm so proud that I get to call them my friends! Never in a gazillion years could I have ever dreamed this would happen to me." Tag adroitly turned from one camera to smile into another. "In all my born days, I could only fantasize about meeting the brilliant Michael Weiss. The fact that he's skating on my very first special is just beyond anything imaginable!"

"And stars, all the way from Russia, Marina Anissina and Gwendal Peizerat! Aren't they the greatest? Yes, they are, and they're here to skate on my show! Isn't that just too incredibly awesomely exciting. I am so way over the moon about them being with me! And that darling little, er," he faltered for a moment, but caught himself, "brilliant spinning machine, Timothy Goebel! He's here too!

"Now, before we do what we love to do best, I just want to take a tiny moment to say that I'm happy to fill in for Kurt Chrysler. Hope you're feeling better, my friend! But enough of talking. It's time to skate!"

The music surged to an energizing jubilee and Tag bounded back across the ice, doing split jumps and double Axels until the director finally yelled, "Cut!"

"Christ, those lights are too fucking hot!" Tag bellowed from center rink. He retreated to his dressing room. While the Zamboni laid a fresh coat of water on the ice, he changed into his next costume. He dressed in a cowboy outfit for a number in which he would explain to the audience that he had first become interested in skating when he was a little kid. His self-written script laid it on thick. He would explain that while the other kids in the slum neighborhood where he lived were playing *Make the Old West Hell for Native Americans*, he had tried to create a more beautiful world by learning to figure skate.

As part of the number, there would be a large screen on which a film would be projected. It was, ostensibly, a grainy home movie of

Tag, as a six-year-old. One minute the boy in the movie would be shooting his play pistol and shouting, "Pew! Pew!" his sound for bullets ricocheting off rocks in the western frontier. The next minute he was in blue jeans and a heavy wool sweater, falling on the ice and getting back up, over and over. The section was meant to segue into the present-day Tag, doing jumps and spins.

"Places, people," the assistant director called again. Tag emerged from his dressing room and wound his way down the hall to the rink. "Water, God damn it," he yelled at a production assistant, who quickly reached into an ice bucket and withdrew a pintsize bottle of Evian. "It's all wet!" Tag complained as he unscrewed the top and took a long pull from the bottle. He twisted the cap back on and dropped it to the floor.

"Aren't you ready, yet?" Tag demanded of the director, who was chewing Tums antacid tablets.

"Just waiting for you, Tag," the director said.

"Are you?" Tag snapped.

The director ignored him.

Tag stepped out onto the ice and skated to his mark.

"And . . . action!" the director called.

Immediately, as if the toggle for a light switch had been flipped on, Tag changed personalities. He was now the Julia Roberts of men's figure skating. "Oh my gosh!" he gushed, almost hyperventilating, pretending that there was no break in the taping since his last jump, although he'd changed clothes. "I'm having so much fun! I hope that you are too! Now, I want you to come with me on a journey back to when I was a boy, when all I could do was dream about growing up and being a real-life star . . ."

Looking directly into the camera, Tag began to tell the story. He offered his most sincere demeanor, and the large screen behind him filled with video images.

"I always felt different than other kids," he said, with a trace of sadness in his voice. "I was big for my age. I guess that's why I didn't have many friends. However, I soon found something special that I could do that made me very popular."

Suddenly the entire arena of stagehands and skaters filled with laughter. Tag was so into his playacting that he took only a slight notice of the uproar.

On the large screen behind him, the video displayed Tag in a scene from *Leaves of Ass*. He was brandishing his fully erect cock, slapping it against another man's ass.

On the ice he was saying, "I found that with a lot of practice, I could be really and truly good at something. This made the other kids want to play with me."

The entire arena was screaming with laughter, as they watched Tag drilling his shaft into a muscle man on a bench press. The man had his legs in the air and the back of his heels resting on a weight bar.

Finally becoming aware of the laughter, Tag saw his director behind the camera, giving rolling hand signals that Tag interpreted to mean that he should ignore the cacophony and just continue his monologue.

"I worked really hard . . ."

The video showed Tag sweating profusely as he hammered the guy's ass.

"People liked what I did . . ."

On screen, the man shot his load.

"I, myself, couldn't get enough of it . . ."

The screen switched to Tag in a bubbling Jacuzzi with two other studs, both of whom had their cocks in his face. He took turns sucking each of them.

"And I gave them my all . . ."

Now he was bent over the side of the hot tub, his ass in the air, impaled, one guy driving at him from behind, while the other forced his cock into Tag's mouth.

"But all those hours of hard work and discipline . . ."

The scene changed again. This time Tag was on his back, his wrists tied to a rusted metal bedsprings, gagged with a leather belt. A muscled, mustached, and tattooed man was ramming his ass with an enormous dildo.

This time, the uproar grew so loud that Tag flashed with anger. He wheeled around and screamed, "Shut the fuck up! You've ruined my monologue! I'm fucking . . ."

Then he saw himself on screen.

In that instant, the sound technician turned up the volume. The air of the arena was rent with the sound of Tag moaning as the hairy-chested man ordered him to "take that cock you little son-of-a-bitch. You want it. You know you want it, you little fucking cocksucker."

"What the fuck is going on!" Tag demanded, turning from the director to the stage manager to the chorus kids to the co-stars. "Where'd you get that?" he cried. "That's private! You're not supposed to have that! *Where* the fuck did you get that!"

"I gave it to them." Kurt skated onto the ice and was immediately met with wild applause from the cast and crew. He blew them kisses and bowed to them in appreciation.

"What's he doing here?" Tag screamed at the director. "This is my show! He's not in the cast! He's not supposed to be here. It's a closed set!"

"It's the other way around, my oh-so-clever little protégé," Kurt said. "There's been another sudden cast change. It's *you* who's not in the show. Since it is a closed set, I guess you'll have to leave."

"I'm not going anywhere. Where's Harlan! Get me fucking Harlan!" Tag demanded. "This is my big break! I made it happen and not you or anyone else can take it away from me! Where's Harlan! Fuck all of you. Get me Harlan!"

"Please! I heard you the first time," a voice called from the darkness behind the bright lights of the videotaping equipment. "And would you kindly dispense with the word fucking, when used in the same sentence as my good name?"

"Harlan?" Tag demanded. "What's going on? They're trying to destroy me. They've got some filthy porno tape pretending it's me, and are trying to kick me off my show!"

Harlan called back. "This is Kurt's show. It always has been, and it always will be," Harlan sighed.

"We'll just see about that!" Tag cried. He turned to the cast and chorus kids. "After what Kurt said about you in the *Enquirer*, you don't want to work with him, do you? He isn't the squeaky-clean queer that America loves," Tag continued. "He's mean spirited and two faced! He turned on all of you! Now you have the chance to pay him back for how mean he was to you! Michael, what do you say?"

Michael skated up to Tag. "You don't think anyone believes the stories they run in that rag, do you?"

"Outta my face, you asshole," Tag declared. "Marina," he begged of the Russian skater. "In America we stick with our friends."

"In Russia vee feed to dog leftover of jerk like you."

Tag was mortified. He turned to face Kurt, Harlan and the direc-

tor. "You guys are featherweights when it comes to fucking someone over. I've had way more practice. That video has been doctored.
I'll swear to it."

"Relax, Tag," Kurt said. "You won't have to testify to your pious
past. Because it's so moot. I have the entire Tag collection. It's a
wonder that you ever found the time to practice skating!"

Kurt glided onto the ice and addressed his audience of skaters
and tech people. "You're all in for a treat! Think of me as Ralph Ed-
wards!" He looked over at his nemesis and called out, "Tag Tempkin.
This is your life!"

The stagehands erupted into applause. The lights faded, the
speaker system came to life. "Hello, Tag," an old woman's shaky
voice said. "I wish I could say that you were a sweet boy growing
up. But I can't. How about the time you ran for Student Council
President and sent blanket e-mails to the whole school, with an attached jpeg of your chief rival, Lucy Fine? She was a nice fat girl,
and had lovely dark curly hair. You made her out as having three
breasts and a penis. That wasn't very nice. I hoped you'd change,
but you're still an egomaniacal asshole. And that's a tough thing
for a mother to say about her son."

A fanfare from the orchestra played. Kurt then called out in his
best announcer's voice, "Ladies and gentlemen, Mrs. Leonard
Schnellman. Tag's mother!"

Applause filled the air, as a short woman of about sixty years,
appeared on a red carpet that had been rolled out onto the ice. She
walked out, waving, and took a seat on a riser that was originally
intended as a place for the guest skaters to wait until called to
skate.

Kurt took the microphone again. "From the distant past to a
more recent time . . ."

"Hey fucker," a male voice boomed. "Although I didn't expect
you to be anything more than a play toy, I seriously didn't expect
you to turn around and be tellin' my record label that I was a Satan
worshiper! Hell, my background's in gospel music. You could'a
said I was a homo and that'd be okay at the Grand Ole Opry. But
you can't be runnin' 'round talkin' cults and voodoo and shit in the
South, for cryin' out loud. No way, man. The Good Book says,
'Don't ever fuck with a country singing star's career.' So I'm here to
help you reap your rewards. Fry in hell you little jerkoff."

Applause accompanied Derek Laramie as he, too, walked down the red carpet and took his place on the riser. He kissed Tag's mother on the cheek and took a seat beside her.

"Hey, guy," another male voice now announced. "*Semper Fi*, and all that Marine shit. I always wondered what happened to you. Remember blowing me in the men's room at a Shell service station in Barstow? Then you asked if I wanted to make fifty bucks getting another blowjob at a friend's apartment. Getting paid to fuck? Sounded way cool. I just didn't know you were recording the whole thing, then selling videos of me to all the other gay Marines—or at least the ones who weren't doing the same thing. Got us in a shit-load of trouble, man. I just wanted to be here to help some people make you pay for all that lying and conniving."

"Ladies and gentleman," Kurt called out, "a couple of nice guys from the United States Marine Corps!"

Wild applause ensued as two Marines who had been discharged from the service for being caught making porn, marched down the red carpet. "We'll be waitin' for you outside, Tag," the spokesman called out. As if giving a twenty-one-gun salute, the men simulta-neously flipped Tag their middle fingers.

"You're not a real popular guy, Tag," Kurt spoke through his hand-held mic. "We've got more fun guests for you. See if you can identify this voice."

"Hey, Tag," another man's voice spoke out. "We had a few swell times together. Of all my students, you always showed the most promise for becoming a professional skater. Looks like I was right. I'd be mighty proud of you, if it wasn't for the fact that in all the ar-ticles I've read, and in this evening's introduction, you claimed to be self-taught. Don't I deserve a little credit? Especially since you owe me approximately forty-two thousand dollars for the skating lessons. We agreed to take it out in trade, but I never got so much as a handful of your dick. You gave it away to all the other skaters. Not that I think it's anything special."

"Ladies and gentlemen, Coach Josh Embry!" Kurt called out, as the man waved and also took a seat on the riser. Kurt turned to Tag, who was being restrained in his seat by Jay, Garry, and Amber. "Well my less than fine, less than friend, is there anything you'd like to add?" He pointed the microphone toward Tag's lips.

Tag sat without making a sound.

"You know, Tag, somehow you remind me of Norman Bates at

the end of *Psycho*," Kurt said over the P.A. "But just to show you that we're a forgiving group, we've made one concession. Unlike your scheme to make Amber, Jay, and Garry retire, we're taking pity on you. We're sending you back to *the drain*. Ernie's company has one gig left this season, and we all want you to take your final bow in, of all things, the Butt-head costume. Someone left it in a men's restroom. But someone else was kind enough to return it to the show. Kerry Benjamin can't wait to see you again." Kurt sniggered.

Wild applause erupted. Tag hung his head over his chest.

"Your former co-stars will be joining me on this television special," Kurt said. "After that, we're touring Europe starting next month. We'll send you a card."

Tag smiled good-naturedly. "It doesn't get much more humiliating than this, does it?" he said. "I mean, you've got my momma here, my whole past more or less. Guess there's nothing left for me to do. Except . . ."

A long silence filled the arena, as Kurt, Jay, Garry, and Amber waited for a revelation to issue forth from Tag. He didn't say a word. Instead, he skated toward the exit in the rink barrier wall. Then he disappeared.

Chapter Thirty-four

"That was such a kick!" Amber had to catch her breath. "Maybe ol' Tag was right in that magazine article when he said that I was just phoning in my performances in *Gold on Ice*. I think I stopped doing the hard stuff 'cause the people seemed happy enough with whatever I did. Can't fake it for TV though."

"It's like the good ol' days, when I was competing," Jay agreed, panting beside Amber. "Notice I didn't freak out during my quad? I'm skating better than ever. Garry, too."

He handed a white terry cloth towel to his friend whose four minutes of strenuous jumps and spins caused him to heavily perspire through his white T-shirt, the cotton fabric pasted to his lithe body.

"I'm sure that we all looked great skating together." Garry breathed heavily, trying to steady his pulse.

"Hell, that was so much fun, I'd do it a couple of dozen more times," Jay beamed. "I'm ready to rock 'n' roll!"

Kurt skated over to the trio. He gave Garry a deep kiss. "Hey, listen you guys," he said, coming up for air. "The director says we've got another five minutes to fill. I think I've got a terrific idea. It's kind of bold, but hear me out."

The quartet huddled together as Kurt made a proposal.

* * *

"Ya think people will be cool with this?" Jay asked skeptically. "How about like sponsor types? And *TV Guide*? I'm terrified of their *Cheers & Jeers* column."

"Hey, it's HBO, viewers expect something original and daring from a cable network," Kurt maintained.

"How about you and Garry doing it?" Jay suggested.

"I'm on the ice too much as it is. Gotta give my guests a little time to sparkle. The secret of success on television is to not give away too much of yourself. The host should only be seen as the one around whom everyone else revolves. Keep 'em wanting more. KnowhatImean?"

"What about you and Amber?" Jay continued to examine all possibilities.

"Don't be silly," Amber smiled and took another sip from her bottle of Evian. "You guys should do it. I'm like Kurt. I'm on way too much. Heck, I still get paid the same as you, but with less work. It'll really be good for publicity and ratings. Maybe Kurt'll have us back again. Yes?"

"Absolutely," Kurt smiled. "In fact, there's talk of bringing variety television to HBO, only making it a weekly skating show with musical guests and comedy stuff, like the old *Carol Burnett Show*, or *Ed Sullivan*. I'm kind of in line to be the host, if it really goes to series. I have a feeling that a lot depends on how well this show does when it airs. Let's go for broke. Hell, who'd have thought *The Osbornes* would be such a hit. Next season every network could be copying us."

"If you're cool with this, so am I," Jay said.

"Ditto," Garry offered.

"Okay, it's settled," Kurt said. "The first network televised *pas de deux* on ice between two men. How about skating to the theme from *Love Story*? A good one? Any other ideas?"

"Anything's fine with me," Jay shrugged, not having time to give it any thought.

"We'll turn the camera on and you can just improvise. I'll have the choreographer watch. He might make a few suggestions for a couple of different positions."

"How provocative do you want us to get?" Garry asked.

"Use your imaginations. Just do what comes naturally. You guys are both sexy beasts. The melody is really pretty, so just go with the flow and pretend that you're two beautiful men who are in love with each other. Hell, you don't even have to pretend. Just so long as Garry thinks of *me*, when he's caressing the ice," Kurt chuckled, and made a face that said, *maybe this isn't such a good idea after all.*

"Not to worry. I'll have him home at a decent hour, Mrs. Chrysler," Jay teased. "So, should we change costumes for this? Are you going to roll tape now?"

"In a bit. Run over and see Bob Mackie. He's in the exercise room, with the production's fitness trainer. He'll get you into something sexy. We'll meet back here in an hour and go from there. Okay? Gotta talk to the director about the music."

Kurt turned to glide off the ice, then stopped. "By the way, Peggy and Dick called up. They're in town for an Oprah show. If you don't mind they wanted to know if they could stop over and watch the finale. I told 'em it was okay. Any objections? They might bring Oprah, too."

Jay made a face that expressed a huge level of discomfort. "You sure Peggy's forgiven me for . . . you know?"

"You're the one she wants to see the most," Kurt explained. "Said she's been meaning to write to you, but decided she wanted to talk to you in person."

"Why do I feel as though I'm being summoned to the boss's office," Jay said. "Okay. Sure. It's fine. I've wanted to see Peggy again too. I've just been too embarrassed to make contact."

"And I know it's okay with Garry if Dick comes along," Kurt smiled. "You've always wanted to meet him. It's my present to you." Kurt then skated away to join the director who was consulting with the choreographer.

"I'll run and change," Amber announced. "I wanna be all comfy when I watch this historic moment in television history," she smiled. "*Love Story*, eh? Why not 'Natural Love,' or 'What I Did for Love.' You could make that into a real ratings grabber." She shrugged her shoulders and her shimmering beaded costume reflected the overhead lights, giving her a radiant glow. "Audiences will get the message."

Amber, Jay, and Garry all skated away together toward the opening in the rink barrier. "Don't start without me," Amber called to her friends as she walked cloddishly on her skate guards toward her dressing room. Her friends veered off toward the makeshift exercise room.

From the corner of Jay's eye, he noticed one of the Russian inter-
preters walking toward them with someone who he immediately
recognized as one of the boy skaters from the corps. The young
man wasn't hard to miss. In fact, Jay had noticed his brilliance on
the ice during practice. His good looks and almost effete carriage
made him a standout.

"Mister Jay. Mister Garry." The Russian spoke in broken English.
"Someone wants meet you," he smiled, his arm on the boy's shoulder. "I introduce you, Wade."

The young man beamed as he shook hands with Jay and Garry.
"This is the most fulfilling moment of my life," he said. "I'm an ar-
dent admirer." He had practiced saying that, even before Sergei
spotted him intently watching the two stars with undivided attention earlier in the day. Sergei had cast his own eyes on Wade and sidled up to him after the chorus number in which the younger man
was just one of twenty other skaters acting as atmosphere for
Michael Weiss's performance.

It didn't take the Russian long to seduce Wade.

"We noticed how great you skate," Jay said to Wade. "Why'd
you turn pro? You could have been a hell of a competitor."

"I figured if my heroes, Jay Logan and Garry Windsor, could
turn pro, so could I."

Jay and Garry smiled warmly. Their gaydar was working over-
time and both picked up on Wade's obvious sexual vibrations. It
was in his blue eyes, and in his wide smile, and the way his T-shirt
clung to the contours of his body.

"I was beside myself when I got to audition for this special and
actually booked the job. Am I doing a good job so far? I really want
to be of value to you and the show," he said.

"Yeah," Jay said. "Great. Haven't heard any complaints, so I
guess everything's peachy. What's the choreographer say?"

"He seems cool," Wade said. "Even though I'm distracted by
being on the same ice as you two. This is like my every dream come
true. Oh my gosh!"

Jay and Garry gave each other a quick horror-filled look. Their
respective cocks, having been summoned to duty by the sight of
Wade, suddenly became flaccid. "Er, great meeting you, Wade," Jay
said with a forced smile.

"Yeah, it's been great," Garry added. "But we've gotta get fitted
for another number."

"Good luck."

"Have a great day."

"See ya 'round."

Jay and Garry quickly retreated to find Bob Mackie.

Garry laughed. "The memory of Tag is like those corny spy movies, the ones where the telephone rings and when someone answers it, someone else says a secret word that makes the other person turn into a psycho. Say, 'oh my gosh,' and we both go insane. We've gotta desensitize ourselves to Tag!"

The camera panned over to a smiling Peggy Fleming and Dick Button seated in the front row of the arena. Oprah Winfrey sat beside them. They were surrounded by screaming fans, wildly applauding.

The music swelled again as Kurt Chrysler did a layback spin into a slow scratch spin. Then he stopped and faced the camera.

He smiled as only Kurt Chrysler, America's most romantic figure skater, could smile. He exuded warmth and friendliness, and sincerity. "This has been another hot time on the ice for us," he said, trying to control his rapid breathing. "But before we say goodnight, I'd like to welcome back to the ice, my dear friends, the talented and sexy Jay Logan and Garry Windsor. They've got a special program they've choreographed, just for you."

As an orchestral fanfare arrangement filled the arena, the director signaled to switch to a camera that was in the third balcony. From that distance, the entire rink was in frame. The violin section of the orchestra began to vibrate, as the camera moved in to find two male skaters at the center of the rink, staring into each other's eyes.

They began to move to the measure of the music. With their chins up, their knees slightly bent, both men simultaneously pushed against the ice with the inside edges of their left blades. Shifting their weight, and keeping their backs properly arched, they leaned into their first maneuver and completed mirrored triple Salchows. The audience applauded wildly as Jay and Garry proceeded to score the ice together on thin rails of steel.

Within four months there were billboards across the country picturing Kurt Chrysler and announcing his new special for HBO. Full page ads in *TV Guide* and the *New York Times* showed Kurt in freeze-frame as he glided on one leg, performing a spiral across the ice. Tag sneered when he saw Kurt's image taking up the entire side of a twenty-story office building on Sunset Boulevard

At the Pickwick ice rink, in Burbank, California, Tag walked up to the box office and slapped down six dollars for a skate pass. He shook his head as he thought, *Ironic. A few months ago, I was paid to be on the ice.*

Tag walked into the lobby of the rink complex with his skate bag slung over his right shoulder. Wending his way past a stampede of rowdy boys in full hockey gear and mothers escorting their little girls to figure skating classes, he tried to recall the last time that he had to share the ice with amateurs.

Quickly remembering, he smiled again. It was that morning in Clarksville. For weeks he had planned that *accidental* meeting, knowing that *Gold on Ice* was coming to town and Jay Logan would be practicing at the IceBox. He had had complete confidence that it would be easy for him to befriend the star, and he was just as certain that he'd get into the show—at the very least as a pick up skater. However, he hadn't factored Garry Windsor and his cocky boyfriend Kurt into the equation. *I won't be so stupid this time,* he said to himself.

Tag looked around the vast, black rubber floor lobby. He spied whom he was searching for standing beside the skate rental shop counter. He sized up the imperious-looking young man wearing a black T-shirt that emphasized a strong upper body, who was speaking animatedly into a cell phone.

"Mr. Warren?" Tag said as he walked up to the man, offering his hand and most seductive smile. "I'm Tag Tempkin. Here for the audition?"

The man's arrogant demeanor melted as he enjoyed the view of Tag's thick blond hair touching his broad shoulders and his tight, white T-shirt tucked into equally tight blue jeans. "Call me Dennis," the man said, smiling. Checking himself, he abruptly asked, "Can you skate as well as Harlan says? Kristi Yamaguchi's chorus boys have got to be a cut above."

Tag was tempted to reel off his credits, particularly *Gold on Ice,* and to berate Dennis for his obvious ignorance. But he needed a job. And Harlan, providing one last favor (with an I.O.U. for a blowjob from Tag), had arranged for him to audition. He could tell that Dennis was undressing him with his eyes. Tag flashed his most dazzling smile and said, "Gosh Mr. Warren. I certainly wouldn't want to disappoint you—or Miss Yamaguchi."

Just then, a young, exotically beautiful woman, wearing white skates and an elegant fire-red costume with glittery hand-sewn beading, and revealing one bare shoulder, walked by. Dennis abruptly looked away from Tag and smiled up at the woman who smiled back and said, "I won't be disappointed with him." She continued on through the double doors leading to the ice arena.

Dennis appeared irritated. "The queen has spoken," he said in a huff. "Guess you're hired for the commercial. You'd damn well better be good."

"I'm the best," Tag retorted snippily. Then, returning to his docile disposition, he added, "So I've been told by a few people."

Dennis pursed his thin lips and gave Tag another long lascivious once-over.

"Mr. Warren," Tag said, looking as forlorn as possible, "I'm all alone out here in L.A. I want to do really well in Hollywood, especially for you and your commercial." He looked down at the floor. "I know that you're very important and very busy, but do you think that I could impose upon you to offer me some of your wisdom?"

Dennis's smile returned. "Wisdom?"

"You are kind of famous for being one of the nice guys in town," he lied. Tag was well aware that Dennis had a reputation for using the proverbial *casting couch*.

"Yeah, well, okay. Why don't we grab a drink at *The Abby* after the rehearsal," Dennis suggested, trying to play indifferent.

"Awesome," Tag grinned and bobbed his head. He started to walk toward the doors leading to the rink, then turned around. "Or, if you'd let me, as an expression of my appreciation I could get some take-out Chinese and bring it to your place." Tag noticed the outline of Dennis's dick as it grew in his pants. His eyes and smile let Dennis know that he was aware of the reaction—and he approved.

This time when he turned to leave he smiled evilly and thought, *Fuck Kurt, Jay, Garry and Amber. And fuck Harlan and Ernie, too. Let 'em have their ice. Making it in this town is just a matter of me fucking the right guys.* He turned around and waved. *Dennis damn well better be Somebody.*

*   *   *

At last, the new Kurt Chrysler television special was scheduled to air. The week of the event, the muscle of HBO's publicity machine was evident everywhere. *Spankable Studs!* roared the cover of *The Advocate*, with a cover story on Kurt. DROOLS OF APPROVAL was the banner headline of *Genre*, in which Garry and Kurt were profiled as gay marriage role models. NICE POOPERS! shouted *Unzipped*, with a photo spread of Kurt wearing nothing but a leather hat, and holding a skate to hide his ample dick. In other publications Jay and Garry were pictured performing a hand-to-hand lasso lift, with Jay's strong arms holding Garry high above his head. Kurt was freeze-framed coming out of a scratch spin.

Chrysler's Ice pummeled the competition and easily won its time slot when it aired. Every major glossy magazine, including *TV Guide*, hailed the show and its stars. HBO won raves for its commitment to programming performing arts and pushing the boundaries of what is acceptable entertainment.

Kurt handed out copies of the magazines to Garry, Jay and Derek, and Amber who, along with her new boyfriend/manager, all settled in to the large common room of the Connecticut home Kurt shared with Garry. "Looks like we're going to series," he announced to his weekend guests.

"This is going to be tons of work," Jay said.

"And we moved back here just so that Kurt and I could spend all of our time together," Garry added.

"Be careful of what you wish for, my dear," Kurt smiled, tousling Garry's hair. "We're going to be together twenty-four-seven. Think you can stand me?"

Garry smiled and sipped from a flute of champagne.

It was autumn. The late afternoon air outside was crisp. The foliage was at its kaleidoscopic peak of beauty. Amber and her new love had commented when they arrived that the views from every floor-to-ceiling window were the most breathtaking they'd ever seen. "Like a Thomas Kincaid," Amber said.

Kurt and Garry's personal assistant, Scott, had baked fresh bread, the aroma from which filled every room and gave the house an authentic Norman Rockwell aura. Scott had also unobtrusively set out silver trays of homemade petit fours, and arranged for every conceivable personal toiletry in the guest bedrooms. He stacked the CD player's carousel with Garry and Kurt's favorite recordings: vintage Linda Ronstadt, Judy Garland, the Carpenters, and the cast recordings of *Camelot* and *My Fair Lady*.

As the conversation turned to their wish list of guests for upcoming shows, each skater took a turn playing casting director.

Amber said, "Do you think if I begged and begged, Janet Lynn might return to the ice? Not! Well, failing that, I would love to see John Misha Petkevich on the show."

Garry was an open book. To no one's surprise he said that no series with weekly figure skating could possibly be complete without an appearance from Dick Button.

"As long as he keeps his trap shut and just skates!" Derek said, offering his own take on the show. "And what about me for a guest?" He started singing "Make a Smiley Face for Jesus," before Jay flicked at his head with his cocktail napkin.

Kurt raised his champagne flute to his lips. "All great ideas," he said. "As a matter of fact, our assistant, Scott, has come up with some terrific suggestions too. Even thought of the Protopovs. How could he even know about them?" Kurt looked around the vast room and into the adjoining kitchen. "Where is Scott? He should be part of this discussion. I tell you, that man is amazing."

"He's indispensable," Garry smiled.

"He takes care of us, as if we were his personal mission in life. The guy thinks only of our needs," Kurt smiled.

Just then, Scott arrived with another bottle of Cristal. "Refills?" he beamed. "Dinner will be in about half an hour."

"Scott is a sensational cook, too," Kurt complimented him. "Just wait until you taste his nuts in the morning!"

The room burst into laughter.

"No! No!" Kurt realized what he'd said. "I mean his homemade *doughnuts!*"

Garry rolled his eyes. "Kurt's a laugh riot, isn't he? He's making this poor boy blush. Wouldn't want to scare him away. I mean, he's just so handy to have around."

"Thank goodness he's also a fitness trainer," Kurt continued. "Keeps us in shape so we can eat his gourmet meals and not have to worry about getting so heavy that we crash through the ice."

As the evening wore on, the group reminisced about what a difference a year had made. What had often seemed to be the worst possible scenario for their lives and careers, turned out to be the best. Garry recounted how his skating club had abandoned him, but that he would never have otherwise had the opportunity to become befriended by Jay Logan and Amber Nyak.

Amber said, "I hate to bring it up, but if it hadn't been for that little rat Tag, we wouldn't have been reintroduced to Kurt. And, maybe, Garry and Kurt wouldn't be our hosts this weekend. And for sure we'd still be in that dinky *Gold on Ice* instead of skating on television."

Scott spoke up too, telling the guests about the year of working for producer Harlan Wahlberg and how, if it hadn't been for Kurt coming to the executive offices that morning—again because of Tag—he'd probably still be fetching coffee and being verbally abused instead of running Kurt and Garry's home. Scott looked at Kurt with deep appreciation. Kurt returned the look.

The connection shared between Kurt and Scott wasn't lost on Garry. But as Garry frequently reminded himself, *I will never love anybody the way that I love Kurt. And Kurt will never love another man the way he loves me.*

While the others laughed about their incredible experiences of the past, Scott busied himself with stoking the fire, changing the CD disk carousel, lighting candles and setting carafes of wine on the dining room table.

The warm ambiance of love and comfort and the bonds of friendship between everyone present caused each of them to realize how grateful they were, for all the circumstances that had brought them to this moment of genuine contentment.

"To the converging paths of our lives." Garry raised his flute of champagne.

"And to the strength it took for each of us to go down those paths," Kurt added. "And never giving up hope."

"And," trumpeted Scott, "To *Gay Blades*, the most *original* programming ever on television. Emmys for everybody!"